Welcome to Your Life

WELCOME TO YOUR LIFE

Writings for the Heart of Young America

Edited by David Haynes and Julie Landsman

MILKWEED EDITIONS

The characters and events in this book are fictitious. Any similarity to real persons, living or dead, is coincidental and not intended by the author.

Distributed by Publishers Group West

Published 1998 by Milkweed Editions
Printed in the United States of America
Cover design by Adrian Morgan, Red Letter Design
Cover painting by Lisa Erf
Interior design by Mary Ellen Buscher
The text of this book is set in Veljovic.
98 99 00 01 02 5 4 3 2 1
First Edition

Milkweed Editions is a not-for-profit publisher. We gratefully acknowledge support from Elmer L. and Eleanor J. Andersen Foundation; James Ford Bell Foundation; Bush Foundation; Dayton's, Mervyn's, and Target Stores by the Dayton Hudson Foundation; Doherty, Rumble and Butler Foundation; Dorsey and Whitney Foundation; General Mills Foundation; Honeywell Foundation; Jerome Foundation; McKnight Foundation; Minnesota State Arts Board through an appropriation by the Minnesota State Legislature; Creation and Presentation Programs of the National Endowment for the Arts; Norwest Foundation on behalf of Norwest Bank Minnesota, Norwest Investment Management and Trust, Lowry Hill Norwest Investment Services, Inc.; Lawrence and Elizabeth Ann O'Shaughnessy Charitable Income Trust in honor of Lawrence M. O'Shaughnessy; Oswald Family Foundation; Piper Jaffray Companies, Inc.; Ritz Foundation on behalf of Mr. and Mrs. E. J. Phelps; John and Beverly Rollwagen Fund of the Minneapolis Foundation; St. Paul Companies, Inc.; Star Tribune Foundation; James R. Thorpe Foundation; and generous individuals.

Library of Congress Cataloging-in-Publication Data

Welcome to your life : writings for the heart of young America / edited by David Haynes and Julie Landsman.
p. cm.
Summary: A collection of stories, poems, and memoir selections of new work from the last ten to twenty years including multiracial and multiethnic writings.
ISBN 1-57131-017-7 (pbk.)
1. Children's literature, American. [1. Literature—Collections.] I. Haynes, David, 1955- . II. Landsman, Julie.
PZ5.W44 1998
810.8'09283—dc21

98-19341
CIP
AC

This book is printed on acid-free paper.

This book is dedicated to all our students
and our colleagues in education,
from whom we have learned so much.

CONTENTS

Section III: The Body

Section IV: Fathers

Section V: Generations

Section VI: Music

Foreword

One of the biggest thrills of my writing life came when I was approached at a southern California bookstore, after I had given a reading from my novel about a black firefighter struggling to be a father. A young woman with long black hair and skin the color of toasted pecans smiled shyly and asked me to sign another book, my first collection of stories, published by Milkweed Editions. "I live here, in this neighborhood," she told me, pointing at the cover. "I never read about my life or my neighborhood until someone gave me your book. I heard friends talking."

Her high school English teacher had given her my book. The young woman was part black, part Chicano, from a city thirty miles from mine, but she said she knew everyone in the stories. It was the first time she felt comfortable enough to enjoy fiction, she said, the first time she felt that thrill of recognition.

I knew exactly what she was talking about, because I spent many years searching for writing that made me feel the same way, that made me say, "I know these people. I know this place." I never thought my kind of community, my kind of friends and family, would exist on paper.

Throughout high school, I read the classic authors we were offered, sometimes with resistance. Though I loved Charles Dickens and Stephen Crane and Emily Dickinson, I longed to read dialogue like I heard every day in playgrounds and yards, to see descriptions of places I walked after school. That never happened until, in the public library, I stumbled across Toni Cade Bambara, whose teenage black characters lived in New York but somehow talked like people I knew. Her stories were a revelation to me. Some time later I found *Fat City,* the novel by Leonard Gardner set in central California, in a tough rural landscape that I recognized immediately, and I finally realized that I could write about the people and arroyos and yards I knew, about the kinds of places no one might ever visit.

But had anyone given me a book like *Welcome To Your Life,* I would have learned this and gained some confidence much earlier. I would also have been enthralled by the different worlds the book lets us know, all of the universes in America. Gary Soto's poem takes me to a part of California I know so well, while Patricia Smith's poems, even though they are set in Chicago, bring back many teenage memories of house parties and nondancing pain soothed by Motown music. This summer, I watched a man from Oaxaca, Mexico, sign his name X, and when I read Pat Mora's poem, I felt my fingers clutch the pencil, too. I have friends who share the dilemma of the mixed-race narrator in Susan Ito's story, and I have often gone for ribs at a place like the one in William J. Harris's poem.

This collection is the kind of thing Milkweed Editions does best. I loved the surprising humor, and the youthful narrators, and the poignant tones. I loved the challenges inherent in many of these pieces. Nothing is easy here, and for that I was grateful, because nothing is easy in real life, and that's what we've got in these pages. I am impressed with the range of writers assembled by David Haynes and Julie Landsman, both veteran teachers, and the kind of teachers who have now given an inspirational book to many readers.

I look forward to giving this book to my own three daughters, who look like that young woman who approached me at the bookstore, and who love to read. In these wonderful stories, poems, and essays, I hope my daughters and many other readers find that thrill of recognition I still remember. You may know the people these words conjure up, or you may be just now meeting them, but you won't forget them. They remind me of the old friends and newly arrived relatives who bring us stories, some fresh and some often told, and from whom we always learn the most important things about life.

—Susan Straight
Riverside, California

Welcome to Your Life

Insider/Outsider

William J. Harris

Rib Sandwich

I wanted a rib sandwich

So I got into my car
and drove as fast as I could
to a little black restaurant-
bar
and walked in
and so doing
walked out
of
America

and didn't even
need a passport

Katharine Harer

Tunnels

American tourists are looking for new ways to spend their dollars. They are flocking to Vietnam to see the tunnels, the ones used by the Vietcong in their long and clever victory. The Americans want to go down under the ground. They want to crawl on their bellies dragging their jogging suits across the earth. They want to sit in the small intestines of the tunnels and talk to each other. They want to imagine what it was like.

But they are frustrated in their desire. They cannot fit in the narrow passages. Their Western bodies are too large, too well-fed, to wedge inside and come out the other end. The solution is to dig out the tunnels, enlarge them, renovate history. This will be done.

[The information in this poem comes from a talk given by Vietnamese journalist, Nguyen Qui Duc, in San Francisco, November 1993.]

w. r. rodriguez

DEMOCRACY

it was decided by the noisier of the people who are delegated such powers by those who just don't give a damn that america was not such a bad place after all it being july and who needs heat or hot water in this weather anyway and at night when everyone is out the tenements don't look quite so bad and who sees them in the daytime when everyone is sleeping away the heat and the war was good for the economy reducing unemployment by sending the men to war and creating jobs for the women who could work for the guys who did not go to war and who were making big bucks and the underground economy was providing enough luxury items to go round and so it was decided by the noisier of the people who are delegated such powers by those who just don't give a damn that america was not such a bad place after all to celebrate by doing what would have been done anyway as it had become a tradition for the fourth of july so each side sent out its scouts to chinatown and little italy to gather up as much firepower as could be bought or stolen and to smuggle it and stockpile it and to distribute it at just the right time which was sunset on the fourth of july when it was decided by the noisier of the people who are delegated such powers by those who just don't give a damn that america was not such a bad place after all to celebrate by doing what would have been done anyway as it had become a tradition and so the two armies of teenagers too young for draftcards or too mean by means of their criminal records for military service assumed positions on their respective rooftops the ruddy irish above their red-bricked tenements and the swarthy puerto ricans and leftover italians above their brown-bricked tenements and it was decided by the noisier of the people who are delegated such powers by those who just don't give a damn that america was not such a bad place after all to celebrate by doing what would have been done anyway as it had become a tradition that the war at home had begun which was signaled by a single rocket's red glare which began the shooting of bottle rockets and m-80s and strings of firecrackers and sizzlers which went on for hour after hour keeping the old ladies and babies awake and driving the dogs crazy they cowered in corners like shell-shocked veterans though casualties were light as the street was wide and nothing more than a sputtering rocket ever hit the other side mostly everything landed in the street which was by mutual decision a free fire zone and anyone or anything in it an enemy to both sides and mostly there was no one in it except a few unfortunate passersby unaware of this great fourth of july tradition and a line of parked cars which would be pockmarked by morning when the sidewalks were covered with red white and blue paper and the air reeked of sulfur and it was decided that everyone should cease fire and get some chow and shut-eye and rest up for the night when it was decided by the noisier of the people who are delegated such powers by those who just don't give a damn that america was not such a bad place after all to celebrate by doing what would have been done anyway as it had become a tradition and the sun went up and down on the ceasefire and the irish and the puerto ricans and the leftover italian guys and their girls and their mothers and fathers and sisters and brothers got back out on our street to hang out to rock babies to gamble to play loud music to drink to gossip to party and to wait to wait to wait for a job for a baby for a draft notice which had become a tradition in not such a bad place after all

Sekou Sundiata

Blink Your Eyes

(Remembering Sterling A. Brown)

I was on my way to see my woman
but the Law said I was on my way
thru a red light red light red light
and if you saw my woman
you could understand.
I was just being a man.
It wasn't about no light
it was about my ride
and if you saw my ride
you could dig that too, you dig?
Sunroof stereo radio black leather
bucket seats sit low you know,
the body's cool, but the tires are worn.
Ride when the hard times come, ride
when they're gone, in other words
the light was green.

I could wake up in the morning
without a warning
and my world could change:
blink you eyes.
All depends, all depends on the skin,
all depends on the skin you're living in

Up to the window comes the Law
with his hand on his gun
what's up? what's happening?
I said I guess
that's when I really broke the law.

He said *a routine, step out the car*
a routine, *assume the position.*
Put your hands up in the air
you know the routine, like you just don't care.
License and registration.
Deep was the night and the light
from the North Star on the car door, déjà vu
we've been through this before.
why did you stop me?
Somebody had to stop you.
I watch the news, you always lose.
You're unreliable, that's undeniable.
This is serious, you could be dangerous.

I could wake up in the morning
without a warning
and my world could change:
blink you eyes.
All depends, all depends on the skin,
all depends on the skin you're living in
New York City, they got laws
can't no bruthas drive outdoors,
in certain neighborhoods, on particular streets
near and around certain types of people.
They got laws.
All depends, all depends on the skin
all depends on the skin you're living in.

Susan K. Ito

ORIGAMI

I take my place, hesitantly, among the group of Japanese women, smile back at the ones who look up from their task to nod at me. Their words float around me like alphabet soup, familiar, comforting, but nothing that I clearly understand. The long cafeteria table blooms with folded paper birds of all colors: royal purple, light gray, a small shimmering silver one. They're weaving an origami wreath for Sunday's memorial service, a thousand cranes for the souls of those who died at Tule Lake's internment camp.

I spread the square of sky-blue paper flat under my hands, then fold it in half. So far, this is easy. I'm going to follow all the directions. It's going to be a perfect crane, *tsuru,* flying from my palm. Fold again, then flip that side of the triangle under to make a box. Oh no. What? I didn't get that. I'm lost. The women around me keep creasing, folding, spreading, their fingers moving with easy grace. My thumbs are huge, thick, in the way of these paper wings that are trying to unfold but can't.

My heart rises and flutters, beating against its cage in panic, in confusion. I try to retrace my steps, turn the paper upside down, in reverse. It's not working. I want to crumple the paper into a blue ball, an origami rock.

But instead I unfold the paper with damp, shaking fingers. I persevere. *Gambaro.* Don't give up. I'm going to make this crane if it kills me. I'm going to prove that I can do this thing, this Japanese skill. I'm going to pull the coordination out of my blood, make it flow into my fingers. I have to.

But what if I can't? Then it only proves the thing that

I fear the most, don't want to believe. That I'm not really Japanese. That I'm just an impostor, a fake, a watered-down, inauthentic K-mart version of the real thing.

༄

I remember the summer when I was nineteen years old. Waitressing at the Gasho restaurant in upstate New York, the centuries-old farmhouse brought over, beam by beam, from Japan. It took over forty-five minutes to dress for work each day, from the white Japanese underthings, pure snowy cotton, to the stiff red and gold *obi.* My mother helped me, turning me around in front of the mirror, her pride making her tall as she fussed over me. I put up my hair, an elegant round sculpture full of air, with red lacquered chopsticks holding it all together. I shuffled around the house in my wooden *geta* clogs, practicing small dainty bows toward the dog, my parents, various pieces of furniture.

It didn't matter that I was making less than minimum wage, that I was putting in more time getting dressed and commuting up the New York Thruway than I was actually working. I was proud.

I still remember that one July night, the frogs singing in the garden behind the restaurant, the moonlight shining like wetness on the stone lantern. I stood in the back doorway of the kitchen, listening to the chefs shouting in Japanese, the dishwashers howling in Spanish. The smell of miso soup and green onions floated in the steam of the kitchen.

I passed through the swinging dining room doors and called out to the next party on the waiting list. "Harrison?"

A short woman with champagne-colored curls waved enthusiastically in my direction. I greeted the group of eight people as they milled around the bar, clinking glasses of emerald green. Midori on ice. I led them to the horseshoe-shaped table with the flat steel grill in the middle, handed them each a steaming towel.

"Good evening," I said, smiling. "Welcome to Gasho."

The customers took the towels, pressed them into their faces, wiped their hands. They made small sounds of pleasure as the steam softened their skin. One man, wearing a beige polyester jacket, did not unroll his towel. He stared at me with reddened eyes and chewed on the end of a toothpick.

"Wait a minute," he said.

"Yes? Is there something wrong?" Sometimes a towel came out of the steamer cold, or not moist enough.

"You're not Japanese, are you?" The man looked up and down, craned his neck to look at the back of me.

"Pardon?" I faltered.

"This is supposedly a Japanese restaurant." He swept his arm up in a wide circle, and I could see a ring of perspiration soaked into his shirt. "I read that brochure in the bar. It's supposed to be an antique farmhouse that was built in Japan."

"The farmhouse is authentic," I murmured. My face was getting hot. "It was shipped here directly from Osaka."

"And what about you?" he demanded. "Where were *you* shipped from?"

I felt the blush draining out of my face, and my fear became so intense I thought my body would fail me. I imagined the blood pooling at my feet and then completely seeping out my soles, leaving me standing in a puddle of my own blood, my half-authentic, tainted blood.

I nearly lost my balance. I stood there, holding the tray of heaped up towels, tottering on my *geta*. "I'm half-Japanese." Just a whisper.

"Half?" he scoffed. "Hey. I come to a Japanese restaurant, I expect to have a Japanese waitress." He gestured toward petite, silky-haired Kimi passing out bowls of rice at the next table. He didn't have a clue, and I didn't tell him, that she was from Korea, and no more Japanese than he was.

He shook his head in disgust. "No, sir, if I wanted to be served my dinner by someone like you . . ." he looked me up and down again, "I'd have gone to McDonald's."

⑥

I stop, unfold everything, smooth the paper out on the table, take a deep breath, start again. My sweat is starting to make the paper all slick and even more unmanageable.

It must be those paternal genes that make me so klutzy, I tell myself. I take stock of all the ways his shadow marks my body. The dark hair that pushes up, unwanted, through the skin of my forearms, my legs, sometimes my belly, or worse, under my chin. No Japanese has to deal with this. I long for the smooth gold skin of my Nisei adoptive parents, the way they tan like caramels under the sun. My skin reddens into a dusky burnt color, and I know it's those delicate European genes that can't take the heat. Then there are the freckles. The huge flat feet, the bushy eyebrows. I blame him and his ancestors for all the parts of me that I hate.

People ponder my lineage. What *are* you, anyway? they ask. They've guessed my roots to be Puerto Rican, Jewish, Italian, Hawaiian, Irish (the freckles). My pencil hovers over the forms that say, *check one for Ethnicity.* One? I mark Asian, defiantly, and then feel guilty, humiliated. It's a lie. A half-lie, anyway.

⑥

I'm ready to give up. Hundreds of origami birds are piled into a mountain of color, spiky wings and beaks poking out like hatching newborns. What difference will it make if I don't complete this one? There are more than plenty for the memorial service.

I look down once again at the failed sculpture in my hands. There are so many folds in the blue paper, the color is starting to wear away at the creases. My would-be crane, still an awkward triangle, is scarred with white lines. I fold it again and again, over into itself, until finally something squat and deformed finally emerges. I shove it into my pocket and get up from the table when I notice the little *oba-san* sitting next to me. Her gray-white head, with its round rice-bowl haircut, the kind little children have, barely reaches my shoulder.

Her knotty, bent fingers are working a piece of pale butter-yellow paper. The folds she makes are gross, awkward, and her eyes are huge with concentration behind her spectacles. She doesn't seem to be having much more success than me, but I know it's not for lack of experience.

Finally she places her lopsided product in front of her and sighs. "This is no *tsuru,*" she mutters. "Looks more like sick chicken."

I take my crane out of my pocket and sit it down next to hers. They make a sort of clumsy, humble symmetry on the table. *Oba-san* looks up at me with a tiny hint of smile behind her round glasses. She reaches for my sleeve, sways a little bit, and I help her to her feet. She and I walk slowly to the kitchen. It's time for tea.

Pat Mora

Señora X No More

Straight as a nun I sit.
My fingers foolish before paper and pen
hide in my palms. I hear the slow, accented echo
   How are yu? I ahm fine. How are yu?
of the other women who clutch notebooks
and blush at their stiff lips resisting
sounds that float gracefully as
bubbles from their children's mouths.
My teacher bends over me, gently squeezes
my shoulders, the squeeze I give my sons,
hands louder than words.
She slides her arms around me:
a warm shawl, lifts my left arm
onto the cold, lined paper.
"*Señora,* don't let it slip away," she says
and opens the ugly, soap-wrinkled fingers
of my right hand with a pen like I pry open
the lips of a stubborn grandchild.
My hand cramps around the thin hardness.
"Let it breathe," says this woman who knows
my hand and tongue knot, but she guides
and I dig the tip of my pen into that white.
I carve my crooked name, and again at night
until my hand and arm are sore,
I carve my crooked name,
my name.

Faye Moskowitz

Excerpt from *A Leak in the Heart*

I get the blues at Christmas like a lot of other people, but I don't need analysis to find the roots of my depression. Somehow the concept of separation of church and state hadn't trickled down yet to Jackson, Michigan, when I was raised there in the late thirties and early forties. At any rate, Christmas was a miserable time for a Jewish child in those days, and I still recall the feeling.

The pressure would begin in late November, after the new clothes for Yom Kippur and Rosh Hashanah, after the begging on Halloween, after the kosher turkey for Thanksgiving. One day Miss Lukens would strip the bulletin board of its brown-and-black gobblers and black-and-white pilgrims with their axes. Stacks of red-and-green construction paper jammed the supply cabinet, and I knew I was in for it.

Oh, we had Hanukkah, of course: great platters of steaming potato pancakes, and dreidels, and all the cousins lining up by age so the uncles could dole out quarters and half dollars and even dollars, maybe, to the older kids; but how could a homely *latke* compete with mince pie and plum pudding? I can remember the Christmas preparations so clearly and can feel, even now, my Gentile friends bubbling like seltzer water as the days were ticked off on the Advent calendar that hung behind Miss Lukens's desk.

On the first school day in December we spread back numbers of *The Citizen Patriot* on our desks while whoever was Miss Lukens's current favorite doled out blobs of delicious smelling white paste, scooped from a large jar with a wooden tongue depressor or Dixie cup spoon. We smeared the cool, smooth paste on strips of red or green paper, formed strips into rings, then slipped rings into rings until each of us trailed a paper chain onto the floor.

It was on a paper-chain day in Miss Lukens's class that I began to have my troubles with Christmas. There I was, threading a green strip through a red ring when Peggy Lucille Harsch popped a glob of paste into her mouth and whispered, "You killed our Lord."

"No, I didn't," I answered automatically. What child admits to any accusation the first time? But if my enthusiasm wasn't dampened already, that did it. I didn't know what she was talking about, but I was sure she was probably right.

The days passed, clean snow fell on soiled slush, thawed a little, and then froze into treacherous ruts. Stores stayed open late and folks grumbled that shopkeepers were starting Christmas earlier than ever. Some nights my parents and I walked downtown after dark, snowflakes whirling like moths in the street lamps' halos and the packed ice hard as diamonds under our feet. In the town square, a crèche appeared with a naked baby Jesus stretching out his little wooden arms. Though I didn't know if he was "Our Lord" or not, I suspected he was, and I felt guilty as anything.

Outside the shops, members of the Salvation Army stamped their feet and rang their bells energetically to keep the circulation going. I mistook their red uniforms for Santa Claus outfits and was more confused than ever when my mother dropped a dime into one of the kettles. If we didn't celebrate Christmas, then why were we giving money to Santa Claus? Maybe she felt guilty too.

In Kresge's five-and-ten, coat unbuttoned, thighs jumping with the transition from ax-blade cold to down-quilt warmth, I headed for the music department to listen to my ideal, the yellow-bobbed pianist, bang out the arrangements of sheet music handed to her by prospective customers. Even here, I was troubled. How could I grow up to be a piano player at Kresge's if I would have to play carols at Christmas?

Overnight, twinkling decorations sprang up like great jeweled mushrooms: here a Santa climbed a chimney, there a front door was festooned with greens. I dreaded going home to my house, naked as an angleworm in all that glitter. More than that, I hated going to school, where even Miss Lukens had to concede that her students were too keyed up to learn anything that wasn't sugar-coated with Christmas.

One day she announced we were each to bring in our favorite psalms to write out on the Christmas cards we were making. The stomachache, part of my digestive system by then, intensified. OK, I give up, I told myself. I'll bring in my favorite psalm, but what's a psalm? My mother was no help. "Sahm?" she said in Jewish. "Sahm is poison." I was ashamed to ask Ruth Mary, my best friend, and though I was already old enough to use a dictionary, hours of research yielded no "som" or "sam" or any other variant I could think up.

We wrote letters to Santa Claus. What was I to do—write to Judah Maccabee? I crossed my fingers and wrote to Santa. Handmade Christmas presents were not a sin, I told myself, making up the rules as I went along. I would pretend they were Hanukkah gifts even if we didn't exchange gifts at home. So I sewed pen wipers for my dad and found a snowman in a magazine to decorate the holders for kitchen matches that were the gifts for our mothers. The Christmas tree in our classroom grew more beautiful every day, draped with strung popcorn, cranberries, and our paper chains. To me, it was like Snow White's fatal apple, more attractive than I could admit, but evil nevertheless.

When Miss Lukens read us the story of Christmas, my confusion was complete. If Jesus was a Jewish baby, like my brother, for instance, then what was all the trouble about? Why couldn't I celebrate his birthday the way my friends did? Still, I knew there was a catch somewhere, a piece of the puzzle missing that no one would help me find. Then Miss Lukens chose me to be a class representative in the choral group that was to sing carols outside the door of every classroom in the school.

I went home that afternoon and told my mother I felt sick. She put her lips to my forehead and said, "You have no fever. What's the matter with you?" What was the point of telling her my troubles? The only time she had ever come to school was to register me for kindergarten, and then she had answered, "Faygie," when the teacher asked my name, so that even now in third grade I was still called Peggy, the closest match my kindergarten teacher had been able to achieve. The worst of it was I *wanted* to sing the carols; they were the loveliest songs I had ever heard. I took to my bed, hid under the comforter, and refused to go to school.

No candy scent of cocoa, no image of oatmeal swimming in butter and cream, could budge me from my self-imposed exile. My father sat on the edge of the bed in his work clothes, late for the shop, I knew, to give me what comfort he could. By Sunday, my parents were ready to call in Dr. Ludwig, a ceremony usually reserved for the terminally ill. I broke down then and blurted it all out—the guilt, the envy, the anger—and my parents talked to me for hours, gently dealing with one more problem brought on by living outside the Jewish ghetto. In the end, my father softened and told me, "Sing the Christmas songs, but don't say Jesus' name." And so I stood outside the classrooms, my voice blending with that of my friends in the glorious old carols, careful always to omit any forbidden words.

Decades later, I still feel left out at Christmas, but I sing the carols anyway. You might recognize me if you ever heard me. I'm the one who sings, "La-la, the la-la is born."

Charles Baxter

GRYPHON

On Wednesday afternoon, between the geography lesson on ancient Egypt's hand-operated irrigation system and an art project that involved drawing a model city next to a mountain, our fourth-grade teacher, Mr. Hibler, developed a cough. This cough began with a series of muffled throat-clearings and progressed to propulsive noises contained within Mr. Hibler's closed mouth. "Listen to him," Carol Peterson whispered to me. "He's gonna blow up." Mr. Hibler's laughter—dazed and infrequent—sounded a bit like his cough, but as we worked on our model cities we would look up, thinking he was enjoying a joke, and see Mr. Hibler's face turning red, his cheeks puffed out. This was not laughter. Twice he bent over, and his loose tie, like a plumb line, hung down straight from his neck as he exploded himself into a Kleenex. He would excuse himself, then go on coughing. "I'll bet you a dime," Carol Peterson whispered, "we get a substitute tomorrow."

Carol sat at the desk in front of mine and was a bad person—when she thought no one was looking she would blow her nose on notebook paper, then crumple it up and throw it into the wastebasket—but at times of crisis she spoke the truth. I knew I'd lose the dime.

"No deal," I said.

When Mr. Hibler stood us in formation at the door just prior to the final bell, he was almost incapable of speech. "I'm sorry, boys and girls," he said. "I seem to be coming down with something."

"I hope you feel better tomorrow, Mr. Hibler," Bobby Kryzanowicz, the faultless brown-noser, said, and I heard

Carol Peterson's evil giggle. Then Mr. Hibler opened the door and we walked out to the buses, a clique of us starting noisily to hawk and raugh as soon as we thought we were a few feet beyond Mr. Hibler's earshot.

@

Since Five Oaks was a rural community, and in Michigan, the supply of substitute teachers was limited to the town's unemployed community college graduates, a pool of about four mothers. These ladies fluttered, provided easeful class days, and nervously covered material we had mastered weeks earlier. Therefore it was a surprise when a woman we had never seen came into the class the next day, carrying a purple purse, a checkerboard lunchbox, and a few books. She put the books on one side of Mr. Hibler's desk and the lunchbox on the other, next to the Voice of Music phonograph. Three of us in the back of the room were playing with Heever, the chameleon that lived in a terrarium and on one of the plastic drapes, when she walked in.

She clapped her hands at us. "Little boys," she said, "why are you bent over together like that?" She didn't wait for us to answer. "Are you tormenting an animal? Put it back. Please sit down at your desks. I want no cabals this time of the day." We just stared at her. "Boys," she repeated, "I asked you to sit down."

I put the chameleon in his terrarium and felt my way to my desk, never taking my eyes off the woman. With white and green chalk, she had started to draw a tree on the left side of the blackboard. She didn't look usual. Furthermore, her tree was outsized, disproportionate, for some reason.

"This room needs a tree," she said, with one line drawing the suggestion of a leaf. "A large, leafy, shady, deciduous . . . oak."

Her fine, light hair had been done up in what I would

learn years later was called a chignon, and she wore gold-rimmed glasses whose lenses seemed to have the faintest blue tint. Harold Knardahl, who sat across from me, whispered "Mars," and I nodded slowly, savoring the imminent weirdness of the day. The substitute drew another branch with an extravagant arm gesture, then turned around and said, "Good morning. I don't believe I said good morning to all you yet."

Facing us, she was no special age—an adult is an adult—but her face had two prominent lines, descending vertically from the sides of her mouth to her chin. I knew where I had seen those lines before: *Pinocchio.* They were marionette lines. "You may stare at me," she said to us, as a few more kids from the last bus came into the room, their eyes fixed on her, "for a few more seconds, until the bell rings. Then I will permit no more staring. Looking I will permit. Staring, no. It is impolite to stare, and a sign of bad breeding. You cannot make a social effort while staring."

Harold Knardahl did not glance at me, or nudge, but I heard him whisper "Mars" again, trying to get more mileage out of his single joke with the kids who had just come in.

When everyone was seated, the substitute teacher finished her tree, put down her chalk fastidiously on the phonograph, brushed her hands, and faced us. "Good morning," she said. "I am Miss Ferenczi, your teacher for the day. I am fairly new to your community, and I don't believe any of you know me. I will therefore start by telling you a story about myself."

While we settled back, she launched into her tale. She said her grandfather had been a Hungarian prince; her mother had been born in some place called Flanders, had been a pianist, and had played concerts for people Miss Ferenczi referred to as "crowned heads." She gave us a knowing look. "Grieg," she said, "the Norwegian master, wrote a concerto for piano that was . . ."—she paused—"my mother's triumph at her debut concert in London." Her eyes searched the ceiling. Our eyes followed. Nothing up there but ceiling tile. "For reasons that I shall not go into, my family's fortunes took us to Detroit, then north to dreadful Saginaw, and now here I am in Five Oaks, as your substitute teacher, for today, Thursday, October the eleventh. I believe it will be a good day: all the forecasts coincide. We shall start with your reading lesson. Take out your reading book. I believe it is called *Broad Horizons,* or something along those lines."

Jeannie Vermeesch raised her hand. Miss Ferenczi nodded at her. "Mr. Hibler always starts the day with the Pledge of Allegiance," Jeannie whined.

"Oh, does he? In that case," Miss Ferenczi said, "you must know it *very* well by now, and we certainly need not spend our time on it. No, no allegiance pledging on the premises today, by my reckoning. Not with so much sunlight coming into the room. A pledge does not suit my mood." She glanced at her watch. "Time *is* flying. Take out *Broad Horizons.*"

൭

She disappointed us by giving us an ordinary lesson, complete with vocabulary and drills, comprehension questions, and recitation. She didn't seem to care for the material, however. She sighed every few minutes and rubbed her glasses with a frilly handkerchief that she withdrew, magician-style, from her left sleeve.

After reading we moved on to arithmetic. It was my favorite time of the morning, when the lazy autumn sunlight dazzled its way through ribbons of clouds past the windows on the east side of the classroom and crept across the linoleum floor. On the playground the first group of children, the kindergartners, were running on the quack grass just beyond the monkey bars. We were doing multiplication tables. Miss Ferenczi had made John Wazny stand up at his desk in the front row. He was supposed to go through the tables of six. From where I was sitting, I could smell the Vitalis soaked into John's plastered hair. He was doing fine until he came to six times eleven and six times twelve. "Six times eleven," he said, "is sixty-eight. Six times twelve is . . ." He put his fingers to his head, quickly and secretly sniffed his fingertips, and said, "seventy-two." Then he sat down.

"Fine," Miss Ferenczi said. "Well now. That was very good."

"Miss Ferenczi!" One of the Eddy twins was waving her hand desperately in the air. "Miss Ferenczi! Miss Ferenczi!"

"Yes?"

"John said that six times eleven is sixty-eight and you said he was right!"

"*Did* I?" She gazed at the class with a jolly look breaking across her marionette's face. "Did I say that? Well, what *is* six times eleven?"

"It's sixty-six!"

She nodded. "Yes. So it is. But, and I know some people will not entirely agree with me, at some times it is sixty-eight."

"When? When is it sixty-eight?"

We were all waiting.

"In higher mathematics, which you children do not yet understand, six times eleven can be considered to be sixty-eight." She laughed through her nose. "In higher mathematics numbers are . . . more fluid. The only thing a number does is contain a certain amount of something. Think of water. A cup is not the only way to measure a certain amount of water, is it?" We were staring, shaking our heads. "You could use saucepans or thimbles. In either case, the water *would be the same.* Perhaps," she started again, "it would be better for you to think that six times eleven is sixty-eight only when I am in the room."

"Why is it sixty-eight," Mark Poole asked, "when you're in the room?"

"Because it's more interesting that way," she said, smiling very rapidly behind her blue-tinted glasses. "Besides, I'm your substitute teacher, am I not?" We all nodded. "Well, then, think of six times eleven equals sixty-eight as a substitute fact."

"A substitute fact?"

"Yes." Then she looked at us carefully. "Do you think," she asked, "that anyone is going to be hurt by a substitute fact?"

We looked back at her.

"Will the plants on the windowsill be hurt?" We glanced at them. There were sensitive plants thriving in a green plastic tray, and several wilted ferns in small clay pots. "Your dogs and cats, or your moms and dads?" She waited. "So," she concluded, "what's the problem?"

"But it's wrong," Janice Weber said, "isn't it?"

"What's your name, young lady?"

"Janice Weber."

"And you think it's wrong, Janice?"

"I was just asking."

"Well, all right. You were just asking. I think we've spent enough time on this matter by now, don't you, class? You are free to think what you like. When your teacher, Mr. Hibler, returns, six times eleven will be sixty-six again, you can rest assured. And it will be that for the rest of your lives in Five Oaks. Too bad, eh?" She raised her eyebrows and glinted herself at us. "But for now, it wasn't. So much for that. Let us go on to your assigned problems for today, as painstakingly outlined, I see, in Mr. Hibler's lesson plan. Take out a sheet of paper and write your names in the upper left-hand corner."

For the next half hour we did the rest of our arithmetic problems. We handed them in and then went on to spelling, my worst subject. Spelling always came before lunch. We were taking spelling dictation and looking at the clock. "Thorough," Miss Ferenczi said. "Boundary." She walked in the aisles between the desks, holding the spelling book open and looking down at our papers. "Balcony." I clutched my pencil. Somehow, the way she said those words, they seemed foreign, mis-voweled and mis-consonanted. I stared down at what I had spelled. *Balconie.* I turned the pencil upside down and erased my mistake. *Balconey.* That looked better, but still incorrect. I cursed the world of spelling and tried erasing it again and saw the paper beginning to wear away. *Balkony.* Suddenly I felt a hand on my shoulder.

"I don't like that word either," Miss Ferenczi whispered, bent over, her mouth near my ear. "It's ugly. My feeling is, if you don't like a word, you don't have to use it." She straightened up, leaving behind a slight odor of Clorets.

At lunchtime we went out to get our trays of sloppy joes, peaches in heavy syrup, coconut cookies, and milk, and brought them back to the classroom, where Miss Ferenczi was sitting at the desk, eating a brown sticky thing she had unwrapped from tightly rubber-banded waxed paper. "Miss Ferenczi," I said, raising my hand. "You don't have to eat with us. You can eat with the other teachers. There's a teachers' lounge," I ended up, "next to the principal's office."

"No, thank you," she said. "I prefer it here."

"We've got a room monitor," I said. "Mrs. Eddy." I pointed to where Mrs. Eddy, Joyce and Judy's mother, sat silently at the back of the room, doing her knitting.

"That's fine," Miss Ferenczi said. "But I shall continue to eat here, with you children. I prefer it," she repeated.

"How come?" Wayne Razmer asked without raising his hand.

"I talked to the other teachers before class this morning," Miss Ferenczi said, biting into her brown food. "There was a great rattling of the words for the fewness of the ideas. I didn't care for their brand of hilarity. I don't like ditto-machine jokes."

"Oh," Wayne said.

"What's that you're eating?" Maxine Sylvester asked, twitching her nose. "Is it food?"

"It most certainly *is* food. It's a stuffed fig. I had to drive almost down to Detroit to get it. I also brought some smoked sturgeon. And this," she said, lifting some green leaves out of her lunchbox, "is raw spinach, cleaned this morning."

"Why're you eating raw spinach?" Maxine asked.

"It's good for you," Miss Ferenczi said. "More stimulating than soda pop or smelling salts." I bit into my sloppy joe and stared blankly out the window. An almost invisible moon was faintly silvered in the daytime autumn sky. "As far as food is concerned," Miss Ferenczi was saying, "you have to shuffle the pack. Mix it up. Too many people eat . . . well, never mind."

"Miss Ferenczi," Carol Peterson said, "what are we going to do this afternoon?"

"Well," she said, looking down at Mr. Hibler's lesson plan, "I see that your teacher, Mr. Hibler, has you scheduled for a unit on the Egyptians." Carol groaned. "Yessss," Miss Ferenczi continued, "that is what we will do: the Egyptians. A remarkable people. Almost as remarkable as the Americans. But not quite." She lowered her head, did her quick smile, and went back to eating her spinach.

૬

After noon recess we came back into the classroom and saw that Miss Ferenczi had drawn a pyramid on the blackboard, close to her oak tree. Some of us who had been playing baseball were messing around in the back of the room, dropping the bats and gloves into the playground box, and Ray Schontzeler had just slugged me when I heard Miss Ferenczi's high-pitched voice, quavering with emotion. "Boys," she said, "come to order right this minute and take your seats. I do not wish to waste a minute of class time. Take out your geography books." We trudged to our desks and, still sweating, pulled out *Distant Lands and Their People.* "Turn to page forty-two." She waited for thirty seconds, then looked over at Kelly Munger. "Young man," she said, "why are you still fossicking in your desk?"

Kelly looked as if his foot had been stepped on. "Why am I what?"

"Why are you . . . burrowing in your desk like that?"

"I'm lookin' for the book, Miss Ferenczi."

Bobby Kryzanowicz, the faultless brown-noser who sat in the first row by choice, softly said, "His name is Kelly Munger. He can't ever find his stuff. He always does that."

"I don't care what his name is, especially after lunch," Miss Ferenczi said. *"Where is your book?"*

"I just found it." Kelly was peering into his desk and with both hands pulled at the book, shoveling along in front of it several pencils and crayons, which fell into his lap and then to the floor.

"I hate a mess," Miss Ferenczi said. "I hate a mess in a desk or a mind. It's . . . unsanitary. You wouldn't want your house at home to look like your desk at school, now, would you?" She didn't wait for an answer. "I should think not. A house at home should be as neat as human hands can make it. What were we talking about? Egypt. Page forty-two. I note from Mr. Hibler's lesson plan that you have been discussing the modes of Egyptian irrigation. Interesting, in my view, but not so interesting as what we are about to cover. The pyramids, and Egyptian slave labor. A plus on one side, a minus on the other." We had our books open to page forty-two, where there was a picture of a pyramid, but

Miss Ferenczi wasn't looking at the book. Instead, she was staring at some object just outside the window.

"Pyramids," Miss Ferenczi said, still looking past the window. "I want you to think about pyramids. And what was inside. The bodies of the pharaohs, of course, and their attendant treasures. Scrolls. Perhaps," Miss Ferenczi said, her face gleeful but unsmiling, "these scrolls were novels for the pharaohs, helping them to pass the time in their long voyage through the centuries. But then, I am joking." I was looking at the lines on Miss Ferenczi's skin. "Pyramids," Miss Ferenczi went on, "were the repositories of special cosmic powers. The nature of a pyramid is to guide cosmic energy forces into a concentrated point. The Egyptians knew that; we have generally forgotten it. Did you know," she asked, walking to the side of the room so that she was standing by the coat closet, "that George Washington had Egyptian blood, from his grandmother? Certain features of the Constitution of the United States are notable for their Egyptian ideas."

Without glancing down at the book, she began to talk about the movement of souls in Egyptian religion. She said that when people die, their souls return to Earth in the form of carpenter ants or walnut trees, depending on how they behaved—"well or ill"—in life. She said that the Egyptians believed that people act the way they do because of magnetism produced by tidal forces in the solar system, forces produced by the sun and by its "planetary ally," Jupiter. Jupiter, she said, was a planet, as we had been told, but had "certain properties of stars." She was speaking very fast. She said that the Egyptians were great explorers and conquerors. She said that the greatest of all the conquerors, Genghis Khan, had had forty horses and forty young women killed on the site of his grave. We listened. No one tried to stop her. "I myself have been in Egypt," she said, "and have witnessed much dust and many brutalities."

She said that an old man in Egypt who worked for a circus had personally shown her an animal in a cage, a monster, half bird and half lion. She said that this monster was called a gryphon and that she had heard about them but never seen them until she traveled to the outskirts of Cairo. She wrote the word out on the blackboard in large capital letters: GRYPHON. She said that Egyptian astronomers had discovered the planet Saturn but had not seen its rings. She said that the Egyptians were the first to discover that dogs, when they are ill, will not drink from rivers, but wait for rain, and hold their jaws open to catch it.

ɞ

"She lies."

We were on the school bus home. I was sitting next to Carl Whiteside, who had bad breath and a huge collection of marbles. We were arguing. Carl thought she was lying. I said she wasn't, probably.

"I didn't believe that stuff about the bird," Carl said, "and what she told us about the pyramids? I didn't believe that, either. She didn't know what she was talking about."

"Oh yeah?" I had liked her. She was strange. I thought I could nail him. "If she was lying," I said, "what'd she say that was a lie?"

"Six times eleven isn't sixty-eight. It isn't ever. It's sixty-six, I know for a fact."

"She said so. She admitted it. What else did she lie about?"

"I don't know," he said. "Stuff."

"What stuff?"

"Well." He swung his legs back and forth. "You ever see an animal that was half lion and half bird?" He crossed his arms. "It sounded real fakey to me."

"It could happen," I said. I had to improvise, to outrage him. "I read in this newspaper my mom bought in the IGA about this scientist, this mad scientist in the Swiss Alps, and he's been putting genes and chromosomes and stuff together in test tubes, and he combined a human being and a hamster." I waited, for effect. "It's called a humster."

"You never." Carl was staring at me, his mouth open, his terrible bad breath making its way toward me. "What newspaper was it?"

"The National Enquirer," I said, "that they sell next to the cash registers." When I saw his look of recognition, I knew I had him. "And this mad scientist," I said, "his name was, um, Dr. Frankenbush." I realized belatedly that this name was a mistake and waited for Carl to notice its resemblance to the name of the other famous mad master of permutations, but he only sat there.

"A man and a hamster?" He was staring at me, squinting, his mouth opening in distaste. "Jeez. What'd it look like?"

୭

When the bus reached my stop, I took off down our dirt road and ran up through the backyard, kicking the tire swing for good luck. I dropped my books on the back steps so I could hug and kiss our dog, Mr. Selby. Then I hurried inside. I could smell brussels sprouts cooking, my unfavorite vegetable. My mother was washing other vegetables in the kitchen sink, and my baby brother was hollering in his yellow playpen on the kitchen floor.

"Hi, Mom," I said, hopping around the playpen to kiss her. "Guess what?"

"I have no idea."

"We had this substitute today, Miss Ferenczi, and I'd never seen her before, and she had all these stories and ideas and stuff."

"Well. That's good." My mother looked out the window in front of the sink, her eyes on the pine woods west of our house. That time of the afternoon her skin always looked so white to me. Strangers always said my mother looked like Betty Crocker, framed by the giant spoon on the side of the Bisquick box. "Listen, Tommy," she said. "Would you please go upstairs and pick your clothes off the floor in the bathroom, and then go outside to the shed and put the shovel and ax away that your father left outside this morning?"

"She said that six times eleven was sometimes sixty-eight!" I said. "And she said she once saw a monster that was half lion and half bird." I waited. "In Egypt."

"Did you hear me?" my mother asked, raising her arm to wipe her forehead with the back of her hand. "You have chores to do."

"I know," I said. "I was just telling you about the substitute."

"It's very interesting," my mother said, quickly glancing down at me, "and we can talk about it later when your father gets home. But right now you have some work to do."

"Okay, Mom." I took a cookie out of the jar on the counter and was about to go outside when I had a thought. I ran into the living room, pulled out a dictionary next to the TV stand, and opened it to the Gs. After five minutes I found it. *Gryphon:* "variant of griffin." *Griffin:* "a fabulous beast with the head and wings of an eagle and the body of a lion." Fabulous was right. I shouted with triumph and ran outside to put my father's tools in their proper places.

Miss Ferenczi was back the next day, slightly altered. She had pulled her hair down and twisted it into pigtails, with red rubber bands holding them tight one inch from the ends. She was wearing a green blouse and pink scarf, making her difficult to look at for a full class day. This time there was no pretense of doing a reading lesson or moving on to arithmetic. As soon as the bell rang, she simply began to talk.

She talked for forty minutes straight. There seemed to be less connection between her ideas, but the ideas themselves were, as the dictionary would say, fabulous. She said she had heard of a huge jewel, in what she called the antipodes, that was so brilliant that when light shone into it at a certain angle it would blind whoever was looking at its center. She said the biggest diamond in the world was cursed and had killed everyone who owned it, and that by a trick of fate it was called the Hope Diamond. Diamonds are magic, she said, and this is why women wear them on their fingers, as a sign of the magic of womanhood. Men have strength, Miss Ferenczi said, but no true magic. That is why men fall in love with women but women do not fall in love with men: they just love being loved. George Washington had died because of a mistake he made about a diamond. Washington was not the first *true* President, but she didn't say who was. In some places in the world, she said, men and women still live in the trees and eat monkeys for breakfast. Their doctors are magicians. At the bottom of the sea are creatures thin as pancakes who have never been studied by scientists because when you take them up to air, the fish explode.

There was not a sound in the classroom, except for Miss Ferenczi's voice, and Donna DeShano's coughing. No one even went to the bathroom.

Beethoven, she said, had not been deaf; it was a trick to make himself famous, and it worked. As she talked, Miss Ferenczi's pigtails swung back and forth. There are trees in the world, she said, that eat meat: their leaves are sticky and close up on bugs like hands. She lifted her hands and brought them together, palm to palm. Venus, which most people think is the next closest planet to the sun, is not always closer, and, besides, it is the planet of greatest mystery because of its thick cloud cover. "I know what lies underneath those clouds," Miss Ferenczi said, and waited.

After the silence, she said, "Angels. Angels live under those clouds." She said that angels were not invisible to everyone and were in fact smarter than most people. They did not dress in robes as was often claimed but instead wore formal evening clothes, as if they were about to attend a concert. Often angels *do* attend concerts and sit in the aisles where, she said, most people pay no attention to them. She said the most terrible angel had the shape of the Sphinx. "There is no running away from that one," she said. She said that unquenchable fires burn just under the surface of the earth in Ohio, and that the baby Mozart fainted dead away in his cradle when he first heard the sound of a trumpet. She said that someone named Narzim al Harrardim was the greatest writer who ever lived. She said that planets control behavior, and anyone conceived during a solar eclipse would be born with webbed feet.

"I know you children like to hear these things," she said, "these secrets, and that is why I am telling you all this." We nodded. It was better than doing comprehension questions for the readings in *Broad Horizons.*

"I will tell you one more story," she said, "and then we will have to do arithmetic." She leaned over, and her voice grew soft. "There is no death," she said. "You must never be afraid. Never. That which is, cannot die. It will change into different earthly and unearthly elements, but I know this as sure as I stand here in front of you, and I swear it: you must not be afraid. I have seen this truth with these eyes. I know it because in a dream God kissed me. Here." And she pointed with her right index finger to the side of her head, below the mouth where the vertical lines were carved into her skin.

Absentmindedly we all did our arithmetic problems. At recess the class was out on the playground, but no one was playing. We were all standing in small groups, talking about Miss Ferenczi. We didn't know if she was crazy, or what. I looked out beyond the playground, at the rusted cars piled in a small heap behind a clump of sumac, and I wanted to see shapes there, approaching me.

୧

On the way home, Carl sat next to me again. He didn't say much, and I didn't either. At last he turned to me. "You know what she said about the leaves that close up on bugs?"

"Huh?"

"The leaves," Carl insisted. "The meat-eating plants. I know it's true. I saw it on television. The leaves have this icky glue that the plants have got smeared all over them and the insects can't get off 'cause they're stuck. I saw it." He seemed demoralized. "She's tellin' the truth."

"Yeah."

"You think she's seen all those angels?"

I shrugged.

"I don't think she has," Carl informed me. "I think she made that part up."

"There's a tree," I suddenly said. I was looking out the window at the farms along County Road H. I knew every barn, every broken windmill, every fence, every anhydrous ammonia tank, by heart. "There's a tree that's . . . that I've seen . . ."

"Don't you try to do it," Carl said. "You'll just sound like a jerk."

୧

I kissed my mother. She was standing in front of the stove. "How was your day?" she asked.

"Fine."

"Did you have Miss Ferenczi again?"

"Yeah."

"Well?"

"She was fine. Mom," I asked, "can I go to my room?"

"No," she said, "not until you've gone out to the vegetable garden and picked me a few tomatoes." She glanced at the sky. "I think it's going to rain. Skedaddle and do it now. Then you come back inside and watch your brother for a few minutes while I go upstairs. I need to clean up before dinner." She looked down at me. "You're looking a little pale, Tommy." She touched the back of her hand to my forehead and I felt her diamond ring against my skin. "Do you feel all right?"

"I'm fine," I said, and went out to pick the tomatoes.

Coughing mutedly, Mr. Hibler was back the next day, slipping lozenges into his mouth when his back was turned at forty-five-minute intervals and asking us how much of his prepared lesson plan Miss Ferenczi had followed. Edith Atwater took the responsibility for the class of explaining to Mr. Hibler that the substitute hadn't always done exactly what he, Mr. Hibler, would have done, but we had worked hard even though she talked a lot. About what? he asked. All kinds of things, Edith said. I sort of forgot. To our relief, Mr. Hibler seemed not at all interested in what Miss Ferenczi had said to fill the day. He probably thought it was woman's talk: unserious and not suited for school. It was enough that he had a pile of arithmetic problems from us to correct.

For the next month, the sumac turned a distracting red in the field, and the sun traveled toward the southern sky, so that its rays reached Mr. Hibler's Halloween display on the bulletin board in the back of the room, fading the pumpkin head scarecrow from orange to tan. Every three days I measured how much farther the sun had moved toward the southern horizon by making small marks with my black Crayola on the north wall, ant-sized marks only I knew were there.

And then in early December, four days after the first permanent snowfall, she appeared again in our classroom. The minute she came in the door, I felt my heart begin to pound. Once again, she was different: this time, her hair hung straight down and seemed hardly to have been combed. She hadn't brought her lunchbox with her, but she was carrying what seemed to be a small box. She greeted all of us and talked about the weather. Donna DeShano had to remind her to take her overcoat off.

When the bell to start the day finally rang, Miss Ferenczi looked out at all of us and said, "Children, I have enjoyed your company in the past, and today I am going to reward you." She held up the small box. "Do you know what this is?" She waited. "Of course you don't. It is a Tarot pack."

Edith Atwater raised her hand. "What's a Tarot pack, Miss Ferenczi?"

"It is used to tell fortunes," she said. "And that is what I shall do this morning. I shall tell your fortunes, as I have been taught to do."

"What's fortune?" Bobby Kryzanowicz asked.

"The future, young man. I shall tell you what your future will be. I can't do your whole future, of course. I shall have to limit myself to the five-card system, the wands, cups, swords, pentacles, and the higher arcanes. Now who wants to be first?"

There was a long silence. Then Carol Peterson raised her hand.

"All right," Miss Ferenczi said. She divided the pack into five smaller packs and walked back to Carol's desk, in front of mine. "Pick one card from each one of these packs," she said. I saw that Carol had a four of cups and a six of swords, but I couldn't see the other cards. Miss Ferenczi studied the cards on Carol's desk for a minute. "Not bad," she said. "I do not see much higher education. Probably an early marriage. Many children. There's something bleak and dreary here, but I can't tell what. Perhaps just the tasks of a housewife life. I think you'll do very well, for the most part." She smiled at Carol, a smile with a certain lack of interest. "Who wants to be next?"

Carl Whiteside raised his hand slowly.

"Yes," Miss Ferenczi said, "let's do a boy." She walked over to where Carl sat. After he picked his five cards, she gazed at them for a long time. "Travel," she said. "Much distant travel. You might go into the army. Not too much romantic interest here. A late marriage, if at all. But the Sun in your major arcana, that's a very good card." She giggled. "You'll have a happy life."

Next I raised my hand. She told me my future. She did the same with Bobby Kryzanowicz, Kelly Munger, Edith Atwater, and Kim Foor. Then she came to Wayne Razmer. He picked his five cards, and I could see that the Death card was one of them.

"What's your name?" Miss Ferenczi asked.

"Wayne."

"Well, Wayne," she said, "you will undergo a great metamorphosis, a change, before you become an adult. Your earthly element will no doubt leap higher, because you seem to be a sweet boy. This card, this nine of swords, tells me suffering and desolation. And this ten of wands, well, that's a heavy load."

"What about this one?" Wayne pointed to the Death card.

"It means, my sweet, that you will die soon." She gathered up the cards. We were all looking at Wayne. "But do not fear," she said. "It is not really death. Just change. Out of your earthly shape." She put the cards on Mr. Hibler's desk. "And now, let's do some arithmetic."

6

At lunchtime Wayne went to Mr. Faegre, the principal, and informed him of what Miss Ferenczi had done. During the noon recess, we saw Miss Ferenczi drive out of the parking lot in her rusting green Rambler American. I stood under the slide, listening to the other kids coasting down and landing in the little depressive bowls at the bottom. I was kicking stones and tugging at my hair right up to the moment when I saw Wayne come out to the playground. He smiled, the dead fool, and with the fingers of his right hand he was showing everyone how he had told on Miss Ferenczi.

I made my way toward Wayne, pushing myself past two girls from another class. He was watching me with his little pinhead eyes.

"You told," I shouted at him. "She was just kidding."

"She shouldn't have," he shouted back. "We were supposed to be doing arithmetic."

"She just scared you," I said. "You're a chicken. You're a chicken, Wayne. You are. Scared of a little card," I singsonged.

Wayne fell at me, his two fists hammering down on my nose. I gave him a good one in the stomach and then I tried for his head. Aiming my fist, I saw that he was crying. I slugged him.

"She was right," I yelled. "She was always right! She told the truth!" Other kids were whooping. "You were just scared, that's all!"

And then large hands pulled at us, and it was my turn to speak to Mr. Faegre.

6

In the afternoon Miss Ferenczi was gone, and my nose was stuffed with cotton clotted with blood, and my lip had swelled, and our class had been combined with Mrs. Mantei's sixth-grade class for a crowded afternoon science unit on insect life in ditches and swamps. I knew where Mrs. Mantei lived: she had a new house trailer just down the road from us, at the Clearwater Park. She was no mystery. Somehow she and Mr. Bodine, the other fourth-grade teacher, had managed to fit forty-five desks into the room. Kelly Munger asked if Miss Ferenczi had been arrested, and Mrs. Mantei said no, of course not. All that afternoon, until the buses came to pick us up, we learned about field crickets and two-striped grasshoppers, water bugs, cicadas, mosquitoes, flies, and moths. We learned about insects' hard outer shell, the exoskeleton, and the usual parts of the mouth, including the labrum, mandible, maxilla, and glossa. We learned about compound eyes, and the four-stage metamorphosis from egg to larva to pupa to adult. We learned something, but not much, about mating. Mrs. Mantei drew, very skillfully, the internal anatomy of the grasshopper on the blackboard. We learned about the dance of the honeybee, directing other bees in the hive to pollen. We found out about which insects were pests to man, and which were not. On lined white pieces of paper we made lists of insects we might actually see, then a list of insects too small to be clearly visible, such as fleas; Mrs. Mantei said that our assignment would be to memorize these lists for the next day, when Mr. Hibler would certainly return and test us on our knowledge.

Andrea Lee

The Days of the Thunderbirds

When the Thunderbirds arrived at Camp Grayfeather, Ellen, Chen-cheu, and I were waiting for them, lounging on the splintery steps of the recreation hall. Behind us a big fly with a weary August note to its buzz banged against the screen door. In front of us, under a level evening sun, the straw-colored Delaware countryside—pointedly referred to as "Wyeth Territory" in the camp catalogue—rolled off from our own wooded hillside toward the bluish haze that was Maryland. It was a Tuesday and just after dinner, the tranquil period in a camp day when the woods are filled with the soft clanging of bells announcing evening activities and the air still holds a whiff of tuna casserole. After dinner was supposed to be journal-writing time for the three dozen or so fourteen-year-olds who made up the rank and file at Grayfeather, but Chen-cheu, Ellen, and I had slipped out of our tent in order to witness the coming of the Thunderbirds. It was an event we were awaiting with the same kind of horrified delight as that with which biblical adolescents—as deep in glandular boredom as we ourselves were—must have greeted a plague of serpents. The Thunderbirds were a black teenage gang, one of many that battled in the close brick streets of Wilmington, and through some obscure adult arrangement they were coming to spend a week with us at camp.

"Do you think they'll have knives, Sarah?" Chen-cheu asked me, rubbing an array of chigger bites on her ankle.

Chen-cheu was the camp beauty, a Chinese-American girl from Oberlin, Ohio, whose solid-cheeked, suntanned face had an almost frightening exotic loveliness above her muscular swimmer's shoulders. She had, however, a calm, practical personality that belied her thrilling looks, and she talked with a flat midwestern accent, as if she'd been brought up in a soddy.

"Nah," I said. "Gangs use guns these days."

In fact my only knowledge of the habits of gangs came from seeing the movie *West Side Story,* but like the other black kids at Grayfeather, most of us the overprotected or horribly spoiled products of comfortable suburban childhoods, I had been affecting an intimate knowledge of street life ever since I'd heard about the Thunderbirds.

"Maybe we'll end up massacred," said Ellen in a hopeful voice, unwrapping a stick of gum.

Ellen was always chewing gum, though it was against camp rules; she had come to Grayfeather with about a thousand packages of Wrigley's hidden in her trunk, and even, to the derision of her bunkmates, made little chains of the wrappers. She chewed so much that her father, a Reform rabbi in Baltimore, once made her walk around a shopping mall with a wad of gum stuck to her forehead. She and Chen-cheu and I had been close friends all summer, a brisk female triumvirate who liked to think of ourselves as Maid Marians, both lawless and seductive. (In reality it was only Chen-cheu who provided the physical charms, since Ellen and I were both peaky, bookwormish types.) The three of us made a point of being on the spot whenever anything interesting or scandalous happened at the camp, and the arrival of the Thunderbirds was certainly the most riveting event of the summer.

They were not the first visitors we'd had at Grayfeather: already we'd played host to a morose quartet of Peruvian flute players and a troop of impossibly pink-cheeked Icelandic scouts. The Thunderbirds represented, however, the most ambitious attempt to incarnate the camp motto, which was "Adventures in Understanding."

As Ellen once remarked, instead of being a tennis camp or a weight-loss camp, Grayfeather was an integration camp. The campers, most of whose fathers were professors, like Chen-cheu's, or clergymen, like mine, had been carefully selected to form a motley collection of colors and religions, so that our massed assemblies at meals, chapel, and campfires looked like illustrations for UNICEF posters.

It was at chapel the previous Sunday that Ned Woolworth, the camp director, had announced the coming of the Thunderbirds.

"During the next week you'll be more than just kids relating to kids," he said, strolling up and down between the rows of split-log benches, scanning our dubious fourteen-year-old faces with his benign, abstracted gaze, his big gnarled knees (his nickname was Monster Legs) working below his khaki shorts. Woolworth was tall and looked like Teddy Roosevelt, and had an amazing talent for not knowing things. He ignored the generally unenthusiastic silence as his campers coldly pondered the ramifications of doubling up in tents with their comrades-to-be, and passed over the muttered lamentations of the camp misfit, a Nigerian diplomat's son named Femi. He read us a few lines from *The Prophet* and then told us we would be like ambassadors, bridging a gap that society had created. It appeared that the staff had already written and gotten permission from all of our parents.

The arrival of the Thunderbirds at Grayfeather was signaled by a grinding of gears and a confused yelling from far down the dirt road that led through six miles of woods to the camp. As Ellen, Chen-cheu, and I poked one another in excitement, a battered yellow school bus covered with a tangle of long-stemmed graffiti rattled into the clearing and swerved into the dusty parking lot beside the rec hall. The bus ground its gears once more, shuddered, and seemed to expire. The doors flew open, and the Thunderbirds poured down the steps into the evening sunlight.

"They're so *small!*" Ellen whispered to me.

There were ten boys and seven girls—the girls forming, as we later found out, a sort of auxiliary unit to the Thunderbirds—brown-skinned teenagers with mature faces and bodies and stunted, childish legs that gave the boys, with their muscular shoulders and short thighs, the look of bantam cocks.

One of the boys came up to Chen-cheu, Ellen, and me and stood rocking on his heels. "Hello, ladies," he said. "My name is Marvin Jones." He wore tight black pants and a green t-shirt that was printed with the words king funk, and he had an astonishing Afro pompadour that bobbed like a cresting wave over his mobile trickster's face. Above his left eye he had dyed a platinum streak in his hair, and down one brown cheek ran a deep scar.

Looking at him, I had the feeling that something unbelievable was happening in front of me. "Hello," said Chen-cheu, Ellen, and I in a faint chorus.

In a minute Ned Woolworth and the rest of the staff were there organizing things. The sleepy little camp clearing with its square of sun-bleached turf and its cluster of low green-painted buildings seemed suddenly frantic and overcrowded. Radios weren't allowed at Grayfeather, but one of the Thunderbirds had brought a big portable receiver that filled the air with a Motown beat. Martha and the Vandellas were singing, their shrill, sweet voices crackling with static, and the Thunderbirds were bouncing to the beat while they eyed the camp, shoved one another, picked up their abbreviated luggage, and shouted back and forth. Meanwhile, the rest of the Grayfeather campers had slipped unobtrusively, even furtively, out of the woods, like an indigenous tribe showing itself to explorers; they settled on the steps and porches of the rec hall to swing their feet and observe. Little Nick Silver, a math whiz from Toughkenamon, Pennsylvania, who at a precocious twelve years old was the youngest kid at camp, sat down next to me. "You have *got* to be joking," he whispered. "They'll eat us for breakfast!"

With the Thunderbirds had come a counselor from the social agency that had sponsored their visit: a tall, sallow white man with thinning curly hair and a weary, skeptical way of regarding the woods, the camp buildings, the evening sky, and his charges. He talked with Ned Woolworth for a few minutes and then climbed back inside the battered school bus, turning around only once to smile sardonically at the Thunderbirds. "See you later, guys," he called out. "Behave yourselves." The Thunderbirds responded with a kind of roar, and then the school bus started up with another wrench of gears and rattled off through the trees.

Once the newcomers had filed down the path into the woods to put their bags away in the tents, one of the counselors rang the evening activities bell. "We'll have introductions at campfire," she announced. "Be friendly!"

We campers simply looked at one another. With the Thunderbirds gone from the clearing, a powerful current of noise and energy had suddenly been shut off. Bats flitted across the darkening sky, and a breeze from the lake carried a smell of damp leaf mold. While the others were lining up, I went over to inspect a far corner of the dining hall, where I'd seen a group of the Thunderbirds clustering. There, carved deeply into the green paint, was a miniature version of the same long-stemmed, weirdly elegant graffiti that had covered the school bus, and that I had seen spray-painted on decrepit city buildings. It read: T-BIRDZ RULE.

Marvin Jones was the leader of the Thunderbirds. At

the get-acquainted campfire, it was his command that galvanized his troops into standing up and stepping forward, one by one, to give their names. ("L.T." "LaWanda." "Doze." "Brother Willy.") He himself stood in the firelight with a crazy tremor running through his body, wearing a rubber-lipped showman's smirk, like a black Mick Jagger. ("Stretch." "Chewy." "Belinda." "Guy.") In the bright circle of hot moving light that baked our faces and knees and left our backs chilled with the damp breath of the big pine grove behind us, we campers studied the Thunderbirds and they studied us. Both groups had the same peculiar expression: not hostility, but a wary reservation of judgment. As bits of ash danced like a swarm of glowing insects in the draft of the fire—a big log-cabin fire, built specially for the occasion by the Wood Crafts class—Ned Woolworth, his cheerful freckled wife, Hannah, and the rest of the staff guided us all through a number of cheers and folk songs.

Most of the counselors looked eager and uneasy. The near-instantaneous grapevine among the campers had already reported that the Thunderbirds had got into trouble immediately after their arrival, as they walked down the path to the boys' tents. Marvin Jones and two others had shinnied up a tall, skinny tree—one of the birches unusual in that area, and beloved by the Nature counselors—swinging on it and pulling it down with their combined weight until it bent over and seemed likely to break. When one of the counselors asked them to stop, Marvin Jones, laughing crazily and hanging on to the birch, responded, "This is the *woods,* man! Ain't *no* law against climbing no tree in the woods!"

That night the Thunderbird girls who had been assigned to share our tent refused to undress until the light was turned out. There were three of them: a pair of tiny, frail-boned sisters named Cookie and June, who had large almond-shaped eyes, hair done identically in an elaborately braided puff over each ear, and small breasts in sharp brassieres that stuck out like pointed Dixie cups through the clinging nylon of their blouses; and Belinda, a stocky girl who looked twenty years old and had a slight squint, straightened hair bleached bright orange-red in the front, and a loud, unbridled tongue—I had heard Belinda laughing and cursing above the others when they got off the bus. She was subdued now, as were Cookie and June, the three of them sitting bolt upright on the tightly stretched army blankets and sheets of the cots that had been set up for them, muttering replies to the kindly chitchat of our counselor, Molly. Molly was from Jamaica, a student with an anxious plump face and a delightful habit of shaking her head at her campers and exclaiming, "Girls, you are becoming hardened in your ways!"

The three Thunderbird girls responded to Molly with a sudden opacity of gaze, glances among themselves, and abrupt fits of shy giggling. We campers were stricken with shyness ourselves: there was none of our usual roughhousing or bedtime ballets in our underwear, or wisecracking about Patty Haas's ugly boyfriend—a standing joke. Instead we undressed quickly in our bunks, turning away from each other, painfully conscious of the contrast between the elaborately equipped trunks from which we drew our pajamas and the small vinyl bags that our guests had brought. Once Molly had turned off the single yellow bulb that illuminated the tent and had strolled off up the path to a late-night staff meeting at the rec hall, the tent was unnaturally silent.

I arranged myself on my lumpy top bunk as I always did—with the sheet over my head to keep off mosquitoes—and breathed in the scent of slightly mildewed canvas from the rolled sides of the tent. From the bunk beneath me, Chen-cheu, a sound and instant sleeper, gave an adenoidal snore, and I could hear little clicks and rustlings that meant that the Thunderbird girls were undressing. There was a cool breeze blowing with a steady rushing sound in the trees, and I wondered what the girls from the city were thinking as they listened, perhaps for the first time in their lives, to the noises of the wild night. Never had I been so aware of the woods as a living place around me: over the stubborn saw of the crickets, I heard two hoots from a white-faced owl who lived in a tree near our tent, and a gradually intensifying gray light in the direction of the lake meant the moon was rising. In my mind the moon mingled with the yellow school bus that had brought the Thunderbirds, and then I found myself sliding quickly out of the vision, knowing that I'd been asleep. What had awakened me was a soft voice; it was the new girl, June, calling out to her sister in a whisper.

"Cookie—Cookie—are you up? I hear a noise."

There was a soft creak as Cookie got up and crept over to her sister's cot. I leaned my head out slightly from my bunk and in the dim moonlight caught a glimpse of the tiny girl, her hair greased and braided for the night, dressed in her underwear. It hadn't occurred to me until then that perhaps the Thunderbird girls didn't have pajamas. "Hush, girl," hissed Cookie to her sister, sitting lightly down on the cot. "Hush up! You want these bitches to hear you?"

"But there's a noise," whimpered June.

"Hush up, girl. It's just trees, that's all. Just trees."

There was silence, and when after a few minutes I edged my head out of the bunk to have another look, I saw that Cookie had lain down on her sister's cot and that the two girls were sleeping with their heads close together on the pillow.

At breakfast Ned Woolworth announced to a chorus of groans from the campers that instead of swimming or canoeing or tennis, we would divide up into small groups for what he called "rap sessions." My group included Ellen; Jackie Murdock, a camper notorious throughout Grayfeather for his prolonged belches at mealtimes; a plump, round-faced Thunderbird named Ricky; and a skinnier Thunderbird named Les, who wore a peculiar rust-colored bowler hat. There was also Marvin Jones, the Thunderbird leader, wearing an army fatigue jacket open to show his gleaming bronze chest; he sat slumped, wiggling his feet, on his face an expression of exaggerated forbearance.

The six of us, with a counselor, met in a grove of pin oaks near the chapel. It was one of those clear, dry, autumnal days that occasionally leap ahead of their time into the middle of August. The sky was a sharp blue, crisp moving shadows checkered the ground, and in the eyes of all the kids sitting there was a skittish, inattentive look, as if they might dash off suddenly into the breezy woods.

A green acorn plopped down near Ricky, the plump Thunderbird sitting beside Ellen. "Wha's that?" he asked her, pointing.

"That's an acorn," said Ellen scornfully, tossing back her red hair. "Didn't you ever see an acorn before?"

"No, Sweet Thighs," said Ricky, giving her a lascivious, cherubic smile that showed a broken front tooth. He picked up the acorn and put it carefully into his pocket.

The counselor in charge clapped her hands. She was a diving coach with a pugnacious sunburnt face and a blunt, bossy way of talking. "This morning we're going to discuss friendship," she said. "We all have friends, so let's talk about them—who they are, and what they mean to us—"

"I don't have friends," interrupted Marvin Jones.

"What?" said the counselor.

"I said I don't have friends," said Marvin Jones, looking at her seriously, the platinum streak in his hair glittering in the sunlight through the treetops. "Yeah, that's right, miss. I mean, shit—'scuse me, miss—I got my *men*. Spike is my *man.* Ricky is my *man,* and J.T., that dude with the sunglasses and the 'Free Africa' t-shirt, he's my *main* man. I mean, them dudes will cut for me. But they don't be no *friends.* And then we got the Thunderbird Queens—I mean our ladies."

"They're not your friends, of course," said the counselor acidly.

"No, like I said, we don't have no friends. We got enemies, though: the Twelfth and Diamond Street gang. You ever hear of them?"

"No."

"Well, that's good, 'cause the T-birds are on top. Wait a minute—I'll show you something."

He gave a curt, imperious nod to Ricky and the other Thunderbird beside him, and an odd tension seemed to seize all three of them. The woods seemed very quiet for a minute. All at once, synchronized, they stood up, snapping their fingers. In high, plaintive voices they broke into words and rhythms that were not quite a song, not quite a chant.

"What the word / Thunderbird . . ."

It was a strange mixture: a bit of Motown, a bit of the interlocking verses all kids use to choose sides for games, a bit of the bouncy silliness of football and basketball cheers, all bound together quite naturally with swearwords—words that we Grayfeather campers all knew and used enthusiastically among ourselves, in spite of what parents and teachers and counselors had to say. The Thunderbird song could have been ridiculous, but instead it was thrilling, carrying with it, to those of us who sat listening, all the resonance of a dangerous young life in the city. It was clear that the song was not intended as an entertainment for us, but was presented as a kind of credential, like the letters scratched into the paint of the rec hall.

Ellen and I punched each other excitedly in the ribs

and tried to remember every word. When the song was finished, Marvin Jones and the other two Thunderbirds flopped down abruptly at the base of a tree, their faces full of restrained pride.

"That was great, fellows," said the counselor. She was trying to seem cordial, but it was clear that she was uncomfortable, almost angry, about what had just happened. "Let's see if you can do a little more talking now, so that we can get to know you."

Marvin Jones picked up a twig from the ground and tapped the toes of his sneakers with it—one, two, three. "Lady, you just got to know us," he said.

Down at the lake that afternoon, Jimmy Terkel, the boating counselor, gave a short briefing on canoeing to an assembled group of campers and Thunderbirds. Terkel was a dark, soft-spoken young man who loved the little irregular lake, with its cedar water and clustering lilies; all summer he had made canoeing into an austere rite, embarking on solitary voyages at dawn or sunset, an angular silhouette at the far corner of the water. The afternoon had grown overcast, and as Terkel talked about water safety and demonstrated the proper way to dip and feather a paddle—the lecture was chiefly for the newcomers, since the campers had been handling canoes all summer—swarms of audacious gnats made forays at our eyes and ears. Suddenly, in the middle of the talk, Marvin Jones strode over to one of the aluminum canoes on the shore and began to push it toward the water. "I want to go for a ride, mister," he said politely to Jimmy Terkel. "I know how to do this. I see it all the time on TV."

Three other Thunderbirds grabbed paddles and rushed over to the canoe, pushing it through the shallows to deeper water and tilting it dangerously when they all climbed in, about fifteen yards from shore. "That's too many in a boat, fellows!" called Jimmy Terkel, coming forward. The gunwales of the overloaded canoe were riding about six inches above the surface of the lake, and the boat shipped water occasionally as the passengers thrashed about trying to position themselves; miraculously, the canoe did not capsize. There was an argument between two of the Thunderbirds ("You on my *arm,* man!") and then the canoe took off with an irregular splayed motion as Marvin Jones and a second Thunderbird paddled with great splashing thrusts.

"Oh, *no!*" Jimmy Terkel muttered, glancing automatically at the heap of orange life preservers on the shore. But no disaster occurred. The canoe made its awkward, lunging way into a cluster of lily pads, and we heard the delighted yells of the novice canoeists as they yanked up the tough-stemmed blossoms, an act that the camp staff, ardent conservationists all, had raised in our minds to the level of a felony. Then the boys in the boat all took off their shirts, and Marvin Jones stood precariously upright to paddle like a gondolier, a big lily coiled dripping around his neck. There was something barbaric and absurd about the sight of him paddling that overloaded canoe, which, as it wobbled heavily over the dark water, seemed a parody of a boat, something out of a nursery rhyme. As I watched it, there came to me out of nowhere a surge of pure happiness. The other campers seemed to feel it as well; the faces of the kids around me were contorted with crazy laughter, and some of them were jumping up and down. Out of the corner of my eye, I saw one of the boys, from pure *joie de vivre,* as it were, pick up a handful of sand and rub it into the hair of his bunkmate. Just for a minute, it seemed that the camp was a place where any mad thing could happen. While Jimmy Terkel stood on the shore with an angry smile on his face, campers and Thunderbirds alike were almost dying with glee. We laughed as if we'd never seen anything so funny.

That was the last, really the only, good time we had with the Thunderbirds. Later that afternoon a scuffle broke out near the camp infirmary between two of the gang members and a stableboy. A burly counselor from Honolulu broke up the fight, which was just a matter of shoving and name-calling. The participants were made to stand face to face and explain themselves, and in the process they quite spontaneously shook hands and apologized. In ten minutes the camp grapevine had telegraphed news of the scuffle to all parts of Grayfeather. It seemed that everyone involved in the fight had laughed it off except for Ned Woolworth, who rushed to the scene and glared at the three boys as if he wanted to knock them all down.

The staff had scheduled a hayride for that night. Normally, the campers looked forward to hayrides: the dusky country roads, shrill with insects; the creaky wagon and plodding, pungent horses; the deep, scratchy hay that offered the opportunity for a little romantic improvisation (though Grayfeather, a camp of overeducated fourteen-year-olds, was notoriously backward in that department). That particular evening, a subtle intelligence flashed through the ranks of the campers, a kind of mass intuition that suggested that things would be much better if we let the Thunderbirds go hayriding on their own. To the bewilderment of our counselors, who had no way of forcing us to accept a treat, all of the campers, gently but immovably, refused to go.

After dinner, Ellen, Chen-cheu, and I, and the other girls from our tent, took part in a desultory sunset game of Capture the Flag as the Thunderbirds and their girls, escorted by Grayfeather staff members, boarded the wagon. An hour and a half later, the returning wagon creaked slowly up to the rec hall. Norah Pfleisch, a plump, excitable junior counselor, rushed inside and burst into tears on the shoulder of Ned Woolworth's wife, Hannah, who was directing a spur-of-the-moment Ping-Pong tournament.

"I've never, *never* had anything like this happen," sobbed Norah, resisting Hannah's efforts to lead her out of the rec hall and away from the fascinated gaze of forty campers. "They—fornicated! They lay in the hay like animals and just . . . did it! It started when we went under the old covered bridge. It was such a beautiful night. Usually we *sing* on hayrides, but this time I didn't know *where* to look, or *what* to listen to!"

We all rushed to the door of the rec hall. Outside, under a clear night sky streaked with meteor showers, the Thunderbirds and their girls, chattering loudly and innocently, were climbing out of the wagon, pulling hay out of each others' clothes.

Things fell apart completely the next day. That morning at swimming class another fight broke out, this one between Femi, the camper from Nigeria, and an agile, pale-skinned, sullen-faced Thunderbird. On the shore in front of the swimming area of the lake, as the white rope and bright floats of the lane dividers bobbed gaily in the morning sun, two counselors held back the two struggling boys in bathing suits, Femi with a swollen nostril leaking blood. "I'll kill that filthy little nigger bastard," panted Femi in his Mayfair accent, wiping his nose with his coal-black arm. "I'll smear his dirty little arse all over the beach. He called me a monkey!"

"He spit on me," the Thunderbird was muttering, scuffling his feet in the sand. "Motherfucker spit on me."

Marvin Jones was called over to make peace. "This ain't no way to act," he began, but his tone was insincere, the tone of a showman bent on pleasing everyone. He sent a quick, shifty grin over to the Thunderbirds standing near him, and one of them suddenly shoved a camper, who went sprawling into the lake. In the boys' swim group a general melee broke out between campers and Thunderbirds, the tanned bodies of the campers mingling wildly with the small, dark, muscular Thunderbirds. The two counselors were themselves dragged in. Pairs of boys bolted, yelling threats, and ran off into the woods.

The girls at the lake, both Thunderbirds and campers, were quickly marched off to our tents, where we were told to sit quietly. Back at her trunk, Chen-cheu looked and found that someone had taken three of her prettiest t-shirts and a new bathing suit. When she complained loudly about it, she found herself surrounded by three Thunderbird girls, including our tentmate Belinda. They began to jostle Chen-cheu and to pluck at her long black hair; Chen-cheu promptly socked Belinda in the stomach. Our counselor Molly came running down the path from the rec hall at precisely the moment when Chen-cheu, propelled by a nasty push, came flying out of the tent to sprawl in the dust and shriek out a string of curses that even Ellen and I had never heard her use. Her beautiful face was contorted and almost purple with rage, but she wasn't crying. None of us were. After that we were separated from the Thunderbird girls.

Meanwhile, the boys were being rounded up. I heard later that a number of them were found grappling in twos and threes in the woods; there were surprisingly few injuries beyond a few black eyes and bloody noses. "We had a plan," one of the boy campers said afterward. "We were going to barricade ourselves in the infirmary and fight 'em off from there. Firebomb them."

The Thunderbird boys, escorted by several strapping counselors called in from a tennis camp across the lake, were confined to the rec hall. By eleven o'clock on a fine, sharp, hot August morning, Camp Grayfeather had settled into a stillness in which the only sounds were those of a sublimely untroubled nature—birdsong; the harsh whirring of cicadas; the light slapping of waves on the lake shore.

None of us was surprised to discover that the Thunderbirds were to be sent home. I sat with nine other girls on the sagging bunks of our tent as Hannah Woolworth, her plump, kindly face pale and drawn with strain beneath its sunburn and freckles, talked to us. "We all feel that it would be better and safer for everyone," she said. "We don't want any of you kids getting hurt."

When she said "you kids," it was clear that she did not mean the Thunderbirds.

I looked at Ellen and Chen-cheu, and they looked back at me. Events were passing, as usual, into the unreachable sphere of adult justice, and though there was a certain relief in that, it also seemed sad. For a day and a half, the Thunderbirds, like a small natural disaster, had given an edge of crazy danger to life at Grayfeather; now the same powers that had brought them to us were taking them away.

"We didn't even get a chance to learn all their names," said Ellen slowly, after Hannah Woolworth had left.

A flicker of resentment ran through the group of girls crowded together in the tent, and Ellen and I began, with an obscure feeling of defiance, to teach the others the song that the Thunderbirds had sung for us under the oak tree the day before.

In about two hours, after we'd eaten a large pile of bologna sandwiches on horrid white bread, sandwiches that the camp cook had provided as a sort of emergency take-out lunch, we heard through the woods the unmistakable sound of a bus. "We've *got* to see this," I said.

Five of us—Ellen, Chen-cheu and I, and two other girls—jumped up and, against the strict instructions left us by our absent counselor, took off toward the rec hall. We didn't take the path but ran dodging like Indian spies through the underbrush, stifling occasional nervous giggles and trying to avoid the poison ivy. When we got to the edge of the clearing, we stood discreetly back in the bushes and observed the scene. The midday sun gave the clearing a close, sleepy feeling. The Thunderbirds, their spirits apparently undaunted, stood in a rambunctious platoon behind a grim-faced Ned Woolworth, and the familiar graffiti-covered school bus was just coming to a halt in the parking lot.

We could see that the same tall, curly-haired man who had delivered the Thunderbirds was coming to pick them up; this time he was wearing a green eyeshade, as if he'd been interrupted during a stretch of desk work. He came quickly down the bus steps and strode over to stand in front of the assembled Thunderbirds. "Well," he said, clapping his hands together, "what the hell have you guys been doing *now?*"

The Thunderbirds, all of them, broke into loud laughter, as if he had just told them the best joke in the world.

"We ain't been doing *nothing,* man," answered Marvin Jones, rocking on his heels. "Just being ourselves!"

The curly-haired man pulled off his visor and sighed so that even we could hear him, fixing his weary, skeptical gaze for a second on Marvin Jones's scarred face, and then on the golden hills and fields of the Delaware countryside rolling into the distance. He talked to Ned Woolworth in a low voice for a few minutes and then turned back to his charges and sighed again. "Come on, get on the bus. We're going back to the city," was all he said to the Thunderbirds.

When we five girls heard the bus start up, we did something we hadn't planned to do. Without any one of us suggesting it, we all took to our heels again and ran through the woods to a dusty crossroads far from the clearing, a spot we knew the bus had to pass. Through some extraordinary, even magical, coincidence the same plan had occurred to all of us. When the bus came rattling up to the crossroads a few seconds after we got there, the five of us, like guerrilla fighters, dashed out of the bushes onto the road. "Stop the bus! Stop for a minute!" we shouted.

The bus slowed and halted, with a squeal of gears, and the Thunderbirds stuck their heads out of the windows. We could see Marvin Jones's platinum streak shining beside Belinda's patch of dyed red hair. "We wanted to sing your song," said Ellen, and without further ado we all began clapping our hands and chanting the profane verses that belonged to the Thunderbirds. "What the word / Thunderbird . . ."

We probably looked ridiculous—five girls in cutoffs, football t-shirts, and moccasins, clapping and trying to perform like a group of tough guys on a city street corner—but we felt natural, synchronized, as if we were doing a good job. When we had finished, the Thunderbirds—still hanging from the windows of the bus—gave us a burst of grave, polite applause. Marvin Jones leaned farther forward out of the window. "That sounded good," he said. "And we're sorry to leave."

The two groups looked at each other, and it seemed for a minute that some obscure misunderstanding was about to be cleared up. Then the bus started up and moved slowly away through the trees.

Getting By

Debra Marquart

Getting Ready

i'm the thousand-change girl, getting ready for school,
standing in my bedroom ripping pants and shirts from my
body, trying dresses and skirts. father, at the bottom
of the steps is yelling, the bus is coming, here comes
the bus. i'm wriggling into jeans—zippers grinding their
teeth, buttons refusing their holes. my brother, dressed-
in-five-minutes, stands in the hall, t-shirt and bookbag,
saying what's the big problem. i'm kneeling in front of
the closet, foraging for that great-lost-other-shoe.
father, downstairs, offers advice. slacks, he's yelling,
just put on some slacks. i'm in the mirror, matching
earrings, nervous fingers putting the back to the front.
downstairs, the bus is fuming in the yard, farm kids
with cowlicks sitting in rows. everything's in a pile
on the floor. after school, mother will scream, get upstairs
and hang up that mess, but i don't care, i'm the thousand-
change girl, trotting downstairs now looking good, looking
ready for school. father, pulling back from the steps with
disgust, giving me the once over, saying, is *that*
what you're wearing?

Natasha Trethewey

White Lies

The lies I could tell,
when I was growing up—
light-bright, near-white,
high-yellow, red-boned
in a black place—
were just white lies.

I could easily tell the white folks
that we lived "uptown,"
not in that pink and green,
shantyfied, shot-gun section
along the tracks. I could act
like my homemade dresses
came straight out the window
of *Maison Blanche.* I could even
keep quiet, quiet as kept,
like the time a white girl said,
squeezing my hand, "now
we have three of us in our class."

But I paid for it every time
Mama found out. She laid her hands
on me, then washed out my mouth
with Ivory Soap. "This is to purify,"
she said, "and cleanse your lying tongue."
Believing that, I swallowed suds
thinking they'd work
from the inside out.

Phillip Lopate

My Early Years at School

In the first grade I was in a bit of a fog. All I remember is running outside at three o'clock with the others to fill the safety zone in front of the school building, where we whirled around with our bookbags, hitting as many proximate bodies as possible. The whirling dervishes of Kabul could not have been more ecstatic than we with our thwacking book satchels.

But as for the rest of school, I was paying so little attention that, once, when I stayed home sick, and my mother had to write a letter of excuse to the teacher, she asked me what her name was and I said I did not know. "You must know what your teacher's name is." I took a stab at it. "Mrs. . . . Latka?" I said, *latka* being the Jewish word for potato pancakes (this was around the time of Hanukkah celebrations). My mother laughed incredulously, and compromised with the salutation "Dear Teacher." As I learned soon after, my teacher's name was actually Mrs. Bobka, equally improbable. She wore her red hair rolled under a hairnet and had a glass eye, which I once saw her taking out in a luncheonette and showing to her neighbor, while I watched from a nearby table with my chocolate milk. Now, can it be possible that she really had a glass eye? Probably not; but why is it that every time I think of Mrs. Bobka my mind strays to that association? She had a hairnet and a very large nose, of that we can be sure, and seemed to have attained middle age. This teacher paid no attention to me whatsoever, which was the kindest thing she could have done to me. She had her favorite, Rookie, who collected papers and handed out pencils—Rookie, that little monster with the middy blouse and dangling curls, real name Rochelle. "Teacher's Pet!" we would yell at her.

Yet secretly I was attracted to Rookie, and admired the way she passed out supplies, as well as the attention she got.

Otherwise, I was so much in a daze, that once I got sent on an errand to a classroom on the third floor, and by the time I hit the stairwell I had already forgotten which room it was. Afterward, Mrs. Bobka never used me as her monitor.

The school itself was a wreck from Walt Whitman's day, with rotting floorboards, due to be condemned in a year or two; already the new annex that was to replace it was rising on the adjoining lot. But in a funny way, we loved the old school better. The boys' bathroom had zinc urinals with a common trough; the fixtures were green with rust, the toilet stalls doorless. In the Hadean basement where we went for our hot lunches, an overweight black woman would dish out tomato soup. Every day tomato soup, with a skim. Sometimes, when the basement flooded, we walked across a plank single file to get to the food counter. And that ends my memories from first grade.

In the second grade I had another teacher, Mrs. Seligman, whose only pleasure was to gossip with her teacher pals during lineups in the hall and fire drills (when *we* were supposed to be silent). Such joy came over her when another teacher entered our classroom—she was so bored with the exclusive company of children, poor woman, and lived for those visits.

By second grade, I had been anonymous long enough. One day we were doing show-and-tell, wherein each child bragged how he or she had been to the beach or had on a new pair of tap shoes. My parents had just taken me to see the movie *Les Misérables,* and Robert Newton as the tenacious gum-baring Inspector had made a great impression on me. Besides, I knew the story backwards and forwards, because I had also read the Classics Illustrated comic book version. As I stood up in front of the class, something possessed me to elaborate a little and bend the truth.

"Mrs. Seligman, I read a book called *Les Misérables* . . ."

She seemed ready to laugh in my face. "Oh? Who is it by?"

"Victor Hugo." I stood my ground. There must have been something in my plausible, shy, four-eyed manner that shook her. Her timing was momentarily upset; she asked me to sit down. Later, when there was a lull in the activity, she called me over to her desk.

"Now tell me, did you honestly read *Les Misérables?* Don't be afraid to tell the truth."

"Yes! it's about this man named Jean Valjean who . . ." and I proceeded to tell half the plot—no doubt getting the order confused, but still close enough to the original to give this old war-horse pause. She knew deep down in her professional soul that a child my age did not have the vocabulary or the comprehension to get through a book of that order of complexity. But she wanted to believe, I felt. If I stumbled she would dismiss me in a second, and I would probably burst into tears. Yet even then I knew (children know it better than adults) that in telling a lie, fidelity is everything. They can never be absolutely sure if you keep denying and insisting.

Just then one of her teacher pals came in, the awesome Mrs. McGonigle, who squeezed bad boys into wastebaskets.

"Do you know what? Phillip here says that he read Victor Hugo's *Les Misérables.*"

"Really!" cried her friend archly. "And you believe him?"

"I don't know."

"What's it about? *I've* never read it. He must be very smart if he read it and I haven't."

"Tell Mrs. McGonigle the story."

"It's about this man named Jean Valjean who stole a loaf of bread," I began, my heart beating as I recounted his crime, aware that I myself was committing a parallel one. By this time I had gotten more than the attention I wanted and would have done anything to return to my seat. Mrs. McGonigle was scrutinizing me sarcastically with her bifocals, and I was much more afraid of her seeing through my deception than Mrs. Seligman. But it came to me in a dim haze of surprise that Mrs. Seligman seemed to be taking my side; she was nodding, and shushing the other woman's objections. Perhaps nothing so exciting had happened to her as a teacher for months, even years! Here was her chance to flaunt a child prodigy in her own classroom before the other teachers. I told the story as passionately as I could, seeing the movie unroll scene by scene in my mind's eye, a foot away from the desk.

"There's only one way to find out," interrupted Mrs. McGonigle. "We will take him down to the library and see if he can read the book."

My teacher could not wait to try this out. She rose and took my arm. "Now, class, I'm leaving you alone for a few minutes. You are to remain quiet and in your seats!" So they marched me over to the school library. I was praying that the school had no such volume on its shelves. But the librarian produced Victor Hugo's masterpiece with dispatch—as luck would have it, a sort of abridged version for young adults. I knew enough how to sound out words so that I was able to stumble through the first page; fortunately, Mrs. Seligman snatched the book away from me: "See? I told you he was telling the truth." Her mocker was silenced. And Mrs. Seligman was so proud of me that she began petting my head—I, who had never received more than distracted frowns from her all year long.

But it wasn't enough; she wanted more. She and I would triumph together. I was to be testimony to her special reading program. Now she conceived a new plan: she would take me around from class to class, and tell everyone about my accomplishment, and have me read passages from the book.

I begged her not to do this. Not that I had any argument to offer against it, but I gave her to understand, by turning dangerously pale, that I had had enough excitement for the day. Everyone knows that those who are capable of great mental feats are also susceptible to faints and dizzy spells. Insensitive as she was, she got the point, and returned me regretfully to the classroom.

Every day afterward I lived in fear of being exhibited before each class and made to recount the deed that I had not done. I dreaded the truth coming out. Though my teacher did not ask me to "perform" *Les Misérables* anymore, nevertheless she pointed me out to any adult who visited the classroom, including the parents of other children. I heard them whispering about me. I bowed my head in shame, pretending that modesty or absorption in schoolwork made me turn red at the notoriety gathering around me.

So my career as genius and child prodigy began.

"Victor Hugo, *hélas!*" Gide said, when asked to name the greatest poet in the French language. I say "Victor Hugo, *hélas!*" for another reason. My guilt is such that every time I hear that worthy giant's name I cringe. Afterward, I was never able to read *Les Misérables.* In fact, irrationally or not, I have shunned his entire oeuvre.

David Haynes

The Dozens

I'm a very dangerous boy. I've been known to say almost anything.

Sam and Rose—two people who are supposed to be my parents have washed out my so-called fresh mouth with soap more than once, but not since I turned fifteen and turned into an overgrown moose. Just maybe it was my big mouth got us into this mess. I don't think anyone knows or cares. It's been more than a year since all this started. Here we are: right back where we began. Same old Sam and Rose and Marshall. Probably forever and ever and ever.

6

That February day was a bad day from the get go.

Such as:

I walk into this class. World Literature for Sophomore Redneck Pinheads, I think they called it. Miss O'Hare is having Black Studies week in 1986 for the first time in her life, and if she flashed her nasty yellow teeth at me one more time, anyway, I'd have knocked them down her throat. We read—get this—excerpts from *Tom Sawyer.* Aunt Polly sends the nigra Jim to fetch Huck and Becky and Tom for victuals.

Pinheads. Each and every one.

"I thought today," says O'Hare, "that we would have a discussion about Black slang. It has made such an important contribution to our language. Let's brainstorm a list of expressions which I'll record on the board. Shall we? Who will begin?"

I'm sitting there with sixteen or seventeen of them.

Pink cheeked and cheery, looking at each other out of the sides of their eyes. O'Hare, scanning for a sucker, catches my eye, hopefully. I drop out my bottom lip about four inches and look at her as if she's asked me to explain nuclear fission. I want to drool, but that would be a little too much.

Finally, she is saved by sophomore class president Connie Jo Hartberger. "I have heard a few times some of them say the word *crucial.* As a slang word, I mean."

"Very good, Connie Jo," says Ohairy, wiping the sweat from her upper lip. She records it on the top of the list.

Connie Jo beams proudly. Her father is a vice president at General Dynamics. He bought her a Honda because she got a B+ in advanced algebra. She told me how "neat" she thought it was that there were now black kids at her school.

"Who can tell us?" Miss O'Hare pushes on, "Does any one here know what *crucial* means? How is it used?"

She knows better than to call on me. I'd tell her it would be crucial if someone peeled the Youth for Reagan bumper sticker from Connie Jo's Civic and pasted it over her fat butt. That would also be "neat."

The slang lesson limps along. On the board she scrawls a list of ten or so worn out and ancient words: *bad, cool, far out.* Ohairy is beet-faced and stammering.

Buzz Simpkins, from whose daddy's dealership Connie Jo got her Honda, raises his hand up by his thick linebacker neck. Buzz's class election commercial featured farting and belching, and a rousing version of "We Are the World." It was a big hit. He is our sophomore class secretary/treasurer. Quick, Buzz: how many pennies in a dollar?

Miss O'Hare calls on him tentatively.

"I know one," he simpers, "but I don't know that I ought to say it. Haw haw haw."

"Use your discretion," teacher encourages. Not even she will look at him.

The pinheads wait on the edge of their chairs. Miss O'Hare poses, chalk at the ready.

"Here goes nothing." Buzz clears his throat. "Your mama. Haw haw haw."

The chalk freezes on the *Y,* trembling. No one moves. Todd, my red-headed friend who sits behind me, swallows loudly, just as if he knows what to expect.

He does.

The dozens, huh? I stand up. "How about this. Your mammy, your pappy, your whole goddamn family and everyone you know." I get my stuff and walk. I bet they all pissed their pants, too. Every one of them.

So I overreacted. Put up with what I put up with and you'd have an edge on you, too.

Such as:

After all of that, after the wise-ass A.P. Mr. Shannon gives me a letter "trusting you'll show your parents," lets me off with a warning "this time, considering the situation," after I have Todd and our other lame-brained friend Artie forge a suitable ass-kissy response to it, which I then have to edit because Todd has such a foul mouth and because Artie is so illiterate (Artie: "You won't be having no more trouble with our son"; Todd: "We beat Marshall's ass real good when we got your note"), after we ride the school bus across west Saint Louis County, Missouri's finest real estate, through rolling fields, and by green-lawned country clubs, past the landfill to the top of Washington Park, after all of that:

I come through the front door—which is of course wide open even though it is all hours of the day—and there's ma and she says to me, "Do me a favor and fill this up."

No "How are you?" No "Have a good day?" No nothing.

She's got this glass held out to me and there she sits: one hand with the glass, the other stretched before her, arm's length, holding a novel. She is on the green-plaid couch, sitting at an impossible angle with her legs curled to the side like an S. The television set is on—daytime PBS, she watches. Shows about pets and about acrylic painting; it is background noise only. Her eyes never leave the novels. Mysteries with such names as *I Walk the Night,* and *The Bracelets of Bangkok.* She's got on a new dress today. White and frilly, and she's shod with clunky-heeled shoes. Her sharp shiny fingernails are the color of strawberries to match the shoes.

The dress ought to have been a clue to what was up, but I wasn't as good at this stuff then as I am now.

She jiggles the ice in the glass. I walk right by, grinding my Nikes into her yellow, short-shag, stall-to-stall carpeting. I throw my notebooks in my room. Then I go change the TV—to the Flintstones.

She jiggles the glass again. Like a chump I give in and get her some more Kool-Aid. Grape. There is a loud snap as I slam it down on the glass-topped coffee table, right on the crack where Daddy fell into it last New Year's Eve. Another three inches: not a bad addition if I don't say so myself. She ignores the crack and scratches my arm by way of thanks.

"What's for dinner?" I want to know.

"What are you fixing?" she answers.

"Shoot," I say, and go get a snack. I munch some plain Cheerios, catching the little dried circles on my eye teeth and crushing them with my tongue. I lie down and nap in front of the set. Wilma and Barney and Fred wander in and out of my dreams. Dino the dinosaur, on the 26-inch set, is the size of a full-grown cat. Ma stays there posed with the mystery.

When Gilligan comes on, "Look at this," I say to her, "Daddy'll be here soon."

"All right, for Christsake," she seethes. She goes to the kitchen and starts banging stuff around. God knows what dinner will be. Canned corned beef with leftover eggs. Nacho cheeseburger helper. This is a woman who named me after a department store. Marshall Field Finney. Connie Jo Hartberger throws away garbage in bags with my name on them.

From the floor by the TV I can see the top part of her in there wandering aimlessly. "How was school today?" she asks in the pass-through-bar window. Moms are always on that. On with those questions. Dip, dip, dip.

"Fine. Artie and Todd and I poured brown dye in the swimming pool and set the football bleachers on fire."

"That's nice," she says. That's how much she really cares. "Have you by any chance seen anywhere my little portable radio?"

"I'm trying to watch TV," I answer.

Something crashes purposely in the sink. I sit up and meet her eyes. The red claws are spread and taut on the counter, and pointed in my direction. She glares at me, but I don't look away. Her eyes are red, too. I wonder how much sleep she's been getting? Neither of us blinks.

Just then, in walks Daddy. "Still in front of that set, I see. You'll rot your mind."

I don't say a word. Sam wears his striped bibs that make him tall and lean, except he looks around the middle as though he's swallowed a whole salami. All swelled up like a snake that just ate.

"Evening, Sam," she says.

"Rose." He drops on the couch and picks up the paper. Dust rises like steam from his overalls.

"You want a beer, Daddy?" I ask, waving away the cloud. She is already passing a Budweiser through for him.

He closes one giant paw around the can. His fingers meet easily, squeezing out the first swallow and slightly crushing the can. The clay and soot from his fingers mix with the sweat on the can, forming rivers of mud.

"Good day today, Sam?" she asks.

"Fine, Rose," he answers.

Sam. Rose. Not Big Sam, or Rosie, or honey or sweetie. Clue #2, that ought to have been. Unfortunately at the time I am caught up in the Hillbillies. Mr. Drysdale is trying to convince the Clampetts that the climate in southern California is getting colder by turning the air conditioning in the Beverly Hills mansion down as far as it will go. Life was in black and white back then. In real life Sam "tsk, tsks" at the headlines, Rose bangs away in the kitchen, and I am too stupid to figure out what's up.

"If you're going to eat this stuff, best get it now."

5:15. One thing for her—she's always on time.

She's set on the table two plastic plates and two glasses of green liquid. And a casserole.

Daddy scoops up a big helping and starts shoveling it in.

I take a little and test it. Tuna and macaroni. That was it. No sauce. No spice. Nothing.

"You expect me to eat this slop?" I say. I turn the plate over on the table and cross my arms.

"Look here, Sam," she says. "You better tell this little nigger of yours something."

"Ug," Sam gurgles. His mouth is full of the crap.

"Clean it up," she says.

I don't move. Then I get up and open the refrigerator door.

She kicks it closed, hard, with her foot, leaving a half-moon-shaped indentation near the center. "There's your dinner," she says, pointing to the mess.

Big Sam's like he's turned to stone. I go get the Cheerios out of the cupboard again.

"Give me that," she says. She grabs the other side of the box. I pull. The cardboard rips. Cheerios fly and land everywhere: dots, pyramids, and rings all over her sticky linoleum floor. It looks like a code.

"Goddamn you to hell," she says, and bursts into a shaking fit of tears.

I go to my room and slam the door and look at the ceiling a while. I do that a lot. Look at the ceiling. From my bed. It is white and gravelly. If you stare long enough you can see things in it.

I'm not staring long this time. After all: I live here too.

I come out and park in front of the set. Lucy and Ricky. I'll grab some grub when the coast's clear. Sam and Rose are really into it now—a continuation of last night and the last month and forever. I've probably missed the best parts.

"It's those filthy hoodlums he runs with," she's saying. "Thieves and delinquents. Urchins."

A lot she knows. Artie writes thank you notes for the thank you notes he gets, and Todd is afraid of almost everything. Loud noises, shadows, even some common vegetables. What's more, he is even white.

Ma goes right on . . .

". . . and here I am stuck in a crackerbox house with a . . . trash man and a loud mouth child. I could have been something."

"Rose, please," sighs Sam.

"Don't touch me," she sobs. And she starts stomping back and forth from the kitchen to her bedroom, to the toilet, to the closet. Stomp, stomp, stomp.

"My mother tried to warn me," she hollers.

That old line, I think to myself. Sam's at the table with his head in his big hands. Sick from the food, no doubt.

Ma stops behind me after a while and I can feel her eyes on me. I turn slowly. Her face is pale beige and her much too red cheeks are streaked with tears. The blue raincoat drapes over her arm and a purse hangs from her shoulder—a little girl's purse on a long metal chain. Just then I know she is really going.

"I can't anymore," she says to me. "I'm sorry."

I turn back to the TV. "Good riddance," I mumble.

Back in the kitchen she and Sam whisper. "No!" he shouts. He comes and stands in front of the door by which she has placed one packed bag. "No, I won't let you." He blocks the door.

"Get out of my way," she says.

I watch the action in the round mirror just above the set. Sam and Rose—framed in smoky-engraved curlicues and butterflies. They aren't looking at each other. Daddy's closed up like a little boy hiding something behind him in a corner. He's looking around like he doesn't know where to look. Our reflected eyes meet.

Come on Sam: use those big hands. Show her who's the boss round here.

"Please," she says. "Don't make this worse, Sam."

Just as he moves to step out of her way she swings the suitcase back to hit him with it. The Samsonite catches him in the groin and he topples over.

And she is gone.

He lies there a long time. So, finally I go over to him.

"Are you all right?" I ask. "Want another beer?"

"Rose," he whines. "My sweet Rosey."

I tell him to get up.

w. r. rodriguez

JUSTICE

a youth grabbed an old woman's purse fat with tissues and
aspirin and such sundries as old women carry in sagging
purses a desperate youth nice enough not to beat her head
bloody into the sidewalk as muggers of the feeble often do
for the fun of it i suppose and he ran up the hill but one of
the perennial watchers watched it all from her window the
purseless old woman in slow pursuit yelling such curses as
it takes old women a lifetime to learn but it was too dangerous too futile the silent watcher knew to call the police
who might come and rough up someone they did not like
just for the fun of it i suppose or who would talk polite
and feel mad inside and roll their eyes because there was
really nothing they could do and there were murders and
assaults to handle so this silent angry watcher carelessly
but carefully dropped flower pots from her fourth floor
windowsill garden one crashing before one behind and the
third hitting him on the head a geranium i suppose and
closed her window while the huffing grateful old woman
looked up at the heavens to thank the lord and walked off
with her purse laughing when she finally calmed down
and leaving the youth to awaken in the blue arms of the
law and do you know two smiling cops walked up all those
stairs to warn the watcher that if she weren't more careful
with her plants she would get a ticket for littering i suppose

Andre Dubus

A Woman in April

In New York City, the twenty-fifth of April 1988 was a warm and blue day, and daylight savings time held the sun in the sky after dinner and all the way from the restaurant to Lincoln Center, where we were supposed to be at eight o'clock. The way from the restaurant to Lincoln Center was sidewalks, nearly all of them with curbs and no curb cuts, and streets with traffic; and we were with my friend David Novak, and my friend and agent, Philip Spitzer, pushing my wheelchair and pulling it up curbs and easing it down them while I watched the grills and windshields of cars. I call David the Skipper because he was a Marine lieutenant then captain in Vietnam and led troops in combat, so I defer to his rank, although I was a peacetime captain while he was still a civilian. Philip is the brother I never had by blood.

Philip of course lives in New York. I happily do not. Neither does the Skipper. He lives in Massachusetts, and he and his wife drove to New York that day, a Monday, and my daughter Suzanne and son Andre and friends and I came in two more cars, because Andre and I were reading that night at Lincoln Center with Mary Morris and Diana Davenport. In Massachusetts we had very little sun and warmth during the spring, and that afternoon, somewhere in Connecticut, we drove into sunlight, and soon the trees along the road were green with leaves. We had not seen those either at home, only the promise of buds.

At close to eight o'clock the sky was still blue and the Skipper pushed me across the final street, then turned my chair and leaned it backward and pulled it up steps to the

Plaza outside the Center. We began crossing the greyish white concrete floor and, as Philip spoke and pointed up, I looked at the tall buildings flanking the Plaza, angles of grey-white, of city color, against the sky, deepening now, but not much, still the bright blue of spring after such a long winter of short days, lived in bed, in the wheelchair, in physical therapy, in the courthouse losing my wife and two little girls. Philip told us of a Frenchman last year tightrope walking across the space between these buildings, without a net.

Then I looked at the people walking on the Plaza. My only good memories of New York are watching people walk on the streets, and watching people in bars and restaurants, and some meals or drinks with friends, and being with Philip. But one summer I spent five days with him and for the first time truly saw the homeless day after day and night after night, and from then on, whenever I went there, I knew the New York I was in, the penthouses and apartments and cabs and restaurants, was not New York, anymore than the Czar's Russia was the Russia of Chekhov's freed serfs, with their hopes destroyed long before they were born. Still on that spring Monday I loved watching the faces on the Plaza.

Like Boston, New York has beautiful women to look at, though in New York the women, in general, are made up more harshly, and they dress more self-consciously; there is something insular about their cosmetics and clothing, as if they have come to believe that sitting at a mirror with brushes and tubes and vials, and putting on a dress of a certain cut and color starts them on the long march to spiritual fulfillment with a second wind. And in New York the women walk as though in the rain; in Boston many women stroll. But then most New Yorkers walk like people in rain, leaving the stroll to police officers, hookers, beggars and wandering homeless, and teenagers who are yet unharried by whatever preoccupations preoccupy so many from their driving preoccupation with loneliness and death.

Women were on the Plaza, their pace slower as they neared the building, and looking to my right I saw a lovely one. She could have been thirty, or five years on either side of it. She wore a dark brown miniskirt, or perhaps it was black; I saw it and her strong legs in net stockings for only a moment, because they were in my natural field of vision from my chair. But a woman's face is what I love. She was in profile and had soft thick brown hair swaying at her shoulders as she strode with purpose but not hurry, only grace. She was about forty feet away, enough distance so that, when I looked up, I saw her face against the sky.

"Skipper," I said. "Accidentally push me into *her.*"

The forward motion of her legs and arms did not pause, but she immediately turned to me and, as immediately, her lips spread in a smile, and her face softened with it, and her eyes did, all at once from a sudden release in her heart that was soft too in her voice: "I heard that."

She veered toward me, smiling still, with brightened eyes.

"It was a compliment," I said.

The Skipper was pushing my chair, Philip was beside me, and she was coming closer. Then she said: "I know."

She angled back to her first path, as though it were painted there for her to follow, and Philip said: "That *nev*er happens in New York."

"It's the wheelchair," I said. "I'm harmless."

But I knew that was not true. There was no time to explain it then, and anyway I wanted to hold her gift for a while before giving it away with words.

Living in the world as a cripple allows you to see more clearly the crippled hearts of some people whose bodies are whole and sound. All of us, from time to time, suffer this crippling. Some suffer it daily and nightly; and while most of us, nearly all of us, have compassion and love in our hearts, we cannot or will not see these barely visible wounds of other human beings, and so cannot or will not pick up the telephone or travel to someone's home or write a note or make some other seemingly trifling gesture to give to someone what only we, and God, can give: an hour's respite, or a day's, or a night's; and sometimes more than respite: sometimes joy.

Yet in a city whose very sidewalks show the failure of love, the failure to make agape a bureaucracy, a young woman turned to me with instinctive anger or pride, and seeing me in a wheelchair she at once felt not pity but lighthearted compassion. For seeing one of her kind wounded, she lay down the shield and sword she had learned to carry (*I dried my tears / And armed my fears / With ten thousand / shields and spears,* William Blake wrote), and with the light of the sun between us, ten or fifteen feet between us, her face and voice embraced me.

For there is a universality to a wounded person: again and again, for nearly two years, my body has drawn sudden tenderness from men and women I have seen for only those moments in their lives when they helped me with their hands or their whole bodies or only their eyes and lips and tongues. They see, in their short time with me, a man injured, as they could be; a man always needing the care of others, as they could too. Only the children stare with frightened curiosity, as they do at funeral processions and the spoken news of death, for they know in their hearts that they too will die, and they believe they will grow up and marry and have children, but they cannot yet believe they will die.

But I am a particular kind of cripple. In New York I was not sitting on a sidewalk, my back against a wall, and decades of misfortune and suffering in my heart. I was not wearing dirty clothes on an unwashed body. Philip and the

Skipper wore suits and ties. I rode in a nine-hundred-dollar wheelchair, and rolled across the Plaza at Lincoln Center. Yet I do not ask that woman, on seeing my body, to be struck there in the sunlight, to stand absolutely still and silent and hear like rushing tide the voices of all who suffer in body and in spirit and in both, then to turn before my dazzled eyes and go back to her home and begin next morning to live as Mother Teresa, as Dorothy Day. No: she is one of us, and what she said and did on that April evening was, like the warm sunlit sky, enough: for me, for the end of winter, for the infinite possibilities of the human heart.

Thom Tammaro

Remembering Bull DeLisio

Twenty years later, you cannot forget him,
you cannot escape his gaze from another world,
the blurred smile in black and white.
He will be here in your high school
yearbook forever, the memorial page.
These thin black lines measuring
the brevity of his life.
Not enough life to have known life.

You remember:
dusk, old Italians living
near the river's edge
walking in their gardens;
the shiny green smell of tomatoes;
the slap of wooden screen doors
echoing along the river;
the flickering of moths
against bare yellow porch lights;
the boys going down to the river.

Then it happens:
The sudden swirl of the river,
a moment's bubble burst of brightness
before the brilliant dark.
Boys, cold and wet, out of breath,
come running up the hill, crying
"He didn't come up! He didn't come up!"

You remember the rescue team
dragging the river, tossing grapple lines;
the thud of aluminum boats against rock;
the skittering path of searchlights
cutting the falling dark. Then always
the hook winning out over flesh,
the river giving up its kill when ready.

Bull, every summer in a dream
I go down with you, the descent
to the watery nowhere.
Whatever worlds came to you then,
whatever words were lost in the ripples,
whatever life gathered in the swirl,
I carry back to strangers, friends, loved ones,
yesterday, tomorrow, now, now.
And always I rise in the waking.

Dwight Okita

Notes for a Poem on Being Asian American

As a child, I was a fussy eater
and I would separate the yolk from the egg white
as I now try to sort out what is Asian
in me from what is American—
the east from the west, the dreamer from the dream.
But countries are not
like eggs—except in the fragileness
of their shells—and eggs resemble countries
only in that when you crack one open and look inside,
you know even less than when you started.

And so I crack open the egg,
and this is what I see:
two moments from my past that strike me
as being uniquely Asian American.

In the first, I'm walking down Michigan Avenue
one day—a man comes up to me out of the blue and says:
"I just wanted to tell you . . . I was on the plane that
bombed Hiroshima. And I just wanted you to know that
what we did was for the good of everyone." And it
seems as if he's asking for my forgiveness. It's 1983,
there's a sale on Marimekko sheets at the Crate &
Barrel, it's a beautiful summer day and I'm talking to
a man I've never seen before and will probably never
see again. His statement has no connection to me—
and has every connection in the world. But it's not
for me to forgive him. He must forgive himself.
"It must have been a very difficult decision to do what

you did," I say and mention the sale on Marimekko sheets across the street, comforters, and how the pillowcases have the pattern of wheat printed on them, and how some nights if you hold them before an open window to the breeze, they might seem like flags— like someone surrendering after a great while, or celebrating, or simply cooling themselves in the summer breeze as best they can.

In the second moment—I'm in a taxi and the Iranian cabdriver looking into the rearview mirror notices my Asian eyes, those almond shapes, reflected in the glass and says, "Can you really tell the difference between a Chinese and a Japanese?"

And I look at his 3rd World face, his photo I.D. pinned to the dashboard like a medal, and I think of the eggs we try to separate, the miles from home he is and the minutes from home I am, and I want to say: "I think it's more important to find the similarities between people than the differences." But instead I simply look into the mirror, into his beautiful 3rd World eyes and say, "Mr. Cabdriver, I can barely tell the difference between you and me."

Reginald McKnight

The Kind of Light That Shines on Texas

I never liked Marvin Pruitt. Never liked him, never knew him, even though there were only three of us in the class. Three black kids. In our school there were fourteen classrooms of thirty-odd white kids (in '66, they considered Chicanos provisionally white) and three or four black kids. Primary school in primary colors. Neat division. Alphabetized. They didn't stick us in the back, or arrange us by degrees of hue, apartheidlike. This was real integration, a ten-to-one ratio as tidy as upper-class landscaping. If it all worked, you could have ten white kids all to yourself. They could talk to you, get the feel of you, scrutinize you bone deep if they wanted to. They seldom wanted to, and that was fine with me for two reasons. The first was that their scrutiny was irritating. How do you comb your hair—why do you comb your hair—may I please touch your hair—were the kinds of questions they asked. This is no way to feel at home. The second reason was Marvin. He embarrassed me. He smelled bad, was at least two grades behind, was hostile, dark skinned, homely, close-mouthed. I feared him for his size, pitied him for his dress, watched him all the time. Marveled at him, mystified, astonished, uneasy.

He had the habit of spitting on his right arm, juicing it down till it would glisten. He would start in immediately after taking his seat when we'd finished with the Pledge of Allegiance, "The Yellow Rose of Texas," "The Eyes of Texas Are upon You," and "Mistress Shady." Marvin would rub his spit-flecked arm with his left hand, rub and roll as if polishing an ebony pool cue. Then he would rest his head in the crook of his arm, sniffing, huffing deep like black-jacket boys huff bagsful of acrylics. After ten minutes or so, his eyes would close, heavy. He would sleep till recess. Mrs. Wickham would let him.

There was one other black kid in our class. A girl they called Ah-so. I never learned what she did to earn this name. There was nothing Asian about this big-shouldered girl. She was the tallest, heaviest kid in school. She was quiet, but I don't think any one of us was subtle or sophisticated enough to nickname our classmates according to any but physical attributes. Fat kids were called Porky or Butterball, skinny ones were called Stick or Ichabod. Ah-so was big, thick, and African. She would impassively sit, sullen, silent as Marvin. She wore the same dark blue pleated skirt every day, the same ruffled white blouse every day. Her skin always shone as if worked by Marvin's palms and fingers. I never spoke one word to her, nor she to me.

Of the three of us, Mrs. Wickham called only on Ah-so and me. Ah-so never answered one question, correctly or incorrectly, so far as I can recall. She wasn't stupid. When asked to read aloud she read well, seldom stumbling over long words, reading with humor and expression. But when Wickham asked her about Farmer Brown and how many cows, or the capital of Vermont, or the date of this war or that, Ah-so never spoke. Not one word. But you always felt she could have answered those questions if she'd wanted to. I sensed no tension, embarrassment, or anger in Ah-so's reticence. She simply refused to speak. There was something unshakable about her, some core so impenetrably solid, you got the feeling that if you stood too close to her she could eat your thoughts like a black star eats light. I didn't despise Ah-so as I despised Marvin. There was nothing malevolent about her. She sat like a great icon in the back of the classroom, tranquil, guarded, sealed up, watchful. She was close to sixteen, and it was my guess she'd given up on school. Perhaps she was just obliging the wishes of her family, sticking it out till the law could no longer reach her.

There were at least half a dozen older kids in our class. Besides Marvin and Ah-so there was Oakley, who sat behind me, whispering threats into my ear; Varna Willard with the large breasts; Eddie Limon, who played bass for a high school rock band; and Lawrence Ridderbeck, who everyone said had a kid and a wife. You couldn't expect me to know anything about Texan educational practices of the 1960s, so I never knew why there were so many older kids in my sixth-grade class. After all, I was just a boy and had transferred into the school around midyear. My father, an air force sergeant, had been sent to Viet Nam. The air force sent my mother, my sister, Claire, and me to Connolly Air Force Base, which during the war housed "unaccompanied wives." I'd been to so many different schools in my short life that I ceased wondering about their differences. All I knew about the Texas schools is that they weren't afraid to flunk you.

Yet though I was only twelve then, I had a good idea why Wickham never called on Marvin, why she let him snooze in the crook of his polished arm. I knew why she would press her lips together, and narrow her eyes at me whenever I correctly answered a question, rare as that was. I know why she badgered Ah-so with questions everyone knew Ah-so would never even consider answering. Wickham didn't like us. She wasn't gross about it, but it was clear she didn't want us around. She would prove her dislike day after day with little stories and jokes. "I just want to share with you all," she would say, "a little riddle my daughter told me at supper th'other day. Now, where do you go when you injure your knee?" Then one, two, or all three of her pets would say for the rest of us, "We don't know, Miz Wickham," in that skin-chilling way suck-asses speak, "where?" "Why, to Africa," Wickham would say, "where the knee grows."

The thirty-odd white students would laugh, and I would look across the room at Marvin. He'd be asleep. I would glance back at Ah-so. She'd be sitting still as a projected image, staring down at her desk. I, myself, would smile at Wickham's stupid jokes, sometimes fake a laugh. I tried to show her that at least one of us was alive and alert, even though her jokes hurt. I sucked ass, too, I suppose. But I wanted her to understand more than anything that I was not like her other nigra children, that I was worthy of more than the non-attention and the negative attention she paid Marvin and Ah-so. I hated her, but never showed it. No one could safely contradict that woman. She knew all kinds of tricks to demean, control, and punish you. And she could swing her two-foot paddle as fluidly as a big-league slugger swings a bat. You didn't speak in Wickham's class unless she spoke to you first. You didn't chew gum, or wear "hood" hair. You didn't drag your feet, curse, pass notes, hold hands with the opposite sex. Most especially, you didn't say anything bad about the Aggies, Governor Connolly, LBJ, Sam Houston, or Waco. You did the forbidden and she would get you. It was that simple.

She never got me, though. Never gave her reason to. But she could have invented reasons. She did a lot of that. I can't be sure, but I used to think she pitied me because my father was in Viet Nam and my uncle A.J. had recently died there. Whenever she would tell one of her racist jokes, she would always glance at me, preface the joke with, "Now don't you nigra children take offense. This is all in fun, you know. I just want to share with you all something Coach Gilchrest told me th'other day." She would tell her joke, and glance at me again. I'd giggle, feeling a little queasy. "I'm half Irish," she would chuckle, "and you should hear some of those Irish jokes." She never told any, and I never really expected her to. I just did my Tom-thing. I kept my shoes shined, my desk neat, answered her questions as best I could, never brought gum to school, never cursed, never slept in class. I wanted to show her we were not all the same.

I tried to show them all, all thirty-odd, that I was different. It worked to some degree, but not very well. When some article was stolen from someone's locker or desk, Marvin, not I, was the first accused. I'd be second. Neither Marvin, nor Ah-so nor I were ever chosen for certain classroom honors—"Pledge leader," "flag holder," "noise monitor," "paper passer outer," but Mrs. Wickham once let me be "eraser duster." I was proud. I didn't even care about the cracks my fellow students made about my finally having turned the right color. I had done something that Marvin, in the deeps of his never-ending sleep, couldn't even dream of doing. Jack Preston, a kid who sat in front of me, asked me one day at recess whether I was embarrassed about Marvin. "Can you believe that guy?" I said. "He's like a pig or something. Makes me sick."

"Does it make you ashamed to be colored?"

"No," I said, but I meant yes. Yes, if you insist on thinking us all the same. Yes, if his faults are mine, his weaknesses inherent in me.

"I'd be," said Jack.

I made no reply. I was ashamed. Ashamed for not defending Marvin and ashamed that Marvin even existed. But if it had occurred to me, I would have asked Jack whether he was ashamed of being white because of Oakley. Oakley, "Oak Tree," Kelvin "Oak Tree" Oakley. He was sixteen and proud of it. He made it clear to everyone, including Wickham, that his life's ambition was to stay in school one more year, till he'd be old enough to enlist in the army. "Them slopes got my brother," he would say. "I'mna sign up and git me a few slopes. Gonna kill them bastards deader'n shit." Oakley, so far as anyone knew, was and always had been the oldest kid in his family. But no one contradicted him. He would, as anyone would tell you, "snap yer neck jest as soon as look at you." Not a boy in class, excepting Marvin and myself, had been able to avoid Oakley's pink bellies, Texas titty twisters, moon pie punches, or worse. He didn't bother Marvin, I suppose, because Marvin was closer to his size and age, and because Marvin spent five sixths of the school day asleep. Marvin probably never crossed Oakley's mind. And to say that Oakley hadn't bothered me is not to say he had no intention of ever doing so. In fact, this haphazard sketch of hairy fingers, slash of eyebrow, explosion of acne, elbows, and crooked teeth, swore almost daily that he'd like to kill me.

Naturally, I feared him. Though we were about the same height, he outweighed me by no less than forty pounds. He talked, stood, smoked, and swore like a man. No one, except for Mrs. Wickham, the principal, and the coach, ever laid a finger on him. And even Wickham knew that the hot lines she laid on him merely amused him. He would smile out at the classroom, goofy and bashful, as she laid down the two, five, or maximum ten strokes on him. Often he would wink, or surreptitiously flash us the thumb as Wickham worked on him. When she was finished, Oakley would walk so cool back to his seat you'd think he was on wheels. He'd slide into his chair, sniff the air, and say, "Somethin's burnin. Do y'all smell smoke? I swanee, I smell smoke and fahr back here." If he had made these cracks and never threatened me, I might have grown to admire Oakley, even liked him a little. But he hated me, and took every opportunity during the six-hour school day to make me aware of this. "Some Sambo's gittin his ass broke open one of these days," he'd mumble. "I wanna fight somebody. Need to keep in shape till I get to Nam."

I never said anything to him for the longest time. I

pretended not to hear him, pretended not to notice his sour breath on my neck and ear. "Yep," he'd whisper. "Coonies keep y'in good shape for slope killin." Day in, day out, that's the kind of thing I'd pretend not to hear. But one day when the rain dropped down like lead balls, and the cold air made your skin look plucked, Oakley whispered to me, "My brother tells me it rains like this in Nam. Maybe I oughta go out at recess and break your ass open today. Nice and cool so you don't sweat. Nice and wet to clean up the blood." I said nothing for at least half a minute, then I turned half right and said, "Thought you said your brother was dead." Oakley, silent himself, for a time, poked me in the back with his pencil and hissed, "*Yer* dead." Wickham cut her eyes our way, and it was over.

It was hardest avoiding him in gym class. Especially when we played murderball. Oakley always aimed his throws at me. He threw with unblinking intensity, his teeth gritting, his neck veining, his face flushing, his black hair sweeping over one eye. He could throw hard, but the balls were squishy and harmless. In fact, I found his misses more intimidating than his hits. The balls would whizz by, thunder against the folded bleachers. They rattled as though a locomotive were passing through them. I would duck, dodge, leap as if he were throwing grenades. But he always hit me, sooner or later. And after a while I noticed that the other boys would avoid throwing at me, as if I belonged to Oakley.

One day, however, I was surprised to see that Oakley was throwing at everyone else but me. He was uncommonly accurate, too; kids were falling like tin cans. Since no one was throwing at me, I spent most of the game watching Oakley cut this one and that one down. Finally, he and I were the only ones left on the court. Try as he would, he couldn't hit me, nor I him. Coach Gilchrest blew his whistle and told Oakley and me to bring the red rubber balls to the equipment locker. I was relieved I'd escaped Oakley's stinging throws for once. I was feeling triumphant, full of myself. As Oakley and I approached Gilchrest, I thought about saying something friendly to Oakley: Good game, Oak Tree, I would say. Before I could speak, though, Gilchrest said, "All right boys, there's five minutes left in the period. Y'all are so good, looks like, you're gonna have to play like men. No boundaries, no catch outs, and you gotta hit your opponent three times in order to win. Got me?"

We nodded.

"And you're gonna use these," said Gilchrest, pointing to three volleyballs at his feet. "And you better believe they're pumped full. Oates, you start at that end of the court. Oak Tree, you're at th'other end. Just like usual, I'll set the balls at mid-court, and when I blow my whistle I want y'all to haul your cheeks to the middle and th'ow for all you're worth. Got me?" Gilchrest nodded at our nods, then added, "Remember, no boundaries, right?"

I at my end, Oakley at his, Gilchrest blew his whistle. I was faster than Oakley and scooped up a ball before he'd covered three quarters of his side. I aimed, threw, and popped him right on the knee. "One-zip!" I heard Gilchrest shout. The ball bounced off his knee and shot right back into my hands. I hurried my throw and missed. Oakley bent down, clutched the two remaining balls. I remember being amazed that he could palm each ball, run full out, and throw left-handed or right-handed without a shade of awkwardness. I spun, ran, but one of Oakley's throws glanced off the back of my head. "One-one!" hollered Gilchrest. I fell and spun on my ass as the other ball came sailing at me. I caught it. "He's out!" I yelled. Gilchrest's voice boomed, "No catch outs. Three hits. Three hits." I leapt to my feet as Oakley scrambled across the floor for another ball. I chased him down, leapt, and heaved the ball hard as he drew himself erect. The ball hit him dead in the face, and he went down flat. He rolled around, cupping his hands over his nose. Gilchrest sped to his side, helped him to his feet, asked him whether he was OK. Blood flowed from Oakley's nose, dripped in startlingly bright spots on the floor, his shoes, Gilchrest's shirt. The coach removed Oakley's T-shirt and pressed it against the big kid's nose to staunch the bleeding. As they walked past me toward the office I mumbled an apology to Oakley, but couldn't catch his reply. "You watch your filthy mouth, boy," said Gilchrest to Oakley.

The locker room was unnaturally quiet as I stepped into its steamy atmosphere. Eyes clicked in my direction, looked away. After I was out of my shorts, had my towel wrapped around me, my shower kit in hand, Jack Preston and Brian Nailor approached me. Preston's hair was combed slick and plastic looking. Nailor's stood up like frozen flames. Nailor smiled at me with his big teeth and pale eyes. He poked my arm with a finger. "You fucked up," he said.

"I tried to apologize."

"Won't do you no good," said Preston.

"I swanee," said Nailor.

"It's part of the game," I said. "It was an accident. Wasn't my idea to use volleyballs."

"Don't matter," Preston said. "He's jest lookin for an excuse to fight you."

"I never done nothing to him."

"Don't matter," said Nailor. "He don't like you."

"Brian's right, Clint. He'd jest as soon kill you as look at you."

"I never done nothing to him."

"Look," said Preston, "I know him pretty good. And jest between you and me, it's 'cause you're a city boy—"

"Whadda you mean? I've never—"

"He don't like your clothes—"

"And he don't like the fancy way you talk in class."

"What fancy—"

"I'm tellin him, if you don't mind, Brian."

"Tell him then."

"He don't like the way you say 'tennis shoes' instead of sneakers. He don't like coloreds. A whole bunch a things, really."

"I never done nothing to him. He's got no reason—"

"And," said Nailor, grinning, *"and,* he says you're a stuck-up rich kid." Nailor's eyes had crow's feet, bags beneath them. They were a man's eyes.

"My dad's a sergeant," I said.

"You chicken to fight him?" said Nailor.

"Yeah, Clint, don't be chicken. Jest go on and git it over with. He's whupped pert near ever'body else in the class. It ain't so bad."

"Might as well, Oates."

"Yeah, yer pretty skinny, but yer jest about his height. Jest git 'im in a headlock and don't let go."

"Goddamn," I said, "he's got no reason to—"

Their eyes shot right and I looked over my shoulder. Oakley stood at his locker, turning its tumblers. From where I stood I could see that a piece of cotton was wedged up one of his nostrils, and he already had the makings of a good shiner. His acne burned red like a fresh abrasion. He snapped the locker open and kicked his shoes off without sitting. Then he pulled off his shorts, revealing two paddle stripes on his ass. They were fresh red bars speckled with white, the white speckles being the reverse impression of the paddle's suction holes. He must not have watched his filthy mouth while in Gilchrest's presence. Behind me, I heard Preston and Nailor pad to their lockers.

Oakley spoke without turning around. "Somebody's gonna git his skinny black ass kicked, right today, right after school." He said it softly. He slipped his jock off, turned around. I looked away. Out the corner of my eye I saw him stride off, his hairy nakedness a weapon clearing the younger boys from his path. Just before he rounded the corner of the shower stalls, I threw my toilet kit to the floor and stammered, "I—I never did nothing to you, Oakley." He stopped, turned, stepped closer to me, wrapping his towel around himself. Sweat streamed down my rib cage. It felt like ice water. "You wanna go at it right now, boy?"

"I never did nothing to you." I felt tears in my eyes. I couldn't stop them even though I was blinking like mad. "Never."

He laughed. "You busted my nose, asshole."

"What about before? What'd I ever do to you?"

"See you after school, Coonie." Then he turned away, flashing his acne-spotted back like a semaphore. "Why?" I shouted. "Why you wanna fight me?" Oakley stopped and turned, folded his arms, leaned against a toilet stall. "Why you wanna fight *me,* Oakley?" I stepped over the bench. "What'd I do? Why me?" And then unconsciously, as if scratching, as if breathing, I walked toward Marvin, who stood a few feet from Oakley, combing his hair at the mirror. "Why not him?" I said. "How come you're after *me* and not *him?*" The room froze. Froze for a moment that was both evanescent and eternal, somewhere between an eye blink and a week in hell. No one moved, nothing happened; there was no sound at all. And then it was as if all of us at the same moment looked at Marvin. He just stood there, combing away, the only body in motion, I think. He combed his hair and combed it, as if seeing only his image, hearing only his comb scraping his scalp. I knew he'd heard me. There's no way he could not have heard me. But all he did was slide the comb into his pocket and walk out the door.

"I got no quarrel with Marvin," I heard Oakley say.

I turned toward his voice, but he was already in the shower.

I was able to avoid Oakley at the end of the school day. I made my escape by asking Mrs. Wickham if I could go to the rest room.

"'Rest room,'" Oakley mumbled. "It's a damn toilet, sissy."

"Clinton," said Mrs. Wickham. "Can you *not* wait till the bell rings? It's almost three o'clock."

"No ma'am," I said. "I won't make it."

"Well I should make you wait just to teach you to be more mindful about . . . hygiene . . . uh things." She sucked in her cheeks, squinted. "But I'm feeling charitable today. You may go." I immediately left the building, and got on the bus. "Ain't you a little early?" said the bus driver, swinging the door shut. "Just left the office," I said. The driver nodded, apparently not giving me a second thought. I had no idea why I'd told her I'd come from the office, or why she found it a satisfactory answer. Two minutes later the bus filled, rolled, and shook its way to Connolly Air Base. When I got home, my mother was sitting in the living room, smoking her Slims, watching her soap opera. She absently asked me how my day had gone and I told her fine. "Hear from Dad?" I said.

"No, but I'm sure he's fine." She always said that when we hadn't heard from him in a while. I suppose she thought I was worried about him, or that I felt vulnerable without him. It was neither. I just wanted to discuss something with my mother that we both cared about. If I spoke with her about things that happened at school, or on my weekends, she'd listen with half an ear, say something like, "Is that so?" or "You don't say?" I couldn't stand that sort of thing. But when I mentioned my father, she treated me a bit more like an adult, or at least someone who was worth listening to. I didn't want to feel like a boy that afternoon.

As I turned from my mother and walked down the hall I thought about the day my father left for Viet Nam. Sharp in his uniform, sure behind his aviator specs, he slipped a cigar from his pocket and stuck it in mine. "Not till I get back," he said. "We'll have us one when we go fishing. Just you and me, out on the lake all day, smoking and casting and sitting. Don't let Mama see it. Put it in y'back pocket." He hugged me, shook my hand, and told me I was the man of the house now. He told me he was depending on me to take good care of my mother and sister. "Don't you let me down, now, hear?" And he tapped his thick finger on my chest. "You almost as big as me. Boy, you something else." I believed him when he told me these things. My heart swelled big enough to swallow my father, my mother, Claire. I loved, feared, and respected myself, my manhood. That day I could have put all of Waco, Texas, in my heart. And it wasn't till about three months later that I discovered I really wasn't the man of the house, that my mother and sister, as they always had, were taking care of me.

For a brief moment I considered telling my mother about what had happened at school that day, but for one thing, she was deep down in the halls of *General Hospital,* and never paid you much mind till it was over. For another thing, I just wasn't the kind of person—I'm still not, really—to discuss my problems with anyone. Like my father I kept things to myself, talked about my problems only in retrospect. Since my father wasn't around I consciously wanted to be like him, doubly like him, I could say. I wanted to be the man of the house in some respect, even if it had to be in an inward way. I went to my room, changed my clothes, and laid out my homework. I couldn't focus on it. I thought about Marvin, what I'd said about him or done to him—I couldn't tell which. I'd done something to him, said something about him; said something about and done something to myself. *How come you're after* me *and not* him? I kept trying to tell myself I hadn't meant it that way. *That* way. I thought about approaching Marvin, telling him what I really meant was that he was more Oakley's age and weight than I. I would tell him I meant I was no match for Oakley. *See, Marvin, what I meant was that he wants to fight a colored guy, but is afraid to fight you 'cause you could beat him.* But try as I did, I couldn't for a moment convince myself that Marvin would believe me. I meant it *that* way and no other. Everybody heard. Everybody knew. That afternoon I forced myself to confront the notion that tomorrow I would probably have to fight both Oakley and Marvin. I'd have to be two men.

I rose from my desk and walked to the window. The light made my skin look orange, and I started thinking about what Wickham had told us once about light. She said that oranges and apples, leaves and flowers, the whole multicolored world, was not what it appeared to be. The colors we see, she said, look like they do only because of the light or ray that shines on them. "The color of the thing isn't what you see, but the light that's reflected off it." Then she shut out the lights and shone a white light lamp on a prism. We watched the pale splay of colors on the projector screen; some people oohed and aahed. Suddenly, she switched on a black light and the color of everything changed. The prism colors vanished, Wickham's arms were purple, the buttons of her dress were as orange as hot coals, rather than the blue they had been only seconds before. We were all very quiet. "Nothing," she said, after a while, "is really what it appears to be." I didn't really understand then. But as I stood at the window, gazing at my orange skin, I wondered what kind of light I could shine on Marvin, Oakley, and me that would reveal us as the same.

I sat down and stared at my arms. They were dark brown again. I worked up a bit of saliva under my tongue and spat on my left arm. I spat again, then rubbed the spittle into it, polishing, working till my arm grew warm. As I spat, and rubbed, I wondered why Marvin did this weird, nasty thing to himself, day after day. Was he trying to rub away the black, or deepen it, doll it up? And if he did this weird nasty thing for a hundred years, would he spit-shine himself invisible, rolling away the eggplant skin, revealing the scarlet muscle, blue vein, pink and yellow tendon, white bone? Then disappear? Seen through, all colors, no colors. Spitting and rubbing. Is this the way you do it? I leaned forward, sniffed the arm. It smelled vaguely of mayonnaise. After an hour or so, I fell asleep.

I saw Oakley the second I stepped off the bus the next morning. He stood outside the gym in his usual black penny loafers, white socks, high-water jeans, T-shirt, and black jacket. Nailor stood with him, his big teeth spread across his bottom lip like playing cards. If there was anyone I felt like fighting, that day, it was Nailor. But I wanted to put off fighting for as long as I could. I stepped toward the gymnasium, thinking that I shouldn't run, but if I hurried I could beat Oakley to the door and secure myself near Gilchrest's office. But the moment I stepped into the gym, I felt Oakley's broad palm clap down on my shoulder. "Might as well stay out here, Coonie," he said. "I need me a little target practice." I turned to face him and he slapped me, one-two, with the back, then the palm of his hand, as I'd seen Bogart do to Peter Lorre in *The Maltese Falcon.* My heart went wild. I could scarcely breathe. I couldn't swallow.

"Call me a nigger," I said. I have no idea what made me say this. All I know is that it kept me from crying. "Call me a nigger, Oakley."

"Fuck you, ya black-ass slope." He slapped me again, scratching my eye. "I don't do what Coonies tell me."

"Call me a nigger."

"Outside, Coonie."

"Call me one. Go ahead!"

He lifted his hand to slap me again, but before his arm could swing my way, Marvin Pruitt came from behind me and calmly pushed me aside. "Git out my way, boy," he said. And he slugged Oakley on the side of his head. Oakley stumbled back, stiff-legged. His eyes were big. Marvin hit him twice more, once again to the side of the head, once to the nose. Oakley went down and stayed down. Though blood was drawn, whistles blowing, fingers pointing, kids hollering, Marvin just stood there, staring at me with cool eyes. He spat on the ground, licked his lips, and just stared at me, till Coach Gilchrest and Mr. Calderon tackled him and violently carried him away. He never struggled, never took his eyes off me.

Nailor and Mrs. Wickham helped Oakley to his feet. His already fattened nose bled and swelled so that I had to look away. He looked around, bemused, wall-eyed, maybe scared. It was apparent he had no idea how bad he was hurt. He didn't blink. He didn't even touch his nose. He didn't look like he knew much of anything. He looked at me, looked me dead in the eye, in fact, but didn't seem to recognize me.

That morning, like all other mornings, we said the Pledge of Allegiance, sang "The Yellow Rose of Texas," "The Eyes of Texas Are upon You," and "Mistress Shady." The room stood strangely empty without Oakley, and without Marvin, but at the same time you could feel their presence more intensely somehow. I felt like I did when I'd walk into my mother's room and could smell my father's cigars or cologne. He was more palpable, in certain respects, than when there in actual flesh. For some reason, I turned to look at Ah-so, and just this once I let my eyes linger on her face. She had a very gentle-looking face, really. That surprised me. She must have felt my eyes on her because she glanced up at me for a second and smiled, white teeth, downcast eyes. Such a pretty smile. That surprised me too. She held it for a few seconds, then let it fade. She looked down at her desk, and sat still as a photograph.

The Body

Jane Hamilton

When I Began to Understand Quantum Mechanics

My uncle says he has to feed me. Otherwise, he says, my brain will shrivel and rot and one day slip to the floor, and no one will notice because there will be no noise. He laughs and I laugh, but my fear is genuine. I try to improve my mind because I know if my brain fails I will have nothing: I look exactly like my father. Still, my mother tells me that in two years it will be my turn to be in the Miss Beaver Dam Beauty Pageant. It was this summer when my sister Kelly took her turn in the pageant that all the brain food my uncle had been dishing out suddenly became intelligible.

Not that I hadn't had glimmers before. My first conscious glimmer occurred when I was six and Kelly was eight. It was the Fourth of July in our town, which is not Beaver Dam but about eight miles outside city limits, in the country. For the ceremony in the park my mother had taught us the song "All Things Bright and Beautiful" and also the deaf signs to go along with it. My sister and I wore identical green-and-blue-plaid cotton jumpers and white shirts with plaid piping along the collar and cuffs. It was 103 degrees under the blazing sun. We wore blue anklets and saddle shoes, and we had the same glasses, the kind men who are doing heavy industrial work must wear under order of the law. My mother had given us pixie cuts the day before. She played the piano up on the stage with us, out in the park, and we chirped, "All things wise and wonderful, / The Lord God made them all. / Each little flower that opens, / Each little bird that sings"—only something slipped a cog in my even then rotting brain, some random energy in the universe, or possibly a curled dimension uncurled itself and made me sing, "Each little fart that opens . . ." My sister jabbed me in the ribs before I knew what had happened, although I had stopped singing because I didn't know how to sign that strange new word. My mother stopped playing and said in her piano teacher voice, "Let's begin again, girls." We took deep breaths and sang the song perfectly. No one mentioned my slip, not even Kelly, who has always been good, but in retrospect I understand that the error was in some ways like the big bang, that there was a very tiny but non-negligible probability that an explosion would happen and then it did, and voilá, here we are on planet Earth. The same with my goof: the key phrase being "non-negligible probability." However small the chance, I was bound to sing the wrong word.

My mother is baffled by the volume of mail my uncle sends me. I don't see him very often because he's a physicist at the University of Wisconsin and he's forever in his lab, but he tells me things I should know and sends me books to read. He promises that no other fifteen-year-old will have a brain like mine if I keep my nose to the grindstone. Until this summer, I understood almost none of the words, and read them only so when he quizzed me I could come up with the answers. Most people say hello when they see me, but my uncle, breaking through the crowd at our family picnic, for example, comes up to me and says, "What role does the observer play in the Copenhagen interpretation of quantum reality?" I rack my poor brain. I know better than to smile and giggle and shrug my shoulders like Kelly does. "According to the Copenhagen interpretation of quantum reality," I say, stalling, "the observer forces a particle to take a certain path, simply by the act of measuring." My uncle slaps me on the back and says, "You're beautiful." This encourages me. "Yes, you see, until you make a measurement and say, 'This particle passed through Slit A,' each particle seems to be going through both Slit A and Slit B. That's what's called superposition, when a particle exists in both states."

"Uh huh," my uncle says, reaching into a bag of corn chips. "Explain Erwin Schrödinger's famous thought experiment with the cat."

"Um," I say, "okay, so you put a cat in a sealed box with a source of radioactive particles and of course you can't know if the cat is dead or alive until you look and the whole point is—"

"The sloppy joes are ready," my mother says. My uncle and I are locked into each other's gaze, me struggling to recite, he looking into my eyes to see if I comprehend. I try Kelly's trick of blinking a lot. I'm not sure if it's working, but my uncle says, "I'm starved. Let's feed our budding cosmologist."

"You two are definitely weird," my mother says, shaking her head as if she has something in her ear.

My mother will never understand what goes on between my uncle and me. She can't keep herself from asking me the question: "Why aren't you more like Kelly?" I try to be good, I really do. I try to stand up straight and smile at Pastor Volt; I try to tease the children in the nursery after church the way Kelly does, so playfully, but it always comes out in a way that must be odd because the children look at me as if I'm not attached to my body.

It is beyond my mother's dimension that I can spend a Saturday morning in my room reading about the universe. She makes me do things like sign up for the homecoming parade committee, so I can stuff napkins into chicken wire, and keep her company while she watches *Knots Landing*. These activities keep me from the work I know I must do. My uncle hasn't said it, but I know he figures being smart is my only hope since I have my father's bone structure. I have a feeling my uncle knows almost everything. He's very tall; he can see over all the heads and he always stands around with his arms folded across his thin chest, watching. When he tells me I'm beautiful or correct I have a wild urge to run to my room and climb under the covers and beat a saucepan with a wooden spoon.

My mother, blind because she is a mother, thinks both of her daughters will capture the Miss America title, and although she is thoroughly committed to the pageant system I think a small part of her secretly wishes it was hooked into the Miss Universe system because you have to admit Miss Universe sounds much better than Miss America.

I'm not like a lot of girls I know: I really love my mother. It's just that I'm beginning to understand that I might have different plans for myself, and I'm not sure how I'm going to get out of her plans for me. At the quantum level, of course, the edges of things are fuzzy, but for my mother absolutely everything is cut-and-dried. A person behaves. If we don't set the table we don't eat. We learn to play two instruments—the piano and one of our choice. We go out for track and field. We are home by 5:30. After dinner we do our homework. Lights-out by ten. If I tried to explain to my mother that it takes sunlight eight minutes to get to the earth, and therefore I should be able to read until 10:08, she would probably give me that You-are-so-weird look, and then snap off the lights. "I'm strict because I love you so much," she says. We audition for Swing Choir whether or not we can sing. Kelly can. I can't. At seventeen we enter the Miss Beaver Dam Beauty Pageant.

Mostly, I guess, I used to be a classical physicist. I thought God ran the whole show and that once I got smarter I would be able to understand how the whole deal was set up, that it was there for me to figure out, and ultimately comprehensible. The beauty pageant was where I really got shaken up.

We were building toward it all spring and summer. First, my mother enrolled Kelly in voice lessons, even though Kelly can play the piano better than anyone at high school, and it is her real talent. But think about it: how many Miss Americas got to be queen playing the piano? You can come up with a few, but it's pretty unusual. Almost all of them win by singing "Smoke Gets in Your Eyes." So Kelly spent all spring and summer singing that song over and over, perfecting even the moments where there is an absence of noise. I would sit at the dining-room table doing my homework and listening to her every word while she accompanied herself and sang, "They said someday you'll find, / All who love are blind. / When your heart's on fire, / You must realize / Smoke Gets in Your Eyes." The only boy I'd had experience with—that is, I talked to him sometimes—was Kelly's boyfriend, Dwight, and I couldn't imagine Kelly's or my heart bursting into flames over scrawny old Dwight. Still, I knew she was singing the song authentically and I never tired of her pure voice and the sweet, sad words.

We went to the mall so frequently, in pursuit of the perfect evening gown, that I could close my eyes as I walked along and say which store we were passing. My mother had her sketch pad neatly obscured in her pocket and she'd skulk around the dress shops drawing what looked suitable. Then we'd pile into the car and go home so she could make a pattern while it was still fresh in her memory. Then she'd make a sort of dummy dress out of old sheets to see if it was worth putting time and money into good material.

In the end, for the evening gown competition, Kelly wore her prom dress, slightly done over. It was a deep red shiny material, far far too much red for anyone to swallow whole, with a ruffle around the low-slung neck. I hate to say it, but she looked like a Mylar balloon. Although my mother is a good seamstress, it was painfully obvious that the dress was homemade. It was okay for the prom, but definitely not pageant material. Some of the girls were buying $500 evening gowns, but we kept remembering that the judges pay the most attention to talent. And Kelly could sing, so we weren't worried.

As I said, I was still in my Newtonian stage, so I didn't truly understand the fact vital to quantum mechanics: the world shifts when it is measured, and this means you can't make precise predictions about it. The world is composed of probabilities, rather than definite, fixed states.

"What do you mean?" I had asked the page, when I read that the world was composed of probabilities. "You're going to tell me I could look in the mirror and see a fish where my nose should be?" After the pageant I knew that such a thing was not impossible.

By the middle of June we were all highly agitated. It's the classic example of counting your chickens before they hatch. We had all nervously sat before the television, watching the Miss Wisconsin Pageant, knowing deep down that Kelly was going to be there in Oshkosh next year, our Miss Beaver Dam. We wanted to wish her onto the screen; instead there was the current Miss B.D., Cindy Potts, who Kelly's boyfriend Dwight said was a total dogface. Kelly laughed at this remark and then snuggled up against Dwight's chest, which was something I found difficult to watch and impossible not to try to look at, a living example, I guess, of Heisenberg's uncertainty principle.

Also, at the end of June, the Pageant Committee started getting the materials ready for the *Miss Beaver Dam Pageant Program,* a very glossy magazine with the contestants' photos and histories, and pageant lore. We all wrote well-wishes, to be printed on the page opposite the contestant's photo and résumé. Dwight wrote, "Kelly, to me you are the most beautiful girl in the world. I give you the best of my love, always, and I hope I will be doing so for many,

many years to come." My mother tolerates Dwight, but there is no way he is going to be her son-in-law. If he ever got too forward she'd sit him down and give him a firm talking-to. My mother is very effective in her Little Talks. I avoid them at all cost by doing the right thing, as much as I can anticipate what the right thing is. Dwight has no meat on his shoulders or torso, but from the bottom down he's thick, so it's hard to know how to describe his whole self. He persists in trying to grow a mustache, and I can't understand why he doesn't realize there is no hope and just quit. From the moment I first saw him, I knew Kelly was too good for him. Of course my opinion is inconsequential: one time I was sitting on the floor watching television and Dwight came in the room and tripped over me. When he collected himself and tried to locate the offending object, and realized it was a person, he squinted at me, wondering, I guess, who in the world I could be.

For the pageant program I wrote, "I'll be your valet when you go to Atlantic City—you're the greatest! Luv, your sister Bonnie." Mike's Meat Market even wrote "Best Wishes," and Mom and Dad wrote a thing about how proud they were of Kelly, how they hoped she was having a fantastic experience in the pageant, and getting to know all the girls, and growing, and how happy they were that she was their daughter. Grandma wrote, "To the Winner!" We wrote enough to fill the whole page. So that got us revved up.

Then there were the rehearsals, and buying the outfits for the production numbers, and finding the right swimsuit. My mother taught Kelly how to tape her breasts so they'd be uplifted and there'd be some cleavage. And we all watched, especially Dwight, in amazement, when Kelly strutted around the living room in her high heels and her lavender suit. My mother kept clapping the smallest, quickest claps with her hands at her mouth and saying, "I can't believe how great you look." Kelly knew it. Turning around, she gave us a full sixty seconds to contemplate her backside before facing us again.

What exactly was my mother seeing? I know now what the role of the observer is, and that matter takes form only because there is an observer. Probe the world with photons and you see the beautiful Kelly and breakfast on the table. Probe it with, say, neutrinos, those extremely light, probably massless elementary particles, and the world will look like an ocean of subatomic emptiness. I guess it all depends on your perspective. To my mother, Kelly in her swimsuit was pure confection. But I saw things that bothered me, against my will. Kelly had a non-negligible potbelly. Her thighs rubbed together. Her bottom was primarily flat but it puddled down to her thighs and hung there looking just plain sloppy. Her purple heels didn't quite match the suit. Was the world shifting because I was trying to measure it? I shook my head hard to try to get ahold of myself. What was the important fact I wanted to keep in mind? Yes, this was it: the judges give the most weight to the talent portion of the show.

There were ten contestants altogether. They really weren't worth talking about. Most of them were blond. They sang or danced or played instruments and had hobbies galore. They collected John Lennon memorabilia and bred boxer dogs and biked and studied French and wanted to be music teachers and physical therapists. Kelly was the only redhead. She was the only one who was under five feet seven, the only one with green eyes and a dimple on her chin. She was almost the only one who didn't have a perm, but my mother panicked at the last minute and sent her to the hairdresser.

The day of the pageant we sat at the kitchen table while my mother scrambled eggs and flipped sausages. She was going to make sure Kelly had a good breakfast; it was all she could do—then her daughter would be out of her hands. Kelly and I sat on our cold fingers, our shoulders hunched up, and jiggled our limbs. My father came in and said, "How's the present and future Miss Beautiful?"

"Daaaaaaaaaaaad," Kelly said.

"Drink your juice," my mother said, and my sister obediently downed all eight ounces.

None of us uttered another word until after breakfast.

My mother had made a new dress for me, which I couldn't wait to wear. When my dad saw me in it he said I looked like his very own peanut. It was pink with puffy sleeves and a square neck and a tight bodice that sort of squashed what little I had in front, and a full skirt. I had a giant white bow for the top of my head. It all made me feel, well, pretty. I was going to be in the pit turning the pages for the piano player, and although not everyone stares at the page turner, I wanted to look as good as possible.

After my sister had been adequately nourished, her pageant chaperon, Mrs. Vendero, picked her up. Pageant rules said we were allowed no contact with the contestant all day. We wouldn't see her again until she came out onstage for the first production number. We stood in the driveway and each of us took our turn hugging and kissing Kelly, and wishing her luck. My dad said he loved her. Kelly started to cry. "Save those tears for the crowning," I wanted to say, but I kept quiet.

"Pray for me at one," Kelly choked from the backseat as the car pulled out from the driveway. My mother clasped her hands and shook them over her head and nodded vigorously. Kelly's interview on current events was scheduled for after lunch. We had all been watching the six o'clock news like maniacs for a month.

My mother had tasks to keep her busy all day long: she had to hem my dress and finish her own outfit and bake for the family party on Sunday, in honor of Kelly. I had nothing to keep my nervous energy in check. I talked to my uncle on the phone for a while. Naturally he grilled me on the grand unified theory and why gravity doesn't fit in. I couldn't answer any of his questions. Finally I said, "I'm sorry, but I'm too nervous to think. Tonight is Kelly's pageant."

My uncle said, "Christ on a crutch. Poor old Kelly."

"What do you mean?" I asked.

"Listen," he said, "don't let your mother put you through it. Do you know what *pageant* means? Do you know the root of the word?"

"Ah," I said. "No."

"In Shakespeare *pageant* is used as a verb, meaning to imitate, to mimic, but you, Bonnie—you are original—you—"

"I have to go," I said. "You never like anything normal. Don't tell me you won't be proud when Kelly becomes Miss Beaver Dam." I couldn't believe I was talking like my mother to my uncle. "See you soon," I said, and hung up.

My heart was bamming up near my throat. I hadn't listened to what he said but the words had gone in somewhere—what had he said about imitating? For reasons I didn't stop to sort out, I was bothered.

At 4:30 I got in the bathtub and soaked. It was terribly hot but I lay there and imagined myself afterward at Stewart's Supper Club. I imagined myself being there with my sister, the queen. Boys might ask me to dance, simply because of the association. Of course I would say no because I hate to dance and I don't know how, which is one of the things my mother has Talked with me about: how sometimes you have to learn to do things you don't like to get on in life. Still, their asking, and my saying no, and the buffet filled with baloney and olives speared with toothpicks—it all thrilled me. Kelly would be so happy, dancing with Dad, and my mother would be ecstatic; she'd sit at the head table all night long while people came up to congratulate her. The newspaper would do one of those spotlights they do on neat families in the community. My mother would tell them how close we are and they'd take a picture of us around the piano, my mother sitting with her hands splayed over the keys, Kelly standing beside her with her violin, me with my trombone, and my dad with his hands on my mother's shoulders. I fell asleep in the tub. When the door opened and banged against the towel rack I opened my eyes. My mother looked hard at me and said if she'd known I was going to look like a prune she wouldn't have gone to the trouble of making me a new dress.

We got there early and put out programs on the seats in the front row. Then we walked around and examined the decorations up close. The gym had been transformed. The theme was "Born in the U S of A!" The Pageant Committee had erected trellises up on the stage and on both sides of the gym, and then strung red, white, and blue balloons all over them, and at each entrance there were enormous wire baskets, the size of silos, filled with more balloons. The floor had a new coat of wax on it, and you could see yourself in a wavery sort of way. The spotlights were poised like cannons at the back, and the folding chairs were set up in perfect lines, like the grave markers at Arlington. My mother grabbed my hand and whispered, "I wonder how she's doing." She squeezed my fingers and we both shut our eyes and grimaced. My father was outside having a cigarette.

At long last I took my place next to the piano player, Mrs. Pinigus, who helped me out by nodding every time she wanted me to turn the page, so I didn't have to pay too much attention. The gym went dark, and the crowd instantly hushed. Mrs. Pinigus played the tinkling intro, and then in the circle of a single spotlight they started coming out from behind the side curtain. One by one they first stuck out their legs, up to their red garters, and then the rest of their selves followed. They were wearing what we had shopped around so hard to find: cranberry pumps, cranberry leotards, navy blue skirts, cranberry-and-aqua flag scarves around their necks, gigantic blue ball earrings, and blue bowler hats. Kelly was #7. She was smaller than the others, but she was sending off sparks exactly like a star immediately after its initial hydrogen explosion. There was no mistaking her voice as she belted, "I'm proud, I'm proud, I'M PROUD to be from the U S of A!" Her teeth were straighter and whiter and much more enormous than they'd appeared at the breakfast table. She looked like she might be able to devour us all in one mouthful. She did the cancan and then skipped up to the front, giving us a minute to take all of her in, and then she sassily turned her back on us. I had the urge to hug Mrs. Pinigus and jump to my feet and holler with the pleasure of being alive. Kelly onstage did that to a person—her gift was raw energy and affirmation. I had to shiver after she disappeared behind the curtain, taking her radiance into the shadows.

The hosts for the pageant were a former Miss Northshore and her husband, Don. They make a living going around hosting pageants and judging and making new rules. Miss Northshore was glamorous in a mature beauty queen way, although the single sweep of blond curl down the side of her face looked as if it was no longer hair but had been replaced by some more durable material. Don looked completely comfortable in his white tux with the pale pink cummerbund to match her pink sequined gown. They sang "You're the Top," and they nuzzled noses at the end of the song and then kissed, which for some reason made my stomach do a flip. They spent a lot of time welcoming us and thanking everybody and introducing the judges, and apparently I was jiggling my legs again because Mrs. Pinigus put her hand gently on my thigh to make me still. I slapped my hand to my mouth and she smiled. She understood it was my nerves.

6

Finally it was time to introduce the contestants. This was the part of the pageant where the girls come out in fabulous outfits and say a few sentences to let us get to know them. Out came #1, Lesley Anne Meyers, looking like a tramp in a red miniskirt and a V-necked cashmere sweater. Her teeth were tiny and pointed, like a weasel's. She came to the mike and said in a scared high voice, "Dreams really do come true. People who succeed in their work find circumstances to suit them." What a dumb thing to say! She cocked her head and smirked and sailed out under the arch. I endured the next five, who said nothing more profound than gobbledygook, and then out came Kelly. She was wearing the black knit top Mom found for her at Target on sale, and the black-and-white polka-dotted skirt that was all bunched up, practically like a tutu. Her long string of pearls was tied in a knot and she was wearing awfully high black heels. She got to the mike, flashed us all a seductive grin, and then she looked us straight in the eye. "Caring and seeing with the heart is as important as knowledge. I wish to be like no other woman in history. I wish to be myself." She winked and then walked through the trellis arch like she had all the time in the world. Everyone clapped their hands off. Dwight was in the back whistling with his thumb and his first finger in his mouth. The whistle split through the applause and said in its continuous screech what we were all thinking: Kelly, you're a genius, you're beautiful, GO FOR IT!

After they all finished their sentences I was clapping so wildly to try and blow off some steam I didn't notice the apparition onstage. The applause was cut short, so I looked up. There was the old Miss Beaver Dam, Cindy Potts, appearing out of nowhere, standing in her tight black sequined gown in a patch of silver light. When we all realized who it was, we involuntarily rose up clapping, before she'd even done a thing. Don't ask me how she got where she was, because she clearly didn't come out of the mold right. Her lips were so skinny and her mouth so small her mother is probably still to this day cutting up chunks of apple for her. She had an enormous nose, which I'm not going to carry on about because mine is probably bigger than hers; black eyes too close together; and a crop of black hair permed to stand on end in half-formed curls. She sang "Over the Rainbow" dolefully. This was the last time she would sing to an audience as Miss Beaver Dam. I felt the weight of it, for a minute, until I remembered who was going to be wearing that crown in one short hour.

The crowd rose up again in appreciation. She did have a good voice, and clearly she had won on that merit. "So, okay," I said to myself. "Thank you and good riddance." Don and Miss Northshore slunk back out, and Don announced, "My favorite part of the pageant is coming right up."

"Not so fast," Miss Northshore said. "You know the pageant gods in Atlantic City are thinking about doing away with the swimsuit portion."

Don looked stricken and said, "Over my dead body."

While they goaded each other, I prayed for Kelly to suck in her belly and for her eighteen-hour girdle to do its job for just five minutes. Mrs. Pinigus started playing the slow romantic music that weaves all over the keyboard, and the girls began their interminable walk from the back of the stage, the pause before the judges, and then the long rear view, and around again, and then to the exit with their heads turned to the audience, smiling beyond their natural capacity even though no one was going to bother looking above their necks.

Kelly came out and I squinted to see her as I wanted. She didn't have one of those suits that are cut up over the hips, because although I hate to dwell on it, Kelly does have a little excess in her hips and thighs. I could hear her nylons rubbing together as she walked; I could see the fold of blubber at her waist. She was tottering on her high heels, as if the weight of her breasts was going to make her fall on her face. I closed my eyes and listened to Don talk about Kelly, about how wonderfully she plays the piano and how many firsts she has taken at the state music contest, about her volunteer work at the hospital (which my mother makes her do, against her will, and which I will have to do next year), about her wins in track and field, and the National Honor Society. I thought of how my mother loves to tell the stories, time and time again, of Kelly spontaneously singing both verses of "Baa Baa, Black Sheep" when she was eighteen months old, of Kelly ordering Dad to return me to the hospital when I was five days old, Kelly tap-dancing at the Senior Center when she was six and kissing all the old ladies with warts and no teeth. I opened my eyes and looked up at Kelly's continental rear end, and then she turned around. Her ruby lips looked as if they were a neon diner sign on the highway at night—I swear her smile was that dazzling—and I couldn't help yelling "YAY KELLY!" When I realized I had made a fair amount of noise I ducked my head and then looked over at my mother. She was frowning and shaking her head. As a page turner I was part of the performance and wasn't supposed to be partial.

By the time the talent portion came, I had no feeling in my hands, so I was having a terrible time turning the pages. We had a long time for #7. No one before Kelly was astonishing, except in defeat. Melissa Campo creamed her Rachmaninoff; it was not distinguishable as Rachmaninoff, and I know him well because my mother teaches piano, and by the time you're in high school and any good at all she assigns this piece. Melissa massacred the man—had to stop in the middle and completely butchered the end. She was a goner, without a doubt. It was so painful to watch that Mrs. Pinigus put her head down and clutched her nose with her two fists. Lesley Anne Meyers fudged the entrance to "Send in the Clowns" but pretended that everything was perfect. The ballet dancer wasn't even on toe, and the other singers were so negligible that I forgot what they sang the instant after they stopped.

And then it was Kelly's turn. She came out in her black silk pants and a sleek green shirt, which was loose. It rippled when she moved. She sang "Smoke Gets in Your Eyes" as if someone had just put a knife through her heart. She moaned a little before she even started. Even though I'd listened to the song over and over, I heard it as if for the first time. Kelly taught me right then and there what love is all about—nothing more or less than total loss followed by unbearable pain that never quits. She swayed, and her pants followed her legs and her green shirt shuddered. Tears sprang into my eyes and sat there until I blinked, and they spilled over onto my lap. She had it in the bag and everyone in that room knew it.

By intermission my mother's excitement had reached a feverish pitch. Her friends were swarming around her reaching for her hands and shaking them. "Kelly will surely place," they told her and my mother and I modestly nodded in agreement. My mother giggled nervously and said, "Let's just hope she doesn't blow evening gown." Mrs. Pinigus assured her there was no chance.

"I'm going outside before this heat affects my brain," I said. My mother paid no attention. I slipped through the fire exit to the parking lot. The asphalt looked soft and steamy in the dim light, as if it were in danger of melting. I stood against the redbrick school and closed my eyes. I honestly didn't know if I was going to make it to the crowning. Although I knew there was no question about the future queen, the suspense was killing me. I tried to empty my head, to fill it with nothingness, but I couldn't help hearing a familiar voice. I tried to block it out, but it kept coming back to me.

"She bites. Hard."

"She bites?" someone asked the voice.

"She's crazy for it. You should hear her sweet-talking her mother, telling her"—at this point the voice went up an octave—"'Yes, Mom, we'll be home by midnight, Mom, we're going to the eight o'clock movie and out for ice cream and then he has to drop off a loaf of bread by his grandma's and then we'll be home.' Her mom and her sister—we call her the Nun—wave at us and the minute we're at the end of the driveway she dives for my pants. She's crazy for it."

I realized that the voices were coming from around the corner and up above, from the fire escape.

"Like, like last time we went out, she put on that polka-dotted skirt number she was wearing for her sentence thing tonight, and she was attacking me in the backseat of the Vega—she was saying 'God Dwight, Yes Dwight, Sweet Jesus Dwight, Oh harder, harder,' and when she climbed off me, guess what she says? She says, 'Now you know what it's like to screw a ladybug; all ass and wings, ass and wings'—because of the wild skirt she had on."

"Sheeeit," the other voice said.

"And then we go home, and there's her mom—and the Nun, wearing some party dress—watching videos of *As the World Turns,* catching up on the week. And her mom says to us, 'How was the movie, kids? What kind of ice cream did you have?'"

The voices laughed.

I stood there for a second watching the moths bang and

bang against the exit light. The voices were laughing and laughing. I felt my dress. It was still on my body. I walked back into the gym and sat down at the piano. The air was thick with perfume and hair spray and I had to clutch at the piano to keep from suffocating and falling over. When I got my balance I reached up and pulled the bow out of my hair and slipped it underneath me.

The lights went down and Miss Beaver Dam sang her third farewell song. Her black dress made her look like the flat dead salamanders in the drain in our basement. Mrs. Pinigus fumbled at the sheet music while I bit my bottom lip and tried to hold on to the piano bench.

The next time I noticed, they were about ready to announce the finalists. Don and Miss Northshore were joking around because the judges were having trouble making up their minds. Finally an old man with a tobacco-stained mustache and thick glasses handed an envelope to Don. It struck me in that moment of exchange that life is hideous: what right did these blind old men have to judge beauty? I felt violently ill for a second, and then the feeling passed to steady nausea. The contestants were in a straight line, up front, holding each other's hands and trying to be still. They were all smiling so hard they looked mad. The first award, Miss Congeniality, is decided by the girls themselves.

Sheila Dart, the girl who raises boxers and didn't dance on toe, came forward to receive the award. She kept her smile plastered on her face even though we all knew she was hoping for more. Mrs. Pinigus played a drumroll on the piano as Don announced the third runner-up. He said, "Step right up, Melissa Campo!"

What? She had creamed the Rachmaninoff! I couldn't believe my ears. What was more unbelievable was how disappointed she looked. She came to the front and grabbed her certificate. My uncle's small silent words were whirling around in my head, getting larger as they came into focus and finding each other to make sentences, and then stopping right up front and shouting at me: *The fact that the world shifts when it is measured means simply that you cannot make precise predictions about it.* This is the cornerstone of quantum mechanics. Its implications are dire. Heisenberg's uncertainty principle tells us that things aren't as they seem. *Sometimes it is useful to think of particles as waves, and when it's useful we think of waves as particles.* I wasn't feeling at all well. *One can only predict a number of different possible outcomes, each with their own likelihood.* The floor was slipping under my feet and I grabbed at the black keys in front of me. Onstage the girls were still squeezing each other's hands and waiting.

Mrs. Pinigus did her drumroll again and Don said, "The second runner-up will receive a trophy and a scholarship donated by Carson Rubber. And she is, Tina Otto!"

Tina Otto, the girl whose brain weighs slightly more than a dustball.

"And now," Don was saying, "the first runner-up, the lady who will assume Miss Beaver Dam's position should anything, God forbid, happen to her, and who will receive a scholarship donated by the Can Corporation, and a trophy. The winner is . . . Lesley Anne Meyers."

Was I experiencing space and time before the big bang singularity, where predictability breaks down? Had something so large happened out in the universe that we had failed to feel it? I couldn't keep my mind on what was making me sickest. Lesley Anne hugged the girls next to her and wriggled up to the front. I guess she was genuinely pleased, because she knew she had blown her entrance to "Send in the Clowns" and under normal circumstances wouldn't have expected to place. Yet there she was, miraculously, the first runner-up. One swift jab of the kitchen knife and she could have the crown.

"Well, shall we go home now?" Don asked Miss

Northshore. She stamped her foot and swatted his arm. "Oh, all right," he said. "I'll announce the queen." He yawned and stretched.

"And now," Don said, "for the coronation of Miss Beaver Dam 1988." Mrs. Pinigus played her dinner club music. "Miss Beaver Dam 1988 will receive a gift certificate from Diane's Dress Shop, a complete wardrobe for the Miss Wisconsin Pageant, modeling sessions at Tres Chic, and a scholarship from the Beaver Dam Lionesses and Lions Club. Are we all ready?"

The audience groaned. My mother had rolled up her program and I knew if there was any further delay she was going to personally march onstage and club Don to death.

"The title of Miss Beaver Dam 1988 goes to . . . Kelly Brooks!"

Mrs. Pinigus threw her arm around me, drew me close, and then jiggled. I sat perfectly still in the crook of her vibrating arm. My uncle's words screamed at me inside my idiotic head: *The world's attributes seem to vary depending on the vantage point of the observer, somewhat like the location of a wave.* I understood everything. We were in this gym and we were not in this gym, somewhat like the location of a rainbow.

"Isn't she lovely?" Mrs. Pinigus murmured.

No, she was not lovely. She was—she was a—slut.

I looked up and there she was, with too much makeup on and a smile that had somehow gotten twisted with overuse. I always knew I could never be beautiful like Kelly, but I had tried so hard to be good. It all was so clear that I started to cry. The blue paint from *South Pacific* on the trellis hadn't been covered up properly, the BORN IN THE U S OF A sign had gotten bumped and half of it was down, and the floor was littered with programs and styrofoam cups. Everyone was clapping. Kelly was trying to cry and hugging Miss Northshore as Cindy Potts struggled to pin the crown into Kelly's hair. When the crown was secure Kelly came to the front smiling the terrible smile that looked as if it was going to sit there on her face permanently. She stood waving at the crowd, sniffling. My mother was standing motionless with her hands to her face. My father was heading out the door for a cigarette. We were the perfect normal family, vanishing into thin air.

I stumbled over to my mother after the lights came on. My stomach was killing me. I begged her to take me home, and she stamped her foot and snorted, and then my face must have impressed her because she said, "Good Lord, you look awful. What's the matter with you?" Before I could say, "Absolutely nothing," she hooked her elbow around my neck and pulled me to her mouth, and then she whispered, "Can you believe it?"

She arranged to have Dwight drive Kelly and my father to the reception in Dwight's car. She would meet them there after driving me home. On the way, she chattered about how smart the judges were, how well the committee ran the pageant, about how wonderfully Kelly had performed. "For once," my mother said, "the judges really knew enough to judge every category."

Maybe yes, maybe no. I could have told her those old men didn't know anything, that they were senile and blind, but I kept quiet. Rain spattered our windshield and the night inside our van was hot and dark and close. My mother parked and made a dash for the house. Slowly I climbed out. I stood on the gravel looking up into the sky.

"Get out of the rain," my mother yelled from the porch. "Don't you know any better?"

I looked at her, safe and relatively dry, spinning through time and space, if there is such a thing. I held my arms up and water trickled into the puffs of my sleeves. I used to love coming home from band practice after dark and standing right here on the driveway, looking into the house with just one light on at the piano, seeing Kelly's head barely moving as she played some crazy Beethoven sonatas. I took off my pink pumps and headed for the marsh. I knew in my heart that everything had collapsed, but I wanted to feel the cold scummy dirt on my bare feet anyway. I was wondering if, by any small chance, the earth was still solid enough to hold me.

Lorna Crozier

Quitting Smoking

The phone says smoke when it rings, the radio says smoke, the TV smokes its own images until they are dead butts at three A.M. Three A.M. and the *dépanneurs* are open just for you. White cartons, silver cartons that mirror your face. Behind the counters, the young men who work the night-shift unwrap the cellophane as lovingly as you undo the buttons of a silk shirt, your fingers burning.

Your cat is grey. When he comes in from the muddy lane, his paws leave ashes on the floor. The dirty burner on the stove smokes, the kettle smokes, your first, your last cup of coffee demands a smoke. The snow on the step is a long Vogue paper waiting to be rolled. Above the chimneys stars light up and smoke the whole night through.

In Montreal there are stores where you can buy one cigarette. Cars parked outside, idle, exhaust pipes smoking. Women you could fall in love with approach you from the shadows and offer a light. The sound of a match struck on the black ribbon of a matchbox is the sound of a new beginning. In every dark room across the city, the fireflies of cigarettes are dancing, their small bodies burning out.

Dawn and the neon cross on the mountains melts in the pale light. Another day. Blindfolded and one last wish. Electric, your fingers ignite everything they touch—the curtains, the rug, the sleeping cat. The air around your body crackles and sparks, your hair a halo of fire.

Breathe in, breathe out. Your lungs are animals pacing their cages of bone, eyes burning holes through your chest. The shape of your mouth around an imaginary cigarette is an absence you can taste. Your lips acetylene, desire begins and ends on the tip of your tongue.

The grey of morning—smoke from the sun settling on the roofs, the snow, the bare branches of maple trees. Every cell in your body is a mouth, crying to be heard: *O Black Cat; O ageless Sailor, where have you gone? O Craven A, first letter of the alphabet, so beautiful to say, O Cameo. . . .*

David Sedaris

Diary of a Smoker

I rode my bike to the boat pond in Central Park, where I bought myself a cup of coffee and sat down on a bench to read. I lit a cigarette and was enjoying myself when the woman seated twelve feet away, on the other side of the bench, began waving her hands before her face. I thought she was fighting off a bee.

She fussed at the air and called out, "Excuse me, do you mind if we make this a no-smoking bench?"

I don't know where to begin with a statement like that. "Do you mind if *we* make this a no-smoking bench?" There is no "we." Our votes automatically cancel one another out. What she meant was, "Do you mind if *I* make this a no-smoking bench?" I could understand it if we were in an elevator or locked together in the trunk of a car, but this was outdoors. Who did she think she was? This woman was wearing a pair of sandals, which are always a sure sign of trouble. They looked like the sort of shoes Moses might have worn while he chiseled regulations onto stone tablets. I looked at her sandals and at her rapidly moving arms and I crushed my cigarette. I acted like it was no problem and then I stared at the pages of my book, hating her and Moses—the two of them.

The trouble with aggressive nonsmokers is that they feel they are doing you a favor by not allowing you to smoke. They seem to think that one day you'll look back and thank them for those precious fifteen seconds they just added to your life. What they don't understand is that those are just fifteen more seconds you can spend hating their guts and plotting revenge.

૬

My school insurance expires in a few weeks so I made an appointment for a checkup. It's the only thing they'll pay for as all of my other complaints have been dismissed as "Cosmetic."

If you want a kidney transplant it's covered but if you desperately need a hair transplant it's "Cosmetic." You tell me.

I stood around the examining room for twenty minutes, afraid to poke around as, every so often, a nurse or some confused patient would open the door and wander into the room. And it's bad enough to be caught in your underpants but even worse to be caught in your underpants scratching out a Valium prescription on someone else's pad.

When the doctor finally came he looked over my chart and said, "Hey, we have almost the exact same birthday. I'm one day younger than you!"

That did wonders for my morale. It never occurred to me that my doctor could be younger than me. Never entered my mind.

He started in by asking a few preliminary questions and then said, "Do you smoke?"

"Only cigarettes and pot," I answered.

He gave me a look. "*Only* cigarettes and pot? Only?"

"Not crack," I said. "Never touch the stuff. Cigars either. Terrible habit, nasty."

૬

I was at work, defrosting someone's freezer, when I heard the EPA's report on secondhand smoke. It was on the radio and they reported it over and over again. It struck me the same way that previous EPA reports must have struck auto manufacturers and the owners of chemical plants: as reactionary and unfair. The report accuses smokers, especially smoking parents, of criminal recklessness, as if these were people who kept loaded pistols lying on the coffee table, crowded alongside straight razors and mugs of benzene.

Over Christmas we looked through boxes of family pictures and played a game we call "Find Mom, find Mom's cigarettes." There's one in every picture. We've got photos of her pregnant, leaning toward a lit match, and others of her posing with her newborn babies, the smoke forming a halo above our heads. These pictures gave us a warm feeling.

She smoked in the bathtub, where we'd find her drowned butts lined up in a neat row beside the shampoo bottle. She smoked through meals, and often used her half-empty plate as an ashtray. Mom's theory was that if you cooked the meal and did the dishes, you were allowed to use your plate however you liked. It made sense to us.

Even after she was diagnosed with lung cancer she continued to smoke, although less often. On her final trip to the hospital, sick with pneumonia, she told my father she'd left something at home and had him turn the car around. And there, standing at the kitchen counter, she entertained what she knew to be her last cigarette. I hope that she enjoyed it.

It never occurred to any of us that Mom might quit smoking. Picturing her without a cigarette was like trying to imagine her on water skis. Each of us is left to choose our own quality of life and take pleasure where we find it, with the understanding that, like Mom used to say, "Sooner or later, something's going to get you."

Something got me the moment I returned home from work and Hugh delivered his interpretation of the EPA report. He told me that I am no longer allowed to smoke in any room that he currently occupies. Our apartment is small—four tiny rooms.

I told him that seeing as I pay half the rent, I should be allowed to smoke half the time we're in the same room. He agreed, on the condition that every time I light a cigarette, all the windows must be open.

It's cold outside.

Bernard Cooper

Burl's

I loved the restaurant's name, a compact curve of a word. Its sign, five big letters rimmed in neon, hovered above the roof. I almost never saw the sign with its neon lit; my parents took me there for early summer dinners, and even by the time we left—Father cleaning his teeth with a toothpick, Mother carrying steak bones in a doggie bag—the sky was still bright. Heat rippled off the cars parked along Hollywood Boulevard, the asphalt gummy from hours of sun.

With its sleek architecture, chrome appliances, and arctic temperature, Burl's offered a refuge from the street. We usually sat at one of the booths in front of the plateglass windows. During our dinner, people came to a halt before the news-vending machine on the corner and burrowed in their pockets and purses for change.

The waitresses at Burl's wore brown uniforms edged in checked gingham. From their breast pockets frothed white lace handkerchiefs. In between reconnaissance missions to the tables, they busied themselves behind the counter and shouted "Tuna to travel" or "Scorch that patty" to a harried short-order cook who manned the grill. Miniature pitchers of cream and individual pats of butter were extracted from an industrial refrigerator. Coca-Cola shot from a glinting spigot. Waitresses dodged and bumped one another, as frantic as atoms.

My parents usually lingered after the meal, nursing cups of coffee while I played with the beads of condensation on my glass of ice water, tasted Tabasco sauce, or twisted pieces of my paper napkin into mangled animals.

One evening, annoyed with my restlessness, my father gave me a dime and asked me to buy him a *Herald Examiner* from the vending machine in front of the restaurant.

Shouldering open the heavy glass door, I was seared by a sudden gust of heat. Traffic roared past me and stirred the air. Walking toward the newspaper machine, I held the dime so tightly, it seemed to melt in my palm. Duty made me feel large and important. I inserted the dime and opened the box, yanking a *Herald* from the spring contraption that held it as tight as a mousetrap. When I turned around, paper in hand, I saw two women walking toward me.

Their high heels clicked on the sun-baked pavement. They were tall, broad-shouldered women who moved with a mixture of haste and defiance. They'd teased their hair into nearly identical black beehives. Dangling earrings flashed in the sun, as brilliant as prisms. Each of them wore the kind of clinging, strapless outfit my mother referred to as a cocktail dress. The silky fabric—one dress was purple, the other pink—accentuated their breasts and hips and rippled with insolent highlights. The dresses exposed their bare arms, the slope of their shoulders, and the smooth, powdered plane of flesh where their cleavage began.

I owned at the time a book called *Things for Boys and Girls to Do.* There were pages to color, intricate mazes, and connect-the-dots. But another type of puzzle came to mind as I watched those women walking toward me: What's Wrong with This Picture? Say the drawing of a dining room looked normal at first glance; on closer inspection, a chair was missing its leg and the man who sat atop it wore half a pair of glasses.

The women had Adam's apples.

The closer they came, the shallower my breathing. I blocked the sidewalk, an incredulous child stalled in their path. When they saw me staring, they shifted their purses and linked their arms. There was something sisterly and conspiratorial about their sudden closeness. Though their mouths didn't open, I thought they might have been communicating without moving their lips, so telepathic did they seem as they joined arms and pressed together, synchronizing their heavy steps. The pages of the *Herald* fluttered in the wind; I felt them against my arm, light as batted lashes.

The woman in pink shot me a haughty glance, and yet she seemed pleased that I'd taken notice, hungry to be admired by a man, or even an awestruck eight-year-old boy. She tried to stifle a grin, her red lipstick more voluptuous than the lips it painted. Rouge deepened her cheekbones. Eye shadow dusted her lids, a clumsy abundance of blue. Her face was like a page in *Things for Boys and Girls to Do,* colored by a kid who went outside the lines.

At close range, I saw that her wig was slightly askew. I was certain it was a wig because my mother owned several; three Styrofoam heads lined a shelf in my mother's closet; upon them were perched a pageboy, an empress, and a baby doll, all in shades of auburn. The woman in the pink dress wore her wig like a crown of glory.

But it was the woman in the purple dress who passed nearest me, and I saw that her jaw was heavily powdered, a half-successful attempt to disguise the telltale shadow of a beard. Just as I noticed this, her heel caught on a crack in the pavement and she reeled on her stilettos. It was then that I witnessed a rift in her composure, a window through which I could glimpse the shades of maleness that her dress and wig and make-up obscured. She shifted her shoulders and threw out her hands like a surfer riding a curl. The instant she regained her balance, she smoothed her dress, patted her hair, and sauntered onward.

Any woman might be a man; the fact of it clanged through the chambers of my brain. In broad day, in the midst of traffic, with my parents drinking coffee a few feet away, I felt as if everything I understood, everything I had taken for granted up to that moment—the curve of the earth, the heat of the sun, the reliability of my own eyes—had been squeezed out of me. Who were those men? Did they help each other get inside those dresses? How many other people and things were not what they seemed? From the back, the imposters looked like women once again, slinky and curvaceous, purple and pink. I watched them disappear into the distance, their disguises so convincing that other people on the street seemed to take no notice, and for a moment I wondered if I had imagined the whole encounter, a visitation by two unlikely muses.

Frozen in the middle of the sidewalk, I caught my reflection in the window of Burl's, a silhouette floating between his parents. They faced one another across a table. Once the solid embodiments of woman and man, pedestrians and traffic appeared to pass through them.

There were some mornings, seconds before my eyes opened and my senses gathered into consciousness, that the child I was seemed to hover above the bed, and I couldn't tell what form my waking would take—the body of a boy or the body of a girl. Finally stirring, I'd blink against the early light and greet each incarnation as a male with mild surprise. My sex, in other words, didn't seem to be an absolute fact so much as a pleasant, recurring accident.

By the age of eight, I'd experienced this groggy phenomenon several times. Those ethereal moments above my bed made waking up in the tangled blankets, a boy steeped in body heat, all the more astonishing. That this might be an unusual experience never occurred to me; it was one among a flood of sensations I could neither name nor ignore.

And so, shocked as I was when those transvestites passed me in front of Burl's, they confirmed something about which I already had an inkling: the hazy border between the sexes. My father, after all, raised his pinky when he drank from a teacup, and my mother looked as faded and plain as my father until she fixed her hair and painted her face.

Like most children, I once thought it possible to divide the world into male and female columns. Blue/Pink. Roosters/Hens. Trousers/Skirts. Such divisions were easy, not to mention comforting, for they simplified matter into compatible pairs. But there also existed a vast range of things that didn't fit neatly into either camp: clocks, milk, telephones, grass. There were nights I fell into a fitful sleep while trying to sex the world correctly.

Nothing typified the realms of male and female as clearly as my parents' walk-in closets. Home alone for any length of time, I always found my way inside them. I could stare at my parents' clothes for hours, grateful for the stillness and silence, haunting the very heart of their privacy.

The overhead light in my father's closet was a bare bulb. Whenever I groped for the chain in the dark, it wagged back and forth and resisted my grasp. Once the light clicked on, I saw dozens of ties hanging like stalactites. A monogrammed silk bathrobe sagged from a hook, a gift my father had received on a long-ago birthday and, thinking it fussy, rarely wore. Shirts were cramped together along the length of an aluminum pole, their starched sleeves sticking out as if in a halfhearted gesture of greeting. The medicinal odor of mothballs permeated the boxer shorts that were folded and stacked in a built-in drawer. Immaculate underwear was proof of a tenderness my mother couldn't otherwise express; she may not have touched my father often, but she laundered his boxers with infinite care. Even back then, I suspected that a sense of duty was the final erotic link between them.

Sitting in a neat row on the closet floor were my father's boots and slippers and dress shoes. I'd try on his wing tips and clomp around, slipping out of them with every step. My wary, unnatural stride made me all the more desperate to effect some authority. I'd whisper orders to imagined lackeys and take my invisible wife in my arms. But no matter how much I wanted them to fit, those shoes were as cold and hard as marble.

My mother's shoes were just as uncomfortable, but a lot more fun. From a brightly colored array of pumps and sling-backs, I'd pick a pair with the glee and deliberation of someone choosing a chocolate. Whatever embarrassment I felt was overwhelmed by the exhilaration of being taller in a pair of high heels. Things will look like this someday, I said to myself, gazing out from my new and improved vantage point as if from a crow's nest. Calves elongated, hands on my hips, I gauged each step so I didn't fall over and moved with what might have passed for grace had someone seen me, a possibility I scrupulously avoided by locking the door.

Back and forth I went. The longer I wore a pair of heels, the better my balance. In the periphery of my vision, the shelf of wigs looked like a throng of kindly bystanders. Light streamed down from a high window, causing crystal bottles to glitter, the air ripe with perfume. A make-up mirror above the dressing table invited my self-absorption. Sound was muffled. Time slowed. It seemed as if nothing bad could happen as long as I stayed within those walls.

Though I'd never been discovered in my mother's closet, my parents knew that I was drawn toward girlish things—dolls and jump rope and jewelry—as well as to the games and preoccupations that were expected of a boy. I'm not sure now if it was my effeminacy itself that bothered them so much as my ability to slide back and forth, without the slightest warning, between male and female mannerisms. After I'd finished building the model of an F-17 bomber, say, I'd sit back to examine my handiwork, pursing my lips in concentration and crossing my legs at the knee.

One day my mother caught me standing in the middle of my bedroom doing an imitation of Mary Injijikian, a dark, overeager Armenian girl with whom I believed myself to be in love, not only because she was pretty, but because I wanted to be like her. Collector of effortless A's, Mary seemed to know all the answers in class. Before the teacher had even finished asking a question, Mary would let out a little grunt and practically levitate out of her seat, as if her hand were filled with helium. "Could we please hear from someone else today besides Miss Injijikian," the teacher would say. *Miss Injijikian.* Those were the words I was repeating over and over to myself when my mother caught me. To utter them was rhythmic, delicious, and under their spell I raised my hand and wiggled like Mary. I heard a cough and spun around. My mother froze in the doorway. She clutched the folded sheets to her stomach and turned without saying a word. My sudden flush of shame confused me. Weren't boys supposed to swoon over girls? Hadn't I seen babbling, heartsick men in a dozen movies?

Shortly after the Injijikian incident, my parents decided to send me to gymnastics class at the Downtown Athletic Club, a brick relic of a building on Grand Avenue. One of the oldest establishments of its kind in Los Angeles, the club prohibited women from the premises. My parents didn't have to say it aloud: they hoped a fraternal atmosphere would toughen me up and tilt me toward the male side of my nature.

My father drove me downtown so I could sign up for

the class, meet the instructor, and get a tour of the place. On the way there, he reminisced about sports. Since he'd grown up in a rough Philadelphia neighborhood, sports consisted of kick-the-can, or rolling a hoop down the street with a stick. The more he talked about his physical prowess, the more convinced I became that my daydreams and shyness were a disappointment to him.

The hushed lobby of the Athletic Club was paneled in dark wood. A few solitary figures were hidden in wing chairs. My father and I introduced ourselves to a man at the front desk who seemed unimpressed by our presence. His aloofness unnerved me, which wasn't hard considering that no matter how my parents put it, I knew that sending me here was a form of disapproval, a way of banishing the part of me they didn't care to know.

A call went out over the intercom for someone to show us around. While we waited, I noticed that the sand in the standing ashtrays had been raked into perfect furrows. The glossy leaves of the potted plants looked as if they'd been polished by hand. The place seemed more like a well-tended hotel than an athletic club. Finally, a stoop-shouldered old man hobbled toward us, his head shrouded in a cloud of white hair. He wore a T-shirt that said INSTRUCTOR, but his arms were so wrinkled and anemic, I thought I might have misread it. While we followed him to the elevator—it would be easier, he said, than taking the stairs—I readjusted my expectations, which had involved fantasies of a hulking drill sergeant barking orders at a flock of scrawny boys.

We got off the elevator on the second floor. The instructor, mumbling to himself and never turning around to see if we were behind him, showed us where the gymnastics class took place. I'm certain the building was big, but the size of the room must be exaggerated by a trick of memory, because when I envision it, I picture a vast and windowless warehouse. Mats covered the wooden floor. Here and there, in remote and lonely pools of light, stood a pommel horse, a balance beam, and parallel bars. Tiers of bleachers rose into darkness. Unlike the cloistered air of a closet, the room seemed incomplete without a crowd.

Next we visited the dressing room, empty except for a naked, middle-aged man. He sat on a narrow bench and clipped his formidable toenails. Moles dotted his back. He glistened like a fish.

We continued to follow the instructor down an aisle lined with numbered lockers. At the far end, steam billowed from the doorway that led to the showers. Fresh towels stacked on a nearby table made me think of my mother; I knew she liked to have me at home with her—I was often her only companion—and I resented her complicity in the plan to send me here.

The tour ended when the instructor gave me a sign-up sheet. Only a few names preceded mine. They were signatures, or so I imagined, of other soft and wayward sons.

When the day of the first gymnastics class arrived, my mother gave me money and a gym bag (along with a clean towel, she'd packed a banana and a napkin) and sent me to the corner of Hollywood and Western to wait for a bus. The sun was bright, the traffic heavy. While I sat there, an argument raged inside my head, the familiar, battering debate between the wish to be like other boys and the wish to be like myself. Why shouldn't I simply get up and go back home, where I'd be left alone to read and think? On the other hand, wouldn't life be easier if I liked athletics, or learned to like them? No sooner did I steel my resolve to get on the bus, than I thought of something better: I could spend the morning wandering through Woolworth's, then tell my parents I'd gone to class. But would my lie stand up to scrutiny? As I practiced describing phantom gymnastics—And then we did cartwheels and, boy, was I *dizzy*—

I became aware of a car circling the block. It was a large car in whose shaded interior I could barely make out the driver, but I thought it might be the man who owned the local pet store. I'd often gone there on the pretext of looking at the cocker spaniel puppies huddled together in their pen, but I really went to gawk at the owner, whose tan chest, in the V of his shirt, was the place I most wanted to rest my head. Every time the man moved, counting stock or writing a receipt, his shirt parted, my mouth went dry, and I smelled the musk of sawdust and dogs.

I found myself hoping that the driver was the man who ran the pet store. I was thrilled by the unlikely possibility that the sight of me, slumped on a bus bench in my T-shirt and shorts, had caused such a man to circle the block. Up to that point in my life, lovemaking hovered somewhere in the future, an impulse a boy might aspire to but didn't indulge. And there I was, sitting on a bus bench in the middle of the city, dreaming I could seduce an adult. I showered the owner of the pet store with kisses and, as aquariums bubbled, birds sang, and mice raced in a wire wheel, slipped my hand beneath his shirt. The roar of traffic brought me to my senses. I breathed deeply and blinked against the sun. I crossed my legs at the knee in order to hide an erection. My fantasy left me both drained and changed. The continent of sex had drifted closer.

The car made another round. This time the driver leaned across the passenger seat and peered at me through the window. He was a complete stranger, whose gaze filled me with fear. It wasn't the surprise of not recognizing him that frightened me; it was what I did recognize—the unmistakable shame in his expression, and the weary temptation that drove him in circles. Before the car behind him honked, he mouthed "hello" and cocked his head. What now, he seemed to be asking. A bold, unbearable question.

I bolted to my feet, slung the gym bag over my shoulder, and hurried toward home. Now and then I turned around to make sure he wasn't trailing me, both relieved and disappointed when I didn't see his car. Even after I became convinced that he wasn't at my back (my sudden flight had scared him off), I kept turning around to see what was making me so nervous, as if I might spot the source of my discomfort somewhere on the street. I walked faster and faster, trying to outrace myself. Eventually, the bus I was supposed to have taken roared past. Turning the corner, I watched it bob eastward.

Closing the kitchen door behind me, I vowed never to leave home again. I was resolute in this decision without fully understanding why, or what it was I hoped to avoid; I was only aware of the need to hide and a vague notion, fading fast, that my trouble had something to do with sex. Already the mechanism of self-deception was at work. By the time my mother rushed into the kitchen to see why I'd returned so early, the thrill I'd felt while waiting for the bus had given way to indignation.

I poured out the story of the man circling the block and protested, with perhaps too great a passion, my own innocence. "I was just sitting there," I said again and again. I was so determined to deflect suspicion from myself, and to justify my missing the class, that I portrayed the man as a grizzled pervert who drunkenly veered from lane to lane as he followed me halfway home.

My mother listened quietly. She seemed moved and shocked by what I told her, if a bit incredulous, which prompted me to be more dramatic. "It wouldn't be safe," I insisted, "for me to wait at the bus stop again."

No matter how overwrought my story, I knew my mother wouldn't question it, wouldn't bring the subject up again; sex of any kind, especially sex between a man and a boy, was simply not discussed in our house. The gymnastics class, my parents agreed, was something I could do another time.

And so I spent the remainder of that summer at home with my mother, stirring cake batter, holding the dustpan, helping her fold the sheets. For a while I was proud of myself for engineering a reprieve from the Athletic Club. But as the days wore on, I began to see that my mother had wanted me with her all along, and forcing that to happen wasn't such a feat. Soon a sense of compromise set in; by expressing disgust for the man in the car, I'd expressed disgust for an aspect of myself. Now I had all the time in the world to sit around and contemplate my desire for men. The days grew long and stifling and hot, an endless sentence of self-examination.

Only trips to the pet store offered any respite. Every time I went there, I was too electrified with longing to think about longing in the abstract. The bell tinkled above the door, animals stirred within their cages, and the handsome owner glanced up from his work.

I handed my father the *Herald.* He opened the paper and disappeared behind it. My mother stirred her coffee and sighed. She gazed at the sweltering passersby and probably thought herself lucky. I slid into the vinyl booth and took my place beside my parents.

For a moment, I considered asking them about what had happened on the street, but they would have reacted with censure and alarm, and I sensed there was more to the story than they'd ever be willing to tell me. Men in dresses were only the tip of the iceberg. Who knew what other wonders existed—a boy, for example, who wants to kiss a man—exceptions the world did its best to keep hidden.

It would be years before I heard the word *transvestite,*

so I struggled to find a word for what I'd seen. *He-she* came to mind, as lilting as *Injijikian*. *Burl's* would have been perfect, like *boys* and *girls* spliced together, but I can't claim to have thought of this back then.

I must have looked stricken as I tried to figure it all out, because my mother put down her coffee cup and asked if I was OK. She stopped just short of feeling my forehead. I assured her I was fine, but something within me had shifted, had given way to a heady doubt. When the waitress came and slapped down our check—"Thank you," it read, "dine out more often"—I wondered if her lofty hairdo or the breasts on which her nametag quaked were real. Wax carnations bloomed at every table. Phoney wood paneled the walls. Plastic food sat in a display case: fried eggs, a hamburger sandwich, a sundae topped with a garish cherry.

Diane Glancy

If Not All These

What's it like to pass from this world?

Is it a tunnel with a light at the end? A field in which your father waits and you talk to him again? Is it a drop into a well? A step you forgot was there jarring your teeth? Possibly death is a long trail to the far corner of the prairie. Sometimes wolves still howl.

Maybe death is a structure of language outside the voice. A getting-out-of-the-body like the chores you never wanted to do.

Here comes death wearing a white hat and a Lone Ranger mask.

Or an acquaintance whose name you can't remember when it's time to introduce him. Maybe death is riding a horse for the first time and not getting thrown.

A burst of gladiolas from an amphora.

Could death be the laundry chute in the old house where you sent your overalls? Even the cat.

Maybe it's the dust-bowl. Or lunar desolation. The edge of the highway from which you can't step back.

Maybe death is a morning when you wake and remember it's your birthday. No—the first day of school you dreaded but find it's not so bad. And soon you get into it. You put on your pinwheel skirt. Your halo like an old propeller beanie. You flap your Teflon wings and soon you're far above the Rio Grande.

Andrew Cozine

Hand Jive

I walk north on Campbell Avenue away from Jefferson Park Elementary School and Mrs. Hansen's third-grade class. I am walking the half mile to Grandma's house. Heat waves shimmer up off the four lanes of asphalt to my left. Off on my right, toward the park, the steady, buzzing hum of cicadas electrifies the afternoon. It is a hundred degrees out, give or take, unusual but not too unusual for the middle of May in Tucson, Arizona. I am taking care not to step on the cracks in the sidewalk. When I step on a crack, I do the thing: I count out loud from one to five, over and over, until it is safe to stop. *One, two, three, four, five . . . one, two, three, four, five.* The hum of the cicadas is drowned out by the engine noise from a wave of cars traveling southbound; the cars pass, and the hum picks up again right where it left off. The white heat of the sun burns into my skin. I walk past the Catalina movie theater and into the shopping center parking lot just as a group of older kids comes out of the Walgreens. I don't know these kids, I've only seen them around on the playground. They are laughing and shouting, making me nervous. I'm afraid they'll try to make me cry. The heat and the buzzing and the shouts of these kids makes it hard to concentrate. I know I'll slip up. I slip up. *One, two, three, four, five . . .*

I wait at the stoplight at Grant Road, hoping the other kids won't come my way. I don't want to wait with them. I don't know what they'll do. If they did try anything, my dad would do something about it. He would call their parents or call the school or go and have a talk with somebody. He would protect me. But what if something happened to Dad? I see my father spread out on the ground, red-faced, an oily, bloody wound spreading out across his chest. Eyes glazed, mouth wide open. Dead. That's a bad thing to think you're a bad boy what if something really happened because you thought a thing like that? I do the thing, the other thing, to stop it from coming true: *I remember my ESP. I remember my ESP. I remember my ESP. I remember my ESP. I remember my ESP.*

The kids go off a different way. I am all alone at the curb, watching and waiting, still not sure after dozens of crossings just when I'm allowed to go. The cars hiss and swish as they pass. Radios blare from open windows. I wait for five minutes, ten minutes. Sweat trickles down my cheeks and my clothes are sticky and wet against my skin. I am thinking, When I get across the street I will get a Baskin-Robbins. When I get across the street I will go to The Book Stop and buy a book by the man who wrote *James and the Giant Peach.* When I get across the street I will go to Lown's Costumes and get some snap pops or a plastic dog barf, but I can't spend my whole allowance. I stare at the cracks in the sidewalk in front of me. The white glare begins to blur and the world gets foggy at the edges. *When I get, but I can't, I can't, what did I forget, what what did I oh no oh no what did I forget what did I forget I'm bad I'm bad what now what now oh no oh no oh no.* The pavement bucks up under my feet; I am swaying side to side. My heart is pushing up against my throat *heart attack heart attack like Grandpa* and my throat gets tight like my heart is trapped there blocking the air *I can't breathe I can't breathe help help I can't . . . help. . . .* The cars are close, too close, there's a horn honking and my feet are tripping forward *what did I do what did I do?* I know I did something, something very very bad. I know I'll pay for it, they'll say, What's wrong with you, William? My body is stopping short, lurching back the other way. I make a list: one, you didn't leave your sister at school, Grandma picked her up early; two, you weren't supposed to ride the bus home; three, you didn't forget a note for a field trip; four, you didn't have Spanish class after school; five. . . . It helps.

When I can see and breathe and move again, I shut my eyes and pray and run.

꩜

I am not crazy because of the words I say, and I am not stupid because I don't know how to cross the street. Brad Hubert and I are the smartest boys in the third grade. He does math a little better and I am the better reader. They separated us, put Brad in Miss Horner's third-grade class, even though we are friends. I am glad. I don't like competition; it makes me too nervous. I suspect they think we are the smartest boys in the whole school, that we could do sixth-grade work if they let us. Brad would want to move up to the sixth grade, I bet; I would not. I like to be where I'm supposed to be, where it's easy to be the best. The other kids come to me for help, even in math; one day I told them all to leave me alone, I was falling behind, and Mrs. Hansen called me up to her desk and told me to help them. She told me I had to, because I was smartest.

On the first day of third grade, I had to get up and go to the bathroom three times. I just get nervous a lot. Mrs. Hansen looked down at me the third time and said, "What's wrong with you, William? Do you have a problem?"

I still go to the bathroom a lot, but not three times. Not counting recess. Mrs. Hansen never asks what's wrong with me anymore. I think she thinks I'm okay.

I'm okay.

꩜

I walk down our driveway in the late afternoon to get the mail for Mom. She didn't work at the hospital today, so we didn't go to Grandma's house. The sun has fallen behind the big hill across the street, so the driveway and the house and the desert behind the house are painted in cool blue, quiet shadow. It is more peaceful here in the foothills, miles away from school and town. The only sounds are the cooings and twitterings of doves, quail, cactus wrens. And the voice, of course. The voice is a pain in the butt. It is me, but it's not me. I never do what it tells me to do, it's only trying to get me in trouble, but the voice is smarter and older than me, and sometimes it tricks me. It speaks with authority, so I listen.

Throw the mail away.

"No."

Throw some of the mail away. Throw away that, and that.

"No. Shut up."

If you won't throw out the mail, you have to ride your bike off the end of the driveway.

"Shut up. Lalalalalalalalala shut up shut up shut up I'm not listening lalalalala."

I pass gas. Just a little. It slips out accidentally. Just in case God is watching, I do my other thing: *Excuse me, excuse me, excuse me, excuse me, excuse me.* Five times, ten times, twenty-five times. Always in multiples of five. I don't want any trouble.

Good, the voice says. *Now: the mail or the bike.*

The bike, I decide.

You have to ride as fast as you can. You have to start back up the road there to build up speed.

Okay, I decide. I take the mail in and ride my bike out to the designated starting line. It is a Schwinn Spirit of Seventy-Six, red, white, and blue. I take three deep breaths and start pedaling. Faster, faster. Forty yards, thirty yards, twenty, ten, don't stop, don't stop, don't think, don't think . . . go!

The end of our driveway, the part the voice refers to, is

a concrete structure built up over a dry riverbed that runs parallel to the road. It is a five- or six-foot drop from the top of the concrete to the sand and rocks below. There are paloverde and mesquite tree limbs scattered over the surface of the riverbed, heavy and covered with thorns, but the rocks, some as big as pumpkins, are the real danger. I try to aim as I fly off the end of the concrete and feel the bike falling away below me, but the momentum I've built up is more powerful than I've figured on and I sail past the spot where I'd hoped to land. I close my eyes and let my body go limp, and I'm already crying from fear as I hit the rocks and dirt on my side and roll, roll. Sand scrapes at my face and forces its way into my mouth. My head hits a rock and I hear popping noises in my neck; pins of light swim up out of the darkness and swirl in dizzy patterns. Sharp sticks like pencils jab into my arms and legs and, in the second before I stop moving, I sense a deeper shadow over me, something moving at me, heavy and powerful, at great speed. The bike. I throw my arms up over my head just as it hits me, a blow that knocks the wind out of me all over again. The handlebars jab into my ribs and I still, seventeen years later, carry the scar where a spinning pedal dug into my forearm. Thirty seconds of panic follow as I struggle to regain my breath; then, purple-faced, I limp back to the house with a sprained ankle and cuts and bruises everywhere.

I hope you're happy, I think. The voice is silent.

That night, Mom and Dad and I are sitting in the family room, listening to classical music, and I start to cry. What's wrong with me, they want to know. I tell them that the classical music makes me feel strange. I try to explain it but I can't find the right words, and I just get more and more confused. There's no way to tell them that I feel sad and hollow and empty inside because I know the music should make me feel happy, but I don't feel anything at all.

People say it's beautiful like they say a sunset is beautiful, but to me it's just music, it's just a sunset. The sunset and music are just there, they're not anything. Like me. I can't explain it. I feel numb.

Mom and Dad look at me curiously. That's a funny thing for an eight-year-old to be thinking, they say. And they're thinking more than that. They're wondering what's wrong with their son, what they did to deserve this, what they will do with me now. I'm ruined. I'm a bad egg. I'm a freak.

I go to bed and lie in the dark, staring at the top bunk. The voice comes and I tell it, beg it, will it to go away.

It stays.

૭

In fourth and fifth grade things are worse. The voice is louder now and harder to control. Everything has to be repeated in five multiples of five, at the very least, to keep bad things from happening. Sometimes I have to excuse myself one hundred and twenty-five times for a single belch or fart. I try to convince the voice to let me just think out the repetitions in my head, but usually it makes me recite them out loud. Even then, I mumble in my smallest whisper. I try to convince myself that nobody notices. But I am cheating. The voice knows I am cheating; Grandpa Kiel, my mother's father, has another heart attack. *I'm sorry. I'm sorry.* At the hospital, the doctor comes into the little white room and tells us Grandpa is dead, and everyone is crying but me. I try to think about Grandpa. Grandpa used to tell me stories. He used to play his old jazz records for me: Bix Beiderbecke, Charlie Parker, the Dukes of Dixieland. I know this is sad, I see the word, "sad," hovering in the air before me, but all I feel is numb. Numb, empty, a little bit guilty, but not too guilty because I know it's only partly my fault. I did all my repetitions, every time, just like the voice told me. I only cheated a little. *Only partly only partly only partly only partly only partly.*

Ryan Brooks is my best friend now, and my sister Nancy and I go to his house after school instead of to Grandma's. Mom pays Ryan's mom to watch us. I like it at Ryan's house because it's more comfortable than school. At school my old friends, Joey and Mike and John, don't hang out with me anymore; they like to play football and I don't. My girlfriend, Celia Parks, breaks up with me because she wants me to be Christian, and I tell her I was raised a Presbyterian and I'm staying a Presbyterian, and that's that. The breakup makes me sad, but I can't break with God. God would make me pay. My teacher, Mr. Peltier, looks at me funny because I'm losing my smartness; I'm not living up to the things I'm sure Mrs. Hansen and Mrs. Ek told him about me. All of it makes me nervous. Everything makes me nervous. But afternoons at Ryan's go by in the same pleasant way, day in and day out. We watch TV, we play superheroes, we walk to the schoolyard and play softball. We visit a girl down the street, Sarah, who has a retarded brother. The retard sits in front of the television and says, Fuck you fuck you fuck you shut up shut up shut up. *Family Feud* is his favorite show. *Treat him like you would anybody else,* Sarah's mom tells us. Sometimes the retard goes swimming with us, and I try to stay away from him so his freak germs don't swim through the water and soak into my skin. It's like when I had to stay at the weird family's house when Mom and Dad went out of town and they told me to take a shower. I pretended to take a shower but I really just turned on the water and sat on the toilet. I stay away from freaky people's water; I've got troubles of my own.

One day Ryan's little brother, Petey, decides he's in love with a little girl named Robin. We sing "Rockin' Robin" because it's fun to watch him turn red and go into fits. I can do it more than Ryan because Petey hits Ryan but he doesn't hit me. One time, though, I take it too far. We are out in the front yard, Ryan, Petey, Sarah, my sister Nancy, and I. I am singing the song and laughing and Petey tells me to stop, he begs, he pleads, but it's too much fun, too, too funny, and even when I try to stop I can't. *You'd better quit it,* he warns me, like he's got something up his sleeve. Some secret weapon. I keep on. *You better watch out.* I laugh. Petey chases me around but he doesn't hit me. He starts imitating me, this little second-grader, he hangs his head and shuffles around and starts to mumble: *Excuse me excuse me excuse me excuse me excuse me. . . .* I feel my face go red and start to burn. I feel shaky all over and dizzy, light-headed. Ryan's mom comes out of the house at a fast trot. *Peter,* she yells. *Stop it. Stop that right now.* She grabs her son and shakes him. *I never, never want to hear you do that again.*

Ryan's mom drags Petey inside the house. But it's too late. We stand on the lawn in a little circle, heads down, silent. I can't pretend anymore that nobody knows, that everybody thinks I'm normal. *Treat him like you would anybody else.* I am just like the retard. I am a freak and I think it's a secret. They let me go to school, they let me read my books, go to friends' houses, ride my bike. But the whole time, they are watching me. They are letting me think I am just like anybody else.

But I am not the same. Not the same at all.

୬

Everything changed in the summer before sixth grade. We moved to a new house a couple of miles away, and this meant a new school district and a new school, new teachers, new friends. I had a new routine: I could bike to my new school, and after school I could walk to friends' houses or invite them over to mine. The distance between school and home was no longer prohibitive. At around the same time, the voice went away. It just vanished, so mysteriously and unobtrusively that I didn't notice its absence for nearly a year. And, much in the same way, I stopped needing my verbal repetitions, my chants, my prayers, whatever they were. I was free. There was suddenly much more time in a day to get things accomplished: I formed a secret club with my friends; I competed in speech competitions and spelling bees; I started listening to the Beatles and the Rolling Stones a lot; and I watched M*A*S*H every afternoon, curling up calm and serene before the television with no unpleasant voices or compulsions to distract me.

But my problems weren't over, not by a long shot. Something had to replace the voice and the behaviors, and it turned out to be something worse and more freakish by far.

In sixth grade I rediscovered the hand jive.

The hand jive actually originated when I was around five years old, in an amusing and fairly harmless way. I was a big Mister Rogers fan; I wanted to be just like him and to have my own television program when I grew up. When I had to go to the bathroom, number two, I played out this fantasy: I would sit on the toilet and, watching myself in the bathroom mirror on the opposite wall, I'd play talk-show host. My *nom de guerre* was The Superdoozie Man, after the code word my parents had developed for bowel movements:

"Hello, welcome to The Superdoozie Man. I'm The Superdoozie Man, William Samuels. I hope everyone out there is having a great day. You should feel very special because you are a very special person. A lot of you kids send letters to me and call me up and you want to know, Are superdoozies bad? Should I feel bad for having superdoozies? No, superdoozies are totally natural. They are also called stools, or BMS. You should never call them poops, because you might get spanked. The Superdoozie Man never says bad words. Sometimes bad words just come out by accident, though, and you can't help it. Yesterday I called my uncle a bad word, but I didn't mean to. I said, 'Uncle David, you gucking, lucking, chucking, bucking . . .' and then I said a bad word by accident. 'F-U-C-K-ing,' in case you didn't know. But don't ever say that word. After Uncle David left, Dad spanked me. But your parents don't spank you because they hate you. They spank you because they love you. They love you very much because you are a very special person." Et cetera.

I believed I could see all my viewers through the TV camera, just like the lady on *Romper Room* said she could. I believed I was the Voice of Authority. I believed I would be a great role model. I believed that parents would admire me and that I would make God and my family proud. The more I became immersed in my role, the more excited I became. I began to duck my head down and let my eyes fall out of focus, imagining my adult self on a television screen. One day, I felt an urge to hold my breath and constrict my vocal folds; i.e., to push the air trapped inside me up against my throat and hold it there, feel it burning my lungs. It is the thing people do when they lift something heavy, when they push out a bowel movement, when a woman has a baby. At the same time, I began to bend my arms at the elbows and flap them wildly, very very quickly, and then pull them in tight against my chest until the knuckles of my hands were pressing against my mouth. Flap out, pull in, flap out, pull in, alternating every five or ten seconds and keeping that air pressing tight against my throat. Occasionally, I would let loose with a sound effect or a tiny, excited squeak.

Before long, I was making up stories, movies, TV

shows, cartoons, whenever I went to the bathroom. And the arm-flapping and constriction of my vocal folds helped me simulate the same kind of excitement I imagined the viewer of my special programs might experience. For as long as I kept it up, I was lost in a totally private, totally satisfying world. I squeaked out theme songs, mood music, as I watched the images and narratives play out in my head, all the while pumping my arms furiously and sending blood racing to my brain. I was escaping into outer space, and it was as if all that body motion was required to launch my imagination and hold it suspended in those dark, isolated dream worlds.

I was fascinated. I was terrified.

The hand jive was born.

୭

Back to third grade. Some of this may seem unrelated, but in my mind it all fits together perfectly:

Gina Betts, the neighbor girl who baby-sits us sometimes, is leading me out to our clubhouse in the desert. There's a growing feeling of excitement, but I don't know why. Gina is in the eighth grade at a private Catholic school, Saints Peter and Paul, and she is in love with a boy named Phil. All of her problems would be solved if she could just talk to Phil but, no, this is impossible. I only know the facts; I do not attempt to understand them.

"Gina, look, there's a tarantula."

"Come on."

"You told me to show you if I found a tarantula."

"Just come on. Hurry up."

Gina leads me under the branches of a paloverde and we skid on our butts down Slide Rock to the riverbed and the fort. I am getting really excited; anything better than a huge, hairy spider has got to be pretty good. As it turns out, Gina has to go to the bathroom; she moves off into the weeds and drops her jeans and panties. Tinkles. "Don't you want to look?" she asks me finally.

I look. I look closer. I touch. Not as good as a tarantula, maybe, but hey, it's something new.

"Now you," she tells me. I eagerly strip down and let her look, look closer, touch.

"It's a lot smaller than my dad's," she says.

"It gets bigger," I tell her. "And it's going to grow."

"It's supposed to have hair."

I look down. "I don't know," I say, skeptically.

Gina leads me back over to the shade of the paloverde and we sit together. She shows me how to kiss like a movie star, with our mouths open. Her mouth is exciting and strange, especially the tongue. I like it. When she gets bored, we pull apart and head back home. "We have a secret now," Gina tells me as we walk through the deep sand of the riverbed. "Don't ever tell anybody our secret. If you don't, we can keep on doing it."

"Okay," I tell her.

A few weeks later, Gina and I have all kinds of new secrets. We are going steady, for one, and she has given me a little silver going-together ring. I am not supposed to tell anyone what it means. We go on a date together to see *Return of the Pink Panther.* Nobody knows it's a real date but us. Her mom drives; the movie is good. I like the way Peter Sellers kung-fu fights with his Oriental cook. Gina has told me how people make babies, she has told me about "rubbers"; we have make-out sessions in my closet when she baby-sits. She gives me all her older brother's *Mad* magazines and makes me promise never to tell anyone anything. I like having secrets with her; I am tired of my own secrets. I know we are doing something wrong, something that is not normal, but, God knows, I'm used to that. It's good to have a little company.

The hand jive is driving me crazy. It has spread to my

bedroom, where I hand jive while I draw superhero comic books. I am Colossal Kid, Joey Carroll is Super Star, Joey's friend Jerry is Black Lightning. Brad Hubert is Boy, a stupid name, and his Boy character is too powerful, has too many superpowers. But everyone got to make up their own name and powers, so what can I do? It is hard, though, coming up with supervillains who can give us a run for our money while Boy's around. I draw pages and pages of stories, adventures we will act out on the playground tomorrow, and when Dad walks in I am deep into the hand jive, squealing and flapping.

"Son," he says. "Time for dinner. What are you doing?"

"Nothing," I say. "Drawing comics."

My voice sounds funny. Dad sees the embarrassment, the shame, in my face, and he leaves it alone. This happens every time Dad or Mom catches me at the hand jive; there is uncomfortable silence and then both parties act as if nothing was happening at all. This time, he turns without a word and marches back to the kitchen. Soon they will learn to knock before entering; they don't want to catch me any more than I want to be caught.

Weeks pass, and one day Gina and I are out playing in the driveway. "I see you from my bathroom window," Gina says. "I see you when you stand in front of your garage."

"I don't know what you're talking about," I tell her, but already I'm getting nervous.

"You stand there and flap your arms around. You make funny noises."

It is getting hard to breathe. My heart moves up and pushes against my throat. "No, I don't," I say.

"I watch you," Gina says. "I think it's funny."

I deny it again, but she's got me dead-to-rights. Mom had suggested that I spend more time outdoors, so I had moved the hand jive to the front yard. I only do it a couple of hours a week, maybe, and I had thought no one could see me. The houses on top of the hill looked so far away, fifty yards at least, and Gina's bathroom window, the only window in her house facing ours, is fogged over with a special kind of glass. I had thought I was safe.

"I'm going to tell your mom," Gina says.

"No, no," I tell her. "No, don't, Gina, please." Gina is angry because I lost her brother's *Mad* magazines, and now he's back from the army and he wants them. Gina only smiles and walks up the driveway and into our house. I turn and run through the backyard and out into the desert. I run through the first line of trees and saguaros and out into the riverbed, the "wash," as we call it, and I keep running the half mile through it to the big hill and up it and onto the dirt road that leads deep into the foothills at the edge of the mountains. The sky is dark and grumbling. A slight rain begins to fall and I keep running. I run one mile, another half mile. I will run forever. I am not wearing shoes, I almost never do, and as I head up the steepest incline in the dirt road I step on a nail and it drives up into my foot. I shriek and fall into the weeds at the road's edge and lie there, sobbing, soaking wet. Every few minutes, I reach down and try to work the nail loose, but it won't come. I try to imagine growing up in my house, with them knowing about me, about my problem, my condition, and I can't. I know I will never go back.

An hour passes and the rain falls harder. I stop crying because it starts to hurt. Through the sheets of rain, I see Mom walking up the dirt road a hundred yards off. She is calling for me, and when she sees me she runs up the incline to where I am. Nancy, my little sister, told her when I ran off, and she has come to get me. I show her the nail and she pulls it loose. I am crying again.

"What's wrong, William? What is it?"

What's wrong, what's wrong. Everything's wrong. I can't feel a sunset, I can't feel music. I hear a voice in my head, and it pesters me and tells me to do bad things. I have to excuse myself fifty times when I belch or pass gas. I have to remember my ESP, over and over, all the time. I play hand jive with myself. I'm tired. I'm tired.

"You know, Mom. You know what's wrong with me."

"Tell me, honey."

Gina didn't really tell her at all. She was just scaring me.

"I said 'goddamnit' to Nancy," I tell Mom. It's true, too; I did say this, but it was several days before. "Gina said she was gonna tell on me."

Mom smiles. "It's okay, honey. It's okay. Just don't do it again."

I was going to tell Mom about Gina and me, about how we are engaged now and how we've been going steady for a month. But Gina has protected my secret and now I will protect her secret. Our secret. Because the hand jive is a lot like sexual feeling to me, and it will stay that way as I grow up. It is forbidden, exciting, disturbing, wrong. I know I'm strange for wanting to do it, but I can't stop wanting, I can't stop doing it. I am sick and awful, but I am the only one who knows just how sick and awful I am.

The skies are cracking, bellowing, and sheet lightning breaks across the clouds to the west of us. I stand and lean against Mom's shoulder, and she walks me home.

૭

Around this time, my parents go to a Marriage Encounter to examine their marriage and discover ways to strengthen their family unit. It is a two- or three-day retreat, the one where I stay with the weird people and only pretend to use the shower, and when they return some changes are made. One of the changes involves Mom and Dad taking each of us kids out, individually, on family nights. Mom and Dad alternate with each child; Dad takes me out one week, and two weeks later I go out for a night with Mom. We do fun things together each time. I don't remember any of the things I do with Mom, though. Dad and I go miniature golfing one night, but we can't go to the go-cart place because Dad hears it is prohibitively expensive. One weekend Dad and I go camping together: it rains on our hike, we get lost, I get a bee sting on my hand that provokes an allergic reaction, and it rains so much during the night that we have to ditch our tent and sleep in the back of the car. I laugh a lot. I love my dad; he is always very funny when these things happen, and I have a great time. It is one of the best weekends of my life.

A few weeks or months later, Dad is driving me home from someplace. I am still in the third grade. We are on Speedway Boulevard, in the middle lane, and I watch the Magic Carpet miniature golf course go by on our right. Dad is telling me about sexual love, because it is *time,* and he is telling me about heterosexuals and homosexuals. He tells me that people get diseases from sexual love, that they grow lumps on their sexual organs and that, eventually, their brains can melt from these diseases. These are things that Gina didn't know. Suddenly afraid, I tell him that my friend Joey and I have touched each other's organs and rubbed them against each other. I tell him we were pretending to be a man and woman, that I don't think I sexual-love Joey. My father gives me a curious, worried look, and then he tells me it is probably okay, that I probably don't have any diseases, but that I should never do that kind of thing again. I ask him to examine my penis for irregularities anyway (I have suspected for some time that the shape, size, and color of my penis are extremely abnormal—Gina let me know it was too small and bald—and now my worst fears are practically confirmed.) I also ask him not to tell Mom about everything, and he says he won't, and I ride home next to him thinking about how much of my brain may have already melted and oozed down into the rest of my body. At home, Dad spends a lot of time wandering around the kitchen, talking to Mom, doing other things before getting around to the examination, and I sit in front of the television watching a show about Digby the Giant Dog and not even seeing it. Everything is a foggy, anxious blur. *Come on, Dad, come on,* I think. I listen to my brain sizzling away; I listen to it drip, drip, drip. Finally he takes me to my bedroom and examines me and tells me I am just fine, and then he reminds me not to do that sort of thing ever again, and that if I want to I should come talk to him. I am relieved. But then he gives me that look again, that curious, worried look, and I almost wish I hadn't said anything and taken my chances.

What was he thinking when he gave me that look? I know what he thought, what he still thinks, what he thinks all the time. He thinks I am growing up to be a very strange boy, a boy he doesn't know and doesn't really want to. A boy who plays naked with other boys. A boy who sits around in his room drawing comics, flapping his arms and making strange noises deep in his throat as he plans out the action and creates sound effects. That stuff, especially. A boy who doesn't like sports, who only plays soccer because he's told to, a boy who likes to go out in the desert by himself and do God Knows What. A boy who says *excuse me* fifty times in a row, for nothing. A very strange boy, indeed.

I stay in my room after he leaves and shut and lock the door. I close the blinds and sit down with my comics, and I hand jive my funny feelings away.

௬

In sixth grade, I've forgotten all about the hand jive. Everything is better, everything is fine. I play with Jay Hardtke and Adam Zele. Mr. Thompson is angry because I don't take things seriously enough. My report card shows almost straight Cs. I have to go in for parent-teacher-student conferences. I'm having too much fun. I have so much potential, and I'm frittering it away. When am I going to grow up and take some responsibility? I'm always late to class in the mornings. It's as if I don't even care.

I love the word "frittering." It just sounds like a lot of fun. It sounds just like what I'm doing. And I don't hear the voice. I don't have to excuse myself or remember my ESP five or twenty-five or a hundred and twenty-five times. I ride my bike on the motocross trail some bigger kids have made in the desert near my house. I go swimming at Skyline Country Club and watch the pretty, tanned older ladies in their tiny swimsuits. I tell jokes and make everybody laugh. And I don't care. I don't care. I don't care.

Near the end of the second quarter before Christmas break, I start thinking about Ronnie Newman. Ronnie is the biggest loser in the school. He is skinny, loaded with acne, ugly and stupid, and he's failed sixth grade five times. *Five* times. He is the sort of kid you know is headed for prison or worse. Not a tough, delinquent kid, just a weirdo. A Ted Bundy in the making. A Jeffrey Dahmer Jr. The last kid you'd want to end up being like. Mr. Thompson calls me into the classroom during break one day and has me sit up close to him at his desk. William, he tells me, I like you a lot. I *like* you. But you're blowing it. And you know what I mean. I know how smart you are, you can't pretend with me. I've talked to you and talked to you, and I've given you more chances than anybody else. And I'll give you one last chance. But if you don't get your act together, I'm going to put you in the remedial learning classroom after Christmas break, and they'll hold you back this year. I mean it. You'll be in there with Ronnie Newman. You'll be held back with Ronnie Newman. Do you want to be like Ronnie Newman?

The Cs on my last report card, it turns out, have become Ds and, some of them, Fs. Mr. Thompson really is going to ship me out. I pedal home as fast as I can, crack all of my books, some of them for the first time, and I start to study. My chest constricts and my breathing quickens. My heart is back up there, beating against my throat. I study five and six hours a night to catch up on a semester's worth of social studies, reading, English, geography, math. I ace every test, every one, from that day forward. I contribute to classroom discussions, I volunteer for the toughest reading list in the sixth grade. I take makeup exams and ace those, too, and Mr. Thompson smiles and squeezes my shoulders and makes me want to go at it even harder.

At semester's end, I've earned myself five As and two Bs, and one of those Bs is a B-plus. Mr. Thompson makes a speech to the class with tears in his eyes. Dad and Mom take me out for dinner. Not knowing what else to do, unable to stop, I start diving into my assignments for the next semester. I study on Christmas Eve.

And, just like that, the hand jive is back.

๑

I begin high school at Amphi High in the fall of 1981, and the hand jive is still with me. It is actually getting worse. I walk home from the bus stop with Ray Farley, a funny, popular kid, but he is too cool to hang out with the likes of me. We laugh and joke while we walk, but then he walks up his driveway and disappears. When Ray transfers out of Amphi, Geyr Greve transfers in, and I walk home with Geyr instead but the situation is the same. We throw rocks at each other as we walk, and that's fun, but then he walks on up his driveway and leaves me to my afternoon. I go to the kitchen and get a snack, and then I go to my bedroom and lock the door. Then I go into my bathroom and lock that door, too. And I hand jive. Hours pass. Outside the bathroom window, there is an old, rotting saguaro cactus skeleton. The skeleton's gray, weathered ribs rise up to a black, knobby point, and I imagine sometimes that Dad and Mom have allowed scientists to install a hidden camera in the knob so they can observe me. I always wonder why they haven't confronted me about all the time I spend in the bathroom, and this scenario provides some explanation, at least. I imagine turning on the television one day and seeing a PBS documentary all about me and my abnormalities. I know this is a paranoid, ridiculous notion, but I close the blinds on the window just in case. I crouch in the near darkness, shut out the world, and do my thing.

Amphitheater High School is a massive public school, population twenty-two hundred. I feel lost there; I am quiet, shy, unsure of myself most of the time. I feel I am five or ten different people crammed into a single body. My sharpest high school memories, in fact, read like the memories of a cross section of Amphi's population, like the recollections of a whole student body. I am highly active in drama class and more or less asleep everywhere else. I win the Best Actor award for my role in *You Can't Take It with You,* but I'm called into the assistant principal's office and threatened with suspension for cutting classes. I test into the "genius club" at Amphi, but I never attend a single meeting. I am sarcastic, cynical, sometimes mean. I submit to an underground humor magazine. I work out at the gym every day and make fun of Lippy Ford, the wrestler who lights cats on fire for fun on Saturday nights. Once, during squat reps, Lippy pulls the pin out of my Nautilus machine for a joke and the metal, unpadded footbar at the end of the leg extension bars swings back at me to carve permanent grooves in my shins. Another time he throws me up against my locker and sticks a loaded gun in my chest, cocks it, rubs the trigger with a greasy finger, laughs, and walks away. I keep making fun of him. I know I'm fairly good-looking, and I am willing to screw anything that moves. The really popular and pretty girls, though, look at me with a kind of wistful pity. I don't realize it's my seventies "retro" look: dirty blue jeans, cheap button-down oxfords, and a "disco" hairdo, parted straight down the middle. So I resign myself to dating wrestling cheerleaders instead of football cheerleaders, voluptuous freaks instead of pretty, nice girls. Louise Chandler is both wrestling cheerleader and voluptuous freak; she smokes, listens to punk bands, and sneaks out her window at night to hang out in gay bars. One night, while I'm nibbling on her boobs in a backroom at a party, she begs me to rape her; I try my best, but I break down when she screams and cries and really struggles. She dumps me, disgusted. I am chosen to dance the senior jitterbug with our homecoming queen, the prettiest girl in school, and we take first prize. I throw a party at my boss's real estate office late one night and end up spread-eagled against the wall outside, ten police officers surrounding me with loaded assault rifles and barking dogs. I join the choir. I learn the trick of dating girls from other schools, nice, pretty girls who think I'm cute and sweet and don't have to worry about what their friends will think. Because their friends will never see me. This trick also makes two-timing easy and worry-free, for me and probably for them as well. I join the advanced Madrigal choir. I smoke grass. Disgusted with cheesy yearbook photos, I pose in the back of a convertible with a gorgeous brunette who feeds me grapes and strokes my hair. In our yearbook I am voted Best Actor in the Senior Class and, in the category of Class Clown, or so goes the rumor, I take second to Paul Potts. The ultrapopular Rawls girls drive me to school in their cherry red Mustang, but I am so intimidated by their glamour that I never, in nine months of twenty-minute rides, ever utter a word. Everyone looks at me the same way I look at myself: I'm a lot of bodies and a nobody, a funny, impressive kid who's almost but not quite worth getting to know.

I avoid my parents. I keep that door locked. I read

underground comic books and jerk off. The hand jive is my very best friend. No matter how hot and uncomfortable it gets at school, on the worst "nobody" days, I know it'll be okay.

I can come home and hand jive, hand jive, hand jive, all night long.

The last hand jive I remember hits me in the spring semester of my freshman year at college. I am sharing a room with Phil Green, an ultraconservative straitlaced kid from Fort Collins, Colorado. I have just bought the new REM album *Fables of the Reconstruction,* and as I listen I get more and more excited. REM is the greatest, man; I love those murky mixes, that anxious, hard-driving beat, and Michael Stipe's tentative growls and murmurs. I kneel down on the hard tile floor beside my bed, and my arms start in with their tight, fast flapping. I grow red in the face, and I envision myself up on the stage singing unintelligibly just like Stipe. I have Stipe's voice, I am in Stipe's body. I am ultracool. I just know I'm wearing black, and all the women love it. I am jiving, I am jiving, all, of course, to the most thunderous applause.

Phil Green opens the door and walks in and stares. Our eyes meet. I am kneeling there beside the bed, my arms frozen in mid-flap. He mumbles an apology. I say, "Oh, Jesus, Phil, you scared the hell out of me." And then there's nothing more to say. Phil grabs something off the desk, whatever he came in for, and leaves. And I realize, as I kneel alone in the dark, quiet room, that I can never, never do this thing again. I can't stand letting other people see it, and I can't stand to see it in myself.

When I was a little boy Dad told me that, when he was growing up, he liked to make strange, high-pitched squeaks when he was excited, too. That was the closest he ever came to discussing the hand jive with me. I wonder whether it is genetic; I wonder how my own kids will turn out. Mostly, though, I think about Dad. Sometimes, when he gets really excited about something, he shakes his arms a couple or three times and lets out a little yelp and gets red in the face. I wonder if he had the one hard moment, at some point, that I had, when he realized the world just wouldn't accept a hand-jiving man. I always thought his frenetic little bursts of excitement were sort of silly and stupid, but that was before I stopped my hand jive. I see them now for what they are, or what they are to me, anyway: a surrogate, a substitute. I find myself firing off these crazy yips and yelps more and more often these days. I get these strange little bursts of energy, and I've just got to let them loose. Smoking also helps a little.

I think, too, about all the time I lost to hand jiving while I was growing up. By my estimate, I spent a good year of my life, all told, doing the hand jive. It got me nothing. I imagined whole movies in my head, but I never got a good idea for a story or a play or a film script out of any of them. During junior high and high school, I mostly only envisioned short scenes of extravagant action and violence, the Hollywood formula: big guns, exploding cars, hot babes, and careless expletives. It did foster in me, though, a very active imagination, a very large and very real dream world, and I feel sometimes when I'm writing as though I'm tapping into that world, that feeling, again.

It feels good, but I can't explain why. That was sort of the point; hand jiving took me to a world beyond judgment, beyond reproach, beyond criticism. It was the ultimate passive, illusory escape. I don't know where the hand jive came from, where it went, or what it was, really, other than a nearly total waste of time and an embarrassment.

And I've tried to discover why I needed such an absolute, self-annihilating escape, but I believe now I may never come close to the truth.

But it made me different, it made me special, it made me freakish. Like Prince Randian, the quadriplegic who rolled and lit his own cigarettes, or like Martin Laurillo the Neck-Twistin' Man or Legless Alvina Gibbs, I was different from everyone else in the world. Like any of those old Coney Island or Barnum and Bailey freaks who continue to fascinate me today, I carried with me everywhere a lonely, secret pride. I knew the whole truth about myself and believed I would horrify and repulse anyone who glimpsed that truth. The faces of those old human misfits, in the aging photographs I collect and in the 1932 MGM film *Freaks,* stare at me with that knowledge that I hid for so long from the rest of the world. Or I wish and pretend they knew, because they were kindred spirits who might have welcomed me into their fold. *We accept you, we accept you. One of us, one of us.* I live in Brooklyn now, and it's an easy ride on the F train to Coney Island. It's as far away from New York City as you can get on the B, D, F, and N subway trains, the end of those lines, and I go there some afternoons and listen to the barker at the freak show. Sometimes I pay to see the freaks: Painproof Man, Elastic Lady, the Human Blockhead. They are different from me, these people who have imposed freakishness upon themselves, but they are the only kinds of freaks allowed by law to hop on a stage. I like their easygoing pride and arrogance. I like the way they share their freakishness with the world as if it's a miraculous, beautiful secret, and assert at the same time their normalcy, their humanity, through the very fact that they're standing there before us, flesh and blood. Living, breathing people, like all of us but slightly different. Slightly special.

So here I go, mounting the stage for the first time, if only in print. I can hear that barker now, and he annoys me:

So here he is, folks, the Hand-jiving Man. An exhibitionist by nature, he can no longer hide his strange, twisted secret from the world. It is yours to see, ladies and gentlemen, live onstage and absolutely uncensored. He has spent years of his life on other worlds, and now you can see what his body does in his absence. A freakish, uncontrollable explosion of energy, folks, for your eyes only. He wants your sympathy, he wants your understanding, he wants to witness your wonder and pleasure, and if he can make a few bucks by exploiting his condition that is just fine by him. The man with no shame. Come on in, folks. Step right this way.

The barker annoys me because everything he says is true. I could never hop on a real stage, though, willing or no. It would not be much of a show. I cannot physically simulate the hand jive. Friends who have read parts of this piece have asked me to try, and I do, but I feel odd, self-conscious, and my arms will not react properly. My heart and mind must lead; my body follows. And I do not want to make an authentic leap into that world again. It is a mindless void, a stupid habit, but for me it obviously had its attractions. I have made a break from it, and I don't want to be seduced again.

For twenty years, it has been my proud, beautiful, odd, horrific secret. And sometimes, when I'm feeling awfully normal, awfully lonely, or awfully anxious, I have to admit that I almost miss it.

FATHERS

Mary Macrina Young

Poem for My Father

Out near Burnside
I'm driving the car
past muddy flooded creeks.
Sky pools in the dregs,
sky survives the watershed
carrying cattle tracks
and treads of balers
under the bridge.
I'm driving out here
with the tire gauge
I got from you
in my pocket.
At the filling station,
among men,
I know something about cars
and I will be alright.

Lucille Clifton

SAM

if he could have kept
the sky in his dark hand
he would have pulled it down
and held it.
it would have called him lord
as did the skinny women
in virginia. if he
could have gone to school
he would have learned to write
his story and not live it.
if he could have done better
he would have. oh stars
and stripes forever,
what did you do to my father?

Gary Soto

Braly Street

Every summer
The asphalt softens
Giving under the edge
Of boot heels and the trucks
That caught radiators
Of butterflies.
Bottle caps and glass
Of the forties and fifties
Hold their breath
Under the black earth
Of asphalt and are silent
Like the dead whose mouths
Have eaten dirt and bermuda.
Every summer I come
To this street
Where I discovered ants bit,
Matches flare,
And pinto beans unraveled
Into plants; discovered
Aspirin will not cure a dog
Whose fur twitches.

It's sixteen years
Since our house
Was bulldozed and my father
Stunned into a coma . . .
Where it was,
An oasis of chickweed

And foxtails.
Where the almond tree stood
There are wine bottles
Whose history
Is a liver. The long caravan
Of my uncle's footprints
Has been paved
With dirt. Where my father
Cemented a pond
There is a cavern of red ants
Living on the seeds
The wind brings
And cats that come here
To die among
The browning sage.

It's sixteen years
Since bottle collectors
Shoveled around
The foundation
And the almond tree
Opened its last fruit
To the summer.
The houses are gone,
The Molinas, Morenos,
The Japanese families
Are gone, the Okies gone
Who moved out at night
Under a canopy of
Moving stars.

In '57 I sat
On the porch, salting
Slugs that came out
After the rain,

While inside my uncle
Weakened with cancer
And the blurred vision
Of his hands
Darkening to earth.
In '58 I knelt
Before my father
Whose spine was pulled loose.
Before his face still
Growing a chin of hair,
Before the procession
Of stitches behind
His neck, I knelt
And did not understand.

Braly Street is now
Tin ventilators
On the warehouses, turning
Our sweat
Toward the yellowing sky;
Acetylene welders
Beading manifolds,
Stinging the half-globes
Of retinas. When I come
To where our house was,
I come to weeds
And a sewer line tied off
Like an umbilical cord;
To the chinaberry
Not pulled down
And to its rings
My father and uncle
Would equal, if alive.

Luci Tapahonso

I Am Singing Now

the moon is a white sliver
balancing the last of its contents
in the final curve of the month
my daughters sleep
in the back of the pickup
breathing small clouds of white in the dark
they lie warm and soft
under layers of clothes and blankets
how they dream, precious ones, of grandma
and the scent of fire
the smell of mutton
they are already home.

i watch the miles dissolve behind us
in the hazy glow of taillights
and the distinct shapes of hills and mesas loom above
then recede slowly in the clear winter night.

i sing to myself
and think of my father
teaching me, leaning toward me
listening as i learned.
"just like this," he would say
and he would sing those old songs

into the fiber of my hair,
into the pores of my skin,
into the dreams of my children

and i am singing now
for the night
        the almost empty moon
        and the land swimming beneath cold bright stars.

Maria Hinojosa

There Was Nothing Else I Could Do

IQ says he's known throughout all of New York City. Maybe not him, but certainly his tag. He was born in the Philippines and started hanging out when he was about twelve years old. Crews back then were only into graffiti and dancing. The beef was over who were the best dancers, who were the best writers, and the fights were almost never violent. Things changed almost all of a sudden, says IQ. It wasn't enough to be a good dancer or writer, you had to know how to fight. And being a short guy, IQ was tested pretty early on. He got respect then because people could see that even though he was one of the smallest guys around, he wasn't afraid of stepping to anyone. And he usually won.

But at home, IQ was never good enough to please his parents. Unless it was an A or a first prize, everything IQ did barely got a reaction.

In 1989, IQ had one of his worst fights. Forty-first had some beef with one of its rival gangs and they had a showdown at a 7-Eleven. But that night, IQ was almost abandoned by his crew. He and two other guys were left alone to fend off an entire crew. He got hit over the head several times by someone wielding a crowbar. The doctors couldn't believe his skull hadn't been cracked open. They gave him thirty-six stitches.

On the street, Shank, Coki, and the rest of the crew said they would take one guy out from the enemy crew for every stitch in IQ's head. But IQ said enough was enough, though after losing that fight, his rep was never the same. For the first time in his life, he felt he had to carry a weapon. He doesn't believe in guns. Instead he carries a hammer in his coat pocket.

IQ got married not long after that fight and had a baby. Less than a year after his son was born, he got a divorce. Now he works in the mail room of a company, lives with his in-laws but doesn't speak to his ex-wife, and raises his son. On the weekends, IQ still chills at the park with his boys, reminiscing about the old days.

MH: How do you want to raise your son? How much do you think you'll tell him about hanging out with the crews?

IQ: He's only two now. He's innocent. I don't want him to get into it. Writing on the walls, if he did that, I'd just tell him to watch out. I don't want him to get into fighting. For me, it was hard 'cause there's nothing else that I'm good at, except graffiti, and if you do graffiti, the competition starts out friendly and then becomes violent. My brothers are into sports. A lot of the kids who play sports, that's all they're into and so hopefully he'll grow into something like that. I mean, me? There was nothing else I could do.

MH: What are you going to do for your son that's different?

IQ: I'll try to be there more for him. I think my parents did a pretty good job. I mean, no one in my family has ever been arrested. For my kid, I want to do everything I can to show him I care for him 'cause I really don't think I got that from my parents. I mean, they never hit us, but if we did something bad they would just yell and not talk to us for a while. But in my kid's case I want to scold him and guide him, too. Explain to him why I'm mad. My parents never explained why they did things. I mean, I think they were good parents, but look what happened to me. I mean, they don't really know much about me.

They didn't know I wrote on walls until a few years ago, and by then I was almost not doing it anymore. They didn't know who my friends were, my girlfriends, or anything. I think they're changing now with my little brothers. But they never told me about safe sex or anything, and that's why I have a kid. They should have been more supportive. Like if I was doing something good, they should praise me for it, and if I was doing bad, then I would want them to say something about it. 'Cause I used to come home drunk and stuff. Maybe they should have waited up for me. My brother sometimes had to carry me home 'cause I was so wasted.

MH: So what do you dream about for your son?

IQ: I always hoped that I could afford to move to a nicer area. I mean, I live in an OK area, but these days, being a hood is in style. But maybe in a small southern town or something like that. I used to live in a small town. Maybe we should have stayed. I probably would have been completely out of trouble then. Maybe if we would have stayed there by now I'd be an artist or something. I know I did things that were wrong and I shouldn't have done things. I mean, writing on walls is OK, but there was no real reason to fight or rob people. I had money. And the fights didn't have to happen. I let them happen. I guess I did it to get a rep. And in the beginning some of my boys had never seen me fighting so they would want to see me do something. But later I didn't have to fight if I didn't want to. Then it was my choice. In the beginning, they'd see me walking and see this little man and say I was nothing. Big guys would come up to me and if I beat them down then they would remember that, and my friends would remember that. And that got me respect. Then later

I would be the one that would set up the fights. People from our enemy crew would come to me and say they had a beef with one of my boys, and I would make sure to set up a one-on-one.

MH: So a lot of the times for the crew it was one-on-ones and kind of decent? No tricks?

IQ: At the beginning it was bum rushes, but then both crews wanted to stop that and it was one-on-ones for a while. It's like boxing on TV. You see who's the better guy and then that's it. But if it's a bum rush then you don't know who's there and what they're carrying. Then it's not even fair. Five guys stomping on one guy. I mean, it's not good to fight, but at least one-on-ones are fair.

My little brothers have avoided it. They just have a couple of friends they hang out with, and I never hear them getting into fights or starting fights. They don't even hang out in the same spot. Like if it was me and my boys, we'd just find maybe a store or something and hang right there for maybe the whole night. Like on a corner, we'd just sit there near a phone or a store. My brothers have things to do. They do positive things. They're musicians. There's no reason to fight about music so they just don't do anything I did. We went to the same school, knew the same people, and I came out different. Maybe they were just closer to my parents than I was. Maybe they just feel like they don't have to be at the center of attention. They just do other stuff. Play video games and stuff. But I don't know anything about computers and video games or music. I don't do anything. I hang out at the handball court, but I don't do nothing. I never even play. No sports. I'm just the guy that's sitting there drinking or writing on the walls. I think I'm boring. A lot of my friends are like that, too. There's nothing that we're good at so we just hang around. And if you're good at fighting that's what you do.

I used to be good at writing graffiti, but then the city made it real difficult for us to do that. I don't like to fight anymore and I wish there was still a way to do more graffiti. It's not thrilling to do it anymore. Now it's like secretive. I used to do it right in the daytime, right in front of people. Before, I used to do real intricate stuff and take my time 'cause I didn't care if the police would come. But now I do 'cause if I get arrested how is that gonna look to my son? Who's gonna take care of him? I don't like all of these responsibilities when all my friends are just hanging out and doing the things we used to do.

I wish I was sixteen, young and carefree. Not have to work and just get money from my parents. Back then it was easier to get away with a lot of those things. And also we were defending our territory. The reason we did that is 'cause there was really nothing else we did except hang out on that block. And as you get older you see people trying to hang out on your block and you don't like them hanging there. The block is yours, it's your property and you don't like people to step on it. If intruders leave without a fight, that's good, but if they want to fight then you have to defend it 'cause it's your place.

MH: Is it your place?

IQ: No, not really. It's the city's. But that's how we feel. Say something happened, like a robbery, they'd blame us for it. But some people would stick up for us and say we were defending the block and the property. I think that's how a lot of us felt. We felt we were doing good for the block 'cause we were protecting it from outsiders. And since we were always on that block, nothing would ever happen on that block. We knew the whole block so it would be impossible for someone to get by without getting caught. But then we, 41st, got together with FTS and then it wasn't just the block, it was all of Flushing that we were protecting. And then there was competition about who was the biggest crew. Or 'cause one crew was crossing out another crew. And then it gets real big and one person's beef becomes everyone's beef.

MH: Do you think it's a good thing that kids defend their territory?

IQ: I think it's a good thing that they don't like outside people damaging their area or causing trouble.

MH: Do you want your son defending . . . ?

IQ: No. I just hope he doesn't even have to defend himself. I doubt he won't have to, but I hope he doesn't have to. I know he will. I guess it's just wishful thinking.

Li-Young Lee

The Gift

To pull the metal splinter from my palm
my father recited a story in a low voice.
I watched his lovely face and not the blade.
Before the story ended, he'd removed
the iron sliver I thought I'd die from.

I can't remember the tale,
but hear his voice still, a well
of dark water, a prayer.
And I recall his hands,
two measures of tenderness
he laid against my face,
the flames of discipline
he raised above my head.

Had you entered that afternoon
you would have thought you saw a man
planting something in a boy's palm,
a silver tear, a tiny flame.
Had you followed that boy
you would have arrived here,
where I bend over my wife's right hand.

Look how I shave her thumbnail down
so carefully she feels no pain.
Watch as I lift the splinter out.
I was seven when my father
took my hand like this,
and I did not hold that shard

between my fingers and think,
Metal that will bury me,
christen it Little Assassin,
Ore Going Deep for My heart.
And I did not lift up my wound and cry,
Death visited here!
I did what a child does
when he's given something to keep.
I kissed my father.

Ethan Canin

Star Food

The summer I turned eighteen I disappointed both my parents for the first time. This hadn't happened before, since what disappointed one usually pleased the other. As a child, if I played broom hockey instead of going to school, my mother wept and my father took me outside later to find out how many goals I had scored. On the other hand, if I spent Saturday afternoon on the roof of my parents' grocery store staring up at the clouds instead of counting cracker cartons in the stockroom, my father took me to the back to talk about work and discipline, and my mother told me later to keep looking for things that no one else saw.

This was her theory. My mother felt that men like Leonardo da Vinci and Thomas Edison had simply stared long enough at regular objects until they saw new things, and thus my looking into the sky might someday make me a great man. She believed I had a worldly curiosity. My father believed I wanted to avoid stock work.

Stock work was an issue in our family, as were all the jobs that had to be done in a grocery store. Our store was called Star Food and above it an incandescent star revolved. Its circuits buzzed, and its yellow points, as thick as my knees, drooped with the slow melting of the bulb. On summer nights flying insects flocked in clouds around it, droves of them burning on the glass. One of my jobs was to go out on the roof, the sloping, eaved side that looked over the western half of Arcade, California, and clean them off the star. At night, when their black bodies stood out against the glass, when the wind carried in the marsh smell of the New Jerusalem River, I went into the attic, crawled out the dormer window onto the peaked roof, and slid across the shingles to where the pole rose like a lightning rod into the night. I reached with a wet rag and rubbed away the June bugs and pickerel moths until the star was yellow-white and steaming from the moisture. Then I turned and looked over Arcade, across the bright avenue and my dimly lighted high school in the distance, into the low hills where oak trees grew in rows on the curbs and where girls drove to school in their own convertibles. When my father came up on the roof sometimes to talk about the store, we fixed our eyes on the red tile roofs or the small clouds of blue barbecue smoke that floated above the hills on warm evenings. While the clean bulb buzzed and flickered behind us, we talked about loss leaders or keeping the elephant-ear plums stacked in neat triangles.

The summer I disappointed my parents, though, my father talked to me about a lot of other things. He also made me look in the other direction whenever we were on the roof together, not west to the hills and their clouds of barbecue smoke, but east toward the other part of town. We crawled up one slope of the roof, then down the other so I could see beyond the back alley where wash hung on lines in the moonlight, down to the neighborhoods across Route 5. These were the neighborhoods where men sat on the curbs on weekday afternoons, where rusted, wheel-less cars lay on blocks in the yards.

"*You're* going to end up on one of those curbs," my father told me.

Usually I stared farther into the clouds when he said something like that. He and my mother argued about what I did on the roof for so many hours at a time, and I hoped that by looking closely at the amazing borders of clouds I could confuse him. My mother believed I was on the verge of discovering something atmospheric, and I was sure she told my father this, so when he came upstairs, made me look across Route 5, and talked to me about how I was going to end up there, I squinted harder at the sky.

"You don't fool me for a second," he said.

He was up on the roof with me because I had been letting someone steal from the store.

From the time we first had the star on the roof, my mother believed her only son was destined for limited fame. Limited because she thought that true vision was distilled and could not be appreciated by everybody. I discovered this shortly after the star was installed, when I spent an hour looking out over the roofs and chimneys instead of helping my father stock a shipment of dairy. It was a hot day and the milk sat on the loading dock while he searched for me in the store and in our apartment next door. When he came up and found me, his neck was red and his footfalls shook the roof joists. At my age I was still allowed certain mistakes, but I'd seen the dairy truck arrive and knew I should have been downstairs, so it surprised me later, after I'd helped unload the milk, when my mother stopped beside me as I was sprinkling the leafy vegetables with a spray bottle.

"Dade, I don't want you to let anyone keep you from what you ought to be doing."

"I'm sorry," I said. "I should have helped with the milk earlier."

"No," she said, "that's not what I mean." Then she told me her theory of limited fame while I sprayed the cabbage and lettuce with the atomizer. It was the first time I had heard her idea. The world's most famous men, she said, presidents and emperors, generals and patriots, were men of vulgar fame, men who ruled the world because their ideas were obvious and could be understood by everybody. But there was also limited fame. Newton and Galileo and

Enrico Fermi were men of limited fame, and as I stood there with the atomizer in my hand my mother's eyes watered over and she told me she knew in her heart that one day I was going to be a man of limited fame. I was twelve years old.

After that day I found I could avoid a certain amount of stock work by staying up on the roof and staring into the fine layers of stratus clouds that floated above Arcade. In the *Encyclopedia Americana* I read about cirrus and cumulus and thunderheads, about inversion layers and currents like the currents at sea, and in the afternoons I went upstairs and watched. The sky was a changing thing, I found out. It was more than a blue sheet. Twirling with pollen and sunlight, it began to transform itself.

Often as I stood on the roof my father came outside and swept the sidewalk across the street. Through the telephone poles and crossed power lines he looked up at me, his broom stokes small and fierce as if he were hoeing hard ground. It irked him that my mother encouraged me to stay on the roof. He was a short man with direct habits and an understanding of how to get along in the world, and he believed that God rewarded only two things, courtesy and hard work. God did not reward looking at the sky. In the car my father acknowledged good drivers and in restaurants he left good tips. He knew the names of his customers. He never sold a rotten vegetable. He shook hands often, looked everyone in the eye, and on Friday nights when we went to the movies he made us sit in the front row of the theater. "Why should I pay to look over other people's shoulders?" he said. The movies made him talk. On the way back to the car he walked with his hands clasped behind him and greeted everyone who passed. He smiled. He mentioned the fineness of the evening as if he were the admiral or aviator we had just seen on the screen. "People like it," he said. "It's good for business." My mother was quiet, walking with her slender arms folded in front of her as if she were cold.

I liked the movies because I imagined myself doing everything the heroes did—deciding to invade at daybreak, swimming half the night against the seaward current—but whenever we left the theater I was disappointed. From the front row, life seemed like a clear set of decisions, but on the street afterward I realized that the world existed all around me and I didn't know what I wanted. The quiet of evening and the ordinariness of human voices startled me.

Sometimes on the roof, as I stared into the layers of horizon, the sounds on the street faded into this same ordinariness. One afternoon when I was standing under the star my father came outside and looked up to me. "You're in a trance," he called. I glanced down at him, then squinted back at the horizon. For a minute he waited, and then from across the street he threw a rock. He had a pitcher's arm and could have hit me if he wanted, but the rock sailed past me and clattered on the shingles. My mother came right out of the store anyway and stopped him. "I wanted him off the roof," I heard my father tell her later in the same frank voice in which he explained his position to vegetable salesmen. "If someone's throwing rocks at him he'll come down. He's no fool."

I was flattered by this, but my mother won the point and from then on I could stay up on the roof when I wanted. To appease my father I cleaned the electric star, and though he often came outside to sweep, he stopped telling me to come down. I thought about limited fame and spent a lot of time noticing the sky. When I looked closely it was a sea with waves and shifting colors, wind seams and denials of distance, and after a while I learned to look at it so that it entered my eye whole. It was blue liquid. I spent hours looking into its pale wash, looking for things, though I didn't know what. I looked for lines or sectors, the diamond shapes of daylight stars. Sometimes, silver-winged jets from the air force base across the hills turned the right way against the sun and went off like small flash bulbs on the horizon. There was nothing that struck me and stayed, though, nothing with the brilliance of white light or electric explosion that I thought came with discovery, so after a while I changed my idea of discovery. I just stood on the roof and stared. When my mother asked me, I told her that I might be seeing new things but that seeing change took time. "It's slow," I told her. "It may take years."

The first time I let her steal I chalked it up to surprise. I was working the front register when she walked in, a thin, tall woman in a plaid dress that looked wilted. She went right to the standup display of cut-price, nearly expired breads and crackers, where she took a loaf of rye from the shelf. Then she turned and looked me in the eye. We were looking into each other's eyes when she walked out the front door. Through the blue-and-white LOOK UP TO STAR FOOD sign on the window I watched her cross the street.

There were two or three other shoppers in the store, and over the tops of the potato chip packages I could see my mother's broom. My father was in back unloading chicken parts. Nobody else had seen her come in; nobody had seen her leave. I locked the cash drawer and walked to the aisle where my mother was sweeping.

"I think someone just stole."

My mother wheeled a trash receptacle when she swept, and as I stood there she closed it, put down her broom, and wiped her face with a handkerchief. "You couldn't get him?"

"It was a her."

"A lady?"

"I couldn't chase her. She came in and took a loaf of rye and left."

6

I had chased plenty of shoplifters before. They were kids usually, in sneakers and coats too warm for the weather. I chased them up the aisle and out the door, then to the corner and around it while ahead of me they tried to toss whatever it was—Twinkies, freeze-pops—into the sidewalk hedges. They cried when I caught them, begged me not to tell their parents. First time, my father said, scare them real good. Second time, call the law. I took them back with me to the store, held them by the collar as we walked. Then I sat them in the straight-back chair in the stockroom and gave them a speech my father had written. It was printed on a blue index card taped to the door. DO YOU KNOW WHAT YOU HAVE DONE? it began. DO YOU KNOW WHAT IT IS TO STEAL? I learned to pause between the questions, pace the room, check the card. "Give them time to get scared," my father said. He was expert at this. He never talked to them until he had dusted the vegetables or run a couple of women through the register. "Why should I stop my work for a kid who steals from me?" he said. When he finally came into the stockroom he moved and spoke the way policemen do at the scene of an accident. His manner was slow and deliberate. First he asked me what they had stolen. If I had recovered whatever it was, he took it and held it up to the light, turned it over in his fingers as if it were of large value. Then he opened the freezer door and led the kid inside to talk about law and punishment amid the frozen beef carcasses. He paced as he spoke, breathed clouds of vapor into the air.

In the end, though, my mother usually got him to let them off. Once when he wouldn't, when he had called the police to pick up a third-offense boy who sat trembling in the stockroom, my mother called him to the front of the store to talk to a customer. In the stockroom we kept a key to the back door hidden under a silver samovar that had belonged to my grandmother, and when my father was in front that afternoon my mother came to the rear, took it out, and opened the back door. She leaned down to the boy's ear. "Run," she said.

૬

The next time she came in it happened the same way. My father was at the vegetable tier, stacking avocados. My mother was in back listening to the radio. It was afternoon. I rang in a customer, then looked up while I was putting the milk cartons in the bottom of the bag, and there she was. Her gray eyes were looking into mine. She had two cans of pineapple juice in her hands, and on the way out she held the door for an old woman.

૬

That night I went up to clean the star. The air was clear. It was warm. When I finished wiping the glass I moved out over the edge of the eaves and looked into the distance where little turquoise squares—lighted swimming pools—stood out against the hills.

"Dade—"

It was my father's voice from behind the peak of the roof.

"Yes?"

"Come over to this side."

I mounted the shallow-pitched roof, went over the peak, and edged down the other slope to where I could see his silhouette against the lights on Route 5. He was smoking. I got up and we stood together at the edge of the shingled eaves. In front of us trucks rumbled by on the interstate, their trailers lit at the edges like the mast lights of ships.

"Look across the highway," he said.

"I am."

"What do you see?"

"Cars."

"What else?"

"Trucks."

For a while he didn't say anything. He dragged a few times on his cigarette, then pinched off the lit end and put the rest back in the pack. A couple of motorcycles went by, a car with one headlight, a bus.

"Do you know what it's like to live in a shack?" he said.

"No."

"You don't want to end up in a place like that. And it's damn easy to do if you don't know what you want. You know how easy it is?"

"Easy," I said.

"You have to know what you want."

For years my father had been trying to teach me competence and industry. Since I was nine I had been squeeze-drying mops before returning them to the closet, double-counting change, sweeping under the lip of the vegetable bins even if the dirt there was invisible to customers. On the basis of industry, my father said, Star Food had grown from a two-aisle, one-freezer corner store to the largest grocery in Arcade. When I was eight he had bought the failing gas station next door and built additions, so that now Star Food had nine aisles, separate coolers for dairy, soda, and beer, a tiered vegetable stand, a glass-fronted butcher counter, a part-time butcher, and, under what used to be the rain roof of the failing gas station, free parking while you shopped. When I started high school we moved into the apartment next door, and at meals we discussed store improvements. Soon my father invented a grid system for easy location of foods. He stayed up one night and painted, and the next morning there was a new coordinate system on the ceiling of the store. It was a grid, A through J, 1 through 10. For weeks there were drops of blue paint in his eyelashes.

A few days later my mother pasted up fluorescent stars among the grid squares. She knew about the real constellations and was accurate with the ones she stuck to the ceiling, even though she also knew that the aisle lights in Star Food stayed on day and night, so that her stars were going to be invisible. We saw them only once, in fact, in a blackout a few months later, when they lit up in hazy clusters around the store.

"Do you know why I did it?" she asked me the night of the blackout as we stood beneath their pale light.

"No."

"Because of the idea."

She was full of ideas, and one was that I was accomplishing something on the shallow-pitched section of our roof. Sometimes she sat at the dormer window and watched me. Through the glass I could see the slender outlines of her cheekbones. "What do you see?" she asked. On warm nights she leaned over the sill and pointed out the constellations. "They are the illumination of great minds," she said.

௳

After the woman walked out the second time I began to think a lot about what I wanted. I tried to discover what it was, and I had an idea it would come to me on the roof. In the evenings I sat up there and thought. I looked for signs. I threw pebbles down into the street and watched where they hit. I read the newspaper, and stories about ballplayers or jazz musicians began to catch my eye. When he was ten years old, Johnny Unitas strung a tire from a tree limb and spent afternoons throwing a football through it as it swung. Dizzy Gillespie played with an orchestra when he was seven. There was an emperor who ruled China at age eight. What could be said about me? He swept the dirt no one could see under the lip of the vegetable bins.

The day after the woman had walked out the second time, my mother came up on the roof while I was cleaning the star. She usually wore medium heels and stayed away from the shingled roof, but that night she came up. I had been over the glass once when I saw her coming through the dormer window, skirt hem and white shoes lit by moonlight. Most of the insects were cleaned off and steam was drifting up into the night. She came through the window, took off her shoes, and edged down the roof until she was standing next to me at the star. "It's a beautiful night," she said.

"Cool."

"Dade, when you're up here do you ever think about what is in the mind of a great man when he makes a discovery?"

The night was just making its transition from the thin sky to the thick, the air was taking on weight, and at the horizon distances were shortening. I looked out over the plain and tried to think of an answer. That day I had been thinking about a story my father occasionally told. Just before he and my mother were married he took her to the top of the hills that surround Arcade. They stood with the New Jerusalem River, western California, and the sea on their left, and Arcade on their right. My father has always planned things well, and that day as they stood in the hill pass a thunderstorm covered everything west, while Arcade, shielded by hills, was lit by the sun. He asked her which way she wanted to go. She must have realized it was a test, because she thought for a moment and then looked to the right, and when they drove down from the hills that day my father mentioned the idea of a grocery. Star Food didn't open for a year after, but that was its conception, I think, in my father's mind. That afternoon as they stood with the New Jerusalem flowing below them, the plains before them, and my mother in a cotton skirt she had made herself, I think my father must have seen right through to the end of his life.

I had been trying to see right through to the end of my life, too, but these thoughts never led me in any direction. Sometimes I sat and remembered the unusual things that had happened to me. Once I had found the perfect, shed skin of a rattlesnake. My mother told my father that this indicated my potential for science. I was on the roof another time when it hailed apricot-size balls of ice on a summer afternoon. The day was hot and there was only one cloud, but as it approached from the distance it spread a shaft of darkness below it as if it had fallen through itself to the earth, and when it reached the New Jerusalem the river began throwing up spouts of water. Then it crossed onto land and I could see the hailstones denting parked cars. I went back inside the attic and watched it pass, and when I came outside again and picked up the ice balls that rolled between the corrugated roof spouts, their prickly edges melted in my fingers. In a minute they were gone. That was the rarest thing that had ever happened to me. Now I waited for rare things because it seemed to me that if you traced back the lives of men you arrived at some sort of sign, rainstorm at one horizon and sunlight at the other. On the roof I waited for mine. Sometimes I thought about the woman and sometimes I looked for silhouettes in the blue shapes between the clouds.

"Your father thinks you should be thinking about the store," said my mother.

"I know."

"You'll own the store some day."

There was a carpet of cirrus clouds in the distance, and we watched them as their bottom edges were gradually lit by the rising moon. My mother tilted back her head and looked up into the stars. "What beautiful names," she said. "Cassiopeia, Lyra, Aquila."

"The Big Dipper," I said.

"Dade?"

"Yes?"

"I saw the lady come in yesterday."

"I didn't chase her."

"I know."

"What do you think of that?"

"I think you're doing more important things," she said. "Dreams are more important than rye bread." She took the bobby pins from her hair and held them in her palm. "Dade, tell me the truth. What do you think about when you come up here?"

In the distance there were car lights, trees, aluminum power poles. There were several ways I could have answered.

I said, "I think I'm about to make a discovery."

After that my mother began meeting me at the bottom of the stairs when I came down from the roof. She smiled expectantly. I snapped my fingers, tapped my feet. I blinked and looked at my canvas shoe-tips. She kept smiling. I didn't like this so I tried not coming down for entire afternoons, but this only made her look more expectant. On the roof my thoughts piled into one another. I couldn't even think of something that was undiscovered. I stood and thought about the woman.

Then my mother began leaving little snacks on the sill

of the dormer window. Crackers, cut apples, apricots. She arranged them in fan shapes or twirls on a plate, and after a few days I started working regular hours again. I wore my smock and checked customers through the register and went upstairs only in the evenings. I came down after my mother had gone to sleep. I was afraid the woman was coming back, but I couldn't face my mother twice a day at the bottom of the stairs. So I worked and looked up at the door whenever customers entered. I did stock work when I could, stayed in back where the air was refrigerated, but I sweated anyway. I unloaded melons, tuna fish, cereal. I counted the cases of freeze-pops, priced the cans of All-American ham. At the swinging door between the stock-room and the back of the store my heart went dizzy. The woman knew something about me.

In the evenings on the roof I tried to think what it was. I saw mysterious new clouds, odd combinations of cirrus and stratus. How did she root me into the linoleum floor with her gray stare? Above me on the roof the sky was simmering. It was blue gas. I knew she was coming back.

೯

It was raining when she did. The door opened and I felt the wet breeze, and when I looked up she was standing with her back to me in front of the shelves of cheese and dairy, and this time I came out from the counter and stopped behind her. She smelled of the rain outside.

"Look," I whispered, "why are you doing this to me?"

She didn't turn around. I moved closer. I was gathering my words, thinking of the blue index card, when the idea of limited fame came into my head. I stopped. How did human beings understand each other across huge spaces except with the lowest of ideas? I have never understood what it is about rain that smells, but as I stood there behind the woman I suddenly realized I was smelling the inside of clouds. What was between us at that moment was an idea we had created ourselves. When she left with a carton of milk in her hand I couldn't speak.

૯

On the roof that evening I looked into the sky, out over the plains, along the uneven horizon. I thought of the view my father had seen when he was a young man. I wondered whether he had imagined Star Food then. The sun was setting. The blues and oranges were mixing into black, and in the distance windows were lighting up along the hillsides.

"Tell me what I want," I said then. I moved closer to the edge of the eaves and repeated it. I looked down over the alley, into the kitchens across the way, into living rooms, bedrooms, across slate rooftops. "Tell me what I want," I called. Cars pulled in and out of the parking lot. Big rigs rushed by on the interstate. The air around me was as cool as water, the lighted swimming pools like pieces of the daytime sky. An important moment seemed to be rushing up. "Tell me what I want," I said again.

Then I heard my father open the window and come out onto the roof. He walked down and stood next to me, the bald spot on top of his head reflecting the streetlight. He took out a cigarette, smoked it for a while, pinched off the end. A bird fluttered around the light pole across the street. A car crossed below us with the words JUST MARRIED on the roof.

"Look," he said, "your mother's tried to make me understand this." He paused to put the unsmoked butt back in the pack. "And maybe I can. You think the gal's a little down and out; you don't want to kick her when she's down. Okay, I can understand that. So I've decided something, and you want to know what?"

He shifted his hands in his pockets and took a few steps toward the edge of the roof.

"You want to know what?"

"What?"

"I'm taking you off the hook. Your mother says you've got a few thoughts, that maybe you're on the verge of something, so I decided it's okay if you let the lady go if she comes in again."

"What?"

"I said it's okay if you let the gal go. You don't have to chase her."

"You're going to let her steal?"

"No," he said. "I hired a guard."

૬

He was there the next morning in clothes that were all dark blue. Pants, shirt, cap, socks. He was only two or three years older than I was. My father introduced him to me as Mr. Sellers. "Mr. Sellers," he said, "this is Dade." He had a badge on his chest and a ring of keys the size of a doughnut on his belt. At the door he sat jingling them.

I didn't say much to him, and when I did my father came out from the back and counted register receipts or stocked impulse items near where he sat. We weren't saying anything important, though. Mr. Sellers didn't carry a gun, only the doughnut-size key ring, so I asked him if he wished he did.

"Sure," he said.

"Would you use it?"

"If I had to."

I thought of him using his gun if he had to. His hands were thick and their backs were covered with hair. This seemed to go along with shooting somebody if he had to. My hands were thin and white and the hair on them was like the hair on a girl's cheek.

During the days he stayed by the front. He smiled at customers and held the door for them, and my father brought him sodas every hour or so. Whenever the guard smiled at a customer I thought of him trying to decide whether he was looking at the shoplifter.

And then one evening everything changed.

I was on the roof. The sun was low, throwing slanted light. From beyond the New Jerusalem and behind the hills, four air force jets appeared. They disappeared, then appeared again, silver dots trailing white tails. They climbed and cut and looped back, showing dark and light like a school of fish. When they turned against the sun their wings flashed. Between the hills and the river they dipped low onto the plain, then shot upward and toward me. One dipped, the others followed. Across the New Jerusalem they turned back and made two great circles, one inside the other, then dipped again and leveled off in my direction. The sky seemed small enough for them to fall through. I could see the double tails, then the wings and the jets. From across the river they shot straight toward the store, angling up so I could see the V-wings and camouflage and rounded bomb bays, and I covered my ears, and in a moment they were across the water and then they were above me, and as they passed over they barrel-rolled and flew upside down and showed me their black cockpit glass so that my heart came up into my mouth.

I stood there while they turned again behind me and lifted back toward the hills, trailing threads of vapor, and by the time their booms subsided I knew I wanted the woman to be caught. I had seen a sign. Suddenly the sky was water-clear. Distances moved in, houses stood out against the hills, and it seemed to me that I had turned a corner and now looked over a rain-washed street. The woman was a thief. This was a simple fact and it presented itself to me simply. I felt the world dictating its course.

I went downstairs and told my father I was ready to

catch her. He looked at me, rolled the chewing gum in his cheek. "I'll be damned."

"My life is making sense," I said.

When I unloaded potato chips that night I laid the bags in the aluminum racks as if I were putting children to sleep in their beds. Dust had gathered under the lip of the vegetable bins, so I swept and mopped there and ran a wet cloth over the stalls. My father slapped me on the back a couple of times. In school once I had looked through a microscope at the tip of my own finger, and now as I looked around the store everything seemed to have been magnified in the same way. I saw cracks in the linoleum floor, speckles of color in the walls.

This kept up for a couple of days, and all the time I waited for the woman to come in. After a while it was more than just waiting; I looked forward to the day when she would return. In my eyes she would find nothing but resolve. How bright the store seemed to me then when I swept, how velvety the skins of the melons beneath the sprayer bottle. When I went up to the roof I scrubbed the star with the wet cloth and came back down. I didn't stare into the clouds and I didn't think about the woman except with the thought of catching her. I described her perfectly for the guard. Her gray eyes. Her plaid dress.

After I started working like this my mother began to go to the back room in the afternoons and listen to music. When I swept the rear I heard the melodies of operas. They came from behind the stockroom door while I waited for the woman to return, and when my mother came out she had a look about her of disappointment. Her skin was pale and smooth, as if the blood had run to deeper parts.

"Dade," she said one afternoon as I stacked tomatoes in a pyramid, "it's easy to lose your dreams."

"I'm just stacking tomatoes."

She went back to the register. I went back to stacking, and my father, who'd been patting me on the back, winking at me from behind the butcher counter, came over and helped me.

"I notice your mother's been talking to you."

"A little."

We finished the tomatoes and moved on to the lettuce.

"Look," he said, "it's better to do what you have to do, so I wouldn't spend your time worrying frontwards and backwards about everything. Your life's not so long as you think it's going to be."

We stood there rolling heads of butterball lettuce up the shallow incline of the display cart. Next to me he smelled like Aqua Velva.

"The lettuce is looking good," I said.

Then I went up to the front of the store. "I'm not sure what my dreams are," I said to my mother. "And I'm never going to discover anything. All I've ever done on the roof is look at the clouds."

Then the door opened and the woman came in. I was standing in front of the counter, hands in my pockets, my mother's eyes watering over, the guard looking out the window at a couple of girls, everything revolving around the point of calm that, in retrospect, precedes surprises. I'd been waiting for her for a week, and now she came in. I realized I never expected her. She stood looking at me, and for a few moments I looked back. Then she realized what I was up to. She turned around to leave, and when her back was to me I stepped over and grabbed her.

I've never liked fishing much, even though I used to go with my father, because the moment a fish jumps on my line a tree's length away in water I feel as if I've suddenly lost something. I'm always disappointed and sad, but now as I held the woman beneath the shoulder I felt none of this disappointment. I felt strong and good. She was thin, and I could make out the bones and tendons in her arm. As I led her back toward the stockroom, through the bread aisle, then the potato chips that were puffed and stacked like a row of pillows, I heard my mother begin to weep behind the register. Then my father came up behind me. I didn't turn around, but I knew he was there and I knew the deliberately calm way he was walking. "I'll be back as soon as I dust the melons," he said.

I held the woman tightly under her arm but despite this she moved in a light way, and suddenly, as we paused before the stockroom door, I felt as if I were leading her onto the dance floor. This flushed me with remorse. Don't spend your whole life looking backwards and forwards, I said to myself. Know what you want. I pushed the door open and we went in. The room was dark. It smelled of my whole life. I turned on the light and sat her down in the straight-back chair, then crossed the room and stood against the door. I had spoken to many children as they sat in this chair. I had frightened them, collected the candy they had tried to hide between the cushions, presented it to my father when he came in. Now I looked at the blue card. DO YOU KNOW WHAT YOU HAVE DONE? it said. DO YOU KNOW WHAT IT IS TO STEAL? I tried to think of what to say to the woman. She sat trembling slightly. I approached the chair and stood in front of her. She looked up at me. Her hair was gray around the roots.

"Do you want to go out the back?" I said.

She stood up and I took the key from under the silver samovar. My father would be there in a moment, so after I let her out I took my coat from the hook and followed. The evening was misty. She crossed the lot, and I hurried and came up next to her. We walked fast and stayed behind cars, and when we had gone a distance I turned and looked back. The stockroom door was closed. On the roof the star cast a pale light that whitened the aluminum-sided eaves.

It seemed we would be capable of a great communication now, but as we walked I realized I didn't know what to say to her. We went down the street without talking. The traffic was light, evening was approaching, and as we passed below some trees the streetlights suddenly came on. This moment has always amazed me. I knew the woman had seen it too, but it is always a disappointment to mention a thing like this. The streets and buildings took on their night shapes. Still we didn't say anything to each other. We kept walking beneath the pale violet of the lamps, and after a few more blocks I just stopped at one corner. She went on, crossed the street, and I lost sight of her.

I stood there until the world had rotated fully into the night, and for a while I tried to make myself aware of the spinning of the earth. Then I walked back toward the store. When they slept that night, my mother would dream of discovery and my father would dream of low-grade crooks. When I thought of this and the woman I was sad. It seemed you could never really know another person. I felt alone in the world, in the way that makes me aware of sound and temperature, as if I had just left a movie theater and stepped into an alley where a light rain was falling, and the wind was cool, and, from somewhere, other people's voices could be heard.

Dan Chaon

FITTING ENDS

There is a story about my brother Del which appears in a book called *More True Tales of the Weird and Supernatural.* The piece on Del is about three pages long, full of exclamation points and supposedly eerie descriptions. It is based on what the writer calls "true facts."

The writer spends much of the first few paragraphs setting the scene, trying to make it sound spooky. "The tiny, isolated village of Pyramid, Nebraska," is what the author calls the place where I grew up. I had never thought of it as a village. It wasn't much of anything, really—it wasn't even on the map, and hadn't been since my father was a boy, when it was a stop on the Union Pacific railroad line. Back then, there was a shantytown for the railroad workers, a dance hall, a general store, a post office. By the time I was growing up, all that was left was a cluster of mostly boarded-up, run-down houses. My family—my parents and grandparents and my brother and me—lived in the only occupied buildings. There was a grain elevator, which my grandfather had run until he retired and my father took over. "PYRAMID" was painted in peeling block letters on one of the silos.

The man who wrote the story got fixated on that elevator. He talks of it as "a menacing, hulking structure" and says it is like "Childe Roland's ancient dark tower, presiding over the barren fields and empty, sentient houses." He even goes so far as to mention "the soundless flutter of bats flying in and out of the single, eyelike window at the top of the elevator," and "the distant, melancholy calls of coyotes from the hills beyond," which are then drowned out by "the strange echoing moan of a freight train as it passes in the night."

There really are bats, of course; you find them in every country place. Personally, I never heard coyotes, though it is true they were around. I saw one once when I was about twelve. I was staring from my bedroom window late one night and there he was. He had come down from the hills and was crouched in our yard, licking drops of water off the propeller of the sprinkler. As for the trains, they passed through about every half-hour, day and night. If you lived there, you didn't even hear them—or maybe only half-heard them, the way, now that I live in a town, I might vaguely notice the bells of the nearby Catholic church at noon.

But anyway, this is how the writer sets things up. Then he begins to tell about some of the train engineers, how they dreaded passing through this particular stretch. He quotes one man as saying he got goosebumps every time he started to come up on Pyramid. "There was just something about that place," says this man. There were a few bad accidents at the crossing—a carload of drunken teenagers who tried to beat the train, an old guy who had a heart attack as his pickup bumped across the tracks. That sort of thing. Actually, this happens anywhere that has a railroad crossing.

Then came the sightings. An engineer would see "a figure" walking along the tracks in front of the train, just beyond the Pyramid elevator. The engineer would blow his horn, but the person, "the figure," would seem not to notice. The engineer blasted the horn several more times, more and more insistent. But the person kept walking; pretty soon the train's headlights glared onto a tall, muscular boy with shaggy dark hair and a green fatigue jacket. They tried to brake the train, but is was too late. The boy suddenly fell to his knees, and the engineer was certain he'd hit him. But of course, when the train was stopped, they could find nothing. "Not a trace," says our author. This happened to three different engineers; three different incidents in a two-year period.

You can imagine the ending, of course: that was how my brother died, a few years after these supposed sightings began. His car had run out of gas a few miles from home, and he was walking back. He was drunk. Who knows why he was walking along the tracks? Who knows why he suddenly kneeled down? Maybe he stumbled, or had to throw up. Maybe he did it on purpose. He was killed instantly.

The whole ghost stuff came out afterward. One of the engineers who'd seen the "ghost" recognized Del's picture in the paper, and came forward or something. I always believed it was made up. It was stupid, I always thought, like a million campfire stories you'd heard or some cheesy program on TV. But the author of *More True Tales of the Weird and Supernatural* found it "spine-tingling." "The strange story of the boy whose ghost appeared—two years before he died!" says a line on the back cover.

૬

This happened when I was fourteen. My early brush with tragedy, I guess you could call it, though by the time I was twenty-one I felt I had recovered. I didn't think the incident had shaped my life in any particular way, and in fact I'd sometimes find myself telling the story, ghost and all, to girls I met at fraternity parties. I'd take a girl up to my room, show her the *True Tales* book. We'd smoke some marijuana and talk about it, my voice taking on an intensity and heaviness that surprised both of us. From time to time, we'd end up in bed. I remember this one girl, Lindsey, telling me how moved she was by the whole thing. It gave me, she said, a Heathcliff quality; I had turned brooding and mysterious; the wheat fields had turned to moors. "I'm not mysterious," I said, embarrassed, and later, after we'd parted ways, she agreed. "I thought you were different," she said, "deeper." She cornered me one evening when I was talking to another girl and wanted to know if I wasn't a little ashamed, using my dead brother to get laid. She said that she had come to realize that I, like Heathcliff, was just another jerk.

6

After that, I stopped telling the story for a while. There would be months when I wouldn't speak of my brother at all, and even when I was home in Pyramid, I could spend my whole vacation without once mentioning Del's name. My parents never spoke of him, at least not with me.

Of course, this only made him more present than ever. He hovered there as I spoke of college, my future, my life, my father barely listening. When we would argue, my father would stiffen sullenly, and I knew he was thinking of arguments he'd had with Del. I could shout at him, and nothing would happen. He'd stare as I tossed some obscene word casually toward him, and I'd feel it rattle and spin like a coin I'd flipped on the table in front of him. But he wouldn't say anything.

I actually wondered, back then, why they put up with this sort of thing. It was surprising, even a little unnerving, especially given my father's temper when I was growing up, the old violence-promising glares that once made my bones feel like wax, the ability he formerly had to make me flinch with a gesture or a well-chosen phrase.

Now I was their only surviving child, and I was gone—more thoroughly gone than Del was, in a way. I'd driven off to college in New York, and it was clear I wasn't ever coming back. Even my visits became shorter and shorter—summer trimmed down from three months to less than two weeks over the course of my years at college; at Christmas, I'd stay on campus after finals, wandering the emptying passageways of my residence hall, loitering in the student center, my hands clasped behind my back, staring at the ragged bulletin boards as if they were paintings in a museum. I found excuses to keep from going back. And then, when I got there, finally, I was just another ghost.

ɕ

About a year before he died, Del saved my life. It was no big deal, I thought. It was summer, trucks were coming to the grain elevator, and my brother and I had gone up to the roof to fix a hole. The elevator was flat on top, and when I was little I used to imagine that being up there was like being in the turret of a lighthouse. I used to stare out over the expanse of prairie, across the fields and their flotsam of machinery, cattle, men, over the rooftops of houses, along the highways and railroad tracks that trailed off into the horizon. When I was small, this would fill me with wonder. My father would stand there with me, holding my hand, and the wind would ripple our clothes.

I was thinking of this, remembering, when I suddenly started to do a little dance. I didn't know why I did such things: my father said that ever since I started junior high school I'd been like a "-holic" of some sort, addicted to making an ass out of myself. Maybe this was true, because I started to caper around, and Del said, "I'd laugh if you fell, you idiot," stern and condescending, as if *I* were the juvenile delinquent. I ignored him. With my back turned to him, I began to sing "Ain't No Mountain High Enough" in a deep corny voice like my father's. I'd never been afraid of heights, and I suppose I was careless. Too close to the edge, I slipped, and my brother caught my arm.

I was never able to recall exactly what happened in

that instant. I remember being surprised by the sound that came from my throat, a high scream like a rabbit's that seemed to ricochet downward, a stone rattling through a long drainpipe. I looked up and my brother's mouth was wide open, as if he'd made the sound. The tendons on his neck stood out.

I told myself that if I'd been alone, nothing would have happened. I would've just teetered a little, then gained my balance again. But when my brother grabbed me, I lost my equilibrium, and over the edge I went. There were a dozen trucks lined up to have their loads weighed, and all the men down there heard that screech, looked up startled to see me dangling there with two hundred feet between me and the ground. They all watched Del yank me back up to safety.

I was on the ground before it hit me. Harvesters were getting out of their trucks and ambling toward us, and I could see my father pushing his way through the crowd. It was then that my body took heed of what had happened. The solid earth kept opening up underneath me, and Del put his arm around me as I wobbled. Then my father loomed. He got hold of me, clenching my shoulders, shaking me. "My sore neck!" I cried out. "Dad, my neck!" The harvesters' faces jittered, pressing closer, I could see a man in sunglasses with his black, glittering eyes fixed on me.

"Del pushed me," I cried out as my father's gritted teeth came toward my face. Tears slipped suddenly out of my eyes. "Del pushed me, Dad! It wasn't my fault."

૬

My father had good reason to believe this lie, even though he and some twelve or more others had been witness to my singing and careless prancing up there. The possibility still existed that Del might have given me a shove from behind. My father didn't want to believe Del was capable of such a thing. But he knew he was.

Del had only been back home for about three weeks. Prior to that, he'd spent several months in a special program for juvenile delinquents. The main reason for this was that he'd become so belligerent, so violent, that my parents didn't feel they could control him. He'd also, over the course of things, stolen a car.

For much of the time that my brother was in this program, I wore a neck brace. He'd tried to strangle me the night before he was sent away. He claimed he'd seen me smirking at him, though actually I was only thinking of something funny I'd seen on TV. Del was the farthest thing from my thoughts until he jumped on me. If my father hadn't separated us, Del probably would have choked me to death.

This was one of the things that my father must have thought of. He must have remembered the other times that Del might have killed me: the time when I was twelve and he threw a can of motor oil at my head when my back was turned; the time when I was seven and he pushed me off the tailgate of a moving pickup, where my father had let us sit when he was driving slowly down a dirt road. My father was as used to hearing these horror stories as I was to telling them.

Though he was only three and a half years older than I, Del was much larger. He was much bigger than I'll ever be, and I was just starting to realize that. Six-foot-three, two-hundred-twenty-pound defensive back, my father used to tell people when he spoke of Del. My father used to believe that Del would get a football scholarship to the state university. Never mind that once he started high school he wouldn't even play on the team. Never mind that all he seemed to want to do was vandalize people's property and drink beer and cause problems at home. My father still talked about it like there was some hope.

When my brother got out of his program, he told us

that things would be different from now on. He had changed, he said, and he swore that he would make up for the things that he'd done. I gave him a hug. He stood there before us, with his hands clasped behind his back, posed like the famous orator whose picture was in the library of our school. We all smiled, the visions of the horrible family fights wavering behind our friendly expressions.

&

So here was another one, on the night of my almost-death.

Before very long my brother had started crying. I hadn't seen him actually shed tears in a very long time; he hadn't even cried on the day he was sent away.

"He's a liar," my brother shouted. We had all been fighting and carrying on for almost an hour. I had told my version of the story five or six times, getting better at it with each repetition. I could have almost believed it myself. "You fucking liar," my brother screamed at me. "I wish I had pushed you. I'd never save your ass now." He stared at me suddenly, wild-eyed, like I was a dark shadow that was bending over his bed when he woke at night. Then he sat down at the kitchen table. He put his face in his hands, and his shoulders began to shudder.

Watching him—this giant, broad-shouldered boy, my brother, weeping—I could have almost taken it back. The whole lie, I thought, the words I spoke at first came out of nowhere, sprang to my lips as a shield against my father's red face and bared teeth, his fingernails cutting my shoulder as everyone watched. It was really my father's fault. I could have started crying myself.

But looking back on it, I have to admit that there was something else, too—a heat at the core of my stomach, spreading through my body like a stain. It made my skin throb, my face a mask of innocence and defiance. I sat there looking at him, and put my hand to my throat. After years of being on the receiving end, it wasn't in my nature to see Del as someone who could be wronged, as someone to feel pity for. This was something Del could have done, I thought. It was not so unlikely.

૬

At first, I thought it would end with my brother leaving, barreling out of the house with the slamming of doors and the circling whine of the fan belt in my father's old beater pickup, the muffler retorting all the way down the long dirt road, into the night. Once, when he was drunk, my brother had tried to drive his truck off a cliff on the hill out behind our house. But the embankment wasn't steep enough, and the truck just went bump, bump down the side of the hill, all four wheels staying on the ground until it finally came to rest in the field below. Del had pointed a shotgun at my father that night, and my father was so stunned and upset that my mother thought he was having a heart attack. She was running around hysterical, calling police, ambulance, bawling. In the distance, Del went up the hill, down the hill, up, down. You could hear him revving the motor. It felt somehow like one of those slapstick moments in a comedy movie, where everything is falling down at once and all the actors run in and out of doorways. I sat, shivering, curled up on the couch while all this was going on, staring at the television.

But the night after I'd almost fallen, my brother did not try to take off. We all knew that if my parents had to call the police on him again, it would be the end. He would go to a foster home or even back to the juvenile hall, which he said was worse than prison. So instead, he and my father were in a shoving match; there was my mother between them screaming, "Oh, stop it I can't stand it I can't stand it," turning her deadly, red-eyed stare abruptly upon me; there was my brother crying. But he didn't try to leave. He just sat there, with his face in his hands. "God damn all of you," he cried suddenly. "I hate all your guts. I wish I was fucking dead."

My father hit him then, hit him with the flat of his hand alongside the head, and Del tilted in his chair with the force of it. He made a small, high-pitched sound, and I watched as he folded his arms over his ears as my father descended on him, a blow, a pause, a blow, a pause. My father stood over him, breathing hard. A tear fell from Del's nose.

"Don't you ever say that," my father roared. "Don't you dare ever say that." He didn't mean the f-word—he meant wishing you were dead, the threats Del had made in the past. That was the worst thing, my father had told us once, the most terrible thing a person could do. My father's hands fell to his sides. I saw that he was crying also.

After a time, Del lifted his head. He seemed to have calmed—everything seemed to have grown quiet, a dull, wavery throb of static. I saw that he looked at me. I slumped my shoulders, staring down at my fingernails.

"You lie," Del said softly. "You can't even look me in the face." He got up and stumbled a few steps, as if my father would go after him again. But my father just stood there.

"Get out of my sight," he said. "Go on."

I heard Del's tennis shoes thump up the stairs, the slam of our bedroom door. But just as I felt my body start to untense, my father turned to me. He wiped the heel of his hand over his eyes, gazing at me without blinking. After all of Del's previous lies, his denials, his betrayals, you would think they would never believe his side of things again. But I could see a slowly creaking hinge of doubt behind my father's expression. I looked down.

"If I ever find out you're lying to me, boy," my father said.

He didn't ever find out. The day I almost fell was another one of those things we never got around to talking about again. It probably didn't seem very significant to my parents in the span of events that had happened before and came after. They dwelt on other things.

On what, I never knew. My wife found this unbelievable: "Didn't they say anything after he died?" she asked me, and I had to admit that I didn't remember. They were sad, I told her. I recalled my father crying. But they were country people. I tried to explain this to my wife, good Boston girl that she is, the sort of impossible grief that is like something gnarled and stubborn and underground. I never really believed it myself. For years, I kept expecting things to go back to normal, waiting for whatever was happening to them to finally be over.

My parents actually became quite mellow in the last years of their lives. My mother lost weight, was often ill. Eventually, shortly after her sixtieth birthday, she went deaf. Her hearing slipped away quickly, like a skin she was shedding, and all the tests proved inconclusive. That was the year that my son was born. In January, when my wife discovered that she was pregnant, my parents were in the process of buying a fancy, expensive hearing aid. By the time the baby was four months old, the world was completely soundless for my mother, hearing aid or not.

The problems of my college years had passed away by that time. I was working at a small private college in upstate New York, in alumni relations. My wife and I seldom went back to Nebraska; we couldn't afford the money at the time. But I talked to my parents regularly on the phone, once or twice a month.

We ended up going back that Christmas after Ezra was born. My mother's letters had made it almost impossible to avoid. "It breaks my heart that I can't hear my grandson's voice, now that he is making his little sounds," she had written. "But am getting by O.K. and will begin lip-reading classes in Denver after Xmas. It will be easier for me then." She would get on the phone when I called my father. "I can't hear you talking but I love you," she'd say.

"We have to work to make her feel involved in things," my father told us as we drove from the airport, where he'd picked us up. "The worst thing is that they start feeling isolated," he told us. "We got little pads so we can write her notes." He looked over at me, strangely academic-looking in the new glasses he had for driving. In the last few years he had begun to change, his voice turning slow and gentle, as if he was watching something out in the distance beyond the window, or something sad and mysterious on TV as we talked. His former short temper had vanished away, leaving only a soft reproachfulness in its place. But even that was muted. He knew that he couldn't really make me feel guilty. "You know how she is," he said to my wife and me, though of course we did not, either one of us, really know her. "You know how she is. The hardest part is, you know, we don't want her to get depressed."

She looked awful. Every time I saw her since I graduated from college, this stunned me. I came in, carrying my sleeping son, and she was sitting at the kitchen table, her spine curved a little bit more than the last time, thinner, so skinny that her muscles seemed to stand out against the bone. Back in New York, I worked with alumni ladies older than she who played tennis, who dressed in trendy clothes, who walked with a casual and still sexy ease. These women wouldn't look like my mother for another twenty years, if ever. I felt my smile pull awkwardly on my face.

"Hello!" I called, but of course she didn't look up. My father flicked on the porch light. "She hates it when you surprise her," he said softly, as if there were still some possibility of her overhearing. My wife looked over at me. Her eyes said that this was going to be another holiday that was like work for her.

My mother lifted her head. Her shrewdness was still intact, at least, and she was ready for us the moment the porch light hit her consciousness. That terrible, monkey-ish dullness seemed to lift from her expression as she looked up.

"Well, howdy," she called, in the same jolly, slightly ironic way she always did when she hadn't seen me in a long time. She came over to hug us, then peered down at Ezra, who stirred a little as she pushed back his parka hood to get a better look. "Oh, what an angel," she whispered. "It's about killed me, not being able to see this boy." Then she stared down at Ezra again. How he'd grown, she told us. She thought he looked like me, she said, and I was relieved. Actually, I'd begun to think that Ezra somewhat resembled the pictures I'd seen of Del as a baby. But my mother didn't say that, at least.

I had planned to have a serious talk with them on this trip. Or maybe "planned" is the wrong word—"considered" might be closer, though even that doesn't express the vague, unpleasantly anxious urge that I could feel at the back of my neck. I didn't really know what I wanted to know. And the truth was, these quiet, fragile, distantly tender people bore little resemblance to the mother and father in my mind. It had been ten years since I'd lived at home. Ten years!—which filled the long, snowy evenings with a numbing politeness. My father sat in his easy chair, after dinner, watching the news. My wife read. My mother and I did the dishes together, silently, nodding as the plate she had rinsed passed from her hand to mine, to be dried and put away. When a train passed, the little window above the sink vibrated, humming like a piece of cellophane. But she did not notice this.

We did have a talk of sorts that trip, my father and I. It was on the third day after our arrival, a few nights before Christmas Eve. My wife and my mother were both asleep. My father and I sat out on the closed-in porch, drinking beer, watching the snow drift across the yard, watching the wind send fingers of snow slithering along low to the ground. I had drunk more than he had. I saw him glance sharply at me for a second when I came back from the refrigerator a fourth time and popped open the can. But the look faded quickly. Outside, beyond the window, I could see the blurry shape of the elevator through the falling snow, its outlines indistinct, wavering like a mirage.

"Do you remember that time," I said, "when I almost fell off the elevator?"

It came out like that, abrupt, stupid. As I sat there in my father's silence, I realized how impossible it was, how useless to try to patch years of ellipsis into something resembling dialogue. I looked down, and he cleared his throat.

"Sure," he said at last, noncommittal. "Of course I remember."

"I think about that sometimes," I said. Drunk—I felt the alcohol edge into my voice as I spoke. "It seems," I said, "significant." That was the word that came to me. "It seems significant sometimes," I said.

My father considered this for a while. He stiffened formally, as if he were being interviewed. "Well," he said, "I don't know. There were so many things like that. It was all a mess by then, anyway. Nothing could be done. It was too late for anything to be done." He looked down to his own beer, which must have gone warm by that time, and took a sip. "It should have been taken care of earlier—when you were kids. That's where I think things must have gone wrong. I was too hard on you both. But Del—I was harder on him. He was the oldest. Too much pressure. Expected too much."

He drifted off at that, embarrassed. We sat there, and I could not even imagine what he meant—what specifics he was referring to. What pressure? What expectations? But I didn't push any further.

"But you turned out all right," my father said. "You've done pretty well, haven't you?"

୬

There were no signs in our childhood, no incidents pointing the way to his eventual end. None that I could see, at least, and I thought about it quite a bit after his death. "It should have been taken care of earlier," my father said, but what was "it"? Del seemed to have been happy, at least up until high school.

Maybe things happened when they were alone together. From time to time, I remember Del coming back from helping my father in the shop with his eyes red from crying. Once I remember our father coming into our room on a Saturday morning and cuffing the top of Del's sleeping head with the back of his hand: he had stepped in dog dirt on the lawn. The dog was Del's responsibility. Del must have been about eight or nine at the time, and I remember him kneeling on our bedroom floor in his pajamas, crying bitterly as he cleaned off my father's boot. When I told that story later on, I was pleased by the ugly, almost fascist overtones it had. I remember recounting it to some college friends—handsome, suburban kids—lording this little bit of squalor from my childhood over them. Child abuse and family violence were enjoying a media vogue at that time, and I found I could mine this memory to good effect. In the version I told, I was the one cleaning the boots.

But the truth was, my father was never abusive in an especially spectacular way. He was more like a simple bully, easily eluded when he was in a short-tempered mood. He used to get so furious when we avoided him. I recall how he used to grab us by the hair on the back of our necks, tilting our heads so we looked into his face. "You don't listen," he would hiss. "I want you to look at me when I talk to you." That was about the worst of it, until Del started getting into trouble. And by that time, my father's blows weren't enough. Del would laugh, he would strike back. It was then that my father finally decided to turn him over to the authorities. He had no other choice, he said.

He must have believed it. He wasn't, despite his temper, a bad man, a bad parent. He'd seemed so kindly, sometimes, so fatherly—especially with Del. I remember watching them from my window, some autumn mornings, watching them wade through the high weeds in the stubblefield out behind our house, walking toward the hill with their shotguns pointing at the ground, their steps slow, synchronized. Once I'd gone upstairs and heard them laughing in Del's and my bedroom. I just stood there outside the doorway, watching as my father and Del put a model ship together, sharing the job, their talk easy, happy.

This was what I thought of, that night we were talking. I thought of my own son, the innocent baby I loved so much, and it chilled me to think that things could change so much—that Del's closeness to my father could turn in on itself, transformed into the kind of closeness that thrived on their fights, on the different ways Del could push my father into a rage. That finally my father would feel he had no choices left. We looked at each other, my father and I. "What are you thinking?" I said softly, but he just shook his head.

Del and I had never been close. We had never been like friends, or even like brothers. Yet after that day on the elevator I came to realize that there had been something between us. There had been something that could be taken away.

He stopped talking to me altogether for a while. In the weeks and months that followed my lie, I doubt if we even looked at each other more than two or three times, though we shared the same room.

For a while I slept on the couch. I was afraid to go up to our bedroom. I can remember those first few nights, waiting in the living room for my father to go to bed, the television hissing with laughter. The furniture, the table, the floors, seemed to shudder as I touched them, as if they were just waiting for the right moment to burst apart.

I'd go outside, sometimes, though that was really no better. It was the period of late summer when thunderstorms seemed to pass over every night. The wind came up. The shivering tops of trees bent in the flashes of heat lightening.

There was no way out of the situation I'd created. I could see that. Days and weeks stretched out in front of me, more than a month before school started. By that time, I thought, maybe it would all blow over. Maybe it would melt into the whole series of bad things that had happened, another layer of paint that would eventually be covered over by a new one, forgotten.

If he really had pushed me, that was what would have happened. It would have been like the time he tried to choke me, or the time he tried to drive the car off the hill. Once those incidents were over, there was always the possibility that this was the last time. There was always the hope that everything would be better, now.

In retrospect, it wouldn't have been so hard to recant. There would have been a big scene, of course. I would have been punished, humiliated. I would have had to endure my brother's triumph, my parents' disgust. But I realize now that it wouldn't have been so bad.

I might have finally told the truth, too, if Del had reacted the way I expected. I imagined that there would be a string of confrontations in the days that followed, that he'd continue to protest with my father. I figured he wouldn't give up.

But he did. After that night, he didn't try to deny it anymore. For a while, I even thought that maybe he had begun to believe that he pushed me. He acted like a guilty person, eating his supper in silence, walking noiselessly through the living room, his shoulders hunched like a traveler on a snowy road.

My parents seemed to take this as penitence. They still spoke sternly, but their tone began to be edged by gentleness, a kind of forgiveness. "Did you take out the trash?" they would ask. "Another potato?"—and they would wait for him to quickly nod. He was truly sorry, they thought. Everything was finally going to be okay. He was shaping up.

At these times, I noticed something in his eyes—a kind of sharpness, a subtle shift of the iris. He would lower his head, and the corners of his mouth would move slightly. To me, his face seemed to flicker with hidden, mysterious thoughts.

When I finally began to sleep in our room again, he pretended I wasn't there. I would come in, almost as quiet as he himself had become, to find him sitting at our desk or on his bed, peeling off a sock with such slow concentration that it might have been his skin. It was as if there were an unspoken agreement between us—I no longer existed. He wouldn't look at me, but I could watch him for as long as I wanted. I would pull the covers over myself and just lie there, observing, as he went about doing whatever he was doing as if oblivious. He listened to a tape on his headphones; flipped through a magazine; did sit-ups; sat staring out the window; turned out the light. And all that time his face remained neutral, impassive. Once, he even chuckled to himself at a book he was reading, a paperback anthology of "The Far Side" cartoons.

When I was alone in the room, I found myself looking through his things, with an interest I'd never had before. I ran my fingers over his models, the monster-wheeled trucks and the B-10 bombers. I flipped through his collection of tapes. I found some literature he'd brought home from the detention center, brochures with titles like "Teens and Alcohol: What You Should Know!" and "Rap Session, Talking about Feelings." Underneath this stuff, I found the essay he'd been working on.

He had to write an essay so that they would let him back into high school. There was a letter from the guidance counselor, explaining the school's policy, and then there were several sheets of notebook paper with his handwriting on them. He'd scratched out lots of words, sometimes whole paragraphs. In the margins, he'd written little notes to himself: "(sp.)" or "?" or "No." He wrote in scratchy block letters.

His essay told of the Outward Bound program. "I had embarked on a sixty day rehabilitation program in the form of a wilderness survival course name of Outward Bound," he had written. "THESIS: The wilderness has allowed for me to reach deep inside my inner self and grasp ahold of my morals and values that would set the standard and tell the story of the rest of my life."

I would go into our room when my brother was out and take the essay out of the drawer where he'd hidden it. He was working on it, off and on, all that month; I'd flip it open to discover new additions or deletions—whole paragraphs appearing as if overnight. I never saw him doing it.

The majority of the essay was a narrative describing

their trip. They had hiked almost two hundred miles, he said. "Up by sun and down by moon," he wrote. There were obstacles they had to cross. Once, they had to climb down a hundred-foot cliff. "The repelling was very exciting but also scarey," he'd written. "This was meant to teach us trust and confidence in ourselves as well as our teammates, they said. Well as I reached the peak of my climb I saw to my despair that the smallest fellow in the group was guiding my safety rope. Now he was no more than one hundred and ten pounds and I was tipping the scales at about two twenty five needless to say I was reluctant."

But they made it. I remember reading this passage several times; it seemed very vivid in my mind. In my imagination, I was in the place of the little guy holding the safety rope. I saw my brother hopping lightly, bit by bit, down the sheer face of the cliff to the ground below, as if he could fly, as if there were no gravity anymore.

"My experience with the Outward Bound program opened my eyes to such values as friendship, trust, responsibility and sharing," Del wrote in his conclusion. "Without the understanding of these I would not exist as I do now but would probably instead be another statistic. With these values I will purely succeed. Without I would surely fail." Next to this he'd written: "Sounds like bullshit (?)".

I don't know that I recognized that distinct ache that I felt on reading this, or understood why his sudden distance, the silent, moody aura he trailed after him in those weeks should have affected me in such a way. Years later, I would recall that feeling—standing over my son's crib, a dark shape leaning over him as he stirred with dreams—waiting at the window for the headlights of my wife's car to turn into our driveway. That sad, trembly feeling was a species of love—or at least of symptom of it.

I thought of this a long time after the fact. I loved my brother, I thought. Briefly.

୭

None of this lasted. By the time he died, a year later, he'd worked his way back to his normal self, or a slightly modified, moodier version. Just like before, money had begun to disappear from my mother's purse; my parents searched his room for drugs. He and my father had argued that morning about the friends he was hanging around with, about his wanting to take the car every night. Del claimed that he was dating a girl, said he only wanted to see a movie in town. He'd used that one before, often lying ridiculously when he was asked the next day about the plot of the film. I remember him telling my mother that the war film *Apocalypse Now* was set in the future, which I knew was not true from an article I'd read in the paper. I remember making some comment in reference to this as he was getting ready to go out, and he looked at me in that careful, hooded way, reminiscent of the time when he was pretending I didn't exist. "Eat shit and die, Stewart," he murmured, without heat. Unfortunately, I believe that this was the last thing he ever said to me.

Afterward, his friends said that he had seemed like he was in a good mood. They had all been in his car, my father's car, driving up and down the main street in Scottsbluff. They poured a little rum into their cans of Coke, cruising from one end of town to the other, calling out the window at a carful of passing teenage girls, revving the engine at the stoplights. He wasn't that drunk, they said.

I used to imagine that there was a specific moment when he realized that he was going to die. I don't believe he knew it when he left our house, or even at the beginning of his car ride with his friends. If that were true, I have to assume that there would have been a sign, some gesture or expression, something one of us would have noticed. If it was planned, then why on that particular, insignificant day?

Yet I wondered. I used to think of him in his friend Sully's car, listening to his buddies laughing, making dumb jokes, running red lights. It might have been sometime around then, I thought. Time seemed to slow down. He would sense a long, billowing delay in the spaces between words; the laughing faces of the girls in a passing car would seem to pull by forever, their expressions frozen.

Or I thought about his driving home. I could see the heavy, foglike darkness of those country roads, the shadows of weeds springing up when the headlights touched them, I could imagine the halt and sputter of the old pickup as the gas ran out, that moment when you can feel the power lift up out of the machine like a spirit. It's vivid enough in my mind that it's almost as if I was with him as the pickup rolled lifelessly on—slowing, then stopping at last on the shoulder where it would be found the next day, the emergency lights still blinking dimly. He and I stepped out into the thick night air, seeing the shape of the elevator in the distance, above the tall sunflowers and pigweed. And though we knew we were outdoors, it felt like we were inside something. The sky seemed to close down on us like the lid of a box.

No one in my family ever used the word "suicide." When we referred to Del's death, if we referred to it, we spoke of "the accident." To the best of our knowledge, that's what it was.

૬

There was a time, right before I left for college, when I woke from a dream to the low wail of a passing train. I could see it when I sat up in bed—through the branches of trees outside my window I could see the boxcars, shuffling through flashes of heat lightning, trailing past the elevator and into the distance, rattling, rattling.

And there was another time, my senior year in college, when I saw a kid who looked like Del coming out of a bar, a boy melting into the crowded, carnival atmosphere of this particular strip of saloons and dance clubs where students went on a Saturday night. I followed this person a few blocks before I lost sight of him. All those cheerful, drunken faces seemed to loom as I passed by them, blurring together like an expressionist painting. I leaned against a wall, breathing.

And there was that night when we came to Pyramid with my infant son, the night my father and I stayed up talking. I sat there in the dark, long after he'd gone to bed, finishing another beer. I remember looking up to see my mother moving through the kitchen, at first only clearly seeing the billowy whiteness of her nightgown hovering in the dark, a shape floating slowly through the kitchen toward me. I had a moment of fear before I realized it was her. She did not know I was there. She walked slowly, delicately, thinking herself alone in this room at night. I would have had to touch her to let her know that I was there, and that would have probably startled her badly. So I didn't move. I watched as she lit a cigarette and sat down at the kitchen table, her head turned toward the window, where snow was still falling. She watched it drift down. I heard her breathe smoke, exhaling in a long, thoughtful sigh. She was remembering something, I thought.

෴

It was at these moments that everything seemed clear to me. I felt that I could take all the loose ends of my life and fit them together perfectly, as easily as a writer could write a spooky story, where all the details add up and you know the end even before the last sentence. This would make a good ending, you think at such moments. You'll go on living, of course. But at the same time you recognize, in that brief flash of clarity and closure, you realize that everything is summed up. It's not really worth becoming what there is left for you to become.

Generations

Li-Young Lee

I Ask My Mother to Sing

She begins, and my grandmother joins her.
Mother and daughter sing like young girls.
If my father were alive, he would play
his accordion and sway like a boat.

I've never been in Peking, or the Summer Palace,
nor stood on the great Stone Boat to watch
the rain begin on Kuen Ming Lake, the picnickers
running away in the grass.

But I love to hear it sung;
how the waterlilies fill with rain until
they overturn, spilling water into water,
then rock back, and fill with more.

Both women have begun to cry.
But neither stops her song.

Thom Tammaro

Innocent Traveler

There was a great storm in the mountains of central Italy that night. Thunder shook the ground, trees trembled, lightning lit up the sky. Rain fell, unrelenting, for hours, making the steep paths slippery and treacherous. In a farmhouse high above the village, a young woman begged her father and mother to offer her suitor the barn for the night. Reluctantly, they agreed and the young man covered himself in straw, slept dry and safe among barn animals, until morning light.

Coming down the mountain path the next morning, the young man came upon a circle of villagers huddled around the stiff, soaked corpse of a young man. Fingers pointed to bullet holes, one in the side of his head and another just above the heart. The dead man's eyes were wide open until someone forced their lids closed for the last time. Later, the murderer was arrested and confessed to the killing, but said the bullets were meant for the young man who courted the woman who lived in the farmhouse high above the village. Two days later the campanile bells echoed above the village where peasants mourned the tragedy of the innocent traveler.

A few years later, the young man and woman were married, and shortly thereafter boarded a ship in Naples and sailed to America. This was 1907. Their youngest daughter was born in 1924, and nine years later the mother died from a brain tumor. And sometime later I became the second child of the youngest daughter and her husband.

This afternoon, coming home through the rain, I remember this story and feel the sanctity of my life. How our coming into this world is precarious, our stay tenuous, our going definite. And so I thank the rain. And I thank the barn animals and the straw that kept my grandfather warm and dry through the night. I am even moved to thank the desperate lover and his jealousy. But most of all I thank the innocent traveler coming down the mountain path in the dark, stepping into my life, unaware of what lay ahead in unrelenting rain.

Penny Harter

THE OLD MAN WHO LOVES BICYCLES

The old man who loves bicycles lives alone in a small gray bungalow. He spends hours polishing his family of seven bicycles: two tiny, four of various middle size (one with balloon tires), and one built-for-two. Daily he takes them outside, turns them upside down, and spins their wheels in the sunlight. Summertime, he eats all his meals with them at his homemade picnic table. Each evening when it is time to sleep he brings them inside his double-length garage and tenderly covers their wheels with old towels—for warmth, for company, and to keep the spiders from starting webs among their spokes. Then he counts them and says good-night.

The local paper decides to feature him. He has offered to repair neighborhood children's bicycles free, and has even given away some bicycles he's rebuilt from old parts. "Why do you love bicycles so?" the young reporter asks him one bright autumn morning out in the back yard as he runs around following the man from bicycle to bicycle, watching him spin their wheels.

"Because of the light," the old man explains, waving an arthritic hand toward the circus of flashing spokes. "And because we go places. We go places!" And he smiles at the reporter and spins around on one foot in the withering grass.

Michael S. Glaser

Preparations for Seder

> *"Therefore, even if all of us were wise, all of us people of understanding, all of us learned in Torah, it would still be our obligation to tell the story of the exodus from Egypt, for redemption is not yet complete."*
>
> —The Haggadah

Preparing schmaltz for matzo balls,
I peel the skin off chickens, scrape yellow fat
from pink meat, think of my father: how he stood
at the elbow of his mother, eating the "cracklings"
she'd hand down from the stove, morsels of meat
fried free of the fat, as she rendered schmaltz
years ago, in Boston.

Today, preparing for Seder, I think of Grandmother
as I salvage these tasty cracklings, relish them
for myself, hand them to my children as I cut more
and more fat from the chicken: how much harder
for her, hot before the wood stove, peeling bits
of fat from the muscle of chickens that ran
free in the yard.

Now the fat is plentiful, preserved with chemicals.
The echo of my father's voice calls out warnings
of carcinogens in the fat of animals and I wonder
what I am doing to myself, my children. But this
is the eve of Passover. I am making matzo balls.

My knife plunges under the skin for more fat.
I will not forsake the traditions of my ancestors.

At the Seder meal, we sip the chicken broth,
then cut into the matzo balls, savory
with marrow and garlic, parsley and schmaltz,
remembering forty years in the desert, the freedom
of the promised land, succulent and dangerous,
bobbing before us like these matzo balls we relish
and eat and praise the taste of, wanting more.

Melanie Braverman

Memoryware

"When the Cossacks came, we were packed and ready to go, we did not wait for them to push us out into the streets like dogs," my grandmother said.

I brought her a smoked fish on a blue plate. I sat down.

"I was the smallest," she said, "my place was on top of the wagon, perched up there level with the eyes of the handsome soldiers. The breath of their white horses came out as white clouds, and I remember the sun feeling warm on my back. I had to pass water but I was too afraid to ask my mother to stop and let me down, and besides, even then I was too proud to squat in front of the soldiers. 'Move on,' the cossacks said and so we moved."

My grandmother ate the skin of the fish, its soft white fat, its flesh.

"The house of my mother's brothers smelled of wood smoke and bachelorhood. We had come a long way to their village, the uncles offered tea but had, they sighed, no sugar to give their only sister. 'Tea without sugar is for peasants,' my mother said. We were a good family, cultured, even our meals of boiled potatoes looked fine with their sprigs of wild onion. My sister fetched the sugar from the wagon, the curve of my bottom impressed on the sack where I'd sat that whole long trip. My uncle slit its off-colored cloth and scooped sugar into a chipped china bowl, but to our surprise the sugar was yellow instead of white, lumpy instead of smooth as it passed through his hand. 'Spoiled?' my uncle asked, stroking his smelly old beard. 'Nonsense,' my mother scolded, 'sugar is sugar,' spooning some into her cup, and then some more. I squirmed in my seat and she swatted at my head like a fly till I stopped."

"What did you do?" I asked my grandmother. She'd picked up the skeleton of the fish between her hands like an ear of corn and was sucking the last of the flesh from the bones.

"I asked for tea," she said.

"But Yaya," I said, "the sugar!"

She took an apple from a wooden bowl and began to peel it slowly with the sharp knife she kept in the pocket of her house dress, red skin coiling onto the blue plate like a spring.

"What is good enough for the mother is adequate for the child," she said, slicing a wedge from the core of the apple and offering it to me without even looking my way.

෴

On Friday nights my grandmother wore a wig that lived a life of its own atop her thinning hair, happy to be off of the styrofoam head and allowed to dance in the breeze as we drove all together into town. Hair and lipstick slightly askew, she looked a little blurry those nights, and I'd let my eyes go in and out of focus on her when I got fidgety in the back seat of the Olds. Every Friday we went to town, and every Friday my grandmother rose during services to mourn the memory of my grandfather. Though I was just a little girl when he died, I could remember the cool pickle crocks he scrubbed and filled with brine in late August, the glads he grew and cut like swords for the table, the way he pinched my cheeks between his fingers like a vise. Now my grandfather was one of the commemorative lights that shone on the Eastern wall of the temple like a movie marquee, illuminating the brass name plates of all the other dead Jews from our towns. When at the end of the service everyone rose to face East toward Jerusalem, I believed those personal lights served to show the way to that mythical place, that foreign home where my grandfather still made pickles and pinched the cheeks of angels. And though she cursed him almost daily under her breath, my grandmother sang the mourner's kaddish with her eyes straight ahead on the altar like arrows fixed on God, and swiped at my grandfather's name plate with a Kleenex as she went down the stairs to eat cake.

Ours was a small temple built along a creek, and in spring the boys rolled their good pants up around their knees and caught crawdads while the girls picked violets for their mothers. The ladies were back-combed and straight-backed, the men all restless in their dark suits, eager to be out in the lobby having a smoke. The Silversteins, the Davidsons, the Goldbergs, the Weisenbergs, the Milkens, and Mrs. Oppenheimer who sang louder than anyone, deep-chested and kindly next to her quiet husband George. We had poppy-seed cake and red punch in the basement of the temple once a week, except those springs when the rains made the creek jump its banks; then the basement was flooded and musty, the rabbi spoke about Noah in his sermons, and we took our refreshment under the glare of spotlights on the higher ground of the front lawn.

Once in midsummer I sat in the sanctuary by myself after the service. The seats in our temple shifted like the ones in fancy theaters, and I tipped myself back to watch the light from the setting sun bounce through the glass onto the golden cover of the ark. I was thinking about the eternal light, which flickered daringly each time the congregation rose and sat. I was thinking about what language God spoke in his everyday life, Hebrew or English. I had drawn a picture of God for myself, one half man in a navy blue suit and one half woman in paisley, my favorite print. It was just for reference, in order to have a clear image in mind when we had our conversations, which was like praying to me. Maybe one half speaks Hebrew and the other English, I was thinking. I closed my eyes, then opened them. "Dear God," I said. "It's me, it's Grace here." The man side of God straightened his tie, the woman side smiled off into the distance. Then a little bat rustled its wings and flew down from the temple rafters, circled and returned to its roost. I'd been watching that bat all evening; that bat was the reason I'd stayed behind after all the others had gone downstairs for cake. *"Boruch atah adonai,"* I tried again. The man God turned his face in my direction.

๑

I lay my hand on my grandmother's face, holding it there like a blind girl new to Braille, taking my time to read the feathery skin. But only the wind came lowing across the plains, sweeping her voice up along with the topsoil and the wastepaper and the leaves. I rubbed my thumb across the surface of her cheek until I couldn't feel either anymore, and then there was nothing left to hold me to myself, feet dangling above the floor like a baby's when I propped myself next to my grandmother on the bed. The night before when I'd said good night, she'd told me a story about a man from her village, mad with grief at the loss of his wife, a girl with an indiscriminate smile who died giving birth to their one child. For days the man wandered from house to house, his pockets full of his wife's trinkets, banging on the doors of women who were touched by the man's grief and willing to overlook the filth of the hands thrust through their open doors, begging. The women asked the man in, sat him by their fires while he told them his story, and fed him what they had in the house, which was not much in those days, a slice of bread perhaps, a cup of broth.

One day as he was fumbling along, the man found a clay jug in the road. He pissed in the dirt, stirred it with a stick, and with the mud he'd made began to plaster his wife's few things to the jug: her thimble, her hairpin, the spoon that had last fed her lovely mouth. Ever after, when the man sat by the fires of the village women, he held the jug to the flickering light, pointing from object to object, telling.

Years passed, and still the man wandered the village, begging bread, begging soup. One day he knocked on a door, only to find smiling at him the face of his long dead wife. So taken aback was he that he forgot all about the rumbling in his belly and stared for a long moment at the woman's face.

"And then what?" I asked my grandmother, kicking my heels anxiously against the side of her bed.

"What happens to everyone," she said. "He died."

"What?" I demanded.

"The truth," she said, patting the sheets with the palms of her hands.

"But who was she?" I said.

"Who knows?" my grandmother said, but I wanted to know. This is a story, I thought, she could be nice for a change, she could make things come out right.

"But the woman still had the jug," I said.

She wrapped her knuckly hand around mine, looking me square in the face as she talked. "Gittl," she said, "you're not a child anymore. The jug was nothing, piss and mud. The story died with the man," she said. "And the story," my grandmother told me, "was everything."

I went to bed and dreamed I was a salmon that night, silver and pink against the clear grey skin of a brook. But instead of having to struggle against the current I only ever had to swim downstream, allowing gravity to hurl me toward some easy end. I don't have to forgive you, I thought as I fell asleep.

Now I reached over and opened the window and

invited every bird I saw to fly in the room and talk to me, to fill the shell of my grandmother with their little exhalations and crusts of bread. But her spirit had already shaken itself free and fled our house like a hobo bent for the thrill of the road. There was my mother outside the door, asking for me to let her in. "Open up," she was calling to me, "open up." Already the house was filling with people and their food. And men had come to take my grandmother, to take my grandmother away.

Susan Straight

TRACKS

As I'm heading down the driveway, I stop the bike because I can see the dripline at the willow tree. It's a problem spot, always too hot because the heat reflects off the white concrete, and I can't get the verbena I planted for ground cover to hide the skinny black hose. Irrigation has to be invisible, so you can't see the money you're spending. That's the point. You don't *need* to see it, or have it be seen, like my cousins with their gold jewelry and El Dog.

In the beginning, the yards I do look really funny, tubing everywhere, circles around trees like I lassoed these scrawny trunks and plants out in the middle of a brown desert, everything flattened by the bulldozers except where the banks cut in steep so we can all fit on the side of the hill.

Two years is the longest it takes to decorate right, let the yard mature, wait for the market to go up by itself. Southern California. Just live here, eat and sleep for long enough, and if you're in the right place, you make money. Do the house up, and you make more. Whenever she happened to see prospective buyers at the second house we sold, Brichée would tell them, "My husband and I love the house, we've just got it to where we want it. We're only moving because of my job."

That's not true—by then I'm tired as hell of the whole place, pouring the cement for the patio, building the deck, matching the colors inside.

The back tire crunches off the curb, and I coast down the street, check out the progress of the Spanish-style three houses down and the Cape Cod next to him. They're slow—still got cement bags piled up, none of their walkways poured yet. On the street, I have plenty of room to ride because no sidewalks are built here. The heat comes straight down my back; the city doesn't do trees here, not like in the old neighborhoods with the huge carobs and elms. It seems even wider here, with the popsicle-stick baby trees and no cars parked in front of the houses. I can fit my truck and Brichée's Honda in the three-car garage.

Brichée won't be home until damn near ten, and I haven't been riding in a long while. It's tax time, end of March, and only 5:30. After four years of this, I know the seasons for accountants. Not that she's ever home early, but tonight there's no question. At the end of our cul-de-sac, I whirl around the corner and see a woman standing at her mailbox, giving me a funny look. A who-the-hell special. Nobody knows me, even though we've been here for a year. I leave at dawn, before anyone except the commuters starting their way to L.A., so I can do most of my banks and offices when it's cool. Out in yards and parking lots all day, especially doing new sprinklers and irrigation, even winter can be too hot in Rio Seco. I usually get home around four, again before most everyone else, take my nap. Then I'm out in the back, trying to keep things under control, staining the deck, staking the trees. I have a half-acre lot, like everyone here, and the weeds are steady trying to kill me.

Riding out of Grayglen makes me dizzy sometimes, the curving short streets until you get to the main road leading down the hill to the city. Cars crank past me once I get to Gardenia. I can see the wooden signs by the side of the street, most of the arrows pointing over the hill the way the cars are going, the yellow lettering carved in: Grassridge, Rosewind, Rivercrest, Haven Hills, Grayglen. After the last, an arrow points at me, where I'm still waiting to pull out. The slope across the road is bare, with a slash down the middle where the rain made a rift, and pepper trees, wild tobacco bushes scattered near the place where the moisture gathers. I see illegals picking the prickly pear cactus, *nopales* in Spanish, I learned from the signs people put up below their houses telling the guys to stay away. The illegals ride ten-speeds down the hill every day, away from all the new tracts they're working.

That was where I started. I bought a three-bedroom in Woodbridge for $89,000 and sold it two years later for 105. In Stonehaven, I bought into the first phase for 126. Six months later, the second phase, on that land I had been watching from my back patio, where tumbleweeds kept flying over my fence, went for 149, and the third phase started at 162. I sold and came back to the better side of the slope for Grayglen.

I hear cricket buzzes near my ears when the wind flaps my lobes; Brichée's always teasing me about my big ears. Gardenia is steep. There isn't any smog for a change, and I can see most of Rio Seco spread out from here. That's the whole idea. The Westside, where my parents live, is past the long arroyo that stretches like spilled green paint in the brown fields. The last couple of days have hit 90 degrees. I follow the strings of gray freeways, the cars close and even as beads on my mother's rosary. Brichée drives from L.A. every night, an hour and a half minimum. Two hours tonight, looks like. All these L.A. people are keeping my prices high, running out here for a cheap house, shaving and putting on makeup in their cars. I won't drive like that. One of the banks out in San Bernardino, about twenty miles away, offered me a contract seven years ago, and my father was cussing mad when I told him I wasn't going to take it. "Boy, I woulda killed for a couple of banks, the easy life. They ain't got but a scrap of lawn to cut, edge, a little trash. Shoot, I thought you had sense."

"This isn't just cutting grass," I told him. "I'm doing

custom landscape, remember? This is a month of driving out there with all the materials, completely different."

"Is the money a different color? Goddamn. And you think you gon buy a house before you old as me?"

I turn at the four-way stop and cross over to Edgewild Estates, a section of custom-builts. All the streets are named after mountains: I drive down Rainier, Matterhorn, Everest. I did two of the houses here, but they didn't want anything too spectacular. Nice border gardens, and for one on Matterhorn I did a beautiful grape arbor in the back, but the front yards were ordinary. Better than most of these I'm passing, though. They look like Singletary's work, the usual boring petunias, marigolds, snapdragons in circle planters near the mailboxes. A couple of bougainvilleas along the cinderblock walls. I stop at my favorite, three weeping willows on a mound, and then head down the newest street, where they've just finished a house I saw months ago only framed. A total brick facade in front, three chimneys twisting and spiraling to a damn turret at the top. A castle. I've never seen anything close. I turn the bike around and come back for another look, stop to check out the patterns on the front walkway. Basketweave bricks, beautiful with the rest. Three chimneys, and it's 90 in March. But yeah, that's it. I look across the street to see a woman in the bay window, staring hard at me. She glares straight at me, doing her best crime-watch frown. I laugh. You build bay windows, river-rock entries, brick facades so people will look, right? But from cars, circling around and around, or from the path where they're *walking* up to the front door for dinner. Not looking like me. I know I should wear the uniform, the damn biking shorts and maybe one of those stupid little caps like Tour de France, but I like to ride in my sweats. My ass looks like two cantaloupes in those tight Lycra shorts. They aren't made for people of African descent. Shit, I keep wearing the sweats even though it's hot because Brichée's always complaining about how I'm going from brownskin to blueblood like my father too quick in the tender years of my life, in the sun.

Just to bother this woman, I get out my little pad of paper and write down the name of the brick contractor from the lawn sign. I always carry the pad and a pen. Since I moved to Grayglen, the cops have stopped me twice talking about, "Somebody reported suspicious activity, loitering, checking out houses."

I laughed real careful. "You want to see what I'm writing?" I showed them the pad, and then I read it, in case they didn't know some of the words. "Wisteria on gazebo, Japanese maple, agapanthus a good color combo." Yeah, right. I want to rob you, so I ride a bike past your house in the middle of the afternoon and write down how I'm going to break in. I see you looking at me, and I keep making notes about the accessibility of your windows and doors.

I turn to go back down the street—you can't ride through, like in Grayglen. You have to go back out the way you came: a closed community. She's still there. Hey, I watch people drive past my yard, slowing around the cul-de-sac to check out the way I painted my garage doors or how nice my roses look against the brick edging. Nobody plants big roses anymore.

Sometimes I can barely stop myself from running out the front door and yelling "Booga booga!" I say to Brichée, "That car will depart at some *high* speeds. There goes the neighborhood." She gets pissed when I talk like that. She's chatted with our neighbors—on the right, a stockbroker, on the left, another accountant. She doesn't run them off. But Brichée's light, bright, and just about right—she's Louisiana. I remember when she showed up at the city college, brothers were falling all over her and her sister Brandy.

Past Edgewild, there's nothing but orange groves.

I pass a dry bank, and the colonies of red ants are tossing up mounds of coarse sand. I watch them carrying bits of palm bark, dry straw, big loads weaving back and forth along the asphalt. Even though they name these places half-nature and half-England, Hampton or Fox or Hunter, this is as close as you get to wilderness before the dozers grade it. I have to break out the Diazinon granules for months because the ants are the worst problem. They eat flowers and stems, where in my parents' neighborhood I only saw them eating regular ant food like sugar and soda. Up here, I find deep holes from ground squirrels; I hear coyotes at night.

I watch to see if the old beat-up house is still here in the next grove, past the canal. I was keeping an eye on it a few months ago. It's gone. I walk around the razed area, where the foundation and chimney are left, with lots of trash from partying rich kids. No For-Sale sign yet, but I look closer at the groves and see the milkweed, straight and perfect as military boys, marching up and down the irrigation furrows.

The old farmhouses spaced in the groves were sturdy, some of them three stories. One old man I met told me that was so the farmers could look out over the tops of the trees and watch for people stealing oranges. I kick the edges of the foundation; the walls are thick, wide, and every room would have touched the outside, had a window. The walls in my house are thin. When Brichée watches *Wiseguy* or *Miami Vice,* I can hear the guns and screeching tires way upstairs in the bedroom I use for an office. I like sitting there, drawing plans, circles for each plant in the flower beds, curving paths and raised rectangular planters. I etch in the leaves sometimes.

When Brichée's in her office, down the hall from our bedroom, I hear her ten-key sounding like the mice that tapped inside the walls when I was small. Everything's thin in this new house. One night she was bitching about the parquet floor—she said another splinter got her, and she was tired of trying to keep the wood shined. "We should have picked tile," she said. "I'm going to get a maid. I see their cars down the street when I'm home late in the morning."

I told her no way, no maid. That was too close. "Don't get black on me," she said. "I'll do it if I want."

"What am I, the field nigger?" I yelled, and then I did something I remember my father doing when he wanted to prove his house was his. I punched the closest door. But when my father did it, the frame shook, and everyone was quiet. My whole damn door caved in, hollow as a wafer cookie. I bought a carved oak door after that—it matched the floor anyway, and it'll recoup the money I spent.

I sit down with my back to the chimney and watch the crows parade and fight in the field across from the grove. My father saw a house as old as this one had been, a small Victorian with all the gingerbread trim, when I was still at city college. He took me downtown to see it. "Take you a belt sander to some of that wood inside, stain it up," he said, standing on the porch, looking in the windows with me. The front room had a built-in china hutch. A mess, but it had potential. "Paint the trim with all them different colors. This the kind of veranda I always thought your mama would like," he said, and it was true; she spent hours outside on the little square cement steps at our house, shelling peas or pulling the husks off corn. "Can't fit but one more woman out there with her," my father would say while we were working on a lawnmower, "and you know she need at least two to talk about me like a dog."

At the old house downtown, he stood next to me, close, and said, "You buy this, you won't be stuck on the Westside, but you won't be far away." I remember looking at the street, ragged at the edges, thinking it could go either way, restored or run-down. "What?" he said. "It's cheap. You want to own, right?"

I'd already thought of Woodbridge then, of location, but I was still saving up the down payment and starting the business. My father died a year after that, left me the down payment—two insurance policies that he'd been paying on for years, since he and my mother had first moved here from Jackson, Mississippi, years before I was born. They'd lived in their house for thirty-one years, bought it for $9,000, paid it off. A $9,000 house in southern California. Everybody, my aunt, cousins, they've all been in the same houses for as long as I can remember. I knew exactly when their plum trees were ready to pick, when they'd call me to come stake the baby fig because the Santa Anas were blowing.

I bought in Woodbridge. I asked Mama to come live with me; I'm the only child. "You can't walk to nothin up there—it ain't no store, no church, nowhere. Uh-uh, baby, don't worry. Sister and them can come here." My aunt Sister and cousin Tarina came to stay with her, and they can all fit in the kitchen to talk at the same time, if not on the steps.

Mama comes to the newest house and laughs at the self-cleaning oven, the garbage disposal, the trash compactor. Brichée loves this house, with the most appliances we've had.

"What is this, self-cleaning?" Mama reads.

"Brichée spilled some barbecue sauce in there one night, and the next day she turned it onto self-clean, came back from work and it was just a little gray ashy spot," I said, pointing to the dial.

"She still have to wipe out the ashy stuff?" Tarina asked.

"Yeah, I guess."

"Why she don't just wipe the damn stuff up in the first place then?"

"Hush," Mama said. "Brichée got all these rinds and peelings in the sink, though. Why you don't put them on your compost heap, Trent? Ain't no need to be grinding them up."

"Mama, nobody keeps compost anymore. It just breeds bugs and disease."

"Shoot, you gon have bugs anyway. Everybody got bugs. Less you got a self-cleaning yard, too," she said, and Tarina cracked up, loving it. On Labor Day, Memorial Day, any of them, Brichée won't come down to Mama's yard for ribs and potato salad and peach cobbler. She says she has bills or accounts to do, but I know it's because Tarina and my cousins always start on her. Tarina looks out the etched-glass pane in the front door, checking out the street. "All y'all got the same kind of houses in this track?"

I know better than to correct her word. "Three models, but each one's slightly different, and that's why the landscaping's so important."

"Huh," she says, looking back at the living room. At Christmas, Tarina told everyone, "Brichée got it so clean and pale in there you don't wanta *walk*. And don't bring no babies, now." The house *was* light—Brichée did this one in cream carpet, cream walls, light-oak picture frames to match the mantel and banister. Pale mauve furniture. Even the living room fireplace was light marble—alabaster, I think she called it. She does the insides, looks at those funny curtains, balloons and valances she says, and I do the outsides.

I used to study the old-money houses my father cut, where the ladies gave teas in their rose arbors. Those gardens have subtle colors, silvery gray and blue salvia, huge cabbage-headed dahlias, bronze chrysanthemums. I read the *Architectural Digest*s, the *Horticulture*s, the high-class stuff. I looked at the hedges, the shapes, the blending colors, before I did mine.

No huge plum trees in the front, no figs or apricots, no beans and tomatoes growing up the side of a chainlink fence. No food in the front yard, because that meant you were raising something you needed. And nothing like morning glories, geraniums, common flowers.

I remembered the gardens at the very top of the hill, the estates that had been there for decades. I did mine English country, with old-fashioned borders and white wooden arches, the trellis for roses, and this time, a gazebo with purple clematis at the sides. Perennials, flowers no one else around here uses, columbine and delphinium and veronica. We always sell in the spring, when everything is blooming. Next year will be the same.

They go fast because it looks like Prince Charles or some earl lives there, as close as I can get it. We'll arrange with the realtor to show people during the day, as usual, when we're gone. If the lookers saw me, they'd bug.

I ride past the last grove, around the corner toward Gardenia again. The cars are still racing, I can hear ahead of me, and the sky lightens up near the edges of the hills, getting deeper above. This whole area will sell, I think, sell fast. I know Rio Seco, all of it, so I watch for my next move. You have to learn the boundaries, the newly-razed trees or cleared fields, the right hills. I tried to tell my cousin Snooter last year when he visited. He rode Brichée's bike, the one she never touches anyway, and I showed him the layout of our tract, told him about location and resale. He started laughing when I shifted gears. "Hey, I used to ride this bike for *keeps,* you forgot?" I told him. "I had to learn to do it right."

"Yeah, Trent, we used to see you *motorvating* home from school on that ten-speed, talking about that was your cruise, man." He pulled next to me. "Let me ax you something, cause you don't never stop. When we were kids, you use to just let go, you know, ride with no hands. When you do that, man, you know what you steering with? Your crotch. Remember?"

He was in my face then, and I couldn't laugh, but my crotch *is* sore now, on the way up the slope, and I have to smile. My legs, too. My father used to holler at me when I said I was tired of pushing the mower. "Go on, you better pass me and improve that shit. Cause if you lag behind, I'ma turn around and run yo ass over."

"You wouldn't tow me, Pops?"

"Shit, I didn't raise you to pull you."

I pump hard up Gardenia, scaring the last of the crows out of the empty field before Grayglen. They join the flock flying down toward the river, over the city. I used to see them every night about this time, when I was standing in my father's yard, and I'd watch them dive at each other when they got mad. Inside Grayglen, an illegal is still swiping circle patterns into the cement of an entry, and past him, I look up my street. All the garage doors are closed. Now I can hear the sprinklers coming on, the clicks of automatic timers starting them up; I pass the vibrating air conditioners, the buzzing pool filters that seem to float heavy in the air. I never put in pools—they're a liability sometimes, not a sure asset. I think of a spa, but then I remember our house has a spa, in the master tub. We've never used it. The dark is coming down fast now, making all the hisses and humming seem louder, and by the time I get close to the end of our street, I see TVs flashing blue through the windows. In each of the yards and driveways I pass, no one is outside.

Lynna Williams

Personal Testimony

The last night of church camp, 1963, and I am sitting in the front row of the junior mixed-voice choir looking out on the crowd in the big sanctuary tent. The tent glows, green and white and unexpected, in the Oklahoma night; our choir director, Dr. Bledsoe, has schooled us in the sudden crescendos needed to compete with the sounds cars make when their drivers cut the corner after a night at the bars on Highway 10 and see the tent rising out of the plain for the first time. The tent is new to Faith Camp this year, a gift to God and the Southern Baptist Convention from the owner of a small circus who repented, and then retired, in nearby Oklahoma City. It is widely rumored among the campers that Mr. Talliferro came to Jesus late in life, after having what my mother would call Life Experiences. Now he walks through camp with the unfailing good humor of a man who, after years of begging hard-scrabble farmers to forsake their fields for an afternoon of elephants and acrobats, has finally found a real draw: his weekly talks to the senior boys on "Sin and the Circus" incorporate a standing-room-only question-and-answer period, and no one ever leaves early.

Although I know I will never be allowed in the tent to hear one of Mr. Talliferro's talks—I will not be twelve forever, but I will always be a girl—I am encouraged by his late arrival into our Fellowship of Believers. I will take my time, too, I think: first I will go to high school, to college, to bed with a boy, to New York. (I think of those last two items as one since, as little as I know about sex, I do know it is not something I will ever be able to do in the same time zone as my mother.) Then when I'm fifty-two or so and have had, like Mr. Talliferro, sufficient Life Experiences, I'll move back to west Texas and repent.

Normally, thoughts of that touching—and distant—scene of repentance are how I entertain myself during evening worship service. But tonight I am unable to work up any enthusiasm for the vision of myself sweeping into my hometown to Be Forgiven. For once my thoughts are entirely on the worship service ahead.

My place in the choir is in the middle of six other girls from my father's church in Fort Worth; we are dressed alike in white lace-trimmed wash-and-wear blouses from J. C. Penney and modest navy pedal pushers that stop exactly three inches from our white socks and tennis shoes. We are also alike in having mothers who regard travel irons as an essential accessory to Christian Young Womanhood; our matching outfits are, therefore, neatly ironed.

At least their outfits are. I have been coming to this camp in the southwestern equivalent of the Sahara Desert for six years now, and I know that when it is a hundred degrees at sunset, cotton wilts. When I used my iron I did the front of my blouse and the pants, so I wouldn't stand out, and trusted that anyone standing behind me would think I was wrinkled from the heat.

Last summer, or the summer before, when I was still riding the line that separates good girls from bad, this small deception would have bothered me. This year I am twelve and a criminal. Moral niceties are lost on me. I am singing "Just as I Am" with the choir and I have three hundred dollars in my white Bible, folded and taped over John 3:16.

Since camp started three weeks ago, I have operated a business in the arts and crafts cabin in the break between afternoon Bible study and segregated (boys only/girls only) swimming. The senior boys, the same ones who are learning critical new information from Mr. Talliferro every week, are paying me to write the personal testimonies we are all expected to give at evening worship service.

୭

We do not dwell on personal motivation in my family. When my brother, David, and I sin, it is the deed my parents talk about, not mitigating circumstances, and the deed they punish. This careful emphasis on what we do, never on why we do it, has affected David and me differently. He is a good boy, endlessly kind and cheerful and responsible, but his heroes are not the men my father followed into the ministry. David gives God and our father every outward sign of respect, but he worships Clarence Darrow and the law. At fifteen, he has been my defense lawyer for years.

While David wants to defend the world, I am only interested in defending myself. I know exactly why I have started the testimony business: I am doing it to get back at my father. I am doing it because I am adopted.

Even though I assure my customers with every sale that we will not get caught, I never write a testimony without imagining public exposure of my wrongdoing. The scene is so familiar to me that I do not have to close my eyes to see it: the summons to the camp director's office and the door closing behind me; the shocked faces of other campers when the news leaks out; the Baptist Academy girls who comb their hair and go in pairs, bravely, to offer my brother comfort; the automatic rotation of my name to the top of everyone's prayer list. I spend hours imagining the small details of my shame, always leading to the moment when my father, called from Fort Worth to take me home, arrives at camp.

That will be my moment. I have done something so

terrible that even my father will not be able to keep it a secret. I am doing this because of my father's secrets.

๑

We had only been home from church for a few minutes; it was my ninth birthday, and when my father called me to come downstairs to his study, I was still wearing the dress my mother had made for the occasion, pink dotted swiss with a white satin sash. David came out of his room to ask me what I had done this time—he likes to be prepared for court—but I told him not to worry, that I was wholly innocent of any crime in the weeks just before my birthday. At the bottom of the stairs I saw my mother walk out of the study and knew I was right not to be concerned: in matters of discipline my mother and father never work alone. At the door it came to me: my father was going to tell me I was old enough to go with him now and then to churches in other cities. David had been to Atlanta and New Orleans and a dozen little Texas towns; my turn had finally come.

My father was standing by the window. At the sound of my patent-leather shoes sliding across the hardwood floor, he turned and motioned for me to sit on the sofa. He cleared his throat; it was a sermon noise I had heard hundreds of times, and I knew that he had prepared whatever he was going to say.

All thoughts of ordering room-service hamburgers in an Atlanta hotel left me—prepared remarks meant we were dealing with life or death or salvation—and I wished for my mother and David. My father said, "This is hard for your mother; she wanted to be here, but it upsets her so, we thought I should talk to you alone." We had left any territory I knew, and I sat up straight to listen, as though I were still in church.

My father, still talking, took my hands in his; after a moment I recognized the weight of his Baylor ring against my skin as something from my old life, the one in which I had woken up that morning a nine-year-old, dressed for church in my birthday dress, and come home.

My father talked and talked and talked; I stopped listening. I had grown up singing about the power of blood. I required no lengthy explanation of what it meant to be adopted. It meant I was not my father's child. It meant I was a secret, even from myself.

In the three years since that day in my father's study, I have realized, of course, that I am not my mother's child, either. But I have never believed that she was responsible for the lie about my birth. It is my father I blame. I am not allowed to talk about my adoption outside my family ("It would only hurt your mother," my father says. "Do you want to hurt your mother?"). Although I am universally regarded by the women of our church as a Child Who Wouldn't Know a Rule If One Reached Up and Bit Her in the Face, I do keep this one. My stomach hurts when I even think about telling anyone, but it hurts, too, when I think about having another mother and father somewhere. When the pain is enough to make me cry, I try to talk to my parents about it, but my mother's face changes even before I can get the first question out, and my father always follows her out of the room. "You're our child," he says when he returns. "We love you, and you're ours."

I let him hug me, but I am thinking that I have never heard my father tell a lie before. I am not his child. Not in the way David is, not in the way I believed I was. Later I remember that lie and decide that all the secrecy is for my father's benefit, that he is ashamed to tell the world that I am not his child because he is ashamed of me. I think about the Ford my father bought in Dallas three years ago; it has never run right, but he will not take it back. I think about that when I am sitting in my bunk with a flashlight, writing testimonies to the power of God's love.

૯

My father is one reason I am handcrafting Christian testimonies while my bunkmates are making place mats from Popsicle sticks. There is another reason: I'm good at it.

Nothing else has changed. I remain Right Fielder for Life in the daily softball games. The sincerity of my belief in Jesus is perennially suspect among the most pious, and most popular, campers. And I am still the only girl who, in six years of regular attendance, has failed to advance even one step in Girls' Auxiliary. (Other, younger girls have made it all the way to Queen Regent with Scepter, while I remain a perpetual Lady-in-Waiting.) Until this year, only the strength of my family connections has kept me from sinking as low in the camp hierarchy as Cassie Mosley, who lisps and wears colorful native costumes that her missionary parents send from Africa.

I arrived at camp this summer as I do every year, resigned and braced to endure but buoyed by a fantasy life that I believe is unrivaled among twelve-year-old Baptist girls. But on our second night here, the promise of fish sticks and carrot salad hanging in the air, Bobby Dunn came and stood behind me in the cafeteria line.

Bobby Dunn, blond, ambitious, and in love with Jesus, is Faith Camp's standard for male perfection. He is David's friend, but he has spoken to me only once, on the baseball field last year, when he suggested that my unhealthy fear of the ball was really a failure to trust God's plan for my life. Since that day I have taken some comfort in noticing that Bobby Dunn follows the Scripture reading by moving his finger along the text.

Feeling him next to me, I took a breath, wondering if Bobby, like other campers in other years, had decided to attempt to bring me to a better understanding of what it means to serve Jesus. But he was already talking, congratulating me on my testimony at evening worship service the night before. (I speak publicly at camp twice every summer, the exact number required by some mysterious formula that allows me to be left alone the rest of the time.)

"You put it just right," he said. "Now me, I know what I want to say, but it comes out all wrong. I've prayed about it, and it seems to be God wants me to do better."

He looked at me hard, and I realized it was my turn to say something. Nothing came to me, though, since I agreed with him completely. He does suffer from what my saintly brother, after one particularly gruesome revival meeting, took to calling Jesus Jaw, a malady that makes it impossible for the devoted to say what they mean and sit down. Finally I said what my mother says to the ladies seeking comfort in the Dorcas Bible class: "Can I help?" Before I could take it back, Bobby Dunn had me by the hand and was pulling me across the cafeteria to a table in the far corner.

The idea of my writing testimonies for other campers—a sort of ghostwriting service for Jesus, as Bobby Dunn saw it—was Bobby's, but before we got up from the table, I had refined it and made it mine. The next afternoon in the arts and crafts cabin I made my first sale: five dollars for a two-minute testimony detailing how God gave Michael Bush the strength to stop swearing. Bobby was shocked when the money changed hands—I could see him thinking, Temple. Moneylenders. Jee-sus!—but Michael Bush is the son of an Austin car dealer, and he quoted his earthly father's scripture: "You get what you pay for."

Michael, who made me a professional writer with money he earned polishing used station wagons, is a sweet, slow-talking athlete from Bishop Military School. He'd been dateless for months and was convinced it was because the Baptist Academy girls had heard that he has a tendency to take the Lord's name in vain on difficult fourth downs. After his testimony that night, Michael left the tent with Patsy Lewis, but he waved good night to me.

For an underground business, I have as much word-of-mouth trade from the senior boys as I can handle. I estimate that my volume is second only to that of the snack stand that sells snow cones. Like the snow-cone stand, I have high prices and limited hours of operation. I arrive at the arts and crafts cabin every day at 2:00 P.M., carrying half-finished pot holders from the day before, and senior boys drift in and out for the next twenty minutes. I talk to each customer, take notes, and deliver the finished product by 5:00 P.M. the next day. My prices start at five dollars for words only and go up to twenty dollars for words and concept.

Bobby Dunn has appointed himself my sales force; he recruits customers who he thinks need my services and gives each one a talk about the need for secrecy. Bobby will not accept money from me as payment—he reminds me hourly that he is doing this for Jesus—but he is glad to be thanked in testimonies.

By the beginning of the second week of camp, our director, Reverend Stewart, and the camp counselors were openly rejoicing about the power of the Spirit at work, as reflected in the moving personal testimonies being given night after night. Bobby Dunn has been testifying every other night and smiling at me at breakfast every morning. Patsy Lewis has taught me how to set my hair on big rollers, and I let it dry while I sit up writing testimonies. I have a perfect pageboy, a white Bible bulging with five-dollar bills, and I am popular. There are times when I forget my father.

On this last night of camp I am still at large. But although I have not been caught, I have decided I am not cut out to be a small business. There is the question of good help, for one thing. Bobby Dunn is no good for detail work—clearly, the less he knows about how my mind works, the better—and so I have turned to Missy Tucker. Missy loves Jesus and her father and disapproves of everything about me. I love her because she truly believes I can be saved and, until that happens, is willing to get into almost any trouble I can think of, provided I do not try to stop her from quoting the appropriate Scripture. Even so, she resisted being drawn into the testimony business for more than a week, giving in only after I sank low enough to introduce her to Bobby Dunn and point out that she would be able to apply her cut to the high cost of braces.

The truth is, the business needs Missy. I am no better a disciple of the Palmer Handwriting Method than I am of Christ or of my mother's standards of behavior. No one can read my writing. Missy has won the penmanship medal at E. M. Morrow Elementary School so many times there is talk that it will be retired when we go off to junior high in the fall. When she's done writing, my testimonies look like poems.

The value of Missy's cursive writing skills, however, is offset by the ways in which she manifests herself as a True Believer. I can tolerate the Scripture quoting, but her fears are something else. I am afraid of snakes and of not being asked to pledge my mother's sorority at Baylor, both standard fears in Cabin A. Missy is terrified of Eastern religions.

Her father, a religion professor at a small Baptist college, has two passions: world religions and big-game hunting. In our neighborhood, where not rotating the tires on the family Ford on a schedule is considered eccentric, Dr. Tucker wears a safari jacket to class and greets everyone the same way: "Hi, wallaby." Missy is not allowed to be afraid of the dead animals in her father's den, but a pronounced sensitivity to Oriental mysticism is thought to be acceptable in a young girl.

Unless I watch her, Missy cannot be trusted to resist inserting a paragraph into every testimony in which the speaker thanks the Lord Jesus for not having allowed him or her to be born a Buddhist. I tell Missy repeatedly that if every member of the camp baseball team suddenly begins to compare and contrast Zen and the tenets of Southern Baptist fundamentalism in his three-minute testimony, someone—even in this trusting place—is going to start to wonder.

She says she sees my point but keeps arguing for more "spiritual" content in the testimonies, a position in which she is enthusiastically supported by Bobby Dunn. Missy and Bobby have fallen in love; Bobby asked her to wear his friendship ring two nights ago, using his own words. What is art to me is faith—and now love—to Missy, and we are not as close as we were three weeks ago.

I am a success, but a lonely one, since there is no one I can talk to about either my success or my feelings. My brother, David, who normally can be counted on to protect me from myself and others, has only vague, Christian concern for me these days. He has fallen in love with Denise Meeker, universally regarded as the most spiritually developed girl in camp history, and he is talking about following my father into the ministry. I believe that when Denise goes home to Corpus Christi, David will remember law school, but in the meantime he is no comfort to me.

Now, from my place in the front row of the choir, I know that I will not have to worry about a going-out-of-business sale. What I have secretly wished for all summer is about to happen. I am going to get caught.

Ten minutes ago, during Reverend Stewart's introduction of visitors from the pulpit, I looked out at the crowd in the tent and saw my father walking down the center aisle. As I watched, he stopped evey few rows to shake hands and say hello, as casual and full of good humor as if this were his church on a Sunday morning. He is a handsome man, and when he stopped at the pew near the front where David is sitting, I was struck by how much my father and my brother look alike, their dark heads together as they smiled and hugged. I think of David as belonging to me, not to my father, but there was an unmistakable sameness in their movements that caught me by surprise, and my eyes filled with tears. Suddenly David pointed toward the choir, at me, and my father nodded his head and continued walking toward the front of the tent. I knew he had seen me, and I concentrated on looking straight ahead as he mounted the stairs to the stage and took a seat to the left of the altar. Reverend Stewart introduced him as the special guest preacher for the last night of camp, and for an instant I let myself believe that was the only reason he had come. He would preach and we would go home together tomorrow. Everything would be all right.

I hear a choked-off sound from my left and know without turning to look that it is Missy, about to cry. She has seen my father, too, and I touch her hand to remind her that no one will believe she was at fault. Because of me, teachers have been patiently writing "easily led" and "cries often" on Missy's report cards for years, and she is still considered a good girl. She won't get braces this year, I think, but she will be all right.

In the next moment two things happen at once. Missy starts to cry, really cry, and my father turns in his seat, looks at me, and then away. It is then that I realize that Missy has decided, without telling me, that straight teeth are not worth eternal damnation. She and Bobby Dunn have confessed, and my father has been called. Now, as he sits with his Bible in his hands and his head bowed, his profile shows none of the cheer of a moment before, and none of the successful-Baptist-preacher expressions I can identify. He does not look spiritual or joyful or weighted down by the burden of God's expectations. He looks furious.

୭

There are more announcements than I ever remember hearing on the last night of camp: prayer lists, final volleyball standings, bus departure times, a Lottie Moon Stewardship Award for Denise Meeker. After each item, I forget I have no reason to expect Jesus to help me and I pray for one more; I know that as soon as the last announcement is read, Reverend Stewart will call for a time of personal testimonies before my father's sermon.

Even with my head down I can see Bobby Dunn sinking lower into a center pew and, next to him, Tim Bailey leaning forward, wanting to be first at the microphone. Tim is another of the Bishop School jocks, and he has combed his hair and put on Sunday clothes. In his left hand he is holding my masterwork, reproduced on three-by-five cards. He paid me twenty-five dollars for it—the most I have ever charged—and it is the best piece of my career. The script calls for Tim to talk movingly about meeting God in a car-truck accident near Galveston, when he was ten. In a dramatic touch of which I am especially proud, he seems to imply that God was driving the truck.

Tim, I know, is doing this to impress a Baptist Academy girl who has told him she will go to her cotillion alone before she goes with a boy who doesn't know Jesus as his personal Lord and Savior. He is gripping the notecards as if they were Didi Thornton, and for the first time in a lifetime full of Bible verses, I see an application to my daily living. I truly am about to reap what I have sown.

૬

The announcements end, and Reverend Stewart calls for testimonies. As Tim Bailey rises, so does my father. As he straightens up, he turns again to look at me, and this time he makes a gesture toward the pulpit. It is a mock-gallant motion, the kind I have seen him make to let my mother go first at miniature golf. For an instant that simple reminder that I am not an evil mutant—I have a family that plays miniature golf—makes me think again that everything will be all right. Then I realize what my father is telling me. Tim Bailey will never get to the pulpit to give my testimony. My father will get there first, will tell the worshipers in the packed tent his sorrow and regret over the misdeeds of his little girl. *His little girl.* He is going to do what I have never imagined in all my fantasies about this moment. He is going to forgive me.

Without knowing exactly how it has happened, I am standing up, half running from the choir seats to the pulpit. I get there first, before either my father or Tim, and before Reverend Stewart can even say my name, I give my personal testimony.

I begin by admitting what I have been doing for the past three weeks. I talk about being gripped by hate, unable to appreciate the love of my wonderful parents or of Jesus. I talk about making money from other campers who, in their honest desire to honor the Lord, became trapped in my web of wrongdoing.

Bobby Dunn is crying. To his left I can see Mr. Talliferro; something in his face, intent and unsmiling, makes me relax: I am a Draw. Everyone is with me now. I can hear Missy behind me, still sobbing into her hymnal, and to prove I can make it work, I talk about realizing how blessed I am to have been born within easy reach of God's healing love. I could have been born a Buddhist, I say, and the gratifying gasps from the audience make me certain I can say anything I want now.

For an instant I lose control and begin quoting poetry instead of Scripture. There is a shaky moment when all I can remember is bits of "Stopping by Woods on a Snowy Evening," but I manage to tie the verses back to a point about Christian choices. The puzzled looks on some faces give way to shouts of "Amen!" and as I look out at the rows of people in the green-and-white-striped tent I know I have won. I have written the best testimony anyone at camp has ever given.

I feel, rather than see, my father come to stand beside me, but I do not stop. As I have heard him do hundreds of times, I ask the choir to sing an invitational hymn and begin singing with them, "Softly and tenderly, Jesus is calling, calling to you and to me. Come home, come home. Ye who are weary, come home."

My father never does give a sermon.

While the hymn is still being sung, Bobby Dunn moves from his pew to the stage, and others follow. They hug me; they say they understand; they say they forgive me. As each one moves on to my father, I can hear him thanking them for their concern and saying, yes, he knows they will be praying for the family.

By ten o'clock, the last knot of worshippers has left the tent, and my father and I are alone on the stage. He is looking at me without speaking; there is no expression on his face that I have seen before. "Daddy," I surprise myself by saying. Daddy is a baby name that I have not used since my ninth birthday. My father raises his left hand and slaps me, hard, on my right cheek. He catches me as I start to fall, and we sit down together on the steps leading from the altar. He uses his handkerchief to clean blood from underneath my eye, where his Baylor ring has opened the skin. As he works the white square of cloth carefully around my face, I hear a sound I have never heard before, and I realize my father is crying. I am crying, too, and the mixture of tears and blood on my face makes it impossible to see him clearly. I reach for him anyway and am only a little surprised when he is there.

Music

Philip Levine

SOLOING

My mother tells me she dreamed
of John Coltrane, a young Trane
playing his music with such joy
and contained energy and rage
she could not hold back her tears.
And sitting awake now, her hands
crossed in her lap, the tears start
in her blind eyes. The TV set
behind her is gray, expressionless.
It is late, the neighbors quiet,
even the city—Los Angeles—quiet.
I have driven for hours down 99,
over the Grapevine into heaven
to be here. I place my left hand
on her shoulder, and she smiles.
What a world, a mother and son
finding solace in California
just where we were told it would
be, among the palm trees and all-
night super markets pushing orange
back-lighted oranges at 2 A.M.
"He was alone," she says, and does
not say, just as I am, "soloing."
What a world, a great man half
her age comes to my mother
in sleep to give her the gift
of song, which—shaking the tears
away—she passes on to me, for now
I can hear the music of the world

in the silence and that word:
soloing. What a world—when I
arrived the great bowl of mountains
was hidden in a cloud of exhaust,
the sea spread out like a carpet
of oil, the roses I had brought
from Fresno browned on the seat
beside me, and I could have
turned back and lost the music.

Patricia Smith

Excerpt from
Life According to Motown

Oh, Mary Mac Mac Mac
All dressed in black, black, black
With silver buttons, buttons, buttons
All down her back, back, back.
She asked her mother, mother, mother
for fifteen cents, cents, cents
To see the elephant, elephant, elephant
Jump the fence, fence, fence.
He jumped so high, high, high
He touched the sky, sky, sky
And he didn't come back, back, back
Till the fourth of July, ly, ly.

—Traditional children's clapping song

When I was nine years old,
growing tall tangled in bitter root,
I could whip my fingers numb with hand jive,
telling tall tales of rhythm and blue black superheroes
who only flew on Fridays
cause that's when the eagle flew.
My small hands put Mary Mac's buttons there,
the nickel and dime also glittered in my brown fist.
My flat singing hands grew red with a necessary music
as I heard my life blare from gaping westside windows.
Dressed in Motor City blues,
even my pain was perfect pain.
Deep, deep, deep in the doo wop, I was a question
that you couldn't answer.

A thin layer of Vaseline and a thick pair of sweatsocks made your legs look bigger, made the muscles of your calves bulge. So when you jumped rope or when you just WALKED, the boys all came around, they sniffed at you like hot, hungry dogs, their pelvises just wouldn't sit still.

And you always had to make your hair look like more hair than it was. First you crammed the pores of your scalp with grease, then you flattened your hair with a pressing comb until it lay flat and black upside your head like ink. I was always trying to work a couple of rubberbands up on my little bit of hair, and the result could have been called pigtails—until the rubberbands popped off, that is.

If you lived on the west side of Chicago in the '60s and your hair was long and wavy and your skin was cream and your legs shone like glass, your ticket was as good as written.

But if you were truly bone black and your hair practically choked on its kinks, you waited for the music to give you a shape.

The Marvelettes made me pretty, Smokey wailed for just a little bit of me, and the Temptations taught me to wait, wait, wait for that perfect love.

Every two weeks, a new 45 hit the streets, but I already knew it, crying in my room under the weight of an imaginary lover, breathing steam onto mirrors, pretend slow dancing in the arms of a seriously fine young thang who rubbed at the small of my back with a sweet tenor.

In the real world the boys avoided me like creamed corn—but I was the supreme mistress of Motown, wise in the ways of love, pretending I knew why my blue jeans had begun to burn.

Those devils from Detroit were broiling my blood with the beat. They were teaching me that wanting meant waiting. They were teaching me what it meant to be a black girl.

Jesús Papoleto Meléndez

OYE MUNDO/SOMETIMES

sometimes (
          when the night air feels *chévere*
) when i can hear the real sound
of *el barrio*
on *la conga*   *y timbales*
coke bottles
& garbage can tops

          when i can feel
          & reallyreally touch
          la música latina/   *africana*

& the fingerpoppin soul
emergin from tears/   sweet tears of laughter

          & i can feel
          a conglomeration of vibrations/
          heat waves
          body waves
          people waves
          of real *gente*
          /& i feel gooooooood

when i can taste the rare culture
of *cuchifritos y lechón*
chitterlins   & black-eyed peas
& corn bread

               & *la pompa* is open
          & cooooooools the hot tar

of summer heated streets
where children play
kick-the-can (
& sirens
cannot be heard)

/sometimes

sometimes
when the last of the ghetto poets
writes of flowers
growin in gutters /& i know it's real

/sometimes

sometimes/ sometimes
when i can almost hear /being echoed back
an answer
to my ghetto cry

sometimes/ sometimes
i run up the fire escape/ not to escape
& climb on the roof
& stand on the ledge
& look down
& yell out
to the midnight world
below
above
around
within:

OYE MUNDO TÚ ERES BONITO!!!

& i forget about the junkies
on the stoop.

Sekou Sundiata

Dijerrido

In your right mind
you say it can't
be done: *the highwire walk*
without the wire.
You exhale and breathe-in
without pause,
for as long as you can feel
one seamless stream.
The music never breaks,
it stops when you stop.
The word for this is dijerrido
and circular breathing,
the switching point
between what you hear
and what you can be led
to believe: wind
moving through wood,
the pressure of blood
against the walls of veins,
the pull of ovum and sperm,
the dreamy mantra of the Interstate
turning into a drowsy hum.
You could like being lost
once you've come this far
what you dream up is deeper
than what you know.
Like the sound the mind makes
at the root, only lower
below habits of thinking, below

the unseen motion
of synapse and hook, of a sigh, of a gaze.
What story does it tell?
Wood and lung and air
at the end of breathing
as we know it to be,
things we cannot explain,
the spells we want to be under.

Patricia Smith

EXCERPT FROM
LIFE ACCORDING TO MOTOWN

So Motown taught me all about men. Men worshipped women. Men couldn't live without women. The men who wailed beneath my phonograph needle were always begging you not to go, whining because you'd left after they'd begged you not to go, or praying out loud that you'd come on home so they could beg you not to go before you left them again.

But I remember my mother coming home from the taverns, dressed in sequins and Chanel, crying because the blues had broken through and touched bone, because she couldn't threaten to leave a man she didn't have.

I remember my friend Debra, her 11-year-old belly tight with the child of her mother's lover. She'd listened to the songs too, and waited along with me for the mindless drone of romance. She remembered him saying "I love you, I love you, really baby, I love you," and that's the way it was supposed to be, wasn't it, even in the movies wasn't it all sweet pain and shivering?

Debra told me she wasn't scared because babies just slipped out of your body while you were sleeping.

No men seemed to be begging my mother and Debra for anything. But I was still awkward, still skinny-legged, still wild by the head, still gawky and uncertain, still a stone fox when no one was around. I wanted so much to believe in the music.

So while the women I knew teetered, fell and crumbled in need of a beating heart, I kept waiting for a man to beg me for something.

It's not like I was asking for much
I didn't wanna be Diana, I just wanted to be Florence
the exact crooner in the background, the one with the hips
the one men winked at while shaking Diana's hand
the one who was so filled with heat and music
that one day her heart just burst instead of broke
I just wanted to be her

There was a time I would have given a fine, light-skinned boy with curly hair several million dollars to simply look like he was about to think about thinking about asking me to dance.

That's what it was all about, a man who looked the way Motown sounded. He'd have the slickest edges. I only got to dance with the ones who sang a wet game in my ear or crooned off key into the side of my face, messing up the lyrics and wetting up my earlobes.

Those fine, "high yella" guys always made my body feel stupid. Lord, I'd see one of them every once in awhile and I'd gaze at him like he was ALL the answers. But the closest I'd come to dancing with one was when he stepped on my toe on the way to somebody else.

If you say Motown didn't teach you to slow dance, you're lying, pure and simple. Oh, you paler types may have done the tea parlor routine to Frankie Valli and the Four Seasons when your folks were around, but I know that as soon as they left you screwed the red bulb into the basement lamp and gave Smokey the rights to your body.

It was easy to pretend I was dancing with a boy everyone else wanted. All I had to do was put on "Ooh, Baby, Baby," wrap my hands around a pillow, bury my lips in it and move my feet real slow.

But pretty soon I had to realize that if I was 16 and waiting to dance, with my legs all greased up and my hair growing nappy under the hot lights, a real cute boy would be off somewhere else, breaking a more beautiful heart.

Afaa Michael Weaver

Improvisation for Piano

after Mood Indigo

Freshly lit cigarette in his mouth,
his collar turned up in the cold,
his face turned wry, and the question,
the awful question hidden beneath.
It is so difficult to see the baby
I sent scooting over to my mother,
laughing out, "He can walk, see."
It is difficult to look in my arms and
remember how he once fit there, how
I could keep the world away from him
if it threatened to hurt him, to rob him.
When I admit that he has been hurt,
that he has been robbed and that I was helpless,
I wonder what register there is for pain.
He is leaving home, and I am sending
another black man into life's teeth and jaws.
All that I know about being black
is some kind of totem knotted with the prints
of my fists beating out a syncopated pain.
I can't begin to tell him how to carve.
I can cry. I can counsel other black men,
but love is its own resistance in
the eye a father shares with his son.

The storm window glass sticks to me
with its cold, and I watch him go under
the big tree up the street and away.
The night is some slow rendition of
Mood Indigo, and the blues takes me

away to some place and frightens the shit
out of me, as I think of how my son will live.
What life will he have without proper
attire, I wonder. I think to run after him,
catch him, and say, "Here, another sweater."
And I know the other sweater is the first time
I saw "nigger" in a white man's eyes.
I know he needs gloves, too, for his hands,
when they stiffen, as he wonders how
blackness colors his life. I close the door.
There is a silence like dead flesh
in the bedroom. My son has left home,
a big, black manchild. I pull my cold feet
under the comforter and swallow sleep medicine.

I slip away hoping there are angels.

Sherman Alexie

POWWOW POLAROID

We were fancydancing, you see.

Step-step, right foot, step-step, left foot, faster, twisting, turning, spinning, changing.

There are photographs taken but only one ever captured the change. It was a white tourist from Spokane. She was lucky, she was quick, maybe it was film developed by the CIA.

She took the picture, the flashbulb burned, and none of us could move. I was frozen between steps, my right foot three inches off the ground, my mouth open and waiting to finish the last sound.

The crowd panicked. Most fled the stands, left the dancers not dancing and afraid. The white woman with the camera raised her arms in triumph, crossed her legs at the ankle, tilted her head to one side.

My four-hundred-pound aunt wept into the public address system. My uncle held his great belly in his hands, walked among the fancydancers, said this:

forgiveness.

Ebony J. Montgomery

Me and My Troupe

WITH THANKS TO QUINCY

break a leg when I get on the stage
the crowd sits quietly
waiting
    me and my troupe of legs
    we come out
    we jam on the earth
    like never before heard
our bodies move
to the rhythm
of the drums
the beat in the song

    our booties shake and bake
    across the floor
    pirouettes on the balls
    of our feet
    the points of our toes

people moving
beautiful as
flowing water
    our spirits soar
    up on that stage
    as we dance and dance and

break a leg

Julie Landsman

Transformations

My reading classes in SAVE, a special project for students who are failing traditional school, are filled with kids from all over the city. These kids are in so much trouble in regular classes that they cannot learn. They disrupt the learning of others. They have destroyed many rooms in fits of uncontrollable temper. After enough of these incidents they are sent to our program, which is housed in a regular high school. Sometimes I have an hour with them, rarely two. By the end of the year some of them will have made enough progress to be allowed back into their neighborhood school.

๑

At my classroom door, Sandy is waiting for me. She is angry because I am later than usual, although first hour doesn't start for another fifteen minutes. Her body slumps against the wall. She turns her face away from me.

"'S'bout time you got here," she mumbles.

Our "honeymoon" time has been over for a few weeks. She tests me each and every morning, first thing, before I have had a chance to put down my books, slip off my coat, take my lunch to the refrigerator in the smoky, windowless lounge across the hall.

When the door swings open, she walks to the table in the middle of the room and settles her body into a chair. She keeps her coat on, holds her purse in her lap. Her back is to me as I arrange my desk, shifting books, setting up worksheets. I check the folders of the kids to make sure everything is ready.

One whole wall of my room is windows that look down on the playing field. Usually, this is the time of day when I gather myself together, but it is hard to draw breath when Sandy is here. It is hard to get ready for Johnny, Danny, and Mitchell. I want to drift, think about the weather or about nothing, think about the squirrel, again at my window.

I turn to Sandy.

"So, how's the niece these days?" I ask.

Without meaning to, she smiles.

"Just fine. She doin' just fine." But Sandy doesn't take off her coat. And her purse stays in her lap.

"I ain't doin' no work today," she says.

I knew that as soon as I saw her slumped against the wall.

Sandy's mother died when Sandy was eight years old. Her father left for Chicago and never came back. Her Aunt Rhonda, who works for the telephone company, has raised Sandy and her sister Lisa for the past seven years. And now Rhonda is also raising Lisa's baby. In the evenings, on the phone, we both puzzle over Sandy's anger, her tantrums, the way she kicks chairs across the classroom when she gets frustrated. Rhonda buys Sandy elegant blouses and long skirts. She says her nieces must never wear pants. She tells me she is raising them "in the ways of the Lord," which means that they go to church every night and both weekend days. I remember my boarding school, the monotony of chapel every morning, prayers every evening, hours of church on Sunday. I remember incense and dark wood, and the restlessness I felt, how I turned and twisted on the wooden pews.

I have told Rhonda how I feel about kids like Sandy: that they need hours to stare out the window, that they need to wear slacks when they want to, and to swear when the going gets rough. Whenever I tell her this, Rhonda sings hymns, right into the telephone. I listen. And when we say goodbye she blesses me. Later, in bed, her hymn rocks me to sleep, a dreamless night.

๑

The first bell rings and the kids begin to wander in. Johnny Washington runs to his seat, talking the whole time. Every part of his body moves at once. He is small for fifteen, with rows of braids woven tight to his head. As always, his clothes are impeccable. He jumps up and kicks over a chair on his way to the pencil sharpener. He tells me that the bus driver shoots baskets with a bunch of kids before school. He's excited.

"I think I'm taller," he says.

"You ain't no taller," says Sandy. "You're still shorter than my cousin, and he only ten years old."

In a rare moment of self-control, Johnny Washington ignores Sandy's comment. He walks up to me and stands directly in front of my desk. He bends close, his hair smelling sweet.

He whispers, "See. My pants are too short. Don't that mean I'm gettin' taller?"

I whisper back, "It could be a sign, unless they shrank in the wash, or you got someone else's pants by mistake."

Johnny's face falls. He turns slowly, sits down hard in his seat, and throws a pencil across the room.

"Jus' had 'em washed," he says.

"Tol' you, little nigger," says Sandy.

Johnny jumps back up and moves toward Sandy. She stands, towering over him. He yells up at her, "Fat-ass lard butt!"

"That's enough, both of you!" I say, as I move quickly out of my seat and walk between them, breaking their eye contact. I quickly search through Johnny's folder for a crossword puzzle. I know he doesn't want to go any further with Sandy. Relieved, he takes the pencil I offer him. He glares under my arm at Sandy, who is still standing. Then he straightens his collar and carefully rolls up his sleeves, pressing each roll neatly and smoothly against his arm, one at a time. Sandy shakes her head as she watches him and slides back down in her chair.

Most days it seems that Johnny is strung like a wire, tight and vibrating. He has such difficulty sitting quietly, letting himself rest. In his previous school he was the center of chaos in classes of thirty students. His teachers always traced their bad days back to Johnny. Books flew across the room, pencils tumbled end over end, dangerously close to the eyes of shy girls in the back row. His failure to read even the simplest words was the source of unrelenting frustration; failing again, he invariably would flip over his desk or hit a student on the head with his textbook on the way back to his seat from the pencil sharpener.

His mother comes to conferences in the clothes of a model. She chews gum, presses the sides of her skirt with her ringed fingers. She has no idea what to do with Johnny. We don't know either and gladly take quiet moments like this one when we get them. Johnny fills in words on the puzzle, making large, child-like letters in each square.

Mitchell comes in, half awake, his hair standing in irregular lumps all over his head, his shirt buttoned wrong, his zipper undone just a little at the top below his beltless waist. He is not wearing socks. Mitchell is too thin; his ankles are bruised dark over the knob of bone that shows above his high-water pants. He is fourteen and cannot read; confronted with sentences, he buries his head in his arms. His mother comes to us in ironed wash dresses and slippers. She tells us that she tries to instill the fear of God in Mitchell. We know she wants to keep him coming home in the evenings, out of trouble, but she doesn't always succeed. Mitchell has occasionally been found by the cops near a house not his own, his friends handing him tape recorders and jewelry out a downstairs window.

"Raggedy ass," mutters Sandy.

"Okay," I say, raising my voice. "No more."

Mitchell folds his arms and stares at his folder. A few more students rush in as the bell rings.

Davey walks softly, choosing a seat away from the rest of the students, and gets to work immediately. This is his second day in my room, and we are still trying to show how well we can get along. I smile at him, touch his shoulder. I remember pictures of my own childhood, our family lined up for snapshots by the beach. My hair was almost white those summers, blondest in the family. Davey looks the way I looked, only prettier. I have heard that at his previous school he had days of uncontrollable tantrums followed by days of total withdrawal. I know that in a few weeks he may display this anger in my room like the rest of them. But for now, he behaves perfectly. His best friend, Karen, a girl with pencil-thin legs and long greasy hair, pops her head in at the door. Davey waves her away. She has many bruises, the other teachers say. Her mother has a history of picking up and moving whenever someone notices. Karen "smokes like a fiend," they say. Now she smiles at me and I smile back.

Davey raises his hand to ask for my help. I sit by him for a moment, show him how to sound out three-syllable words. I ask him to read the first sentence of a short story I have found. He struggles with the words in a voice that is light and soft. He understands what he reads, and I leave him working on the first paragraph, his lips forming each word, his eyes squinting, intense, directed toward the page.

I have never met Davey's mother or father. No one comes to conferences, and there is no phone in his house. No one will open the door when we attempt to make home visits. I sense that he and his girlfriend Karen are on the run many nights. The social worker knows, is trying to find out what their situation is. Davey seems grateful for the warmth of the building on these increasingly chilly September mornings.

Sandy eases out of her coat, plants her feet on the floor, and opens her folder. She is dressed in a blue silk blouse, gold earrings, a black skirt, and low black heels. She refuses to let me listen to her read aloud, but she does begin to fill in words on a worksheet. Once she settles down, Johnny concentrates on his puzzle and Mitchell fingers the flash cards in front of him.

First hour. Monday. Class has begun.

For the next ten minutes everyone works. I drift around the room, asking them to read to me, write for me. I bend over or sit next to them, our shoulders touching. The sunlight spreads across the room while outside the phy ed class plays softball.

The coordinator of the program, Ted Marvin, sticks his head in the door to ask how things are going. Fine, I say, and marvel at my luck. All the kids look studious. Fifteen minutes earlier he would have seen Johnny kick a chair over or throw a pencil. He might have come in for the "lard butt" scene.

"Man's head on a boy's body," mutters Sandy after he has left.

"What?" Davey asks, looking up.

"He's so little, he's got a big ol' man's head on a boy's body," she repeats. Davey looks bewildered and goes back to his book.

Sandy catches my eye and smiles. Her face is wide and beautiful. For an instant the storm in her eyes lessens.

Sandy has a way of finding anyone's most vulnerable physical characteristic. Last week she said something about my breast size, something to the effect that if I turned sideways I'd disappear.

Mitchell has fallen asleep. His shirt rides halfway up his back as he rests his head on the table. I make a note to myself to have a conference with his mother soon. I can't seem to keep him awake for the whole hour. He twitches in his sleep, out cold. A boy picks up the bats on the playing field. Around me I feel the restlessness of classes beginning to end. Johnny spends the last few minutes of class shooting a crumpled-up paper at the wastebasket. The rest of us figure out his percentage. Not bad—92 out of 128.

When the bell rings, Johnny gets up slowly, straightens his collar, shakes out his pants so they fall just above the top of his shoes. He picks up his folder and sets it carefully in the rack on my desk. Then he rushes toward the door, his speed kicking in, his wire strung tight. He bumps into Davey, who, almost dreamlike, is drifting up to my desk.

"Hey, man!" says Johnny, angry for a moment, touchy.

Davey smiles, waves his hand in dismissal. Johnny glares at him, then moves on past and into the hall.

I tap Mitchell on the shoulder to wake him up. He looks bewildered but gets up and stumbles past me. Sandy stands near my desk, unwilling to leave.

"Hate that old lady gym teacher," she says. "Makes me change."

I sympathize, remembering how my classmates and I stared at each other in the huge stall showers in boarding school. I remember wondering if my body would ever look like Sarah Williamson's: large breasts and slim hips.

"Those are the rules," I say. "Now go ahead or you'll be late." I look deliberately down at my attendance book and she reluctantly moves away.

From my doorway I can see Sandy's shape diminishing at the end of the corridor, her coat tight around her shoulders. I remember what Rhonda said about Sandy in one of our first conversations: "She's always been a tough little girl. She's always fightin' for herself or her little sister." Sandy's back is ramrod straight. She moves like royalty, unhurried, carrying herself exaggeratedly upright.

I slouched as a kid. My father would press my shoulders back and tell me not to sag, that I would never be attractive if I hunched over. Kids bump into Sandy, and seem to bounce off her hardness. Yet she seems suddenly vulnerable, as though she must maintain this rigid height because she is afraid of curving, of falling, of feeling.

In September, the students are constantly trying out ways to establish their place in the hierarchy of the classroom, of the school. Davey, the pretty blond boy in first hour, has become restless, gets up unexpectedly and walks around the room, mumbling to himself.

Two weeks after David arrived, I found two police officers waiting at my door. As I struggled with the habitually malfunctioning lock, I nodded to them, and they followed me in, one smiling and picking up my briefcase full of books, lesson plans, and papers.

"We need to see one of your students, David Williams," said the less friendly one, his jaw tight, his thin face all business. "We'd like to wait in here so he won't see us," he said.

"What's he done?" I asked, nervous, getting out my books, setting them in random places on my desk.

"We just need to talk to him," the kinder one said. I wondered, briefly, if cops were always paired like this, a kind one with a hard one, a sweet with a bitter.

"I'd rather you stood outside, or in the office," I said. I didn't want the kids to think I would help the cops trap them, that I was unequivocally on the side of the uniforms.

"What time does he usually come in?" the nice cop asked.

"In about ten minutes. At eight," I answered.

"Okay. We'll come back in fifteen," he said.

Once the kids were settled, the police returned. They stood blocking the door, the nice cop asking to see Davey, as though I hadn't already talked to them, as though I hadn't already taken part.

"Davey?" I called to him at the back of the room, his head bent over his book. When he looked up and saw the cops, panic crossed his face. He seemed deerlike to me, caught. He looked so slight between the two dark uniforms as the police escorted him out.

When Davey came back a half hour later, he turned his chair toward the wall and refused to answer anyone's questions.

⁂

These days, Davey focuses on Johnny, mocks his perfect clothes, his struggle with words, his excited questions. Johnny responds with jeers about Davey's thin T-shirts and torn sneakers.

Sandy is still keeping an immense distance from all of us. She comes in sleepy in the mornings after staying out late at church, or after being up at night with her niece, Jasmine. She keeps her coat wrapped around her body all hour.

For weeks I have struggled to keep Mitchell awake. About the middle of each class his head moves slowly down onto his desk, and in five minutes he drifts off. I keep trying new ways to keep him awake. I sit next to him more often, nudge him, and talk in his ear. A week ago, one of the other teachers in the program was talking about Mitchell.

"I think the child's just plain hungry," she said. "He's not getting anything to eat in the morning."

We arranged to have free breakfast for our students

who qualified. Eighty-eight percent of them were eligible. That first morning, Mitchell sat at the table eating waffles and sausages out of plastic containers. After everyone had eaten, there were five breakfasts left. Mitchell asked if he could have another, and when the coordinator said he could, Mitchell sat alone in the middle of the room, eating a second and a third. I came to see where he was ten minutes into first hour. He turned to me, his chin covered with syrup. He smiled and asked if he could keep eating. I told him to come along soon, that he didn't want to be sick. It must have been my imagination, but when he walked in my door few minutes later it seemed as if a some of his scrawniness was already gone.

Today, Mitchell eats two breakfasts, comes in on time, and works almost all hour, sleeping only during the last five minutes.

௭

Ted Marvin agrees to cover my afternoon classes while I take my first-hour students on an October field trip to the zoo with John Martin's science class. I am rewarding my kids for beginning to settle down. Sandy has been writing short essays about her long-gone father in Chicago. She is working for points again and seems a little more comfortable. Johnny continues to jump around the room knocking over chairs or throwing pencils, but he's reading better and is not so obsessed with his height. And although Mitchell stumbles into class after breakfast, his shirt falling out of his beltless pants, he tries a little harder each day and stays awake the entire hour. Davey turns away from us toward the windows, yet he's trying to get through the book of short stories.

௭

On the bus, the kids stay close to me for the hour-long ride. I overhear Johnny as he asks Mitchell, "That your raggedy ol' house over there?"

We are driving through a South Minneapolis neighborhood on our way to the freeway.

Mitchell grunts, "Yeah."

The house Johnny is talking about has a screen door hanging by one hinge, blowing in the October wind. The steps to the porch are crumbling, as is the paint on the entire house, large chunks of it gone, revealing a cracked yellow surface underneath. In the yard are broken plastic toys and old gasoline cans.

"Raggedy-ass house," Johnny mutters.

Mitchell remains silent. I pretend not to hear but plan to talk to Johnny alone, later.

The neighborhood is typical of this city: low houses, many stucco, single storied. In the alleys in back the garages lean into each other. Small children dart in and out behind trash cans, and dogs pull at chains. These are deceptive streets. They do not look like those of cities on the East Coast, with their high rises and rows of sunless apartments. They are neighborhoods, yet the cold bite of poverty is here, the arctic wind blowing in around the windows in the kitchens.

When the bus pulls into the countryside, I notice that colors have deepened to red and burnt orange. Although many of the trees reach dark bare arms into a clear sky, the blond fields still ripple into waves of light and the breeze is not yet bitter with November chill.

After a while, almost everyone on the bus becomes quiet. Davey has fallen asleep against a window. Sandy stares straight ahead, her purse in her lap, her feet planted firmly on the floor. Johnny and Mitchell whisper to each other and then fall silent. Some of the girls from John's class apply makeup. They smile at Johnny. They think he is cute. He shrugs. He is wearing a fur-collared coat I've never seen before and new baggy wool pants. A boy reads a copy of *The Diary of Anne Frank.* Cars pass us, and from our height I can see couples lighting cigarettes for each other, a single man in a suit speaking into a tape recorder as he drives.

When we get to the zoo, I let my kids split up. Sandy and Johnny stay with me. The rest charge off: first to eat junk food, then to smoke in the bathroom, then to see a few animals. Johnny and Sandy and I go to the water show. We watch dolphins jump through the light, through the sky, through the sun, to catch fish. They swim under a trainer in the pool and ease him up into the blue air. After the show we go to see the nocturnal animals. We are down under the earth and our eyes need to adjust. In the green light, we see gophers and moles moving around their dirt homes.

Small children are running around between us, darting away from their frantic mothers. I do not notice immediately how quiet Sandy and Johnny have become. Sandy edges closer to me. I talk on, pointing out the different shapes of the burrows, the way animal eyes look like red lights in the darkness. Johnny doesn't say a word.

As we stand in front of a window behind which a gopher lives I feel Sandy's hand reaching for mine. At the same moment Johnny grabs my other hand. Neither of them speaks. I am between them, holding their fingers. While we move through the room, stopping at each window, I chatter on, amazed to feel their warm hands in mine. They clutch me, silent. They swallow audibly.

As soon as we reach the light, they drop my hands. Sandy pulls me aside. "Don't you tell no one I grabbed hold of you," she says in a menacing voice. I nod my head. She has no idea that Johnny was holding my other hand the whole time.

Johnny just smiles at me and walks ahead of us to where the lions are pacing the hilly field behind the fence.

He has been with me long enough to know I wouldn't tell anyone. I have something on Sandy now, something tender but secret. There is nothing I can say to reassure her enough. That will come with time.

Johnny runs back and reaches for my hand to drag me toward a pure white polar bear.

"Landsman," he says, "you got to see this honky bear!" He pulls back his hand quickly when he sees Sandy's angry face. I turn to follow him, hear her mumble behind me, "Yeah, Honky. Go see the honky bear!" She sits down on a bench and waits there alone for an hour until we are ready to leave.

૭

A week after our trip to the zoo, the kids hold a dancing contest. Mitchell comes in the morning of the contest smelling of urine. He missed breakfast and throughout first hour his head drops, then rises. He wants to read but can't stay awake.

I notice that Mitchell is wearing a velvet-trimmed jacket and baggy pants pulled in at the waist to keep them on. The kids look at him expectantly. For once Davey doesn't tease him about his clothes. Johnny whispers in his ear, watches him intently.

After classes are over, the fifty-four students in the program gather in the afternoon light of my classroom. The chairs are pushed back against the wall to make plenty of open floor space. When the music starts, Mitchell takes off the jacket and places it on the back of a chair. He rolls up his sleeves and starts to dance. His whole body moves at once. His hands push the space around him into curves. His feet are snakes. Head back, eyes closed, he moves. A change in the beat provokes a change in his step. He pulls the music with him. He pushes it away. He gets down on the floor and swivels on his hips.

The strutters, the taunters, and teasers edge off the floor. The well-dressed, straight-legged, gerry-curled kids move toward the walls, watching as Mitchell moves his hips, hands, and feet around the music. He is unaware of their shining eyes, their shaking heads, their "amens" of approval.

Finally, Trent, the toughest, shouts, "Go, Mitchell! Take it with you!" and then Mitchell smiles, as he takes the music inside, down and around his skinny body.

૯

After that day, though the kids still snicker and Mitchell wears the wrong clothes, something is different. He walks straighter, dances in the middle of class when he finally reads a book, stays awake for the entire hour. Mitchell sings songs in the hall, his church voice clear as a bell in the morning. Johnny and Sandy and Davey smile as they bend over their work, listening to his songs.

૯

When Mitchell's mother, Mrs. Davis, comes to see me about a week after the contest, I am correcting the papers of my first-hour students. A large gray sweater is pulled down over her clean washdress. She breathes heavily with the strain of climbing three flights of stairs. I put out my hand and she encloses it in hers. She smiles.

"Just checkin' on Mitch," she says, seating herself across from me. "Left my daughter in charge of the house so I could come over here."

"Mitchell is doing well, now that he's awake in class," I say. "We've got him on the breakfast program."

"He told me. That's good, that's good. He gets up too late to eat before the bus. So that's a good thing, that breakfast. I'm keepin' him in the house now, too. He got to runnin' around too much this summer. Couldn't settle down in school."

"I'm trying to get him to read more," I say, showing her some worksheets and a book from his folder.

"I know that!" she says and smiles at me. "You do want these children to be readin'!" I smile back. Audrey Davis and I have been working together for two years now, pushing Mitchell to stop fighting and to learn to read. When I first met Audrey, she frightened me by barging into my classroom, picking Mitchell up by his collar, and dragging him out into the hallway, hitting him on the head with a rolled-up newspaper the whole time. The kids said she did the same thing once in front of all Mitchell's friends at the roller rink. "She just snatched his old lazy butt out the crowd and took care of business," said Johnny, his eyes wide the next Monday when I had mused out loud about Mitchell's absence.

Another day last year, when Ted Marvin called to let her know that Mitchell was involved in a fight on the playing field, she showed up in Ted's office, where he was sitting with Mitch, about twenty minutes after his call. When he saw her, Ted said, Mitch's eyes grew large and he jumped up and began running around the desk, trying to keep something between himself and his mother. Audrey followed after him, smacked him once on his head, and then they sat down together to talk about Mitchell's suspension. Since then, Mitch has never been in a fight. And while I find it hard to watch scenes like the ones I've seen between Audrey and her son, I know she cares about him. She pays the bus fare and finds child care for her other kids so she can visit our program at least once a month. Even Johnny has a hint of appreciation in his voice when he describes Mitchell's mother. "She goes after her kids, Landsman—she don't take no shit!"

Audrey fingers the flash cards Mitch is working on, then flips through his book. "He's not gettin' in any fights is he?"

"None," I say. "And after the dancing contest last week, he's doing a lot better. The other kids don't tease him or pick at him as they used to."

Audrey smiles again and relaxes in the chair. "That's one good thing, then. My other ones got problems, and I don't know what to do with Thomas, my oldest. He's dropped out of North High School and just got fired from his job at the Super Valu. I tell you, he's in a nasty mood."

"I think Mitchell is going to have a fine year, so you don't have to worry about him."

"Yeah. I'm glad about that. I just thought when I brought them up here from Gary, they'd settle down, you know."

I nod my head. Although I don't know, not really. I haven't had to move and leave my friends for the sake of my children, and I haven't had to raise four kids all by myself.

Audrey gets up slowly. She shakes my hand again and tells me to call her if there are problems. She heads down the hall to talk to Bart, Mitchell's math teacher. Each month she makes the rounds. Mitchell brings home weekly reports, as well as daily point slips and notes from us. But Audrey Davis believes in sitting across from you, believes in looking at you when she talks, believes in getting the truth.

On the last day of October, John Martin, the science teacher, dressed as a skeleton for Halloween, tells me that Mitchell walked up to him the other day and put his arms around his neck. This in itself is not unusual. John has always had a way of inviting touch from his students who want to be touched, and Mitchell can be affectionate. Mitchell stayed there for a moment, in a long hug while kids moved around the two of them, coming and leaving the room, waving passes in front of John's face. Finally, Mitchell whispered in John's ear, quietly but clear as could be, "Hey, Martin, I don't know what the fuck is goin' on in this class!"

John and I both laughed, and I am still smiling at the image of Mitchell, his long brown arms next to John's pink face, successfully finding the right words.

CONTRIBUTORS

SHERMAN ALEXIE is a Spokane/Coeur d'Alene Indian and the author of ten books of poetry and prose, including *Indian Killer* (Atlantic Monthly Press) and *The Summer of Black Widows* (Hanging Loose Press). He wrote the screenplay for and co-produced, along with ShadowCatcher Entertainment, the feature film *Smoke Signals.*

CHARLES BAXTER was born in Minneapolis, attended Macalester College, and is the author of two novels, *First Light* and *Shadow Play,* four books of short stories, most recently *Believers,* and a collection of critical essays. His fiction has been widely anthologized and translated. Baxter lives in Ann Arbor, Michigan, where he teaches at the University of Michigan.

MELANIE BRAVERMAN has published poetry and fiction in *American Poetry Review, American Voice, Carolina Quarterly,* and other journals. "Memoryware" is an excerpt from her first novel, *East Justice,* which was published by Permanent Press in 1996.

ETHAN CANIN is the author of two collections of stories, *Emperor of the Air* and *The Palace Thief,* and two novels, *Blue River* and *For Kings and Planets.* A former physician, he is now on the faculty of the University of Iowa Writers' Workshop.

DAN CHAON grew up in rural western Nebraska and attended Northwestern and Syracuse Universities. His first book, *Fitting Ends and Other Stories* (Northwestern University Press/Tri-Quarterly Books) was published in 1996. He now lives in the Cleveland area with his wife and two sons.

LUCILLE CLIFTON's books of poetry include *The Terrible Stories* (BOA, 1996), *The Book of Light* (Copper Canyon, 1993), and *Quilting: Poems 1987–1990* (BOA, 1991). She is the only author to have two books of poetry chosen as finalists for the Pulitzer Prize in one year: *Good Woman: Poems and a Memoir 1969–1980* and *Next: New Poems* (both from BOA, 1988). She lives in Columbia, Maryland.

BERNARD COOPER's "Burl's" is from *Truth Serum* (Houghton Mifflin), a collection of memoirs about growing up gay. His work has appeared in *Harper's Magazine, Paris Review, Georgia Review,* and elsewhere. He is currently at work on a collection of short stories and a nonfiction book about studying avant-garde art.

ANDREW COZINE writes and teaches in Tucson. He and his wife are expecting a boy.

LORNA CROZIER has won all of Canada's major literary awards, including the Governor General's Award for Poetry. Her poems have been translated into seven languages, and she has read her work internationally. Born in Saskatchewan, she now lives in British Columbia, where she teaches in the Department of Writing at the University of Victoria. Her latest book, *A Saving Grace,* published in 1996 by McClelland and Stewart, is a series of poems about the 1930s drought and depression on the Canadian prairies.

ANDRE DUBUS is the author of nine books of fiction and two books of essays, most recently *Meditations from a Movable Chair,* published by Knopf in June 1998. He has six children and five grandchildren, and he lives in Haverhill, Massachusetts.

DIANE GLANCY is associate professor at Macalester College in St. Paul, Minnesota. Her third novel, *Flutie,* was published in 1998 by Moyer Bell. A third collection of essays, the *Cold-and-Hunger Dance,* was published by the University of Nebraska Press, also in 1998. A new collection of poetry, *Asylum in the Grasslands,* is forthcoming from Moyer Bell.

MICHAEL S. GLASER chairs the English department at St. Mary's College of Maryland where he also directs the annual literary festival at St. Mary's. He serves as a Maryland Poet-in-the-Schools and in 1995 received the Columbia Merit Award for his service to poetry. His collection of poems, *A Lover's Eye,* is in its second printing, and his chapbook, *In the Men's Room and Other Poems,* was the winner of the 1996 Painted Bride Quarterly chapbook competition. Over two hundred of his poems have appeared in literary journals, anthologies, and newspapers. Glaser lives in St. Mary's City with his wife, Kathleen, and is the proud father of five children.

JANE HAMILTON is the author of the novels, *The Book of Ruth, A Map of the World,* and *The Short History of a Prince.* Her short stories have appeared in *Harper's* magazine.

KATHARINE HARER's book, *Hubba Hubba,* was the winner of the Slipstream Poetry Chapbook Contest for 1995 and is her fourth small-press collection. She teaches at Skyline Community College, just south of San Francisco, and publishes regularly in literary journals. She is currently working on a nonfiction book about baseball.

WILLIAM J. HARRIS teaches African American literature, poetry, and creative writing at Penn State University at University Park. He has published two books of poems, *Hey Fella Would You Mind Holding This Piano a Moment* and *In My Own Dark Way,* is the editor of *The Leroi Jones/Amiri Baraka Reader,* and is the coeditor of *Call and Response: The Riverside Anthology of the African American Literary Tradition.*

PENNY HARTER has published fifteen books of poems, five since 1994: *Shadow Play: Night Haiku, Stages and Views, Grandmother's Milk, Turtle Blessing,* and *Lizard Light: Poems from the Earth.* She has published work in numerous anthologies and magazines worldwide, and her autobiographical essay appears in *Contemporary Authors Autobiography Series, 1998.*

MARIA HINOJOSA is an award-winning journalist, the urban affairs correspondent for CNN, and the host of NPR's *Latino USA.* Her next book, entitled *Raising Raul,* is a motherhood memoir about raising a Latino child in a multicultural society. She lives in New York City with her husband and two small children.

SUSAN K. ITO lives in Oakland, California, where she teaches creative writing at the University of California at Berkeley's extension program. Her work has appeared in many anthologies and journals, including *Growing Up Asian American, Making More Waves,* the *Santa Barbara Review* and *Hip Mama.* She is currently working on her first novel.

ANDREA LEE was born in Philadelphia and received her bachelor's and master's degrees from Harvard University. Her first book, *Russian Journal,* was nominated for a National Book Award and received the 1984 Jean Stein Award from the American Academy and Institute of Arts and Letters. *Sarah Phillips* is her first novel.

LI-YOUNG LEE was born in 1957 in Jakarta, Indonesia. He is the author of two award-winning volumes of poetry, *Rose* and *The City in Which I Love You,* and a memoir, *The Winged Seed.* He lives in Chicago.

PHILIP LEVINE divides his time between Fresno, California, and New York City, where he teaches at New York University in the fall. His book of poetry, *The Simple Truth,* won the Pulitzer Prize in 1995. In April of 1999 he will publish a new book of poems with Knopf entitled *The Mercy.*

PHILLIP LOPATE is the author of three personal essay collections, *Bachelorhood, Against Joie de Vivre,* and *Portrait of My Body,* and the editor of *The Art of the Personal Essay* and *The Anchor Essay Annual.* He teaches at Hofstra University.

DEBRA MARQUART's poetry collection, *Everything's a Verb,* was published by New Rivers Press in 1995. As a collaborating member of The Bone People, she has released two CDs: *A Regular Dervish* (spoken word, jazz poetry) and *Orange Parade* (acoustic rock). Ms. Marquart's work has appeared in *North American Review, River City, Witness, Zone 3,* and *Southern Poetry Review* among others. Ms. Marquart teaches creative writing at Iowa State University and is at work on a collection of short stories about road musicians, *Hunger in the Bones.*

REGINALD MCKNIGHT teaches at the University of Maryland, College Park. He has received an NEA fellowship, an O. Henry Award, the PEN Hemingway Special Citation, the Pushcart Prize, a Whiting Writer's Award, and the Drue Heinz Literature Prize. He is the author of *Moustapha's Eclipse, I Get On the Bus,* and *The Kind of Light That Shines on Texas.*

JESÚS PAPOLETO MELÉNDEZ's career as a poet-teacher has spanned twenty-nine years. He is an original founder of the Nuyorican poets' movement and has twice been selected as one of sixty poets nationwide to facilitate poetry and creative writing workshops through the Writerscorps division of President Clinton's AmeriCorp program. As a performance poet Papoleto has distinguished himself as a dynamic presenter of his works in the oral tradition.

EBONY J. MONTGOMERY graduated from Minneapolis's South High in 1997. She plans to study Cosmetology at the Aveda Institute and then move to New York to study fashion design. Her poem was inspired by Quincy Troupe's "A Poem for Magic" *(Skulls Along the River,* 1984).

PAT MORA, recipient of NEA and Kellogg fellowships, writes poetry, nonfiction, and children's books. The most recent of her five poetry collections is *Aunt Carmen's Book of Practical Saints.* Her family memoir, *House of Houses,* received a Southwest Book Award and the Premio Aztlán Literature Award.

FAYE MOSKOWITZ, George Washington University's English department chair, is the author of *A Leak in the Heart, Whoever Finds This: I Love You,* and *The Bridge Is Love,* and is the editor of *Her Face in the Mirror: Jewish Women on Mothers and Daughters.*

DWIGHT OKITA's poetry book, *Crossing with the Light,* was published by Tia Chucha Press in 1992. In addition to poetry, he also writes screenplays and stage plays. His screenplay *My Last Week on Earth* was a finalist in the Sundance Screenwriters Lab in 1998. His play *The Rainy Season* is published in a collection entitled *Asian American Drama,* published by Applause.

W. R. RODRIGUEZ is the author of *the shoe shine parlor poems et al* (Ghost Pony Press, 1984) and is working to complete *the concrete pastures of the beautiful bronx,* the second of a trilogy of books about his former home.

DAVID SEDARIS is a playwright and regular commentator for National Public Radio. He is the author of the best-selling *Barrel Fever* and *Holidays on Ice,* and *Naked.* He lives in New York City.

GARY SOTO is the author of twenty-seven books, including *Jesse, Buried Onions, Novio Boy,* and *Junior College.* His *New and Selected Poems* was a finalist for both the *Los Angeles Times* Book Award and the National Book Award. He lives in Berkeley, California.

PATRICIA SMITH, a former metro columnist for the *Boston Globe* and reporter for the *Chicago Sun-Times,* is the author of *Africans in America,* the companion book to the PBS series, as well as three volumes of poetry—*Close to Death, Big Towns, Big Talk,* and *Life According to Motown.* A four-time individual champion of the National Poetry Slam, Smith's work has also been published in *TriQuarterly,* the *Paris Review,* and other publications. Her one-woman show "Life After Motown" was produced by Nobel Prize-winner Derek Walcott, and the film of her poem "Undertaker" won a coveted cable Ace Award as part of the Lifetime Women's Film Festival. She is currently working on a novel. And still, she is guided by the bible that is Motown.

SUSAN STRAIGHT was born in 1960 in Riverside, California, where she still lives with her three children. She has published four novels, *Aquaboogie: A Novel in Stories, I Been in Sorrow's Kitchen and Licked Out All the Pots, Blacker Than a Thousand Midnights,* and *The Gettin Place.* Her essays have appeared in *Harper's, Los Angeles Times Magazine, Hungry Mind Review, Family Circle,* and *Westways.* In 1997, she received a Guggenheim fellowship.

SEKOU SUNDIATA is a poet and recording artist who writes for both the page and the stage. His poetry was most recently anthologized in *Flame and Spirit* (Syracuse University Press), *The Language of Life* (Doubleday), and *Aloud* (Holt). His first recording, "The Blue Oneness of Dream," was released to critical acclaim in 1997 on Mouth Almighty/Mercury Records. Sundiata is a professor in the writing program at Eugene Lang College/ New School for

Social Research in New York City. His writing and performing for theater includes "The Circle Unbroken Is a Hard Bop" and "The Mystery of Love" for the American Music Theater Festival. He is currently working on a music theater work entitled "Elijah" in collaboration with composers Craig Harris (U.S.) and Dou Dou Ndiaye Rose (Senegal). Sundiata produces The Talking Book Festival of Literary Arts at the New School, and he is currently co-producing a CD of Tupac Shakur's poetry for Amaru/Interscope. Sundiata is a 1998 master artist-in-residence at the Atlantic Center for the Arts.

THOM TAMMARO, the grandson of four Italian immigrants, was born and raised in the heart of the steel valley of western Pennsylvania. He is professor of multidisciplinary studies and teaches in the M.F.A. program in creative writing at Moorhead State University in Minnesota. He is the author of *When the Italians Came to My Home Town,* a collection of poems (1995), and *Minnesota Suite,* a chapbook of poems (1987). With Mark Vinz, he has coedited two award-winning anthologies, *Inheriting the Land: Contemporary Voices from the Midwest* (1993) and *Imagining Home: Writing from the Midwest* (1995), both published by the University of Minnesota Press. He is the recipient of fellowships in poetry from the Minnesota State Arts Board (1985 and 1991), a Loft-McKnight Award in Poetry (1995), and most recently a Jerome Foundation Travel and Study Grant (1997–98).

LUCI TAPAHONSO is a member of the Diné Nation (Navajo) of New Mexico and is an associate professor of English at the University of Kansas in Lawrence. She is the author of six books, including *Blue Horses Rush In: Poems and Stories,* published by the University of Arizona, which was awarded the 1998 Award for Best Poetry from the Mountains and Plains Booksellers Association. Her work has appeared in many print and media productions, both in the U.S. and internationally. In 1996, she was featured on Rhino Records's CD "In Their Own Words: A Century of American Poetry" and in the films *The Desert Is No Lady* and *Woven by the Grandmothers: An Exhibition of Nineteenth Century Navajo Textiles* (1997), which were released on PBS stations.

NATASHA TRETHEWEY was born in Gulfport, Mississippi, in 1966. Her poems have appeared in *Agni, American Poetry Review, Callaloo, Gettysburg Review, Massachusetts Review, North American Review,* and *Southern Review,* as well as other journals and anthologies. She is an assistant professor of English at Auburn University.

AFAA MICHAEL WEAVER (Michael S. Weaver) is a poet and playwright. His sixth collection of poetry is *Talisman* from Tia Chucha Press. His previous book was *Timber and Prayer.* His new play is *Candy Lips and Hallelujah.* A veteran of fifteen years as a factory worker, he is Alumnae Professor of English at Simmons College in Boston.

LYNNA WILLIAMS, a Texas native, was a political reporter and speechwriter in Texas and Minnesota before she began writing fiction. Her short stories have been published in the *Atlantic, Lear's,* and a number of literary magazines. Her first collection, *Things Not Seen and Other Stories,* was named a Notable Book of the Year by the *New York Times.* She is an associate professor of English/creative writing at Emory University.

MARY MACRINA YOUNG is an artist born in Somerset, Kentucky. She has a son, Micah. Most of her poems happen while she is painting or drawing and are songs before she writes them down. She also works for money as a case manager in a homeless shelter in Louisville, Kentucky.

ACKNOWLEDGMENTS

Alexie, Sherman. "Powwow Polaroid." In *Old Shirts and New Skins.* Los Angeles: American Indian Studies Center (University of California), 1993, 43. Copyright © 1993 by Sherman Alexie. Reprinted with permission from the author.

Baxter, Charles. "Gryphon." In *Through the Safety Net.* New York: Viking, 1985, 165–84. Copyright © 1985 by Charles Baxter. Reprinted with permission from Viking Penguin, a division of Penguin Books USA Inc.

Braverman, Melanie. "Memoryware." In *East Justice.* Sag Harbor, N.Y.: Permanent Press, 1996. Copyright © 1996 by Melanie Braverman. Reprinted with permission from The Permanent Press, Sag Harbor, N.Y. 11963. Previously published in the *American Voice.*

Canin, Ethan. "Star Food." In *Emperor of the Air.* Boston: Houghton Mifflin, 1988, 159–79. Copyright © 1988 by Ethan Canin. Reprinted with permission from Houghton Mifflin Company. All rights reserved.

Chaon, Dan. "Fitting Ends." First published in *TriQuarterly.* Subsequently published in *Fitting Ends and Other Stories* by Dan Chaon, TriQuarterly Books/Northwestern University Press, 1995. Copyright © 1995 by Dan Chaon. All rights reserved; reprinted with permission from Northwestern University Press and the author.

Clifton, Lucille. "sam." In *The Book of Light.* Port Townsend, Wash.: Copper Canyon Press, 1993, 14. Copyright © 1993 by Lucille Clifton. Reprinted with permission from Copper Canyon Press, P.O. Box 271, Port Townsend, WA 98368.

Cooper, Bernard. "Burl's." In *Truth Serum.* Boston: Houghton Mifflin, 1996, 15–27. Copyright © 1996 by Bernard Cooper.

Reprinted with permission from Houghton Mifflin Company. All rights reserved. First appeared in the *Los Angeles Times Magazine.*

Cozine, Andrew. "Hand Jive." Copyright © 1994 by Andrew Cozine. Reprinted with permission from the author. Also published in the *Iowa Review* and *The Best American Short Stories 1995.*

Crozier, Lorna. "Quitting Smoking." In *Angels of Flesh, Angels of Silence.* Toronto: McClelland and Stewart, 1988. Copyright © 1988 by Lorna Crozier. Reprinted with permission from McClelland and Stewart, Inc., the Canadian Publishers. Previously published in *The Party Train* (New Rivers Press).

Dubus, Andre. "A Woman in April." In *Broken Vessels.* Boston: David R. Godine, 1991, 140–44. Copyright © 1991 by Andre Dubus. Reprinted with permission from David R. Godine, Publisher, Inc.

Glancy, Diane. "If Not All These." In *The West Pole.* Minneapolis: University of Minnesota Press, 1997, 196. Copyright © 1997 by Diane Glancy. Reprinted with permission from University of Minnesota Press. Previously published in *The Party Train* (New Rivers Press).

Glaser, Michael S. "Preparations for Seder." In *There's No Place Like Home for the Holidays,* edited by Sandra Haldeman Martz. Watsonville, Calif.: Papier-Mache Press, 1997, 53–54. Copyright © 1997 by Michael S. Glaser. Reprinted with permission from the author and Papier-Mache Press.

Hamilton, Jane. "When I Began to Understand Quantum Mechanics." *Harper's,* August 1989, 41–49. Copyright © 1989 by Jane Hamilton. Reprinted with permission from International Creative Management, Inc. "Smoke Gets in Your Eyes" was written by Otto Harbach and Jerome Kern. Copyright © 1933 by Polygram International Publishing, Inc. Copyright renewed. Used by permission. All rights reserved.

Harer, Katharine. "Tunnels." Copyright © 1996 by Katharine Harer. Reprinted with permission from the author. Previously published in *The Party Train* (New Rivers Press).

Harris, William J. "Rib Sandwich." Copyright © 1977 by William J. Harris. Reprinted with permission from the author. Previously published in *Celebrations,* edited by Arnold Adoff.

Harter, Penny. "The Old Man Who Loves Bicycles." Copyright © 1996 by Penny Harter. Reprinted with permission from the author. Previously published in *The Party Train* (New Rivers Press).

Haynes, David. "The Dozens." In *Right by My Side.* Minneapolis: New Rivers Press, 1993, 1–7. Copyright © 1993 by David Haynes. Reprinted with permission from the author.

Hinojosa, Maria. "There Was Nothing Else I Could Do." In *Crews: Gang Members Talk to Maria Hinojosa.* San Diego: Harcourt Brace, 1995, 55–63. Copyright © 1995 by Maria Hinojosa. Reprinted with permission from Harcourt Brace and Company.

Ito, Susan K. "Origami." Copyright © 1994 by Susan K. Ito. Reprinted with permission from the author. Previously published in *Two Worlds Walking* (New Rivers Press).

Landsman, Julie. "Transformations." Excerpted from *Basic Needs.* Minneapolis: Milkweed Editions, 1993. Copyright © 1993 by Julie Landsman.

Lee, Andrea. "The Days of the Thunderbirds." In *Sarah Phillips.* New York: Random House, 1984, 67–80. Copyright © 1984 by Andrea Lee. Reprinted with permission from Random House, Inc.

Lee, Li-Young. "The Gift" and "I Ask My Mother to Sing." In *Rose.* Rochester: BOA Editions, 1986, 15–16, 50. Copyright © 1986 by Li-Young Lee. Reprinted with permission from BOA Editions, Ltd., Rochester, N.Y.

Levine, Philip. "Soloing." In *What Work Is.* New York: Alfred A. Knopf, 1991, 63. Copyright © 1991 by Philip Levine. Reprinted with permission from Alfred A. Knopf, Inc.

Lopate, Phillip. "My Early Years at School." In *Bachelorhood.* Boston: Little, Brown and Company, 1981, 237–42. Copyright © 1981 by Phillip Lopate. Reprinted with permission from The Wendy Weil Agency, Inc.

Marquart, Debra. "Getting Ready." Copyright © 1996 by Debra Marquart. Reprinted with permission from the author. Previously published in *The Party Train* (New Rivers Press).

McKnight, Reginald. "The Kind of Light That Shines on Texas." In *The Kind of Light That Shines on Texas.* Boston: Little, Brown and Company, 1992, 20–40. Copyright © 1992 by Reginald McKnight. Originally appeared in the *Kenyon Review.* Reprinted with permission from Christina Ward Literary Agency and the author.

Meléndez, Jesús Papoleto. "OYE MUNDO/Sometimes." Copyright © 1998 by Jesús Papoleto Meléndez. Reprinted with permission from the author.

Montgomery, Ebony J. "Me and My Troupe." Copyright © 1998 by Ebony J. Montgomery. Reprinted with permission from the author.

Mora, Pat. "Señora X No More." In *Communion.* Houston: Arte Público Press, University of Houston, 1991, 15. Copyright © 1991 by Pat Mora. Reprinted with permission from Arte Público Press.

Moskowitz, Faye. Excerpt from *A Leak in the Heart.* Boston: David R. Godine, 1985, 58–64. Copyright © 1985 by Faye Moskowitz. Reprinted with permission from Russell and Volkening as agents for the author.

Okita, Dwight. "Notes for a Poem on Being Asian American." In *Crossing with the Light.* Chicago: Tia Chucha Press, 1992. Copyright © 1992 by Dwight Okita. Reprinted with permission from the author.

rodriguez, w. r. "democracy." Copyright © 1994 by w. r. rodriguez. Previously published in *Two Worlds Walking* (New Rivers Press). "justice." Copyright © 1996 by w. r. rodriguez. Previously published in *The Party Train* (New Rivers Press). Both poems reprinted with permission from the author.

Sedaris, David. "Diary of a Smoker." In *Barrel Fever.* Boston: Little, Brown and Company, 1994, 151–54. Copyright © 1994 by David

Sedaris. Reprinted with permission from Little, Brown and Company.

Smith, Patricia. Excerpts from *Life According to Motown.* Chicago: Tia Chucha Press, 1991. Copyright © 1991 by Patricia Smith. Reprinted with permission from the author.

Soto, Gary. "Braly Street." In *New and Selected Poetry.* San Francisco: Chronicle Books, 1995, 24–27. Copyright © 1995 by Gary Soto. Reprinted with permission from Chronicle Books.

Straight, Susan. "Tracks." In *Aquaboogie.* Minneapolis: Milkweed Editions, 1990, 136–45. Copyright © 1990 by Susan Straight.

Sundiata, Sekou. "Dijerrido" and "Blink Your Eyes." Copyright © 1998 by Sekou Sundiata. Reprinted with permission from the author.

Tammaro, Thom. "Innocent Traveler." *North Dakota Quarterly* 63, no. 1 (Winter 1996). Copyright © 1996 by Thom Tammaro. Reprinted with permission from the author.

Tammaro, Thom. "Remembering Bull DeLisio." *Sidewalks* 1, no. 1 (August 1991). Copyright © 1991 by Thom Tammaro. Reprinted with permission from the author and *Sidewalks.*

Tapahonso, Luci. "I Am Singing Now." In *A Breeze Swept Through.* Albuquerque: West End Press, 1987, 4. Copyright © 1987 by Luci Tapahonso. Reprinted with permission from the author.

Trethewey, Natasha. "White Lies." Copyright © 1994 by Natasha Trethewey. Reprinted with permission from the author. Previously published in *Two Worlds Walking* (New Rivers Press) and the *Seattle Review.*

Weaver, Afaa Michael. "Improvisation for Piano." In *Unsettling America,* edited by Maria Mazziotti Gillan and Jennifer Gillan. New York: Penguin Books, 1994, 229–30. Copyright © 1994 by Maria Mazziotti Gillan and Jennifer Gillan. Reprinted with permission from Viking Penguin, a division of Penguin Books USA, Inc.

Williams, Lynna. "Personal Testimony." In *Things Not Seen.* Boston: Little, Brown and Company, 1992, 55–72. Copyright © 1992 by Lynna Williams. Reprinted with permission from Little, Brown and Company.

Young, Mary Macrina. "Poem for My Father." Copyright © 1994 by Mary Macrina Young. Reprinted with permission from the author. Previously published in the *American Voice.*

David Haynes is the author of five works of fiction for adults, including *All American Dream Dolls* (Milkweed Editions, 1997), *Live at Five* (Milkweed Editions, 1996), *Heathens* (New Rivers Press, 1996), *Somebody Else's Mama* (Milkweed Editions, 1995/Harvest Books, 1996), and *Right by My Side* (New Rivers Press, 1994), selected by the American Library Association as one of the Best Books for Young Adults of that year. He is also the author of two novels for children, *The Gumma Wars* and *Business As Usual.* In 1996, Haynes was named by *Granta* magazine as one of the Best Young American Novelists. Haynes has taught middle-school students in the inner city for fourteen years, has served on the leadership team at the experimental Saturn School of Tomorrow, is currently a consultant for the National Board for Professional Teaching Standards in Washington, D.C., and is the visiting writer-in-residence at Southern Methodist University in Dallas, Texas.

Born in Connecticut, **Julie Landsman** received her B.A. from George Washington University, her teacher's certification from Carleton College, and her certification in special education from the University of Minnesota. An educator, writer, and writing teacher, she has been a teacher and behavior specialist in inner-city and suburban schools in the Minneapolis Public School system for twenty years. She has worked in special settings for students with academic and behavioral problems. She has also taught creative writing to students of all ages, including those at the Minnesota High School for the Arts. Landsman is the author of *Basic Needs: A Year with Street Kids in a City School* (Milkweed Editions, 1993) and *Tips for Creating a Manageable Classroom: Understanding Your Students' Basic Needs* (Milkweed Editions, 1994). She edited an anthology of student writings for Fairview Press entitled *From Darkness to Light.* She is presently a consultant and a teacher at Sheridan School in Minneapolis.

Interior design by Mary Ellen Buscher
Typeset in Veljovic
by Stanton Publication Services, Inc.
Printed on acid-free 55# Sebago Antique Cream paper
by Maple-Vail Book Manufacturing

More Anthologies from Milkweed Editions:

Changing the Bully Who Rules the World:
Reading and Thinking about Ethics
Edited by Carol Bly

Clay and Star:
Contemporary Bulgarian Poets
Edited by Lisa Sapinkopf
and Georgi Belev

Drive, They Said:
Poems about Americans and Their Cars
Edited by Kurt Brown

Looking for Home:
Women Writing about Exile
Edited by Deborah Keenan
and Roseann Lloyd

Many Lights in Many Windows:
Twenty Years of Great Fiction and Poetry
from the Writers Community
Edited by Laurel Blossom

Minnesota Writes: Poetry
Edited by Jim Moore
and Cary Waterman

Mixed Voices:
Contemporary Poems about Music
Edited by Emilie Buchwald
and Ruth Roston

The Most Wonderful Books:
Writers on Discovering the Pleasures of Reading
Edited by Michael Dorris and Emilie Buchwald

Mouth to Mouth:
Poems by Twelve Contemporary Mexican Women
Edited by Forrest Gander

Night Out:
Poems about Hotels, Motels, Restaurants, and Bars
Edited by Kurt Brown and Laure-Anne Bosselaar

Passages North Anthology
Edited by Elinor Benedict

The Poet Dreaming in the Artist's House:
Contemporary Poems about the Visual Arts
Edited by Emilie Buchwald
and Ruth Roston

Sacred Ground:
Writings about Home
Edited by Barbara Bonner

Testimony:
Writers of the West Speak On Behalf of Utah Wilderness
Compiled by Stephen Trimble
and Terry Tempest Williams

This Sporting Life:
Contemporary Poems about Sports and Games
Edited by Emilie Buchwald
and Ruth Roston

Transforming a Rape Culture
Edited by Emilie Buchwald, Pamela Fletcher, and Martha Roth

Verse and Universe: Poems about Science and Mathematics
Edited by Kurt Brown

White Flash/Black Rain: Women of Japan Relive the Bomb
Edited and translated by Lequita Vance-Watkins and Aratani Mariko

Milkweed Editions publishes with the intention of making a humane impact on society, in the belief that literature is a transformative art uniquely able to convey the essential experiences of the human heart and spirit.

To that end, Milkweed publishes distinctive voices of literary merit in handsomely designed, visually dynamic books, exploring the ethical, cultural, and esthetic issues that free societies need continually to address.

Milkweed Editions is a not-for-profit press.